The Stick Man

Also by Gillian Bligh

THE CORNELIANS

The Stick Man

Gillian Bligh

Copperstone Books

Gillian Bligh
The Stick Man

First Edition

Published 2003

ISBN 0-9544628-1-5

Published by
Copperstone Books

© 2003 Gillian Bligh

Author contact e-mail: gib@copperstone7.fsnet.co.uk

This novel is a work of fiction.
Characters and names are the product of the
author's imagination. Any resemblance to anybody,
living or dead, is entirely coincidental.

Cover design: Kaarin Wall

Printed in Great Britain
by
The Galliard Press
Great Yarmouth

Gillian Bligh was born and educated in Norfolk.
She now lives with her husband on the Suffolk coast.
She has two daughters and two grandchildren.
When not writing she enjoys painting and
researching her family tree and her links with
William Bligh, Admiral of the Blue, probably
better known for being involved in the famous
Mutiny on the Bounty.

The Stick Man is her second book.

Author's Note

The Suffolk dialect is not easily read or understood by the
uninitiated. For this reason I have used a diluted version –
to retain a flavour of Suffolk without causing hardship
to the reader.

The inspiration for Marcie's Bridge came from a little bridge in
Attleborough, Norfolk, where I spent part of my childhood.

Acknowledgements:

Very special thanks to:

My husband Michael

And

My daughter Suzanne, who, once again,
deciphered my scribble, typed my manuscript
and kept me inspired throughout.

For My Daughter

Suzanne

And

To The Memory of My Parents

Mildred and Frederick Bligh

PART ONE

Cuckoos and Corncockle

CHAPTER ONE

Suffolk, England, 1863

It was on a Tuesday evening in early Summer, that Harnser Elliot first saw Arabella; he was seventeen. He was staring vacantly into the middle distance from his vantage point, high up on a bank, when two tiny, indistinct figures came into view. He saw that both were female and appeared unhurried as they walked toward him down the lane. He moved a little down the grassy slope until a bush obscured him from them. It had been a very hot day; the grass beneath him was cool and lush. He propped himself up on one elbow and casually crossed one ankle over the other, idly rolling a grass stalk between his forefinger and thumb, but did not take his eyes from the pair.

As the ladies drew closer he realized that one was somewhat older than the other and carried an open basket. Every now and then one or the other would stop, stoop down, pluck something from the hedgerow, and put it in the basket. There was no urgency about their task so he supposed they were gathering wild flowers and greenery for pure pleasure.

As they drew level with him, Harnser saw that the lady's companion was very young; nearer to his own age. Her hair was a rich chestnut colour and fell freely around her shoulders as the lowering sun caught the copper highlights. It was being lifted gently from her face by the evening breeze, giving him his first glimpse of her near perfect face.

He continued to watch as they passed him by, appreciating with young male pleasure the way the girl's skirt gently swung from side to side with the movement of her hips. Turning his head he saw them disappear round a bend in the lane. He stood up and stretched his neck as high as he could but saw no more of them.

Harnser was thoughtful as he strolled home. The pair he had seen must live fairly close by, since they were on foot and he had heard no evidence of horses, or a conveyance that might have been waiting for them. This conclusion pleased him greatly and he acknowledged to himself that the move to Little Pecking might turn out better than he had anticipated.

CHAPTER TWO

"Did you enjoy your walk?" Maria turned her head towards her son as he entered the back kitchen door. She knew he had been apprehensive about the move, and was eager for a sign that he was coming to terms with it. "You have been gone quite some time. Did you meet anyone interesting?"

"I met the Vicar on the way through the village; he says he will be round to visit you before long – when you have had time to settle in. He said he was fond of your father and will miss their conversations; apparently he was a frequent visitor to this cottage and hopes to remain so. If he does not manage to call this week he looks forward to seeing us all in church on Sunday morning. I quite liked him, Mother; I think you will too. He seemed genuinely interested in my musical talents and wondered if I would be interested in teaching his son to play the piccolo, for a fee of course. He has lived here for only a year himself."

Harnser did not mention the two ladies he had seen, for some reason he did not want to share that particular piece of information. The image of the young lady was still very clear in his head and he knew he would be making return visits to the scene of his first sighting. He also knew he would fall asleep that night thinking of her chestnut hair and the gentle swinging of her summer skirts.

"Did you mention your post at The Hall to him?"

"Yes, he said the lessons could be at my convenience," and then changing the subject and sitting at the table Harnser said, "The house is quiet tonight."

"Walter is up at The Hall and James is fast asleep." Maria crossed the room, put her arm around her son's shoulders and laid her head close to his. "Just like old times is it not?"

"Yes," he replied, thoughtfully, "just like old times." Then,

"Are you happy, Mother, I mean are you happy living with Walter and James? It is just that Walter is not much like Father and I know how much you loved Father … "

His voice trailed off as he wondered whether or not he should have mentioned the subject and he was filled with a sudden sadness, very much at odds with his feelings of a short while ago when the girl had been on his mind. His throat felt constricted and tears came easily to his eyes as he stared at the scrubbed table and thought of his father. He could hear music; he could always hear music when he thought of him; the soft, relaxing strains of the flute he used to play to them in the evening as his mother sewed. That was his favourite memory – the three of them together – enjoying the music. And then there were the piccolo and the ocarina – the first instrument his father had taught him to play was the ocarina, he had been a willing pupil. How glad he was now that he had learnt his music diligently. He went hardly anywhere without the little instrument.

His mother broke into his thoughts as she tried to answer him truthfully. "Walter is more like your father than you might think. He may be a manual worker but he is very well read and he is kind; he wanted to look after us Harnser and it works both ways. He was devastated when he lost Mary, as well you know. He had no idea how to look after a baby. Helping him with James at the time helped me to cope with my own loss; it was a natural progression to marriage. In the circumstances we have all benefited, do you not think? Little James is like my own son; I could not love him more if he were."

"I was not criticising, Mother, truly," he stood up and put his arms around Maria, "I like Walter, you know that, and as for little James well, who could not love him? It is just that I love you very much, you have been through so much in the last few years and now with Grandpa going well, I worry about you."

"There is no need to concern yourself with my happiness but thank you all the same. I am back in the house where I was born, I have lovely memories of this place too; I feel very close to my parents here but of course I will never forget your father,

I see him all the time in you. She kissed him on the cheek and tightened her arms around him before turning away again, her head full of conflicting thoughts.

She *was* happy to be back in Orchard Cottage and she was not unhappy with Walter, but she *did* still miss Edward; his laughing dark eyes, his enthusiasm for life, his music, his brilliant brain and knowledge. Most of all she missed the *essence* of him; the qualities she could not easily put a name to, the ones that had made him *Edward*. She could see many of those qualities in her son of whom she was so proud. She had not had to encourage him to follow in his father's footsteps as a musician and teacher. His love of music and thirst for knowledge was obviously innate. She was glad too that he had inherited his father's looks. She herself was small and dark haired; she was often teased about her size; '*You do not eat enough to keep a sparrow alive*', was a frequent comment to her '*No wonder you are so little*'. But she had always been little and Edward had liked her so. Harnser, on the other hand, was tall and lean, one could not call him thin, he was strong and had the type of skin that turned very brown in Summer, a good combination with his flaxen hair.

Yes, she thought with pride, my son is very handsome.

CHAPTER THREE

Two days after moving to Little Pecking, Harnser took up his very junior post at The Hall. He was assistant to the schoolmaster.

Silas Midcote was in his middle thirties. His face was a little pasty looking and, when working, he wore a small pair of spectacles. At first sight he appeared dour but, like a lot of dedicated teachers, his face became alive as he imparted knowledge to the next generation of scholars. This was but one of the master's attributes that won the admiration of the younger man.

There were five children at The Hall. Two were not yet old enough to partake in lessons; two were under the sole instruction of Mr Midcote who excelled in Mathematics, English and Latin. That left twelve year old Nicholas. Silas Midcote handed over Nicholas to the young man's charge and Harnser soon realized that the boy had the attention span of a gnat. He also suspected that Nicholas might have been the reason for his being hired. The boy's gaze frequently drifted to the large window, which overlooked the home garden, where an oak tree grew to massive proportions and which had in its shade a long wooden bench. Nicholas was the 'difficult' pupil and Mr Midcote had frequent discussions with the boy's parents regarding his abilities. They were at present wondering whether their son would do better at boarding school. Not a light decision to make due to the fact that his father had been extremely unhappy away at school and had vowed to educate his own children at home.

"Do your best with Master Nicholas", Silas had said on the first morning, "any improvement at all would be appreciated, he is not an easy child to teach." This was a remark that Harnser bore in mind during his first week in the schoolroom. He was keen to make his mark on his superior and his employer so therefore decided to watch the boy closely to try to find out why his concentration was so poor.

Each time Nicholas's eyes strayed from his work Harnser followed his gaze and noticed that the lad was watching 'life'; that is wildlife. Spiders spinning webs, flies buzzing about, the house martins that were nesting under the eaves – whose flight path passed the window – the odd earwig or beetle that scuttled along the floor; all seemed to hold a fascination for him.

Harnser felt a certain empathy with the boy since he was experiencing a similar problem himself. This was his first week at The Hall but his thoughts kept straying to 'the girl'. Where did she live, what was her name, would he see her again? She was becoming a mild obsession to him. He had returned to the lane the evening after first seeing her but could find no house. The following evening he had walked further but his quest was hampered by the crossroads about fifty yards round the bend in the lane; where he had lost sight of them. He did not know which route they had taken so would have to investigate them all.

On the Monday afternoon of the second week Harnser reached a private agreement with Nicholas. If he worked hard and concentrated on his lessons, the last hour of the day could be spent learning about nature and wildlife – the experiment had begun. Nicholas found Homer's odyssey much more palatable when tempered with the life cycle of the Red Admiral butterfly!

"Did you say they were black and white, Sir?" Nicholas asked one day as he labelled his drawing.

"No, chestnut, definitely chestnut with copper highlights," he dreamily replied.

"Are you sure, Sir? I do not think I have seen antennae with copper highlights." There was a confused look on the face of the boy scholar as he studied his young master and imagined antennae with little copper lanterns swinging from their tops. "What *are* highlights, Sir?"

"Er, highlights, Nicholas are the lighter tones that are

perceived when an object has light or sunlight on it, they bring a colour to life and make it more interesting…" he suddenly stopped and stared at his student, "May I ask why you are asking that?"

"Because you said that the antennae were chestnut with copper highlights," the puzzled boy replied.

Harnser's face coloured visibly and he shot a quick glance in the direction of his superior. He realized his thoughts had once again been with the girl, he really must concentrate on his work, he would be dismissed at this rate, before he had had the chance to prove himself. "I am sorry, Nicholas I misunderstood you. I was referring to something entirely different." He smiled at his charge, "Black and white, yes definitely black and white, and I must say that is an excellent drawing. Nature is a fascinating subject is it not? I think you will do well at it. But remember, if your other lessons do not improve we will have to defer nature study until they do."

Although he tried to sound serious and a little stern, Harnser had no doubt that his secret pact with the boy was going to achieve the desired result. The smile he received left him in no doubt that the youngster saw him as an ally, as well as a teacher. He felt somewhat pleased with himself.

Two days later as Silas and Harnser left the Hall, the older man became unusually talkative and seemed somewhat excited, bringing about the perfect opportunity for Harnser to quiz him on local geography.

"I have been wanting to tell someone my news all day," Silas confided unexpectedly as the pair walked down the long drive in the direction of the Gate Lodge. "Yesterday at about six o'clock my wife and I were blessed with the arrival of our first child – a boy." He turned his beaming face towards Harnser and the younger man saw evidence of tears in his eyes.

"Why, that is wonderful, Sir, please accept my heartiest congratulations and also convey them to your wife." His outstretched hand warmly grasped Silas's and he felt an affinity with the man whose pride and happiness shone out, strangely at odds with the serious countenance of his schoolroom demeanour. "May I ask what names you have chosen?"

Silas beamed again, "George – George Silas of course."

"I think that is an excellent choice; strong and regal." He could see that he had chosen the right words.

"There is nothing to beat marriage and a family, Harnser, nothing at all better for a man."

Their familiar evening walk home was taking place at a much faster rate than usual and Harnser realized that Silas was keen to get home to the bosom of his family. If he were going to take advantage of the usually quiet man's good humour, he would have to hurry. He might not get the chance again for a while.

"When you find the right lady," his companion continued, "make sure you hang on to her, do not dither, there are plenty enough young bounders out there ready to act fast if you do not. I nearly came adrift like that myself, being of a somewhat shy nature."

Harnser could easily imagine the situation and realized that he liked Silas.

"I was out for a stroll one evening a week or so back," he ventured tentatively, "down Rookery Lane on the west side of the village. I saw two ladies taking an evening walk but I could see no nearby houses. Are you familiar with that area, Sir?"

"Silas, call me Silas when we are out of the schoolroom. Rookery Lane you say, um now let me think...I should say the nearest dwelling to that would be the Biddemore place."

"The Biddemore place?"

"Yes, old Major Biddemore has a grace and favour home on the edge of Mr Sanderson's estate. He is known round and about as 'Sugar' Sanderson. That is how the family made their money you see – out of sugar in the West Indies."

Harnser was now very interested and wanted to know more. "Where exactly is the Biddemore place? I saw no houses at all despite walking a fair distance."

"It is visible from Rookery Lane in the Winter but with the trees in leaf it is well hidden in Summer. You need to turn right at the crossroads just round the bend there, although I think there is a track across the fields, which cuts quite a distance off

11

the walk". Silas turned toward him with a rare twinkle in his eye, "I take it you took a fancy to one of the young ladies?"

Harnser blushed, he had not realized he had been so transparent. "Only one was young," he confided sheepishly, "and yes, she was very pretty, I – I did not speak; in fact they did not see me, I was just curious as to where they lived." He had said more than he meant to but he did not think that Silas was the sort of person to betray a confidence and he *had* found out a bit more about the girl; well, maybe where she lived. He would venture round that way again this evening and pay more attention to the trees!

The Gate Lodge was in sight when Silas spoke again. "Being a newcomer you are probably unaware of the village grapevine system so I will enlighten you," he smiled at Harnser, "If you want to know anything about anybody around here you go and see Abel, Abel Sawyer. He lives in one of the cottages on the Green; number seven I think. He is a mine of information. He spends a great deal of time in The Bell where he naturally hears all the local news but, in addition to that, he reads any newspaper he can lay his hands on. People pass the papers on to him you see; when they have finished with them, folk like the Doctor and the Vicar, and me of course. Abel spent years at sea and has travelled the world so all in all he is a fascinating person to spend time with. If he is not in The Bell he is usually by the pump house on the Village Green or at home. He welcomes visitors so you need not be shy about calling on him. It is a sad fact of life, Harnser, that few of the villagers can read or write so would not know what was going on in the world but for people like Abel. Go and introduce yourself, it will be the quickest way to let all and sundry know that you are a musician and as you know musicians are always in demand one way or another. Your popularity will be ensured overnight."

They reached the top of the drive and turned towards one another to shake hands. A friendship had been forged. Harnser turned left to walk the one hundred yards or so to Orchard Cottage while Silas turned toward the High Street as he made his way home to School Lane; a fitting address, even though he did not teach at the school.

As Harnser approached home he could see a young boy loitering in the lane, kicking at the roadway – his mother would be none too pleased – and casting furtive glances at the house.

"Can I be of assistance?" Harnser enquired quietly, noticing that the boy appeared troubled.

The boy looked at him worriedly. "Do you live here, Mister?"

"Yes, I am Harnser Elliot, and what is your name?"

"Tom Hubbard."

"I am pleased to meet you, Tom, how can I help?" Harnser's soft voice obviously put the boy more at ease.

"I – I know The Stick Man died but Mother needs some sticks and Granddad never got his walking stick. Mother said sorry he died."

Harnser smiled reassuringly at Tom. "Does your Grand-father's name happen to be Tom as well?"

"Yes, Mister."

"Then I think I can help you. When we moved in recently we found a new walking stick labelled 'Tom' but we did not know whom it was for. The Stick Man as you called him was my own grandfather. Please thank your mother for her condolences."

The boy looked relieved, "It's Granddad's present; he's seventy on Sunday – we've bought him a stick 'cos he's not very safe no more."

"Anymore." Harnser corrected automatically, "he is not safe *any* more."

"No he int, Mister."

Harnser smiled despite himself; the schoolmaster in this village had a job on his hands but then it was common for folk to double their negatives in Suffolk, so it would be the same in any village here about. Dropping aitches and leaving off the ends of words was also very common, in fact the Suffolk dialect was a language of its own. Despite all these factors he liked it and although it was his job to correct children's English he sometimes wished he did not have to.

"You would also like some sticks?"

"A bundle, Mister, I brought a rope 'cos a wheel's off me cart

13

– I can drag em home, it int far."

Maria decided not to charge for the walking stick, it was the last one her father had made so it was somewhat special. She wished she did not have to part with it, but then, she had others to keep; some quite ornate, her father had enjoyed carving.

Within the hour two more small boys had called asking for The Stick Man. News travelled fast. Like it or not, Harnser, as the eldest male Elliot, was now officially The Stick Man of Little Pecking.

The title had come about in a most unusual way. The story was that, one very bad Winter, Maria's grandfather had been taught to play poker by old Lord Haverham. John Porter had been a groundsman at The Hall. He was a widower.

Old Lord Haverham had been left alone while his son and family had attended a wedding in London. They had been prevented from returning home because snow had fallen heavily for a week. The old gentleman had grown crotchety with loneliness and gout. Standing at his front door one day he had hailed the first person he saw – which happened to be John Porter -with the startling question, "I say, my man, do you play poker?"

"No, Sir, I do not." John had replied walking towards his master through the thick snow.

"You cannot do much out there today can you?"

"No, Sir, I'm getting to grips with repairing some of the barns. There's always something to do somewhere."

"How would you like to come into the warm and play poker?"

"I cannot play, Sir, I do not know how." John had felt uneasy.

"I will teach you, man."

John had looked bewildered, he had never set foot in The Hall, he did not know how to respond.

"Well come on," the old man shouted impatiently, "get yourself in here and lets get on with it."

Thereby an unlikely friendship was formed. Lord Haverham taught John how to play poker, then they had some serious games but the old man wanted some excitement. "How do you feel about a wager or two?" he asked one evening as his eyes shone wickedly.

14

"I have nothing to gamble with," replied a worried John.

"I know – I know but I have plenty. Let us agree that if you win you have the pick from the library, how's that? If you lose, you lose nothing."

John could hardly disagree with such an offer.

For the next fortnight as the snow continued to fall the pair continued their one sided gambling. John was quite enjoying himself and began to see how the gentry lost and won so much money. The old man was having fun too, he enjoyed John's company and parted with several books as the younger man's skill improved. Then one night Lord Haverham made a startling offer. If John could win three games in a row the old man would sign over his cottage and an acre of land to him; not only that but he could have any sticks and branches from the estate's home wood that he wanted. "No chopping trees down mind, just what you find on the ground." The Home Wood was extensive although not huge. It covered about twenty-five acres and lay between John's estate cottage and The Hall as well as extending eastwards. Lord Haverham was a much more experienced card player than John, but, he was also much older, with poorer concentration, even so John could not see himself winning the ultimate prize.

Night after night the unlikely pair played cards and John almost gave up hope of becoming a property owner – until the night of the blizzard.

The groundsmen had been working non stop for two weeks just to keep the drive and paths around the house clear but this particular evening, as the card playing progressed, the drifts were piling up.

"You can't go home in that, man, wait until it stops. I doubt you can get into your cottage anyway."

And so the playing continued…and at three o'clock in the morning John won his third game in a row – his house, his land, and all the wood he wanted – in perpetuum…a house and a woodland right to pass on to his children.

Eventually they both fell asleep, but not before John had the written, signed promise in his pocket. The old man kept his word; a gentleman always pays his gambling debts.

It was just as well the weather improved otherwise John Porter could have become the new Lord of the Manor!

"Do you not think it a little demeaning to be referred to as The Stick Man?" Harnser enquired of his mother. "Should we not discourage the name?"

"Walter quite enjoys gathering the wood; he likes to be out in the forest, I doubt he will mind doing the job. Anyway I think it is rather quaint. I can think of worse names to be called." Maria answered quite cheerfully, " And I will get to meet the children which I will quite enjoy."

Harnser was not sure he agreed with her but he did not pursue the subject. Of one thing he was certain, that he did not want to be known by that name himself – even if he did enjoy wandering in the woods – so was quite happy that Walter had offered to take over the role.

CHAPTER FOUR

Later that evening Harnser found the entrance to the track leading across the fields, that Silas had told him about. Opposite the entrance on Rookery Lane he found a signpost – hardly visible in the overgrown hedgerow – with an arm pointing down the track. On closer inspection and only just discernible he read 'Flinton 3 Miles.' He began walking in that direction.

The track was quite narrow with a ridge of grass growing all the way down the middle but it was wide enough for a horse and vehicle, consequently there were passing places cut into the banks at regular intervals.

It was a warm evening with a slight breeze. A vast, spectacular, pink and orange sky was to his left, a magnificent backdrop to a meadow of grass and wild flowers. To his right was a lush, green field of young corn and beyond that, ahead and to the right he could see cows grazing.

Harnser removed his jacket and threw it casually over one shoulder. He began to whistle, he felt relaxed but strangely excited as well. Ahead of him, slightly to the left were the trees – the ones he was sure provided summer privacy to the Biddemore place. Most of them were horse chestnuts but there were several oaks and a selection of others, including beech. From the road they had appeared to be growing quite close together but as he got nearer he could see that that had been an optical illusion. He could not, however, see any sign of human habitation.

He continued on his way, now and again his free hand going to his chest and the ocarina that hung from around his neck on a narrow leather thong. This was a habit of his; he checked now and again to make sure the little instrument had not been lost. It was one of his most treasured possessions.

And then, all of a sudden, it came into view; one of the most beautiful, old, red brick houses he had ever seen, nestling between the trees with the sun caressing its mellow walls, its latticed windows glinting in the soft evening light.

As he stood and gazed in awe at the lovely old house he had the strangest feeling that he was coming home – home from somewhere unknown, where he had triumphed over adversity – home, after a long absence. He had never seen the house before yet it was somehow familiar, familiar to his inner being, restful to his soul.

He had stopped without realizing, but he now began walking slowly ahead – cautiously – quietly – as if he might frighten the sight away, but there it remained, as it had for nearly a century.

As he got closer, more than the house was revealed. A way back from the main building and to the right was a collection of outhouses all in the same red brick.

Presently he came upon a turn off to the left flanked by wooden gates and saw that it led to the house. The gates were open and judging from the surrounding vegetation, they had not been closed for sometime. To the right of the entrance, at an angle, was a large wooden sign. It hung on chains from the crossbar of the two posts and on it was written 'Barcada'. The sign made a creaking noise as it swung gently in the soft evening breeze.

Harnser went to the bank opposite the entrance and found a comfortable place to sit. The house was like a magnet to his eyes. He watched as the sun dropped low, behind and to the left of the building, producing an eggshell blue sky.

Slowly the light faded and it was almost dark when he suddenly shivered and replaced his jacket. He would return to this spot he knew, and not just to try to see the girl. It was at times like this that he wished he could paint, maybe he could; he had never tried, his music lessons had taken up all his spare time. He was not too bad at sketching; perhaps he would buy himself some paints. He would love to transfer to canvas the scene he had witnessed tonight – Barcada Sunset – he would always remember this night, with or without a permanent reminder.

He began the walk home, wondering where the girl was. He had seen no evidence of life at the house and no lighted windows. Perhaps she did not live at the house at all. He would venture further down the lane the next time he came. There were probably many dwellings along the three-mile route to Flinton. Then an extraordinary thought came to him. If she did live at the house why would she have any interest in him, a mere assistant teacher? The house was substantial; the family obviously had means. How stupid he now felt; and disillusioned. He must get her out of his head and concentrate on his studies, how else would he ever aspire to being a schoolmaster? Even so somewhere at the back of his mind he could hear Silas' voice '*old Major Biddemore has a grace and favour home*'.

One did not live in grace and favour homes if one had money! His mood brightened.

Chapter Five

For the third Sunday in succession the girl was not in church. Harnser's heart had leapt when he saw a chestnut head three pews in front of him, but the tresses did not look so thick as he remembered on the girl, and, when the head had turned, he saw that it was not her. The girl in front however liked what she saw in Harnser; it was always exciting to the young village population when newcomers moved in, especially if they were young and good looking. Several times through the service she turned and smiled at him in a flirtatious way. Each time the woman by her side, who Harnser judged to be her mother, gently touched her shoulder and persuaded her to turn back. By the girl's side was a boy and beside him two men, one was elderly.

From his position near the back of the church Harnser had a good view of most of the village population. There were several young ladies around his own age, all taking great interest in him, which amused his mother. Silas was sitting across the aisle, alone; his wife was still resting after childbirth. The congregation sang the last hymn and filed from the church. Harnser blushed visibly as the young ladies passed and cast him furtive, appreciative glances.

Once outside Silas joined the family and addressed the group, "You must *all* call on us and meet our son now that Sally is a little stronger, she much appreciated the gifts, they will come in very handy. She hopes you will all come to Sunday lunch in a few weeks time so that she can thank you properly." He then turned to Maria with a twinkle in his eye. "Your son certainly turned a few heads did he not? I swear the young female congregation is growing week by week. No doubt Vicar Hanley is much indebted to you."

Maria returned his smile; she liked Silas and his wife. She

and Sally would become good friends she knew. She felt she was fitting in with the villagers. Everyone had been very welcoming, but then, she thought, her father had lived here all his life and a lot of the older population remembered her from when she was a girl. She had begun to feel that she had never left.

Harnser became aware of the group to their right. The young girl was still watching him and the boy shot him a cheeky smile. He realized it was Tom Hubbard, he looked slightly different with his face scrubbed and his hair flat. He returned the smile. He thought he should go over and have a word so he excused himself and approached the small group, smiling at Tom as he did so.

"Good morning," he said self consciously, aware of the girl's eyes on him, then, offering his hand to the old man, "Many happy returns of the day; I understand you are seventy today."

The old man beamed, "I am too, or so they tell me. How did y' know that?"

"Because that walking stick," Harnser pointed to the stick on which the old man was leaning, "was the last one my grandfather made." He wished he were not so shy. The girl's eyes were still on him and he knew his face was burning.

"So you're John's boy. A sorry day it was when he went, I miss him, aye I miss him. We allust had a mardle, him and me, yis, I miss him a lot." He smiled sadly, "But I'm proud to have his last walkin' stick, that I am." He fell quiet, obviously thinking of his old friend and Harnser wondered if he should have brought up the subject.

Walter, Maria, James and Silas joined the group and introductions were duly made, then the whole party made their way toward the lych gate. But one young lady, for all her flirtatiousness, had kept strangely quiet – she did not want to appear *too* forward, on the other hand she noticed she was the envy of her peers, had not Harnser Elliot walked from the church with her? And he a teacher at The Hall!

The following morning, in the schoolroom, Harnser amd Silas were surprised by a rare visit by their employer. Lord Haverham entered quietly and made his way to Silas whereupon Harnser watched as the pair engaged in conversation. The exchange was short, after which Lord Haverham nodded in Harnser's direction and took his leave. Silas immediately approached Harnser with a sombre look on his face and the younger man felt that he was in trouble of some sort. All sorts of imaginary forebodings flashed across his mind as the older man crossed the schoolroom toward him, but what he said took him completely by surprise. "The schoolroom will be closed all day on Thursday, Harnser, due to the funeral of Mrs Biddemore, apparently she died yesterday in London; she will be brought home by train tomorrow evening. Lord and Lady Haverham are close friends of the Sandersons. Mrs Biddemore was the late Mr Charles Sanderson's sister. The family have had to curtail their London holiday."

The news spread quickly. The London train was due in at Winford at five o'clock on Tuesday evening. By that time every dwelling on the main road through the village had its front curtains drawn in readiness for Walter Fennel, the Flinton undertaker, to bring Mrs Biddemore home to Oxley House; her birthplace. The Bell Inn doors were also closed at five o'clock but would reopen at six, when the hearse and bereaved party had passed through. Few people were abroad at the time; those that were stopped all activity and bowed their heads as the solemn procession passed by. Harnser knew that the girl could be among them, but he stayed indoors, this was not an appropriate time for him to look for her.

Slowly the village came back to life and groups of people gathered to exchange their views on the sad occasion. Abel Sawyer held court outside The Bell. A good many villagers were employed on the Oxley estate and all had their own tales to tell of the late Mrs Biddemore.

Harnser joined the group.

"Her granddaughter will miss her," said one estate worker, "they were very close, especially since the young lass lost her mother."

22

Harnser listened to the stories attentively. He felt quite guilty that he was interested in the chatter for all the wrong reasons but then he told himself, he had not known the old lady and he felt sure that 'the granddaughter' and 'the girl' were one and the same. He plucked up courage to enter the conversation.

"How old is the granddaughter?" he asked the man who mentioned her, trying not to sound as eager as he was feeling.

"Oh, now let me think, I should say she'd be about sixteen now, maybe older she's quite tall so it's difficult to tell, she's the apple of her father's eye, I know that."

The talker drained his glass and Harnser offered to refill it: an offer that was readily accepted. "Why thank you, thass very kind of you; I know who you are cos Abel told us. Nothin' much git past Abel you know, he hear all the news. I'm Arthur." The young man offered Harnser his hand, who shook it warmly before going off to fill the glass.

Arthur, it transpired, worked for Mr Sanderson but for the majority of his time he was employed in the grounds of the Biddemore place as a Jack of all trades and was happy to tell the relative newcomer all about the family.

"I think I know the house," said Harnser, "I have been familiarizing myself with the village and I came upon a lovely old house called 'Barcada'. Is that the one?"

"Aye it is, thass where I work most of the time. Bin a bit quiet lately cos they've all bin in London. Miss Arabella will be glad to be back I know that much, She's allust glad to git home agin; although I s'pose it's a bit different this time on such a sad occasion."

Arabella, Arabella Biddemore. Harnser said the name over and over in his mind. He now had a name to put to the face and it did not disappoint him. Arabella was a beautiful name, very fitting for the chestnut haired girl who haunted his thoughts and dominated his dreams.

On Wednesday, the main road through Little Pecking saw more traffic than it usually did in a month. Carriage upon carriage passed this way or that as relatives and friends arrived at

Winford railway station and were ferried to Oxley House. Wednesday evening saw Harnser and Arthur at the village green watching the traffic and chatting in low voices. "She's not going in the family vault," Arthur informed him sombrely, "apparently she didn't wish to, she's goin' to be buried with her husband the Major, on top like."

"Was he a major too?" inquired Harnser.

"Oh, yis, there's a paintin' of him hangin' in the drawin' room at Barcada, in full uniform he is – with his horse." He leaned closer to his receptive companion and whispered, "I've sin it through the winder; when passin' of course, not particularly lookin'." He shot Harnser an indignant look, "I'm not a snooper."

"I am sure you are not. It is quite obvious you would notice such things if you are around the house so much. I expect the family are glad they have such an observant man around to keep an eye on things; especially if they leave the house from time to time."

Arthur sat up a little straighter, puffed his chest out a little and widened his eyes. Yes, he thought to himself his new friend was quite right; he was an asset to his employers, he was quite important really, then, getting back to the subject, "He's not *on* his horse, it's just *with* him."

Harnser smiled, he liked Arthur; he was one of those down to earth, trustworthy sort of people.

"Thass a posh one, Harnser, look at that brass work," Arthur indicated a passing carriage, "I bet some poor beggar was workin' hard at that this mornin'; you could see y' face in them doors. My sister Maisie say it's a nightmare up at the house; gettin' rooms ready, makin' up beds, shakin' curtains, they're workin' all hours."

"Your sister works at the house then?"

"At the big house, yis. They're all just about droppin' on their feet but it's extra money and extra food so she dunt mind none. I've bin up there too for the last two days. I've seen so much dust shook out of them winders this week that you'd think they were usually knee deep in the stuff. And they've all

24

bin told to work quiet like, on account of Mrs Biddemore lyin' in rest in the room she was born in." Arthur gave Harnser a wry smile, "She's the only one gettin' any rest up there at the moment, I can tell you. Mind you she's quite a way from the guest bedrooms. Maisie say there's a half mile walk between the two, but I s'pose the quietness is more out of respect, yis that's what it is," he finished reflectively.

"Are you going to the funeral tomorrow, the church is not over large is it?"

"We've all got to meet for prayers in the little chapel, in the grounds, at half past nine; Vicar Hanley's comin' over. Then we've got to walk down to the church in an orderly manner and stand along the driveway while the cortege pass and the service goes on. Some of the senior members of staff are goin' inside at the back. We've been told to remember it's not time off – it's a privilege. Then we've got to go back and resume our duties – quietly. At six o'clock we'll all get a meal in the kitchens – not all together of course – to thank us for the extra work."

Arthur had been staring into the middle distance as he related all this and Harnser could imagine them being given their orders to ensure that the day went smoothly.

"I *have* been given the day off and I have no specific orders, but I know I will be expected to be in evidence somewhere along the route until the service and burial have both taken place. Silas and I will attend together. I expect we will see you, Arthur."

As he got up to take his leave Harnser's jacket fell open just enough to reveal the ocarina.

"What's that you've got there?" Arthur inquired, pointing at the instrument.

"It is an ocarina, I would play you a tune but it is not really appropriate in the circumstances is it?"

"You could play us a hymn tune," one of their neighbours suggested hopefully. And so, as the light faded on the assemblage on the village green, Harnser played the tune of 'Abide with Me' to an appreciative audience. The Vicar, passing coincidently at that very moment, raised his hand to them and then, addressing Harnser, "I will know where to come if my organist is ever sick."

"Yis," muttered one of the group, "and 'e might not make quite so many mistakes."

The next day an air of sobriety cloaked the village. The sky was lightly overcast but rain did not seriously threaten as the sun tried to break through, and occasionally a few soft rays lit the flint walls of the church and flitted over the countryside.

Harnser and Silas took their places alongside the estate workers, house-maids and the more curious of the villagers, and watched as, one by one, the hearse and the carriages stopped outside the church gates to deliver their occupants.

As the doors of the first coach were opened Harnser saw Arabella again. She was helped down onto the roadway, a tall slim figure in black with a veil covering her face; there was no evidence of her chestnut hair but he knew it to be her. She was joined by an elderly man whose arm she took for the walk up the church path behind the pallbearers carrying the light oak coffin of her late grandmother.

A light breeze caught at her cloak and veil making her appear slight and frail. Harnser wanted to run to her side and support her; instead he watched as once again she walked away from him, out of view.

CHAPTER SIX

Arabella picked up the silver framed photograph and studied the face that stared back at her – her grandmother. She missed the gentle old lady very much; she missed her presence in this house and she missed the conversation and tales of her youth; especially those relating to her elopement with the Major. She had never tired of the stories even though she had heard them many times: this she attributed to the way her grandmother had added small, choice details over the years as she deemed Arabella old enough to hear them. Instead of becoming stale and boring over time, the stories had grown along with Arabella until they were rich in detail and had been told with an air of secrecy and excitement.

The old lady, after whom Arabella had been named, would sit with her granddaughter on winter evenings, in front of a roaring fire and tell her the family history. Sometimes Arabella's father would be in the room and sometimes not. When he was present the stories would be factual and to the point; when he was not there, they were embellished with finer feelings, emotion and an air of secrecy. Needless to say the two women had been close – very close.

"My father built this house for me," the old lady would say wistfully; her mind going back in time, her eyes roaming around the lamp-lit room. "He knew that my brother Charles would inherit the House you see and he wanted me close. One day he sat me in front of him on his horse and rode over the estate – I could not have been more than six years old.

" 'Where would you like your house to be built my little Arabella?' he asked me, 'choose anywhere on the estate and your papa will build it for you. I do not want you to move miles away from me when someone steals your heart away'.

" But I did not choose this site on *that* day. We rode the estate many times and for several years until one day, sitting atop my pony, I came over the fields and saw the church nestling among the trees in Little Pecking with the sun soft on its flint walls. 'That is how I want my house to look,' I said assuredly, 'among trees with the evening sun warming the bricks'. And so, after much deliberation, we chose this spot; hidden from the road until you get part way down the lane, does it not look lovely, Arabella, when you happen upon it that way?"

Arabella smiled to herself as she replaced the photograph, "Yes, Grandmother," she said softly, "I like to happen upon it that way too."

Her eyes were moist as they lingered on the familiar face, then she shut them tight, her face crumpled, and the tears fell copiously down her cheeks. She did not hear her father enter the room as she sat sobbing by the petite sofa table but she felt his arm around her shoulders and rose, only to collapse again; her face pressed hard against his tweed waistcoat and the heavy gold chain of his pocket watch. He rocked her comfortingly for maybe five minutes until her sobs subsided, then they supported each other to the sofa and sat quietly together; each knowing the other was away, back in time, thinking of the dear old lady they had just lost.

Arabella Sanderson Senior had been just ten years old when her father began building her house. She had watched with love and interest as the walls went up, the latticed windows went in, the roof went on, the beautiful mahogany staircase was placed and the stables and outhouses took place around. She never tired of watching the men at work as she dreamed of growing up, getting married and having children at 'Barcada'. Her house was so different from Oxley House. The ceilings were low and beamed, whereas Oxley's were high and elegant; the windows were casement and latticed, while Oxley's were tall and sashed; the doors were ledge and braced, with Suffolk latches, Oxley's were panelled. The chimney breastsummer in the sitting room was English oak like most of the other wood in the house. "It is a lady's house," her father had told her proudly, " for the most beautiful young lady in the land."

As the house neared completion the land was measured off – ten acres – and the gardens formed, tilled and planted. Lastly a name had been chosen. "What do you think of 'Barcada', my little Arabella? I saw a house by that name in the West Indies – a rich man's house with a beautiful woman in the garden." So, 'Barcada' it was, all the way from the sugar lands to the Suffolk countryside – an exotic name for a traditional English house, but one that she loved.

The house had stood empty, cared for but uninhabited, waiting for Arabella to grow up and find a husband. The gardens flourished and the little girl spent most of her spare time in or around her house, dreaming of the future, to the delight of her father.

It was six months after her eighteenth birthday that Arabella's life changed so dramatically, with the death of her father, from a heart attack. He had returned home from riding complaining of feeling unwell and had gone to his bedroom to rest; two hours later Arabella's mother, Eliza, had found him lifeless on the landing; he had obviously tried to get downstairs to summon help. The house was plunged into shocked sadness.

Eliza took to her bed where, apart from attending the funeral, she more or less stayed for a month. She never really regained her spirits, becoming a semi-invalid for the rest of her life. Eliza left the running of the estate to her son Charles and told Arabella to be a good girl and do as her brother told her, which she did willingly. Some days her mother would sit on the terrace with her or walk in the garden but she did not wish to socialize, so became something of a recluse. "You must marry only for love, Arabella," she told her daughter on many occasions, "follow your heart, my darling, like I did." And then she would dab at her eyes and stare expectantly at the garden as if she expected her husband to stride up the path and save her at any minute, make her feel young again – happy again – alive again.

Arabella spent most of her time with Eliza, cajoling her into doing this and that, so much so that she hardly ever visited

29

'Barcada'; leaving the staff to keep it aired and clean. Although she still loved the house, it saddened her that her father would never see her living there – that she would never 'ride over' to see him at Oxley as he had intended. Then one night out of the blue some visitors called – Eliza's cousin Oswald whom she had not seen since her husband's funeral, but it was his companion, resplendent in uniform, that most interested Arabella; and with whom she fell instantly and hopelessly in love, much to her brother's dismay.

The visitors stayed for a fortnight, at Eliza's insistence. Oswald tried to rally his cousin so it was up to Arabella to entertain Bertie and show him the estate. She rode with him most days. They laughed and talked and delighted in one another's company – by the end of the visit they had declared their feelings – there was just one problem, Bertie was twenty-two years older than his sweetheart, a fact that horrified her brother Charles.

To begin with, when the situation was realized he tried to reason with his sister. "It is because you have been cooped up so long with your mother, you will get over him and meet someone your own age, we must start entertaining again; please, Arabella, think how Father would feel, think how much it will hurt your mother."

"Mother has always told me to follow my heart," retorted the young girl, "ask her yourself, I'm sure she would approve."

"You are missing a father figure, I have been so busy that I have neglected you but I will rectify the matter, we will get back to normal, you will see."

Arabella's mother did not approve the match but she did not have the strength or the desire to argue the matter with her daughter. She hoped that time and distance would resolve the problem. The Major had returned to Essex. Arabella would settle down; or so she hoped. And if she did not – well – was it so terrible to marry an older man? She was too tired and frail to argue; her daughter's happiness was paramount.

To all outward appearances and in consideration of her mothers health Arabella did 'settle down' – while continuing to correspond with the Major. Charles however became very active on the matter; making enquiries among his friends and acquaintances – enquiries that confirmed his fears: Bertie, it transpired, had a reputation with the ladies and gambled excessively.

Gradually, Arabella won her mother's approval, but only because Eliza could see that her daughter was not just infatuated. Bertie visited often, against the wishes of Charles. The two men were coolly polite to one another, that was all.

Eliza faded away and followed her husband into the family vault. She'd had no will to live without him and, it seemed, had become prone to every illness under the sun.

With his mother's death Charles began, anew, to oppose Arabella's marriage to Bertie. "I will not allow it, Arabella, I am your legal guardian, you have no money until you are twenty-one and I know for a fact that Bertie has no money to speak of. He gambles heavily – did you know?"

"He has his faults, Charles, as have we all, but he loves me and has promised to reform. For my sake please give us your blessing. Mother liked him, why don't you?"

"Of course he won Mother over, he is a ladies man, he could charm the birds from the trees."

"When I am twenty-one I will inherit my money and 'Barcada'. Bertie and I will have a home and an income. I will marry him anyway but I would rather have your blessing".

Charles lowered his eyes, he was about to shatter his sister's dreams and he was not going to enjoy it.

"That is precisely where you are wrong, Arabella. You may be approaching twenty-one and you will inherit your money but you will not inherit Barcada – not if you marry Bertie."

"But it is not up to you, you cannot stop me," she faced her brother, colour high in her cheeks, but she had a cold feeling in her chest, she could sense disaster, her brother had a determined look on his face.

"To all intents and purposes," he began quietly, "Barcada does not exist." Father never added it to his Will so he did not leave it to you. It is part of the estate; as are all the other homes and cottages and, as you well know, the estate was left to me."

31

There, he had said it.

He watched as the blood drained from his sister's face and rushed forward to catch her as she collapsed in a heap at his feet.

Six months later, after an uneventful twenty-first birthday, Arabella eloped with the Major. He had now retired from the army.

For ten years they lived in London but there was too much temptation to gamble and Arabella knew she had to look after her dwindling inheritance, she also missed the countryside, so she persuaded her husband to move to Essex where they bought a farm.

Their son, Bertie, had been born two years after the marriage and was doted on by both parents. He quickly became known as the 'Young Major'. Bertie loved Arabella, his womanising was easily curtailed, but his gambling was a different matter and slowly the money disappeared. The farm did well enough and Arabella always forgave Bertie's 'lapses' as she called them, after all, he did try to resist the temptation to gamble and he did love her so, but she could not prevent him seeing his friends now and again could she? How many people were as happy as they were? It was one long love affair. They doted on each other; nothing else mattered.

By the time Bertie died, Arabella's money had gone, but she had no regrets, they had had a wonderful marriage. She was glad she had followed her heart. Even so she thought about Oxley and Barcada, she wondered how her brother was – if he had married and who was living in her house. Her lifestyle had changed considerably and now she was going back – back to Little Pecking for one day – one very sad day – to bury her husband in the little churchyard where, one day, she would join him.

But as she made the arrangements she knew she would not go near her old home. It would be a journey to the church only, for a small private funeral, then back to the farm.

She had chosen her way.

*The 'Young Major' was thirty years old when he married Eleanor and brought her home to the farm. They had almost given up hope of a family, when **little** Arabella was born and named after her grandmother.*

Shortly afterwards their fortunes changed after five consecutive bad years. The farm was sold and a small market garden was purchased.

Seven years later Charles Sanderson rode into their yard in a handsome carriage and made his elderly sister an offer she could not refuse.

Little Arabella was twelve years old, her grandmother and namesake was seventy.

"Father, wake up". Arabella gently nudged the Major who had fallen asleep by her side. She had not noticed how dark it had grown as she had lost herself in thoughts of her grandmother, nor how chilly – it was still only May and the little evening fire had burned low.

CHAPTER SEVEN

"Do you mind if I go out?" Arabella looked inquiringly at her father. She did not like to leave him alone too much so soon after his mother's death, although he insisted he did not mind. She was the only *family* he had in the house, but Jenny the maid had been with them for years as had Sarah their cook-housekeeper; both women were in their fifties, Sarah lived in, but Jenny lived in an estate cottage a short way down the lane. The only other indoor help was young Marjie, who was younger than her mistress, she too lived in.

"You go out and get some colour in your cheeks, you are looking far too pale," her father planted a kiss on his daughter's forehead and gave her shoulder an affectionate squeeze. "I have to go into Winford this morning to see my solicitor," he hesitated and then much more brightly, "unless of course you come with me, yes, why do you not do that? You could walk by the sea and meet me for lunch at The Royal. That would do you far more good, me too." Her father smiled wryly, "After an hour or so with old Wilkinson-Kibble I shall be in need of some young company." Arabella understood all too well; on rare occasions she had visited the solicitor's office with both her father and grandmother. She had usually waited in a small room while her elders attended their business, even so, the air was always permeated with the musty smell of old books, dust, and woodwork that had seen better days. Other people who had shared the same room with her had not spoken; appearing to be lost in their sombre thoughts while waiting to make their Wills, arrange property transactions or any other of the solemn purposes for which people visit their solicitors. Sometimes, through the open door, she would see a studious looking clerk creep by, walking carefully as if not wanting to disturb the ancient dust, or let anyone be aware of his existence. The only noises were those of muffled voices behind heavy doors, creaking hinges, shuffling paper and measured footsteps on wooden floors. No, she certainly did not fancy spending an hour or so there on this early summer morning. She was pleased she was now old enough to be left to her own devices when her father attended to such matters – she readily accepted his offer, relishing a walk by the sea.

The waves were high and noisy as Arabella approached from The Royal, where her father had left her. There was much more of a breeze by the sea, but she could feel the warmth of the sun through her black mourning cloak.

She stood on the promenade and faced the sea as the wind swept her hair up and away from her face. She could smell the salt and stood for a while just drinking in the freshness with her head up and her eyes closed, she loved it here. Nothing about nature changed, it was comforting that personal calamities went unnoticed by the natural world, the clouds were always there – floating calmly in the sky; the sea was constant, tides in – out; the sun rose in the morning and set at night; the dawn chorus welcomed the day and evensong bid it goodnight. The world continued on its majestic, awe-inspiring way – oblivious to the millions of personal traumas afflicting people all over the globe.

As Arabella stood and watched the sea these thoughts comforted her somewhat. God in his infinite wisdom took care of everything from the smallest creature to the roaring oceans, from the tiniest seed to the majestic heavens – each balancing the other to keep a constant world. We sometimes do not understand why tragedies happen but we have to put our faith in The Almighty and try as best we can to weather the storms. He, after all, knows best. Her grandmother always told her so. She knew in her heart it was the only way.

She descended the steps to the sands, walking towards the waves as they crashed and foamed on the shore. What with the roar of the sea, the noise of the wind and the screaming of the sea gulls as they whirled and swooped around her, it was far from quiet, but it was strangely peaceful, her soul acquired a calmness for the first time in a fortnight.

She began walking along the shoreline watching the gulls bobbing on the swell, seeing the waves hit the break-waters, sending the spray heavenwards as it shattered into millions of sparkling, sun drenched droplets; blowing in the wind so she felt it on her face. She walked for maybe half an hour kicking her feet free of the clumps of seaweed that swirled ashore only to be drawn back again as the waves receded. She felt very close to her grandmother but there was also, strangely, a sense of release; she could almost hear her namesake's voice telling her not to be unhappy; not to forget, but to accept; accept and move bravely into the future – and that made her think of Charles...

The first time she had seen him was at the small farm they owned before coming to Barcada – she was twelve years old – it was a sunday evening. The chickens and dogs had made such a racket that she had gone out to the main yard to see what the fuss was about and found that a handsome carriage with two fine black horses between the shafts, had just arrived. On the side of the carriage, just below the window, on the door, in gleaming gold paint were the words 'Oxley House', and, underneath, a coat of arms, resplendent in red and yellow.

The carriage driver jumped down and opened the door, whereupon a tall elderly man stepped out onto the dusty, stony ground then stood aside to allow a younger man to descend. Arabella had retreated into the shadowy doorway of the big barn, from where she watched as Jack, their only farm hand, went to greet the visitors. She judged the older man to be in his seventies and the younger, in his early twenties. A worried feeling had crept into her stomach – she knew all about Oxley House and her great uncle Charles, and she was sure that that was the identity of their illustrious visitor.

She ran through the barn, out the other side and round to the back door of the house, hoping she would get there before Jack and the visitors reached the front door – she did. Arabella just had time to warn her grandmother of the impending knock as it came upon the door. Moments later her mother was ushering them into the parlour where, for the first time in almost fifty years her grandmother faced her brother.

"Hello, Arabella, you are looking well," the older man said somewhat awkwardly. "This is my grandson and namesake, Charles." He indicated the tall young man by his side who immediately stepped forward with hand outstretched toward his great aunt. The older man continued carefully, painfully aware of the awkward atmosphere, "I wonder if I might have a private conversation with you about matters that have been at the forefront of my mind for sometime now." The man looked expectantly at his ageing sister, not sure what reception to expect. Not receiving an immediate answer he continued hesitantly, but very gently, "We are both getting older, Arabella. There are matters to settle."

The old lady regained her composure and turned her face toward her son and daughter-in-law. "This is Bertie my son and his wife, Eleanor" – then turning her head toward her granddaughter. "This is my granddaughter, Arabella, " she said stretching out her arm to the girl and drawing her closer, then, "perhaps she would like to show your grandson around the farm," she smiled at the girl, "Would you do that for me, dear?" As hands were shaken the girl responded.

"Yes, Grandmother," she said quietly, then looked toward the young man who was studying her intently. She then turned toward the parlour door hoping he would follow her with no need for further conversation – he did.

The two young people walked through the house in silence and reached the inner yard. "I am glad to be out of there," the young man said, not unkindly, "what say you?" he smiled at Arabella. "This must be a big surprise to you. I, of course, have known about the visit for some time. Grandfather has been on tenterhooks about it for days. I think he brought me along for moral support and, of course," he blushed and hesitated here, "so we could meet," he finished self-consciously. "We are second cousins," he added needlessly.

They had walked in silence through the inner yard and barn, and were heading toward the orchards when Charles spoke again. "I suppose I should warn you," he began cautiously, "Grandfather has plans for us."

Arabella shot her companion a quick look and spoke for the first time. "Plans?" she said puzzled, "What do you mean 'plans for us'?"

Charles appeared even more uncomfortable but continued all the same. "I think he wants to arrange our marriage... keep the money in the family and all that – you know..." he finished lamely.

Arabella coloured to her hair roots at the same time as stumbling on a large stone, necessitating Charles grabbing her arm to prevent her falling. She pulled away quickly as she regained her balance and walked ahead. Her heart was thumping madly in her chest as she tried to absorb this amazing piece of information. She was not sure that her great uncle Charles had even known of her existence before this day. And here he was trying to arrange her marriage. Her mind was all over the place, she had not realized that her pace had increased as her thoughts and her feet raced forward. Charles remained close behind, not knowing what to say or do, but eventually he stopped and called her name. She turned reluctantly, her face burning. "You need have no fear, Sir," she said, looking him straight in the eye. "I am sure you can find a far more suitable bride for yourself than me. I assure you I had no hand in this whatsoever. Apart from anything else I am only twelve years old." There, she had said it – stood up to him; she was shaking with the effort and humiliation of it all.

She found a seat for herself on a log, he sat beside her and suddenly she realized that he was just as embarrassed as she herself. They turned toward one another, their brows furrowed, and then suddenly, simultaneously, their faces relaxed, they smiled, then laughed, and then threw back their heads and rocked with laughter as they saw the funny side of it, and tried to imagine what was going on indoors, between their namesakes.

"What did you think of your cousin Charles?" the old lady asked her granddaughter tentatively, when their guests had gone.

"I thought him very handsome." Her parents looked on but did not speak. The room was very quiet with only the clock making its presence known by its ticking; accentuated by the surrounding silence. Arabella did not know how to answer. She had been waiting for this question. If she said she liked him, would she be committing herself to marriage? On the other hand she would be lying if she said she did not like him – she did very much. The visitors had departed some time since and she wondered what had transpired between her grandmother and great uncle. Her mother and father worked very hard to make a living on the farm with only one paid helping hand. She knew they had little money. She also knew her grandmother felt responsible for the hard times they had suffered; after all she was the one who had turned her back on her comfortable lifestyle and eloped with the Major. Had it not been for that, her descendants would be living in luxury – not scraping a meagre living from a little bit of land and selling their produce for what ever they could. She thought of her cousin; he had not treated her condescendingly, although he must have noticed their dire straits. Her elders were waiting patiently. All their eyes were on her; at last she spoke.

Bearing in mind that they were probably ignorant of the fact that she knew the nature of the recent visit, she said quite brightly, "He was very nice, not at all pompous, he took an interest in the farm, which was surprising considering he lives on such a large estate."

She saw their faces relax, she had said the right thing – she waited – there were exchanged glances, then a pregnant pause – eventually her grandmother spoke. "You are old enough now, Arabella to know of our situation. I have told you of the family history and that I turned my back on great wealth to marry your grandfather Bertie. That was my choice and I was very happy with him as well you know, but my money has all gone and your mother and father work far too hard; I feel responsible for their hardship – and yours of course." Arabella made as if to contradict her grandmother but the old lady gently raised her hand and continued. "Hear me out, please dear, I know none of you blame me, and I am grateful but, today, out of the blue, my brother has

39

offered us a solution to our problems." She looked at each one of the listeners before she said softly, "He wants us all to return to Oxley. Age has mellowed him – he wants to make amends. When he first told me I felt the rebelliousness and fire of my youth rise again but, I am getting old and I owe it to all of you to let bygones be bygones."

Her voice started to break and tears rolled down her cheeks but she went on. "He wants me to take up my rightful place at Barcada, the house my father built for me when I was just a little girl. He is willing to pass it to me as Father intended, together with a capital sum to recompense me for withholding it for so many years. He always knew it to be mine. But," her voice rose a little – became stronger, "that is not all. He also wants to settle money on you, Major, you can retire in style." She smiled at her son – the son who had never reproached her for her wilful actions of youth. "You will be able to look after Eleanor as she deserves – she will be able to rest and regain her strength." Eleanor's pale face looked relieved; she did not know how long she could continue working like she did, she prayed that Bertie would accept – after all it was his birthright and he deserved a rest too.

Bertie saw the relief in his wife's face. He could not deny her the rest she needed. If his mother was prepared to forgive her brother then so should he – for his wife and child's sake if nothing else – he quietly nodded in the direction of his mother.

Lastly the old lady turned towards her granddaughter, she took the girl's hand in her own and said gently, "Arabella, you are very young, still a month from your thirteenth birthday, but I would like you to think about something very important. When we all went to Little Pecking to bury your grandfather, my brother Charles made inquiries of the Vicar. He learned you were my granddaughter and also where we lived. He has decided that he would like his grandson to marry my granddaughter thereby pulling the Sanderson family together again once and for all." She paused, waiting for Arabella to respond, strangely she did not, although her face was burning. So Charles had been right. She remembered how they had laughed out in the orchard, sitting side by side on the log. It had been only two hours ago yet it seemed like *a lifetime. Now all of a sudden it had turned serious. It seemed that her family were all in agreement about their return to Oxley, almost as if they **expected** her to agree. She felt a little frightened. Charles was nice but he was much older – had he been consulted on these matters?*

As if reading her thoughts, her grandmother continued. "We all understand how overwhelming this is for you but, please do not refuse too quickly. Apparently Charles is willing to wait for you providing you both have the opportunity to get to know one another and both agree to the union. They thought perhaps five years time, when you are eighteen, although of course it could be sooner...or later...Whenever it is, on the day of your marriage you will have a large sum of money settled on you. You will be independent...well inasmuch as a married woman can be independent. Believe me, Arabella it is well worth thinking about – a very generous offer."

Arabella was thinking. She could not believe that Charles Sanderson, heir to a huge estate, someone who could pick and choose his bride, could be willing to wait for her. Then she felt herself colouring again. He had now met her, was he still willing to go along with his grandfather's plans? He must have found her very childish compared to his usual lady acquaintances. He could, at this very moment be arguing the point with his grandfather. Her face burned at the thought.

Arabella faced her grandmother. "Charles may not be so keen now that he has met me," she said in a small, embarrassed voice.

"Nonsense, you are beautiful, he will be as keen as ever, if not more so."

It took some time to arrange the move but Charles visited often and Arabella found herself dreaming of being mistress of Oxley House, with her handsome husband by her side – in the meantime her namesake was dreaming too – of taking possession, at last, of Barcada.

With the passage of time Arabella became used to the fact that she was officially promised to her cousin in marriage, it actually quite

41

excited her. She had listened to so many of her grandmother's stories about life at Oxley House, that it did not seem an alien place to her; on the contrary she could see the house and estate in her mind and it was somewhat comforting to her to have her future mapped out. She knew that many girls her age would give their eye teeth to have such a secure future waiting for them, and all without the embarrassment – and sometimes humiliation – of waiting to see which young – or worse still, old – man would ask for their hand in marriage. She had been privy to some of the conversations of her older London cousins when she and her family had stayed in the capital – whispered snatches of betrothals, affairs, marriages, pregnancies and ways of how **not** to fall for a child. She remembered how her face always burned when being enlightened about these things; some of which she did not even understand. Nothing ever seemed to be **explained** fully; just hinted at, whispered with a certain amount of giggled interjection, leaving her to imagine the finer details. Mostly she just stored the information in her brain and hoped that she would hear something from them at a later date that would clarify matters – sometimes she did but, even so, she realised she knew very little about this very personal side of life.

She often wondered what it would be like to be **with** a man in the married way. She had once caught a glimpse of her father in his small clothes through a crack in her parent's bedroom door; he had looked so strange – funny even, nothing like his usual self in his comfortable tweeds. She had felt quite embarrassed around him for quite sometime after that, as if she did not really know him. She had realised that her parents had a life apart from her, a strange secret life to which she would never be privy. She thought of herself and Charles sharing a life like that, she coloured to her hair roots and realised she would be quite content to wait for marriage. She tried not to dwell too much on these matters but, like most things one tries not to think about, it frequently popped into her mind and would not easily leave.

She remembered the time, years ago, when she and Jack had happened upon two dogs in the yard; Sandy had half his body up on top of Poppy and was pushing into her. "Stop y' copulatin' in front of Miss Arabella," Jack had shouted running toward them, then added almost to himself, "She'll be in pup agin afore long no doubt".

"Will she really?" Arabella had said quite excitedly, then, with a frown playing on her forehead, "Is that how she gets to have puppies?"

"Yis," Jack had said somewhat uncomfortably, "That's how she gits in pup."

"Poppy did not look very happy," the little girl said worriedly.

"No she dint, but thass the way of life, we all hatta put up with things we dunt like, to git on in the world and git what we want."

"What does Poppy want?" Arabella had asked.

"Why, she want her pups dunt she? Just like you'll want yours one day – babes I mean."

Slowly Arabella had put the pieces of the jigsaw together until she knew the rudiments of 'copulating'. After that incident with the dogs she seemed to see it everywhere – rabbits, horses, cats, even the chickens were at it. She started to creep around the house imagining that she would spin round at any moment to find people copulating! But gradually she had begun to realise that what happened freely outside between animals was a much more secretive affair between men and women. So much so that it was difficult to find out anything at all about it. She had wondered if Charles was any wiser than she herself, after all he was not married either but...once again she preferred not to dwell ...knowing the rudiments was certainly not enough. Sometimes a fuzzy image of Charles in his small clothes and she in her shift would nudge in on her thoughts and hazily metamorphose into the dogs in the yard...and back again...

...yes, she could wait for marriage.

Chapter Eight

"Penny for 'em, Abel." Arthur settled himself into an easy chair at The Bell, opposite the seasoned traveller. It was still early evening so, until Arthur's appearance, Abel had had the room to himself. It was cosy in the chimney corner, the favourite place of the older regulars, and Abel had had his eyes closed. "Where were you drifting off to then?" Arthur continued as Abel opened his eyes and looked around the room, there was a slightly disappointed look on his weather-beaten, old face as he brought his mind back to the present.

"Now wouldn't you like to know," he said secretively, with a twinkle in his rheumy eyes. "Thass one of the nice things about growin' old, young Arthur, you've got a lot of memories stored up here;" he pointed to his head, "and a lot of places you can visit just sittin' quietly and closin' your eyes."

"Well, you must have bin somewhere nice just now; you didn't look too pleased when I brought you back to the present."

"I was on a pacific island, and a beautiful, lithe, native girl was dancing just for me. I could feel the sun on my back and hear the whispering leaves of the tropical trees as the breezes played amongst them. Oh those lovely lissom bodies, Arthur, in their grass skirts and nothing else. They always made up for the storms and the gales and the cold you went through to get there, oh yes, they certainly did, God's reward, that's what we used to say."

"What d' y' mean 'and nothin' else', what about the top half?" Arthur was very interested in this topic of conversation and was already contemplating a life at sea.

"Naked, naked as the day they were born; no inhibitions whatsoever. I wish I could have brought one home. Mind you," he chuckled mischievously here, "I don't know what my sister Aggie would have said if I'd asked her to share her kitchen with

44

a south sea island girl. English women are far too *reserved*, Arthur; they need to let themselves go a bit," he winked at his young companion here, "Do you know what I mean? Although I don't suppose English weather is conducive to dancing around half naked, well, not in the Winter anyhow."

Arthur had not touched his drink; he was trying to imagine the scene that Abel had just described, but was having difficulty. He thought of may-pole dancing and fair dancing, then the waltzes and polkas and the like he'd seen at Oxley House, but he could not imagine any of them being conducted half naked. His brows were knitted together in a puzzled frown as he questioned his learned friend. "What *sort* of dancing did they do for you, Abel?"

Abel laughed as he realized the limited knowledge of dancing his young friend would have. He hauled himself out of his chair, found a small area of clear floor space, and proceeded to imitate a south sea island dancing girl, while Arthur, and a few other lately arrived regulars, fell about laughing.

"I haven't *quite* got the right movement in my hips," Abel spluttered, out of breath and even more red in the face than usual. "You've got to use your imaginations; I'm a young, beautiful, tanned, slender female in nothing but a grass skirt." He clumsily attempted to gyrate his old body around the room with one hand above his bald head and the other waving to one side, as the perspiration ran into his whiskers and his audience tried to catch their breath.

"I don't think that's a sight I'd want to bring to mind too often," spluttered Arthur as he held his aching midriff and fell back into his chair. "I think you need to go back for a few more lessons!"

"Oh, that I could, oh, that I could," panted the old man recovering in his chair. "I shall be sore tomorrow, young Arthur, all on account of you." He took a few deep breaths and a long drink from his ale mug before saying, "What we need now is a tune or two from young Harnser and his oca...oca...rina" he finished breathlessly.

"And so you shall have." Harnser was still fighting for his own breath and chuckling as he came forward from the back of the small room. He had arrived at the beginning of Abel's performance and was eager to learn what had induced the comical exhibition. Having been enlightened by Arthur, Harnser played a few popular tunes before taking his leave for his usual evening walk in the direction of Rookery lane.

He was sitting high up on the bank, opposite the track leading to Barcada, when he saw her again, a solitary figure in black walking alone. Although she was too far distant for him to see her face she appeared sad. He supposed it was the black clothing and the fact that she was by herself. She walked aimlessly, as if lost in thought. As before, Harnser did not like to think he was spying on her. He decided to scramble through the copse and slide down the bank further up the lane around a corner so that he could meet her as if by accident. He was about to do just that when he had an idea to cheer her up. He raised the ocarina to his lips and played two notes – two well practiced notes – imitating a cuckoo. The girl stopped and looked up into the trees. After a while, seeing nothing, she began walking again. Harnser repeated the two notes. Again she stopped, for longer this time, as her eyes searched the overhead branches looking for the elusive bird, the one renowned for being heard far more often than it is seen. Once again Harnser played the two notes then scrambled away to initiate the desired meeting.

Harnser rounded the corner expecting to come face to face with Arabella, but she was still a short way off, walking slowly, still looking up at the trees. He began whistling softly so that he would not startle her. "A lovely evening," he began casually, though his heartbeat belied his outward demeanour, "a lovely evening for a walk," he finished lamely as he approached his beautiful quarry.

His gaze took in her English rose appearance and luxurious hair and he was sure his eyes would give away his feelings. The girl blushed as she lowered her face from the heavens, realizing she was no longer alone. "Are you looking for something?" he continued, amused that he had imitated the cuckoo so well.

"I – I am looking for the cuckoo," Arabella responded nervously, "I have heard it three times now, and it sounded quite close by but I have not caught sight of it." Harnser's piercing blue eyes were captivating her, he had appeared as if from nowhere, she was not used to being alone with young men; she did not think she ought to be speaking to a complete stranger, but something about him put her at her ease. His voice was soft but deep, reassuring somehow, she wondered if she ought to know him, but she could not remember seeing him before. She realized she was staring at him and felt suddenly self-conscious. Blushing profusely she lowered her eyes and dipped her head as she made to pass him. "Good evening, Sir," she said.

Harnser reacted quickly; he did not want her to leave. "Perhaps you would allow me to walk with you," he said hurriedly, then, sensing her nervousness, he added, "I have seen you before – at your grandmother's funeral. I was sorry to learn of your loss." He noticed the hesitation in her step, so gained enough confidence to continue. "My name is Harnser Elliot, I am assistant teacher to Mr Midcote at The Hall." He held out his hand tentatively to the blushing girl and continued softly, "I believe you are Arabella Biddemore."

His heart raced as he waited for the girl to respond. Her colour had risen when he said her name; he had said it with a softness, almost reverence, and he realized that she knew he was attracted to her. Her hand reached for his, but she was not prepared for the affect it had on her, she pulled away abruptly as the searing sensations swept through her body and her heart thudded uncontrollably; at last she spoke.

"Yes, I am Arabella," she said quietly, trying to keep control of her emotions, how did you learn my name?"

"I have recently moved to the area, I know Arthur, he says he works for you." Harnser waited, hardly daring to breathe, then when she did not speak and, in an effort to normalize the conversation, he said, "Cuckoos are very elusive, we may have a long search on our hands."

She smiled shyly, she liked him. "I expect he is in the copse, it

47

is full of wildlife. There is a way in round the corner but I do not venture in too deeply on my own…" her voice trailed off, was she offering him an invitation? She surprised herself as she added, "Did you notice the turn off to the left? There is a little bridge along there, the stream runs right through the copse."

Harnser seized the opportunity, "I often come for an evening walk along here, perhaps I will see you again…it is usually around this time…I would like to see the bridge… maybe tomorrow evening?"

They knew they were dancing around one another, neither wanting to appear too forward but each keen to meet again, there was a strong mutual attraction simmering in an undercurrent of uncertain excitement.

Suddenly Arabella shivered, "It is getting chilly…Father will be wondering where I am…I told him I would not be long…" She was reluctant to leave her new acquaintance and was already looking forward to the following evening – she would wear a warmer cloak.

Harnser took off his jacket and laid it gently around her shoulders amid her murmured protestations. She allowed him to fall into step beside her as she began retracing her footsteps down the track towards Barcada. She was pleased that the trees were in leaf. They would be unobserved from the house until they got quite close. The jacket was warm from his body heat. For reasons unfamiliar to her, this sent her senses spiralling, she could smell his scent on the rough material. Her hand gripped the front edge of the jacket, ostensibly to secure its position, but the action provoked primaeval feelings and repressed excitement, it was almost as if he were touching her and she realized that she wished he were. No words had passed between them since they entered the track. They each knew the other was reluctant to break the spell, their steps had slowed, they had no wish to finish the journey. The house came into view, its lamp-lit windows exuding a welcome, but it was a welcome easily resisted as the fading light cloaked an air of intimacy around the budding sexual awakening of Arabella Biddemore.

CHAPTER NINE

"There it is." Arabella said, pointing ahead, "It is a pretty little bridge, I come here often."

Harnser had been in a state of turmoil for twenty-four hours, wondering if Arabella would meet him. He could not believe his good fortune when he saw her coming down the track. He had walked to meet her, enjoying the gentle swaying of her body. She was wearing a soft, grey, wool dress and carried a warm cloak. She smiled and blushed as they met. "I am prepared for the evening chill this time, I would not want to deprive you of your coat two evenings in a row."

Harnser took the cloak and put it over his arm along with his jacket. "I have a warm leather-lined waist coat." He had wanted to say, 'I could never be cold in your company, your presence alone keeps me warm.' But he had refrained. Instead he said, "It is much warmer tonight, we are having a lovely May are we not?" He thought of her recent bereavement and added quickly, "weather wise I mean."

She glanced across at him, a brief smile playing on her lips, "Yes," she said, "the weather has been lovely," then added, knowing he would understand, "Nice weather helps, does it not?"

They walked in silence along Rookery Lane, listening to the birdsong and the crickets in the verges. The hedgerows were a mass of blossom, mostly hawthorn and crab apple. Stitchwort could be seen along the roadside together with pretty pink corncockle and celandine.

Now they were approaching the bridge.

The little, brick bridge was indeed appealing, the top bricks were rounded, making it comfortable to lean over and watch the water as it trickled on its way. It was quite shallow, allowing the white pebbles on the bed to be seen easily. The relaxing bubbling sound and sun-kissed ripples were mesmerising and the pair watched in silence for some time.

"There is a waterfall the other side," Arabella said, breaking the spell at last. "If you go down beside the bridge over there," she pointed to the other side of the narrow lane, "there is a wide grassy area where you can sit and watch the water tumbling down on to the pebbles."

"It is beautiful," Harnser said dreamily. "How can you bear to share it with anybody? I am glad you have," he added hurriedly, "it is balm to the soul." But even as he said it he knew that he would want to share such a place with Arabella if the roles were reversed. He had the feeling she came here quite a lot; he also thought it unlikely that she had brought anybody else. The thought pleased him. He did not ask the question; her look told him he had no need to. He smiled at her, his eyes were moist, he wanted to wrap his arms around her, bury his face in that beautiful chestnut hair and forget everything save the two of them. He realized she was waiting for him to speak, and to go down to the grass beside the stream. "Shall we have a race first?"

"A race?"

"Yes, on the stream."

He searched on the ground for two twigs. "We will each throw our 'boats' into the stream on this side of the bridge and see which one arrives at the other side first."

The girl laughed as she held out her hand for her 'boat'. Harnser took a small knife from a leather pouch on his belt and scraped the bark off one twig before handing it over. "There, you can have the white one," he said, and laid it on her palm as his eyes caressed her face.

Ten races later, after running back and forth across the lane, the pair were laughing amid playful banter over who had won. "It is good to see you laugh," Harnser said softly, you must do it more often." The girl blushed slightly as she turned to go down to the stream. The slope was quite steep. Harnser went first and held his hand out to her to assist; she took the hand and once again experienced the sharp pleasurable sensations of last evening. Physical contact was of short duration, but even so,

50

long enough to tell them both that this was no ordinary friendship.

Harnser spread his jacket out on the grass and indicated to Arabella to sit down. He joined her at a slight distance. The bank sloped very gently to the stream and the lane was out of view. They sat in quietude as the stream babbled on its way, oblivious to the embryonic, life-changing events silently taking place on its bank.

The sun warmed their faces and played on the ripples. Two large red damselflies appeared before them over the water and entertained them with a spectacular aerial display, while a black bird sang its evensong in the overhead branches.

Arabella was experiencing the weirdest mixture of emotions of her life; she felt safe but at the same time excited. Everything around her spelled serenity, but her mind was working overtime. She thought about everything before she actually said it; not wanting to voice anything that would spoil the magic. It was difficult for her to believe that she had met this young man for the first time only last evening, she felt as if he had been part of her life for as long as she could remember. It seemed impossible that only two days ago, when she had been walking by the sea, she had not known that he existed; why was that so? The peacefulness of her surroundings and the activity of her brain were at odds with one another. She was aware of both as her mind flitted back and forth. The sound of the stream and the birdsong was like soothing background music to the variety of her thoughts and emotions. There was a certain danger about what she was doing that excited her; she was with a strange young man and nobody knew where they were and yet she felt completely safe. She knew she should not be unchaperoned in such circumstances, that fact added to her excitement. Would she tell her father about him? She thought not, not yet anyway. If she told him, would he let her out again on her own? She was asking questions and getting no answers. What would Charles make of her behaviour? She blushed at her thoughts and glanced sideways to make sure her companion had not seen her high colour; he had not, his eyes were closed.

Her mind went back to her betrothed. He had returned home for her grandmother's funeral and then gone back to London, where the family had business interests. He seemed to spend an inordinate amount of time in the capital. She supposed it was because he was young and healthy so did not tire of the travelling, as his father would.

Old Charles Sanderson had died shortly after his sister had moved back to the fold. It was almost as if he could not die until he had put matters right between them. Now there were just Charles and his father Henry left to manage the family fortunes.

Charles was due home in a fortnight's time, she had received a letter yesterday, but the visit would be short – just a week – before he went off again, this time abroad for a few months. Henry always said it did a young man good to travel abroad; broadened one's horizons and was character building. *Plenty of time to settle down,* he would say. She wondered if she would have to accompany Charles on these travels when they were married. Her train of thought came to an abrupt halt. How could she marry Charles now? She realised with shock that the prospect no longer seemed so attractive. She liked him a lot, had even imagined herself to be in love with him – until last night. Charles had never, even on the day they met, evoked such feelings in her that Harnser did and much to her own secret embarrassment, she acknowledged that the thought of sharing a bedroom with *Harnser* did not worry her at all – she must not think of such things…

Harnser's mind was working along parallel lines to his sweetheart's. Was she his sweetheart? He smiled at his thoughts; she was with him was she not? He had not had to use too much persuasion. He thought of the imitated cuckoo call and felt somewhat guilty. He consoled himself that all was fair in love and war, and that he would confess his playful trick to her as just soon as he was sure he had secured her love. He wanted to go to the top of the bridge and shout at the top of his voice that he had found his one true love. He imagined that the birds would stop singing, the breeze would be calmed, and the stream would stop babbling, while he told the whole of the natural world of his good fortune. He imagined all fauna and flora would whisper the news to each other until the complete world was aware of his love for Arabella. Instead he lay quietly in the evening sunshine beside his beautiful quarry and thanked God for his present situation.

Although he wanted to tell the world, he knew he would tell no one – not yet anyway. He had never felt so happy in his life; he did not want the evening to end. He wanted to ply her with questions and learn every little thing there was to know about her, but he knew he would not. He would savour the mysteriousness of her and get to know her gradually, rather like eating a favourite food very slowly so as to enjoy every succulent morsel and then feel very contented with one's lot.

He had made her laugh, he was pleased about that; he knew she had not known much happiness of late. He would continue to make her laugh, he would treasure and cherish her 'til the end of his days – wrap her in his arms and keep her safe always. She would not have to live in 'grace and favour homes'. He would work his fingers to the bone if need be. His heart had never felt so full, she was everything he had imagined her to be – it had been worth the wait.

Now and again he glanced across at her. At one point he noticed her colour was high and wondered what had made it so. She had stirred and he had quickly closed his eyes. He did not want her to think he was staring at her, although he found it very difficult to keep his eyes from her. He thought of the Summer stretched out before them and knew that they would return to this place many times. He did not think of obstacles, he was aware of none. His thoughts were those of a man in love, any problems in the distant future would be surmountable. Their love would conquer all. It would soon be time to go back to the real world, where all the ordinary people went about their ordinary existence, unaware of the *extra* ordinariness of his own. He would be especially nice to everyone, he could afford to be, he wanted everyone to feel as special as he did himself. His life would never be the same again. He knew that in his mind it would always be divided into two separate parts.

There would be life 'before Arabella' and life 'with Arabella...'

He walked her home, her cloak was not so comforting as his jacket had been...the journey was not long enough...tomorrow was too far away...how could they each live another twenty-four hours without seeing each other?

Chapter Ten

"It is nowhere near as warm tonight, would you like to walk so that we do not feel the cold so much?" Harnser was concerned that Arabella always looked so frail.

She read his thoughts by his expression. "I am much stronger than I look," she assured him, "I have never carried much weight but I am very healthy. However it *would* be nice to walk through the copse, we might locate the cuckoo." She smiled sideways at him, melting his heart. "I love to hear the wood pigeons too, do you not think they sound friendly?"

Harnser was feeling somewhat guilty, this was only their third meeting but he felt he must confess to her. They had reached the bridge and after helping her down to the stream he found a sheltered spot, a bit away from the bank, between some thick bushes. "It is quite dry here, Arabella, would you like to sit down, I have something to confess."

She sat, wondering why he looked so serious. He was far too young to be married, maybe he was promised to someone else too. She felt sharp pangs of jealousy at the thought, an alien emotion to her. She had always considered jealousy to be unattractive. She knew she should tell him about Charles. It was strange how she tried not to think of Charles these days. She just wanted to enjoy all these new feelings. She wanted to enjoy being young with this new companion of hers. She was in no hurry to complicate matters. They were doing nothing wrong. She knew he was falling in love with her, it was in his eyes, but she did not want to frighten him away. She had never felt happier in her life. She told herself that she was not deceiving him. He had not asked much about her at all. Much of the time they spent together was in silence, as now, but what an *exhilarating* silence it was. She could almost *taste* the excitement. All these thoughts were flying through her mind as she sat herself down, eager to know what he had to say, but half dreading it as well. She turned towards him. "Well, do not keep me in suspense," she said lightly though her heart was thudding.

Then they both fell quiet as they heard the elusive bird in the copse. "Cuck-oo, cuck-oo."

Harnser laughed out loud. He felt much happier now that he knew there really *was* a cuckoo in the copse.

"What is so funny?"

He lay back, propping himself up on one elbow. "Please do not be angry with me, Arabella for I could not bear it," he began earnestly, then, wanting to get it over with, he continued, "I played a trick on you two evenings ago, but only," he added hastily, "because I so much wanted to get to know you."

He described how he had seen her, briefly twice before and how much he wanted to speak to her. She listened intently, wondering what the trick had been and then he told her how he had imitated the cuckoo to gain her interest, and to give them a topic of conversation when he met her in the lane. He waited, wondering if she would get up and flounce off. She was studying him; she saw how worried he was. She was quite flattered that he had been so interested in her.

"Do it now," she said suddenly.

"Do what?"

"Imitate the cuckoo. It was definitely a bird I heard that evening. I know it was."

"No, really it was me."

"If it was you, you would be able to repeat it. You are teasing me," she blushed, "although I do not know why."

"Close your eyes, Arabella, and the cuckoo will sit upon your shoulder."

She did as she was asked. Harnser fished the ocarina from within his jacket and played the two notes.

Her eyes sprang open in disbelief. She laughed delightedly. "What is *that*," she said pointing to the little instrument, but before he had time to answer. "Do it again, show me please."

Harnser repeated the operation. He was so pleased that she

was not angry with him.

"I cannot believe how realistic it sounds, can I try?"

He had her interest. He showed her how to play the two notes.

"Can you do any more bird sounds?" she said excitedly.

"Close your eyes again. Your friendly wood pigeon is about to pay you a visit."

"It is so lifelike," she laughed, opening her eyes again, "now I shall never know if it is the real thing or you spying on me." She gave him a playful push, smiling into his eyes.

"There is one way to make sure," Harnser said softly, "and that is to spend all your spare time *with* me." He had been overjoyed to see her laughing and smiling. He quickly resumed the light-hearted conversation. "Do you know what a peewit sounds like?" he continued happily.

"Oh yes, can you make that sound too?"

Harnser plucked a blade of grass from the ground beside him. She watched as he stretched the blade between his two thumbs and blew through the gap, producing a perfect imitation of a peewit.

They both laughed as Arabella tried and failed to master the call. "That one sounded quite like a duck," she spluttered as she rocked with laughter after a loud 'squawk' had been emitted from between her thumbs. "I am going to practice every day until I get it right." Then, "What did you say that was called?" she turned her eyes to the little instrument.

"It is an ocarina."

"I have never before seen one."

"Would you like me to play for you?"

"I would love it."

There was no sun, the sky was quite overcast, but the magic was the same as the little stream trickled by, and Harnser played a collection of tunes, some jolly and toe tapping, some haunting and some romantic. As darkness closed in they wandered reluctantly homeward each knowing the Summer would be one to remember – and there was still so much of it ahead of them and they knew so little about one another – sweet anticipation.

57

They reached the gate to Barcada.

"Goodnight, Arabella," Harnser said softly. "Will you meet me again?" But he knew the answer even as she said it.

"Goodnight, Harnser," then looking into his eyes, "until tomorrow."

CHAPTER ELEVEN

For ten consecutive days Arabella met Harnser in the evenings. They went for long walks – mostly through the copse and across the fields on the other side. It was estate land, which Arabella knew well. For her, the meetings were bitter sweet – she had fallen in love at first sight, just as her grandmother had, riding the estate with the Major. She wondered if the two of them had used the same paths and tracks – if they had sat on the same gates, tree stumps and stiles, if they had found the same grassy clearings in the copse and had sat below the little bridge watching the stream and the wildlife. She knew the gates would have been replaced but they would no doubt have been in the same place. She would look at trees and realize they would have been but saplings in her grandmother's day. She still had not mentioned Charles and it was lying heavily on her mind. Harnser was the perfect gentleman. He had not touched her apart from to assist her over stiles and such like. He had not touched her, but she longed for him to do so – only one thing made her hope that he would not – if ever their friendship progressed openly to romance she would have to tell him about Charles and she did not want to do that. Charles belonged to a different world, a real world, the one in which she had grown up.

She and Harnser belonged to a magical world where time stood still and everything was beautiful. She could not join her two worlds together; they were incompatible. Sometimes she and Harnser would lie so close together on the riverbank that she knew she would only have to roll over to be in his arms. She knew if that happened he would seize her tightly and smother her hair in kisses and she would not stop him – so she did not roll over…

She had not told her father about Harnser. He had got used

to her going for long evening walks and had commented on how much better she was looking. He could see that the strolls had had a therapeutic effect on his daughter so did not complain, although he missed her company.

It was fortunate he liked to read.

Charles' homecoming was just four days away. She knew she would have to tell Harnser that she would not be able to see him for a week. How would she get through that week? How would he? She rehearsed what she would say to him. Every time she thought she had got it word perfect she would turn towards him, he would smile, and she would lose her nerve and another day would go by – she would tell him tomorrow. It was still early June – they had all Summer – somehow she knew that the week would still seem like an eternity.

And then the rain came.

Why had they not arranged a meeting place in the event of rain. She could not believe the situation in which she found herself. Three days to go until Charles came home. Could she trust Arthur to take a letter to Harnser? Where would they meet? She would go mad.

The weather had set in – two days to go – she had not seen him for two days, she could not bear it, her heart ached. What was he doing each evening as she played cards, halma and chess with her father and watched at the windows for evidence of the rain ceasing? She had wild thoughts of putting on her cape and riding to his house on some pretext or other while her father looked stunned, looking at the deserted playing table, and unfinished game...wondering to where his daughter had fled.

"I can see you are missing your walks," the major observed as he waited for his daughter to take her turn at the halma board while she stared out at the relentless rain.

"I am sorry, Father," she turned her face towards his concerned gaze and realized that she must tell him; she could not live a lie. The old saying ' the suppression of truth is a suggestion of falsehood' came to mind as she gripped her hands together in her lap, staring at them as she took a deep breath. "I have something to tell you, Father. Something I should have told you before." She raised her eyes, he was listening intently. "I have a new friend, someone my own age whom I have been meeting in the evenings and walking with."

Her father looked relieved. "But that is wonderful, dear, for a moment I thought you were going to give me bad news. What is her name? Am I going to meet her?"

Arabella blushed, how would he take it? He was waiting patiently, she was searching for the right words. "It is a young man, Father. His name is Harnser Elliot and he is a teacher at The Hall."

Her father stared at her, what was she telling him? Was history repeating itself?

Arabella could imagine what he was thinking. "It is all right, Father. Nothing improper is going on. It is all very innocent. It is just so good to have somebody near to my own age to talk with and accompany me whilst walking. He is very much the gentleman and very intelligent. He is a musician and can imitate the birds and…"

Her father put out his hand towards her, smiling as he did so. "It is all right, my dear, I am glad you have found some young company. I know you do not see many people. It is not as if you have old school friends or sisters and brothers. But do you think people might get the wrong impression? You would not want to be the subject of gossip would you? Perhaps I *should* meet him, it might help to put the friendship on a more acceptable footing, if you see what I mean. He could then be termed 'a friend of the family'. What about inviting him to supper one evening after Charles' visit? Maybe he has a lady friend he could bring as well?"

"I *will* invite him, Father. I do not know if he has a friend to bring. He has not lived here long himself. That is one of the reasons we enjoy each other's company. Neither of us knows many local people. Well *I* know them by sight but our position somewhat sets us apart does it not? They do not realize we have lived a very ordinary life. They associate us with Oxley House and grand living – not scraping a living off the land as we did for so many years. I have more in common with them than they think."

"In some ways I agree with you, Arabella, but you must remember that, although we were poor, we differ from them in two very big ways. We have breeding and education. That counts for a lot. You would not feel at home with the village girls, nor they with you."

" I feel comfortable with Harnser…" she began defensively.

"But you said yourself, he is well educated. He must be, if he is teaching at The Hall."

"I suppose I do not fit with either group," the girl said dejectedly. "I sometimes wonder if I am grand enough to be Charles' wife."

"Of course you are, you are of the same family, how can you have doubts about your suitability?"

Arabella saw her father's concern. "It is probably just the rain making my spirits low," she said with a smile. But she realized how little she thought of her future with Charles. She preferred to put it to the back of her mind. It was the future, it was security but somehow it did not belong in her present thoughts. The present was with Harnser. What if it rained tomorrow too, then she did not meet him all next week? He would think she was no longer interested in their walks – she may never see him again. She was experiencing mild panic. What if he saw her out riding with Charles? What would he think? Would she stop and speak to him? Of course she would, he was her friend. How would she introduce Charles? As her cousin – or her betrothed…No they were not officially engaged. She would say he was her cousin. Yes, after all, that was the truth.

If it rained tomorrow she would give Arthur a letter and ask him to deliver it. For all he knew she might want music lessons!

Her breathing became more even, she realized her father was still waiting for her to take her turn at the halma board…she jumped over four 'men', landed in the opposite corner and smiled triumphantly at her kindly opponent.

The rain had stopped at around mid-day giving way to a weak sun that strived to push its way through the grey clouds. It had won the fight by about five o'clock and it was now a fine evening. Arabella turned into the road and strained her eyes to the end of the track where Harnser usually waited for her. Was he there? She could not see clearly. Her spirits had soared when the rain stopped but now she was concerned that if he did not show up tonight she would not see him for another week.

The earth smelled fresh from all the rain. Birds splashed around in the puddles and flew away as she approached, only to continue their bathing further up the lane. Their antics amused her as she manoeuvred her way between the pools, whilst at the same time looking for Harnser. She was having to lift her skirts free of the mud and water, and hoped that Rookery Lane would be better drained. And then she saw him; the now familiar figure that occupied her thoughts and had stolen away her heart. She began to run, then slowed her pace, as she realized that perhaps she should not show such eagerness. She must not lead him to think that there was a future for them. She must tell him about Charles – she would, tonight. But she saw that *he* was running and that pleased her. For one moment she thought he was going to rush up and embrace her, but of course he did not.

He leapt the last few puddles and took both her hands in his.

"I have missed you *so* much, Arabella," he said, his eyes roaming over her face. "I thought the rain would *never* cease."

They stood looking at each other, each drinking in the other. His hands felt so good and warm as they held hers, she was reluctant to pull away. This was the first time he had touched her apart from giving her assistance. This was spontaneous. If she needed a sign that her feelings were reciprocated then this was it.

"I have missed you too," she said softly.

"We must arrange a place to meet in the event of rain," Harnser was talking quickly, as if making up for lost time. "I would like to take you on the river; we can take a picnic and make a day of it, what do you think of the idea, Arabella?"

She gently withdrew her hands, her smile turned to a happy

laugh as she said, "I can see you have been doing a lot of thinking. Yes, a day on the river would be lovely."

She could see that she had made him very happy.

"First things first. Do you know of a suitable meeting place in the rain?"

They both knew that meeting in the rain would change the nature of their relationship. It was one thing to stroll along country lanes together in view of anyone who might pass by – although they rarely saw anyone on the particular routes they took. It was quite another to be thinking of meeting somewhere dry and private. She knew she had to talk to him.

"I *do* know of somewhere suitable," she said slowly, "I will show you when we return, but I must talk to you about something." She blushed and shot a sideways glance at him.

He was watching her intently. Why did he think he was not going to like what she was about to tell him? Something in her tone of voice worried him. He was so frightened of losing her.

"I will not be able to meet you next week," she began cautiously.

"Which day next week?"

"I will not be able to meet you at all next week, I am sorry," she finished sadly.

"What is the problem? Am I meeting you too often? Am I taking up too much of your free time?"

"My cousin Charles is coming home tonight, for a week, before he goes abroad. I will be expected to spend my time with him. It is important to the family." She paused as they turned down towards the bridge. She hoped that he had picked up on the fact that it was not so important to her.

"I do not understand. Could you not meet me once or twice?" Harnser felt quite dejected; it had all gone so smoothly; too easy; too good to be true.

"I would love to meet you, Harnser." Tears sprang to her eyes and trickled down her cheeks. She leaned on the bridge and took out her handkerchief to check her tears. Harnser took it from her hand, wiping her face gently.

"What is it my love? It breaks my heart to see you weep."

"It is all such a mess," she blurted out, sitting on the low part of the wall, "and when you know the whole story you will never want to see me again and I could not bear it."

"Nothing could make me not want to see you, nothing at all – I promise you."

"I have got to marry my cousin Charles."

There, she had told him. She watched as her sweetheart's face drained of colour.

He dropped to his knees beside her, ignoring the wet ground. He gripped her hands tightly.

"You cannot, Arabella. You cannot do this to me. *I* love you. I have said nothing because we have not known each other very long. *I* love you, Arabella."

"And I you," she said simply, through her tears. "Oh Harnser what are we going to do?"

His mind was racing, they could run away. Would she go with him? No, he could not provide for her as he would want to. He could hardly keep himself and he could not ask her to leave her father.

"Why must you marry him?"

Slowly Arabella told him her family history. She told him about her grandmother and the Major, about their years of poverty, and how, after fifty years, the two halves of the family had been reconciled and how, when she married Charles, the family would be joined together once and for all. She finished by saying, "It means so much to so many people Harnser; my father, my Uncle Henry and Aunt Sarah – Charles. The marriage was part of the agreement. How can I disappoint my father, when after all these years, he has regained his birthright. My aunt and uncle and Charles would never speak to us again, the family would be ripped apart for a second time. My grandmother was so happy when we came home to Barcada. I can see no way out. It is my duty, Harnser and now I am going to lose *you*." She again dissolved into tears. "I told myself there was no harm in our friendship so long as that was all it remained, but now I cannot live without you."

Harnser let go of her hands and raised himself off the

ground to join Arabella on the wall. She loved him. He had known it but now she had *said* it. He loved her, she loved him but their world was falling apart. He thought of the surprise he was preparing for her seventeenth birthday next month but most of all he realized how little he could give her compared to Charles. They did *not* live in a grace and favour home; the village gossips had got it wrong. The beautiful house was their own and, in a few years, Arabella would live at Oxley House, and want for nothing, as Charles' wife. She was waiting for his answer, but he knew he could not help her any more than he could help himself. "Do you have *any* feelings for Charles?" he said at last.

"I like him, and respect him. He is my second cousin. He is a good man. I imagined myself in love with him. I have had little experience of young men. Please do not desert me, Harnser, please remain my friend at the very least."

Harnser put his arm lightly around Arabella's shoulders and drew her to him. "I love you with all my heart but I could never give you the life you deserve. I will be whatever you wish me to be and no, Arabella, I will never desert you." He lifted her head to look at him. "How long before your engagement becomes official?" he asked gently.

"A year's time, when I am eighteen."

"Then we have a whole year before I can be accused of anything improper. Shall we promise each other to remain friends and continue meeting at least until then and try not to dwell on the future? That is the best we can hope for my love – one whole year of memories to last us forever. Shall we promise to make the very, very best of it?"

"Yes, Harnser, I promise."

They stood up, it was getting dark. His arms crept around her and held her close. How he had longed for this moment but he had imagined it so differently – as a beginning rather than an end.

"You *will* come to supper next Tuesday and meet Father?"

"Yes."

"You will not go home and have second thoughts? You will

not desert me?"

"No."

She snuggled into his side, she felt safe. She would think no further than her eighteenth birthday. If they met anyone she would hide her face. No one would think it was she. Sweethearts were aplenty in the public lanes. They would have to make sure they kept to estate land, or at least well out of sight.

Arabella steered Harnser past the entrance to Barcada. A little further on she showed him a gap in the hedge. They went through and walked past the back of a barn. The next buildings were stables. There were steps up the side of the building leading to a door half way up. Arabella pointed to it. "That's the hayloft over the stables. You can always meet me in there if the weather is inclement."

He held her tightly. "I will see you in church tomorrow and then on Saturday evening. "I will be thinking of you all next week. You know where I work and where I live. I am not far away if you ever need me." He knew he must not kiss her, but he put his face into her hair and held her tightly before releasing her into the darkness.

His mood was melancholic as he walked home. His future looked bleak, only one thing consoled him – he had a whole year with Arabella, and a lot could happen in a year...

CHAPTER TWELVE

"Harnser."

The call brought him out of his thoughts and he pulled Nellie to a stop. He turned to find Alice Hubbard waving frantically at the side of the road.

"Harnser, I am so pleased to see you, could you possibly give me a ride home?"

"Of course, Alice." He jumped down to relieve Alice of her heavy shopping baskets and helped her up beside him on the driving seat. "I did not see you in the market place."

Alice could not believe her luck. She had spent hours thinking of ways to get Harnser to herself with little success, and here he was like an answer to a prayer when she really *did* need him. They usually exchanged a few words after church on Sundays and the families walked home together. They sometimes met in the village and exchanged pleasantries but she could not seem to get him really interested in her. She spent hours on Sunday mornings fussing with her hair and pinching her cheeks so that she looked her best for him, evoking constant teasing from her family. She had tried to curb her natural flirting and endeavoured to pronounce her aitches and her t's. Harnser spoke so nicely, she knew she would have to persevere if she hoped to win his affection.

"How is your family, Alice?"

"They're all well thank you," she said quietly. This was another thing she had noticed. Ladies always spoke softly whereas common people tended to shout, even when it was not strictly necessary. She remembered her manners and added, "And your family?"

"Yes, we are all well. James is a handful, always up to mischief, but then, he is only four."

Conversation was a little strained. Harnser knew that Alice

was trying hard to impress him, he felt uneasy. Her family tried to push them together at every opportunity. They thought him a good catch. To Harnser's deep embarrassment Alice wore her heart on her sleeve. He made sure he was always kind to her, but it was difficult to be friendly without encouraging her advances.

"We don't see much of you through the week," she said tentatively. "I expect you are busy with your music lessons."

"Yes, I am busy with one thing and another."

The truth was that, apart from the Vicar's son and the children at The Hall, he was not busy with lessons, but it suited him for Alice to think that way. It saved explanation. Actually Alice was helping him in more ways than she knew, for she liked to give the impression – to her family and friends – that she was actually walking out with him; it was a fantasy in which she indulged, hoping that her dreams would turn to reality.

Harnser was also being secretive about where he spent his evenings so the families could be forgiven for their teasing.

The journey passed in relative silence, save for Nellie's snorting and hoof beats. Alice was overjoyed just to be seen with Harnser so did not notice the silence.

Harnser's thoughts were with Arabella. He had seen her in church with all her family but it was Charles that played on his mind. He was handsome, tall and dark – he had bearing. His clothes were, naturally, of very good quality. One looked at him and thought 'money'. More importantly they looked so well together. Charles was attentive to her. Sometimes he touched her lightly, maybe just a hand on her back to guide her through the Sunday throng, but each time, Harnser experienced such pangs of jealousy that it was painful. He could not bear to think of them together for a week, let alone for the rest of their lives. It also sharply brought home to him how unsuitable he himself was as a contender for her hand. When he had thought that Arabella and her father lived on the charity of the Sandersons he had thought, in time, when he had finished his studies, he could liberate her – give her some dignity, but now he realized he was totally out of her league and had merely told himself that which he wished to hear. After a week in Charles' company would she still want to continue their friendship? He suddenly felt mean. He was doing her an injustice. Of course she loved him. She had fallen in love with him despite her rich, handsome cousin. He could not understand *why*, but she *had*.

Charles was making him feel very insecure.

Alice broke into his thoughts, "I shall be seventeen next month." She hoped she was not being too obvious.

"On which date?"

"The nineteenth."

"I shall be eighteen on the seventh."

She smiled, another little bit of information she had gleaned about him.

And Arabella will be seventeen on the seventeenth, he thought to himself. He must finish making her present this week while he had time on his hands. He had started it during the two days of rain and, it was looking good. The next stage was the difficult one – carving their initials – an entwined A and H. It needed thinking about; maybe not entwined. He was feeling pleased with himself, the labour of love was getting him through a difficult week.

Harnser drove past his own home to deliver Alice and her shopping to her gate. She bristled with importance and pride as she alighted from the conveyance. She hoped her family was watching. She hoped the neighbours were watching. This was just too good to be true. Perhaps he went to town every Tuesday. This could be the first of many rides home with Harnser Elliot. He was carrying her baskets to the door. She would live on this happiness for a month at least. She smiled as she thanked him, then watched dreamily as he turned Nellie around and retraced her footsteps along the High Street. She noticed the curtains move in the house opposite and smiled triumphantly.

Little did she know how short-lived her elation would be.

Chapter Thirteen

Saturday dawned at last. Harnser was putting the finishing touches to Arabella's present when his mother burst into the workshop. "Harnser, come quickly, there has been an accident at the brickworks; Arnold Hubbard has been taken to hospital."

"Is he badly hurt?"

"Yes, but we do not know all the facts, apparently his arm has been crushed. Young Tom is distraught. He says can you take his mother and Alice to Winford. He'll have to stay at home with his grandfather."

Harnser grabbed his jacket and ran to the stable where he quickly set about putting Nellie between the shafts of the trap.

"I will come with you Harnser, to bring the trap back. They will need you to stay with them, it could be a long night."

"Where is James?"

"Out with Walter. I will leave a note; not that it will be necessary, bad news travels like wild fire."

In no time at all the sombre little party were on their way to the hospital. Molly and Alice sat huddled together, weeping. "It probably sounds much worse than it is," Harnser said gently, but the look he shot his mother said something else entirely.

"Can we go faster please?" Molly implored, but she knew it was impossible; Harnser was pushing Nellie to her limits. "He'll be dead before we get there she said hopelessly. "He'll be all alone...all alone...all alone..." her voice trailed off as she rocked herself back and forth, one arm clutched tightly round her stomach, her weeping was heartbreaking. "He's going to die, I know it, Alice, oh no, no, no..." They were inconsolable as they sat gripping each other's hands while Maria offered what words of comfort she could.

The grim face of a brickworks foreman met them outside the hospital where he waited to escort them inside. His voice was flat. "I'm afraid it's bad news, Mrs Hubbard. His arm is crushed and burnt. The chain on the kiln door broke. It swung back onto Arnold's arm. We got him here as quickly as we could. He was asking for you."

Molly and Alice sat one side of the bed, Harnser the other. Arnold opened his eyes once or twice just before dawn and let them linger on his wife and daughter. His mouth moved very slightly on one occasion as he tried to speak.

Four hours later, he opened his eyes again. This time tears ran down his face as he said audibly, "I'm so sorry, Molly, so sorry."

Around nine-thirty, as the distant church bells rang out to summon Winfordians to Sunday worship, Arnold Hubbard made his own journey… into the next world.

Seven days later young Tom would abandon his schooling to start work on Slater's Farm.

He was twelve years old.

CHAPTER FOURTEEN

Charles' carriage drew up at the door of Oxley House amidst a
flurry of excitement. It was good to see his parents and family
again. As always at these times he wondered how Arabella would
receive him. She was such a shy little thing – extremely demure.
He thought her quite enchanting in an ethereal sort of way –
quite unlike the ladies of his acquaintance in London, who
were all self-assured. Contrived coyness was often displayed, but
it was known by all parties to be a feminine little wile, put on
solely for young gentlemen.

Arabella had intrigued him since their first meeting. Despite
their reduced means the family had retained their dignity and
pride, and he had found it quite pleasing that the young girl
had not been in the least in awe of him. In fact she had told
him quite forcefully that their desired future marriage had been
in no way encouraged by her. He smiled as he remembered
them laughing together in the orchard as the absurdity of the
situation engulfed them. She might be shy but there was fire in
her spirit too, just enough to be attractive…was she here to
greet him this evening? Then he saw her as she stepped forward
with his parents. His eyes were riveted. She was tall and willowy
but, what struck him most, was how she had blossomed since his
last visit. She looked radiant, a little more colour than he
remembered and her hair was loose. He found it hard to
believe that this was the same girl with whom he had attended
his aunt's funeral less than a month ago. She had been pale and
sad looking, her hair drawn tightly back and hidden in black.
He had stayed just twenty-four hours before returning to
London – and his other life…

He kissed his mother, Sarah, and father then turned to his
future bride, took both her hands in his and kissed her lightly
on both cheeks. As he did so, her hair was caught by the

evening breeze and lightly brushed his face. A subtle scent of lavender aroused his senses. Suddenly the distant marriage, which he tended to look on as a duty, took on a more appealing aspect.

He half wished he were not soon to go abroad.

He smiled warmly, "It is good to see you looking so well, Arabella, I am looking forward to spending some time with you."

"Yes," she responded kindly, "We do not see enough of you." Perhaps it would not be so bad, she thought, making an effort to improve her mood, after all, Charles was nice and he always had lots of interesting things to tell her about his travels. She would try to make the best of the situation, after all, in a little over a year she would be his wife.

As the little welcoming party turned to re-enter the house, Charles lingered outside for a few minutes, Arabella by his side. "You are so fortunate, Arabella to live permanently in the countryside. I am so busy in London that it hardly crosses my mind but, as soon as I step out of the carriage at Oxley I am overwhelmed by the beautiful night scents; one cannot discern them individually but, collectively, they are amazingly seductive. Do you not find it so? I suspect the honeysuckles are the chief contributors. Did you know that Samuel Pepys called honeysuckle 'the trumpet flower whose bugles blow scent instead of sound'? Is that not one of the most beautiful lines of literature ever written, Arabella? I have always held it in my head and, whenever I arrive home, on a summer's evening, it jumps to the forefront of my mind as the evening fragrances once again take me completely, but pleasantly, by surprise."

Arabella was somewhat surprised by Charles' lyrical phraseology. It was the sort of language more usually used by Harnser. But, she reflected dreamily, Harnser would not need to have travelled all the way from London to appreciate the subtle, aromatic qualities of the countryside. Even so, she could not but be pleased that Charles had an unexpected softer side to his nature. It would go a long way toward making their marriage more palatable. It would be better in some ways if she did not *like* Charles; then she would not feel in the least bit as if she were being unfaithful to Harnser. As it was she felt slightly guilty that she found his company, whilst not exciting, pleasantly companionable.

Charles' voice broke into her thoughts. "I suppose we should be going in," he said wistfully, "unless of course you would like a walk in the garden?"

"A walk in the garden would be lovely," Arabella replied quickly. She could easily wait to join the older generation in the house, she knew that quite soon now they would begin to talk of the future – a future that she herself would rather not dwell on.

"You look very nice in green, it suits your hair." Charles was trying to behave more like a suitor than a cousin. It was not difficult, since he found himself warming to Arabella as a bride, but sometimes, as now, she seemed dreamy and contemplative. It was not an unattractive quality; on the contrary, he found this ethereal side of her nature quite charming, almost as if she were floating by his side.

She turned her head and smiled at him, a secretive, enigmatic smile, that made him wonder where her thoughts were...

Her thoughts were with Harnser. She had seen him in church that morning. She had searched every pew thoroughly with her eyes until they had found him and, momentarily, lingered. She hoped her look had conveyed her feelings for him. He had seemed so sad, almost lonely. She had seen the beginnings of a smile as he caught sight of her, but it had disappeared almost immediately as his eyes dwelt on Charles. She tried to see the situation from his perspective and understood his unhappiness. She had wanted to stop and reassure him, tell him she loved him, tell him she could hardly wait for next Saturday. Instead she smiled generally in his direction letting her eyes linger for the merest second lest anyone should suspect.

Out in the churchyard, after the service, her eyes had again sought him out. As usual he was with a little group of family and neighbours and, not for the first time, she noticed the girl. Normally it did not bother her to see the girl, after all, she was just one of his neighbours, but today she noticed that she was quite pretty, a little plumper than she herself, but quite wholesome and, was it her imagination, or was she standing far too close to Harnser? A little pang of cold fear had clutched her heart before she felt the pressure of Charles' hand in the small of her back as he guided her toward their waiting carriage…

Their horses had reached the brow of a small hillock. Somewhere, from far away, Charles' voice had come to her telling her she looked nice in green. Harnser had told her *that* quite often and as she turned her head and smiled she almost expected to see her secret love by her side. Her secret love…is that what he was?…how tantalisingly delicious….she hugged the knowledge to her and thought of the long Summer ahead…she could almost hear the little waterfall as it tumbled on to the pebbles just a mile or two away. Would Harnser go there without her? Would he watch the damselflies and think of her? Or would he spend more time with the plump, wholesome girl, who tended to stand much too close to him?

The call of the peewit cut across her thoughts, bringing her out of her reverie, causing her to turn and turn about. Was it a peewit or was it Harnser with a blade of grass stretched between his thumbs?

"Are you looking for the bird?" Again Charles' voice came from some distant place where she did not really want to go, but knew she must.

"Did you know they have green backs?"

"Who have?"

"Peewits."

"I thought they were black and white."

"Yes, I thought so too until quite recently, but apparently they have a green oily sheen to their backs… and the males have longer crest feathers…Did you know…?" her voice trailed off as Charles laughed out loud… "I am sorry, am I rambling?"

"I would be delighted to learn all about the indigenous bird population at some point in life but, right now, I would like to learn a little about you. What, for instance, is your favourite gem stone?"

She coloured, she had known she could not put off the subject of the engagement for ever but, somehow, right now did not seem an appropriate time to discuss it... especially when her thoughts were with another man.

"I – I have not really thought about it."

He would think she was disinterested in their engagement. She quickly added, "They are all so beautiful are they not? But since you think green suits me so well, I think I would like an emerald in my ring." She could see that she had said the right thing.

"I was hoping you would say that, Arabella. It was what I had in mind. An emerald it will be then."

"Thank you, Charles." She smiled warmly at him but almost at once her thoughts turned again to Harnser. How she wished it were *his* ring she would be wearing next year.

They turned their horses about and headed home to Oxley.

As the huge house came into view Arabella experienced a weird cold feeling that crept along her spine, she shuddered as she thought of spending the rest of her life there, instead of in the warm friendly confines of Barcada.

"It is a beautiful old house is it not? It always gives me a feeling of permanence." Charles had pulled up his horse and was staring proudly at his family home. "One day, Arabella, all this will be ours – ours to pass on to our children."

Suddenly the enormity of the whole situation hit her like a bolt from the blue. She had hardly dared to think of the engagement and the wedding but suddenly she realized that she would be responsible for providing the next heir to Oxley and by the sound of it Charles was expecting her to produce a whole brood of children to ensure the continuation of the Sanderson name. Panic swept over her, a need to escape... and then the grounds of Oxley began to undulate...then spin around as a warm black cloak engulfed her...

When she regained consciousness she was lying on a sofa in

the drawing room with four anxious faces peering down at her. She struggled to rise, only to have a restraining hand placed on her by her father, who was seated beside her. "No, Arabella, you must stay where you are. We have sent for a doctor."

"What happened?"

"You fainted and, if it were not for Charles' prompt action, would have fallen from your horse. Why did you not tell somebody you were feeling unwell?"

"I – I do feel well. I do not need a doctor, Father. I will be fine."

"We will let Dr Miles be the judge of that my dear and, until he gets here, you must stay where you are."

An hour later Dr Miles ordered Arabella to bed where, he said, she must stay for two days rest. As he explained to her father, "The emotional upheaval of the last few weeks has obviously been too much for your daughter. The loss of her grandmother and the excitement of her young man coming home, all within the space of a month, well, even very healthy young ladies can feel 'delicate' at times and quite prone to fainting. So long as she rests for two days I am sure she will make a complete recovery. I will call again on Tuesday."

The last thing Arabella needed was to be confined to her bed for two days, where there would be little to take her mind of her hopeless situation. Oh, if only Harnser could visit her.

Charles dutifully kept her company for great stretches of the day, as did her father. They encouraged her to sleep but she found it difficult. Her head was full of producing heirs, holding dinner parties and pacing the long corridors of Oxley. Or staring wistfully, out of the high windows, over the great swards of the estate toward the friendly little bridge, the waterfall and the copse where the wood pigeons and Harnser waited for her…her eyes filled with tears.

"Please do not cry, Arabella, look, let me read you some poetry to lift your spirits…" Charles read to her, the room grew dim, lamps were lit, which spread a warm flickering glow all around, but Arabella's spirits refused to be lifted.

By Tuesday afternoon, when Dr Miles called, she had begun

to think she would never be happy again. She worried that, because of her melancholy, he would make her stay in bed longer. She explained that she thought her mood might improve if she were allowed out of doors – surprisingly he agreed and, much to her father's concern, suggested a carriage ride along the seafront at Winford.

As soon as she felt the wind in her hair and heard the whispering of the sea on the shore she felt a little better. She even felt guilty for spoiling Charles' visit home. She decided that, for the next three days she would try to make it up to him, after all, he was not responsible for her present predicament and he had been remarkably attentive during her confinement to bed. "I am sorry, Charles, for spoiling your holiday, especially as you will be away for so long. You must be very disappointed in me."

"I am just happy it was nothing serious and that you are feeling better. We have our whole lives ahead of us, Arabella, I am sure I can spare two days to read you poetry."

Those three words 'our whole lives'…why did they have such an affect on her? She shook her head – a physical expression of an emotional decision – she would not dwell on it. If she did she would fear for her sanity. She must be unselfish and put Charles first. They were cousins, as such they could have some fun, she should make him laugh, give him a few nice memories to take away with him, after all – she had a whole Summer to look forward to.

They walked and talked, they laughed at the antics of the gulls and of the children on the beach, they looked for interesting pebbles and found a sovereign, which he said he would keep in a separate compartment of his wallet with a small photograph of her. He would show her photograph to his travelling companions of which, no doubt, there would be many over the coming months, and make them all envious of him having such a beautiful bride-to-be. And when he returned he would give her back the sovereign and she could keep it as a memento of a happy day. Charles was nice, he was family, why was life so complicated?

They lunched, then Charles took her to a little jeweller's shop where he bought her an emerald and diamond brooch. 'To relieve the plainness of her Sunday black mourning coat', he said, and bring out the colour of her eyes. But mostly it was for her seventeenth birthday in a fortnight's time and would one day compliment her engagement ring. But she could have it now, so that he could have the pleasure of seeing her wear it.

Yes, Charles was nice.

They were all at the railway station to see him off, his parents, his uncle and Arabella. He said his farewells to them in turn leaving Arabella to the last. His mother was crying softly, her husband comforted her.

"I will see you in a year's time, Arabella. Thank you for a lovely week. I especially enjoyed the poetry." She knew he was just being kind. He patted his coat in the area of his heart. "I will keep you here until next year when I give you back your sovereign." Suddenly tears sprang to her eyes, she wished she were worthy of him, she felt sad for him. He was going to keep her in his heart while she would spend the Summer with another man. He kissed her and brushed away her tears.

"Goodbye, Charles, I will think of you often." She knew she would; she felt so guilty. She liked him so much, but liking was not loving, was it?

They waved until they could no longer see him leaning from the window – until the train was the merest speck in the distance, she thought of her photograph close to his heart – and the sovereign that would remind him of a happy day.

PART TWO

The Long Hot Summer

CHAPTER ONE

"It is an unusual name."

"What is?"

"Harnser…"

He smiled across at Arabella's bowed head of chestnut tresses, to where she was intent on making a daisy chain. He loved to just watch her. His heart was full of love for her. Sometimes he felt so full of emotion that tears came easily to his eyes and his throat felt constricted. He often wondered what was going on in her head; sometimes, as now, she shared her thoughts with him.

"…the only Harnser I know," she continued thoughtfully, unaware of his eyes upon her, "is a heron…and who would name their child after a heron?" She raised her head and found him watching her. She coloured as she saw the admiration in his eyes – then laughed mischievously, "I suppose there *is* a slight likeness…" She giggled, stretching her neck up as she did so and pulling her arms close to her sides.

Harnser chuckled; he wanted to tickle her…to prolong the giggling and the mood. How he was enjoying these summer evenings.

"My mother," he said presently, "that is who would name her child after a heron, if you do not like the name I have no objection to you using my second name…"

"I love it…really I do," she cut in quickly, worried that she had offended him, "It is very strong and masculine…and unusual," she finished dreamily, "But why did she choose it?"

Harnser smiled, "About four months before I was born my father arrived home one evening and said to my mother, 'There is a young harnser in the garden, by the pond, did you know?' 'No' my mother replied as she surveyed the young bird. 'He's a handsome little fellow isn't he?'

"Well," said Harnser, the bird came back every day and Mother got so used to Father talking about 'young harnser' in the garden that one day she surprised him by saying, 'If we have a boy I would like to call him Harnser, what do you think?'

"My father thought at first that she was joking but gradually warmed to the idea. The strange thing was that a week after my birth 'young harnser' disappeared until the next Spring – unless of course it was a completely different bird – Mother, of course, liked to think it was the same one coming back to check on his namesake."

"That is a really lovely story," Arabella said feelingly, laying down her daisy chain and peering into the distance. "I shall never see a heron again without thinking of you and your family."

Harnser got up from where he had been sitting and picked up the flowers. He doubled them up and put them around Arabella's hair. He looked deep into her eyes and said throatily "...and *I* will never again see *anything* of beauty without thinking of you...and our Summer."

There were two groups of people on the Village Green as Harnser approached. One comprised young villagers which included Arthur, his sister Maisie, Alice Hubbard and a quiet young man by the name of Jack who had wandered over from Flinton; the other group consisted of older inhabitants of Little Pecking, presided over, as usual, by Abel Sawyer. Harnser nodded in the direction of the latter while making his way to join the former. He was pleased to see that Alice's attention was focused on the young man from Flinton but he realised from her frequent slanted looks in his own direction that she was intent on making him jealous. He felt a pang of pity for her; after all, he was familiar with the situation of wanting someone who is unavailable. He decided to be extra nice to her especially as he was in such a good mood himself, it being Arabella's birthday and a beautiful, fine evening to give her her present.

"You look very happy tonight, Alice," he said, giving her a warm, open smile.

"I am booking kisses for my birthday in two days time," the girl responded coquettishly, eyeing him from beneath lowered lids. "Can I add your name to my list?"

The group were all smiling, looking at him expectantly. He hesitated, not wanting to encourage her advances. "Am I not pretty enough for a school teacher to kiss?" she continued, assuming a hurt look.

He relaxed and decided to join in the fun. "You are very pretty, Alice, you know that, I am flattered that you would want a kiss from the likes of me. It is not an offer I get every day, I shall look forward to my kiss although, I think we should be giving *you* presents."

Alice blushed, she had not expected him to say yes but she had wanted to remind him of her approaching birthday. He had taken the wind out of her sails, so to speak, and now all she could think of was kissing Harnser in two days time. She would make sure as many of her girlfriends as possible witnessed the event.

Someone from the other group called over to Arthur and he wandered over to them, only to come back chuckling. "I've got five more kisses booked for you, Alice, well, six really, cos Abel wants two!"

"Uugghh," the girl shrieked, shaking her head vigorously, "I can't have those whiskers near me, they'll bring me out in a rash, they've been all over the place – my mother told me, she said, 'Where Abel and those whiskers have been don't bear thinking about.' "

Everyone laughed at the change in Alice's manner as she contemplated being kissed by Abel in full view of all and sundry. "Don't worry, Alice, we won't let him get carried away and we'll put his head under the pump spout before we let him near you," Arthur reassured her.

Harnser felt sorry for the girl, "Cheer up, Alice, I will go and persuade Abel that kissing young girls would not be good for him at his age, especially young girls as pretty as you." He smiled at her as he took his leave adding, "Do not renege on the rest of us will you?"

"What does he mean?" she asked, looking around at her contemporaries

Quiet Jack found his tongue. "I think it means don't go back on your promise to us," he said self-consciously.

Alice smiled inwardly. That means Harnser *wants* to kiss me she thought happily, but at the same time she turned her full, flirtatious attention to Jack, who had gone up considerably in her estimation – she liked a man of words.

They were approaching Marcie's bridge when Harnser said, "Close your eyes, Arabella and I will guide you down the slope."

She feigned protestation, "I will fall surely."

"I promise you will not, as my life depends on it," he responded light-heartedly; but as he took her hands in his to help her down he wished things were different; that they had a future together. A sadness engulfed him but it was an emotion he had no time to indulge; they must make the most of their year together. He endeavoured to raise his spirits as he guided Arabella towards his present for her. "You can open your eyes now."

She gazed on the bench seat he had made while she was with Charles. There was a bird on each upright at the sides of the backrest and a rose in the middle. There were leaves along the armrests. "It is beautiful, Harnser," Her voice shook with emotion as she continued, "I feel so unworthy of it. You made it when I was with Charles, did you not?"

"You are *very* worthy of it, Arabella, I enjoyed making it for you. Look," he tipped the seat over, where she saw, burnt into the wood on the underside of the seat, A & H 1863 ~ A YEAR TO REMEMBER.

She could not hold back her tears any longer as she fell against his chest, but the tears were those of happiness, "Oh, Harnser I will treasure it always, can I leave it here near the stream, it is my favourite spot."

"Of course, I have put it well back among the bushes so that it is not visible from the road but if you would rather move it nearer to the water…"

"No, it is perfect where it is."

"At the moment only we two and Nellie know of its home."

"Nellie?"

"You do not think I *carried* it all this way early this morning do you?" They laughed; Nellie, they knew, could be trusted with all their secrets.

"I am sorry the carvings are not very good. I could have asked Walter to help but I was too proud, I wanted to do it myself. One day, I will make you a much better one – take more time."

"It is perfect, Harnser, really I would have it at home but…"

"I understand…anyway, I made it for this spot…so that we will have somewhere comfortable to sit when the ground is damp…you see, I will benefit as much as you…and maybe other young lovers who happen upon this spot…that is a nice thought is it not?"

She smiled, he always knew how to make her feel better. How would she ever live in this village without him? Knowing he was close but unattainable? As always when her thoughts went in this direction she experienced mild panic imagining herself riding her horse in the dead of night, hair and cloak flying wildly around her, to meet him in the moonlight by the stream…while her husband and children slumbered, blissfully unaware, at Oxley House. She would go mad – at times like this she always feared she would lose her sanity and be locked away – out of the public eye; a subject of conjecture and gossip in the village and surrounding district. Her moods were swinging up and down – up and down – elation, despair – elation, despair. She put her hand to her head and swayed. Harnser put out his hand to steady her, his voice came to her as if from afar; a gentle, concerned voice, "Are you alright, Arabella? You look very pale, come, sit down a while." His arm was around her shoulders, she was suddenly aware of his closeness – his body heat, she shuddered, as one does when waking up from a nightmare only to find oneself safe in bed. The colour crept back into her face, she laughed nervously. "I am sorry, for a moment I went where we have promised not to – to the future – and it frightened me. Hold me, Harnser, please hold me close…"

Gradually she relaxed and he loosened his hold. Her fingers caressed the carvings on the armrest of the bench seat – her seat. Her head rested on his shoulder. The sounds of the stream and the copse slowly penetrated her mind and she raised herself as she became aware of a frog hopping around their feet. He was a greeny – brown colour, so well camouflaged in fact, that he would probably have remained unseen had it not been for his faint croaking song. She looked for his mate but, unable to spot her, she spied a small tortoiseshell butterfly, which was fluttering around a blackberry bush to her right. Her eyes and ears became more alert as she picked up the sound of a grasshopper and tried in vain to locate it. She gave up and looked sideways at Harnser, who had his head resting on the back of the seat. His eyes were closed.

She sat watching him, her heart full of love for him. Although his eyes were closed, she imagined him to be fully aware of his surroundings. He had told her often enough that he loved to sit or lie in the sun and listen to the wildlife. His flaxen hair flopped casually over one side of his forehead giving her the urge to gently lift it back with her finger – she resisted – she did not want to spoil the moment and anyway she knew it would fall back, as always. She wondered about his hair; it was strange that, for as long as she had known him, his hair had flopped to his eyebrows; no less, no more. She wondered whether he took great pains to keep it that length or if it just grew more slowly at the front. She smiled as she imagined him studying his reflection every morning and taking his scissors to any strand of hair that threatened to exceed the required length.

A gnat alighted on his face – she was about to brush it away when he twitched his face and raised his hand to do likewise – yes, he was fully aware of his surroundings.

She relaxed and put her head back on Harnser's shoulder, she felt his arm tighten around her, giving her a reassuring squeeze – she thought of her birthday...

Sitting down at the breakfast table that morning she had been delighted to find a vase of sweet peas and fern beside her place setting. A card said simply ' Happy Birthday, Miss Arabella ~ with love Jenny'. She knew that these were from Jenny's garden down the lane and when she brought her breakfast in she quite surprised the woman by getting up and giving her a kiss on the cheek. Her father, from his place opposite, had smiled at the gesture, pleased that his daughter had such a sweet nature. "Eat your breakfast first, Arabella, while it is still hot," he had suggested kindly, seeing her eyes on the prettily wrapped parcels to one side of the table.

Breakfast eaten, she had opened her presents; three beautifully embroidered handkerchiefs from Sarah, their housekeeper; a tablet of lavender soap from young Marjie; a leather-bound writing case with accessories, from her future in-laws. She had smiled at the unspoken message the present conveyed to her – and a beautiful gold bracelet from her father. She had ran around the table to give him a warm hug and he had told her lovingly, "You will get the matching watch for your eighteenth next year."

She had felt so happy and close to everyone that she had gone to her bedroom and fastened Charles' brooch to her frock – far too ornate for it really, but it was too warm for outer wear and she would not wear her light mourning coat, for which it was originally intended, until church on Sunday. She had felt momentarily close to Charles as she had fastened the brooch and admired it in the mirror. So much so that she had felt pangs of guilt when wondering if his thoughts were with her today – when hers were predominantly with Harnser. She wondered what he would give her this evening – whatever it was she would love it and cherish it forever – of that she was sure…

And here she was, in her favourite place, on her birthday, with her sweetheart – hardly able to contain her love for him while her future husband continued his tour of Europe – building his character as he prepared to take on the responsibilities of a wife and family – and the running of Oxley Estate.

She shuddered in the evening sunshine causing Harnser to,

once more, enquire as to her well being...and tighten his arm around her...

Presently he said lazily, "Why is it called Marcie's Bridge, do you know?"

"Yes, my grandmother told me the story. It is named after a little girl who lived in a cottage in Rookery Lane – you know the one, on the outskirts of the village with the pretty roof, it is an estate cottage. There had been a murder in the locality and it was the talk of the village. Little Marcie must have overheard conversations about it. She was five years old and had been sent out to play in the garden because her mother was giving birth, but Marcie did not know this. She went back indoors and heard her mother screaming in pain in one of the bedrooms. Thinking that her mother was being murdered she ran away. She was found two days later during a thunderstorm, freezing cold and half starved under this little bridge. When she recovered she said that she had been hiding from the bad man who was hurting her mother. She had been hiding in the copse and sleeping under the bridge. The whole village turned out to look for her. Sadly her mother *did* die, but the baby boy lived and Marcie became a little mother to him. He eventually moved away but Marcie and her father continued to live in the cottage, even after she married. Her father was a carpenter and he taught his new son-in-law everything he knew. The young man's name was John, and he and his father-in-law worked on my grandmother's house, Barcada.

"Marcie and John had four children; you probably know one of them; Old Joe who is always wandering about the village or in The Bell, a very thin man with a long straggly beard. After that the copse and the bridge were known as Marcie's copse and Marcie's bridge."

"That is very sad but it is good to know our little bridge gave her shelter, it probably saved her life. The story has made this place even more special...on a very special day....happy birthday, Arabella."

CHAPTER TWO

One...two...three...four, Harnser could hear the counting from some way off. A small crowd on the green was obviously making the most of Alice's birthday. Jack was kissing the birthday girl as the youngsters counted aloud, measuring the duration of the kiss...seven...eight...nine...

Alice caught sight of Harnser; she pushed Jack away amid protestations of needing to breathe and stood flushed and happy as she waited for her prize of the night. She looked around, most of the young villagers between twelve and twenty were gathered to join in the merrymaking – Alice was popular and village entertainment was in short supply. She had been chased all over the green by the young, and some not so young, men who were taking advantage of the fun, including the regulars drinking outside The Bell.

Harnser gripped the birthday present, he had not known whether to leave it at the Hubbard house along the way or present it on the green...he guessed Alice would prefer it to be given on the green. It had been difficult choosing the present. He did not want it to be too personal, on the other hand he did not want to embarrass her with something mundane in front of her friends – he was aware of her feelings for him and felt he should be kind on her birthday. In the end he had bought three tablets of lavender soap, prettily wrapped and boxed. Much too expensive really but Alice had had a rough time of it lately what with losing her father and everything. He knew young ladies loved lavender soap; even Arabella had been happy to receive a bar from Marjie on her birthday. Even so, he did not want her to get the impression he was anything but a friend.

The little assemblage had fallen silent. Harnser walked the last few steps to the pump house self-consciously. He tried to appear casual as he handed over the little parcel and sat beside her as she opened it. Alice was nervous, her hands shook as she removed the wrapping, she had the weird feeling that time was standing still and that everyone could hear her heart thudding nervously in her chest. As always, when in Harnser's company, her manner changed; she felt almost humble for some reason. Then the box was revealed. She sat staring at it, then opened it to reveal the individually wrapped soaps. Tears sprang to her eyes, what was happening to her? She had meant to be triumphant and flirtatious in front of her friends but, all she could think about was the big, rough bar of carbolic with which all her family washed – as well as using for scrubbing the floors. *Ladies* used lavender soap; there was always the faint aroma of it wafting around ladies in town – and now she had *three* bars of her own. She resolved to never use more than one – for the experience. The others she would keep forever among her small clothes in her chest of drawers, so that she would always smell like a lady.

Everyone had crowded around and gradually the conversation started up again. "You do like it?" asked Harnser tentatively.

"Oh yes, thank you, it's lovely…really lovely," she added quietly, still looking at the present.

"Well?" Harnser said brightly – a bit too brightly but he wanted to get the happy birthday mood back amongst the youngsters.

"Well what?" the dazed girl replied, her feelings all over the place.

"I thought I had a kiss booked." He jumped up and gently removed the present from Alice's hands to the pump house seat. He grabbed both her hands and playfully pulled her to her feet then, putting his arms around her, called to the watching crowd, "Start counting."

Alice, stunned as she was, could not miss her big chance. She clung to Harnser for all her worth, fastening herself to his mouth with a mixture of love, lust and gratitude.

"…ten…eleven…twelve…"

Gently he pushed the girl away, looking at his watch – his father's watch – as he did so. "Enjoy your birthday, Alice, I must rush or I shall be late for my appointment. Goodbye, I am glad you liked your present."

Much to her disappointment, he once more took his leave...as *her* eyes returned to the box of soaps.

"Can you ride?" Arabella said suddenly as they ran out of the copse, down the slope and toward the stream. "I feel I know you so well and then I realize I hardly know anything at all about you," she continued, slightly out of breath from their running.

"Yes, I can ride, but we do not have a horse now...Father had one but, when he died..." his voice trailed off then he added, smiling, "We have Nellie of course but I do not think she would take kindly to anyone but little James riding her. Why do you ask?"

"It promises to be a fine week; I thought we might go for some early morning rides. Father says you can ride his horse..." she hesitated, "if you would like to of course. An early morning ride along the beach maybe...Father is so pleased I have a friend my own age who knows my position...he likes you, Harnser, he likes you a lot. Just last evening he said it was so good knowing I was having some fun with someone young and strong who could be depended upon to look after me – he considers you a friend of the family."

"Are we deceiving him, Arabella?"

"I do not think so."

"I respect your father, it does not make me feel good..."

She quickly broke in and hushed him. "Ssshh, do not worry, my father is quite intuitive, I am sure he knows how we feel and that is why he does not ask. Charles is away, having fun and Father thinks I should be having fun too...he only wants my happiness...plenty of time in the future, he says, for duty and responsibility. He says I should make the most of my young life and who better to spend my time with than a respectable young man like you, who obviously makes me very happy. No, Harnser do not underestimate my father – I know he is aware, he is just very wise, wise enough to know when to say nothing."

"Then I would love to ride with you."

The early morning mist swirled around them and hugged the land as they made their way down the track toward Flinton. There were quite a few people abroad, mainly farm labourers making their way to work. The figures loomed out of the mist and were swallowed by it again after passing. Arabella and Harnser said little on this part of the ride – one did not know who was about or how close they were.

Presently they came to a fork in the road, they veered to the right and took the lane to Cottlefield. They decided that by going this way they could get to the beach quicker and then ride along the sands to Winford and back again.

They heard the sea before they saw it. Arabella drew her horse to a halt. "Listen, Harnser, doesn't that sound beautiful? I could listen to it all day and never grow tired of it. I love to hear it whisper as it laps on the shore but just listen to it today, it sounds wild and happy – just like me." They edged their horses onto the sands carefully as the sound of the ocean grew louder and louder, still they could not see it, the mist was so dense and the tide was out. The gulls swooped overhead calling as always to all who would listen. They reached the firmer sand where they could now see the sea...they stopped and marvelled at the eerie beauty of it all. "What are you thinking about?" she called over to him.

"I am thinking of a poem."

"Tell me please."

"I will tell you later," he flashed her a smile, "I will race you to the pier," and off they went at a gallop.

She reached their destination first, she knew he had let her win although he laughingly denied it, adding, "I am a little out of practice, I will not let you get away so lightly next time."

They headed for the promenade where they found a seat after securing their horses.

"Is it not beautiful down here in the early morning, Arabella, so peaceful despite all the noise," he smiled at her, and at his contradictory terms, but she knew what he meant; she had felt the same when on the beach after her grandmother had died.

They were sitting close together. Now and again a solitary

figure or two would loom out of the mist and disappear again, silently reminding them that they were not alone. They recognized no one; most were too far away and indistinct.

"The poem," she said, "tell me the poem, please."

He knew she liked poetry, she had mentioned it often. He made a mental note to find her a suitable collection for Christmas – a little book that would not be difficult to carry about her person. He imagined her sitting on her bench seat by the stream and waterfall, reading his little book when she was married and unable to be with him. He took her hand and recited the poem: -

Misty Morning

> *The ethereal misty beauty of the sunrise on the shore,*
> *Is a silent shrouded promise of the warmth that lies in store.*
> *Each creature keeps its secrets from whomsoe'er pass by,*
> *Enveloped in the cloudy cloak, safe from prying eye.*
> *So soon to rise and disappear, the mist will float and soar,*
> *The dazzling sun sees everything, and secrets are no more.*

They sat in silence until she said softly, "That is lovely, one could almost imagine the poet is sitting here with us, describing this very scene."

He turned to her with a secretive smile, "Yes, one could," he said happily.

It was a week of early mists, morning rides, sultry days and warm evenings. Sometimes they rode west, to the broads and the marshes; sometimes to the south, down country lanes; and once more to the beach, as on the first day. Each was aware of the passing days of Summer, but neither mentioned the matter. Harnser felt a little guilty about how seldom he had a decent conversation with his mother these days, and how little time he spent with James, but, he balanced these thoughts with the amount of time he would have next year – time for his family and time over. He would make it up to them then. Arabella was his for only a year – he knew his mother would understand if she knew the details of his predicament – as it was she seemed happy enough to know he was happy, even if she thought the reason for his happiness was Alice. This was something else that bothered him. He had not lied to his mother but he *felt* he had lied by omission. Again he consoled himself by the fact that Alice herself was giving people the impression that they were walking out together, so it would not be gentlemanly to contradict her. This train of thought led him to wonder where, and with whom, Alice was spending her evenings. She was being just as secretive as he was, she was obviously not at home twiddling her thumbs. He knew her better than to think that.

CHAPTER THREE

Harnser's head was full of Arabella. What had he thought about before he knew her? These thoughts, and those of their ride that morning to the marshes and water meadows, were vying for pole position in his head as he reached the gate of Orchard Cottage. He wished he were rich and did not have to leave his sweetheart every morning. As soon as they parted he found himself looking forward to the evening when he could see her again, he knew it was just the same for her. Their eyes would lock and hold; the yearning in them clearly visible. Their entwined fingers would slowly pull apart until only the tips were touching and they would walk backwards from each other; neither wanting to turn away to face another long, lonely day.

He was brought slowly out of his reverie by an insistent voice that gradually penetrated his thoughts. "Mr Stickman, why can't you hear me?"

"I am sorry…yes of course I can hear you, how can I help?"

"Mother need some sticks for her copper, she's waitin', she'll git funny mad if I'm not back soon."

Harnser turned his full attention to the small boy by the gate whose eager eyes shone up at him from a none-too-clean face. His hair was tousled as if he had only just risen from his bed but it was his eyes, clear and brown, that held Harnser's attention and, for some peculiar reason, brought a lump to his throat. What chance did these children have in life; deprived, over-crowded, poorly educated, often hungry and yet amazingly cheerful; their cheeky little faces radiating warmth and friendliness. He realized sadly that they had no inkling of what lay ahead and perhaps it was best that the harshness of life would permeate slowly…

"Can I have them then?" the boy said worriedly.

Harnser hurriedly fetched a bundle of sticks, prepared by Walter. He then made a small detour to an outhouse from where he took two apples from the store to give to the boy. Quickly returning he said, "There, those should please your mother, they are best russets."

The boy's eyes shone brighter, "Thanks, Mr Stickman."

Harnser smiled but stayed him with his hand, saying gently "If you *must* call me something other than my Christian name, please call me 'The Piccolo Man', I'd like that better."

Two furrows appeared between the eager, brown eyes as the lad stared back, befuddled before saying, "But Mother don't want no pickaloes today, Mister."

Harnser laughed out loud as the boy's face relaxed and a wide grin spread over it until he too was laughing merrily, even though he did not understand the joke. Maybe, he thought happily, he could tell his mother about it and make her laugh as well – make her laugh *and* give her a best russet apple, theirs, from their one tree, had all been eaten long ago.

Collecting his bag from the cottage Harnser began his walk to The Hall. He had not gone far when he saw young Tom Hubbard approaching at a run from the opposite direction. The boy began shouting to him long before he was within earshot, causing Harnser to hasten his step, thinking something terrible had happened; as far as Tom was concerned, it had.

Tom eventually reached him, out of breath and looking scared. His eyes darted all around as he gasped, "Have you seen a pig?"

"A pig?"

"Yes, a big black and pink pig. He'll kill me he will, I've let his prize pig escape and after he's killed me he'll sack me I know he will, and then me mother'll kill me too cos we need the money."

The outburst would have been funny were it not for the despair on Tom's face.

"Mr Slater won't sack you, he knows how much you need the money and how much your mother depends on you. He will, no doubt, give you a chance to re-capture the pig."

Tears rolled down Tom's face, "I'm not so sure, Ted's already hided me, he say he'll be held jointly to blame, he's all of a muckwash, he say he'll be sacked too. He say Percy'll notice straight off that he's missin'. Percy don't miss much, he's all about – like dung in the field."

Harnser tried not to smile at the comical analogy. He noted the rope in Tom's hand and said hopefully, " I am sure the pig will be found, there are plenty enough people around here capable of catching him, why, if he's not back by this evening, the whole village will no doubt turn out to help – me included."

He half wished he had not volunteered so readily as he thought of Arabella, but he was quite confident that the excitement would all be over long before then. Little did he realize how wrong he could be.

The village was abuzz with the latest news. Harnser wondered how Arabella would respond if he suggested they spend their evening hunting a pig, but he had promised Tom.

As he approached the Village Green he was amazed at the turn out. Old and young alike had congregated to discuss strategy and form groups in order to find the missing animal. It was decided that groups would have more luck then individuals. Small boys were selected to be 'runners' – Harnser noticed his 'pickaloe' boy amongst them – and Abel would sit outside The Bell to mastermind the whole operation. Each group would include a 'runner' and if the pig was found they would run down to the Green to tell Abel so that he could send out runners to the other groups so that they would not keep searching unnecessarily. Every now and then all searchers would return to The Bell for 'refreshment' or be taken some by the runners. It was not difficult to visualize the situation if the pig had not been found by ten o'clock; half the population would be strewn out over the countryside in a drunken stupor and the other half – the womenfolk – would be out on the rampage to drag home their menfolk. Jack and Ada Foley would be rubbing their hands together and thanking the good Lord for this unexpected piece of good luck that promised to inflate their takings beyond their wildest dreams.

It was unanimously agreed that everyone should go out of their way to keep Percy Slater in an optimistic mood in the hope that he would not sack young Tom Hubbard, who lived in fear of pauperising his grandfather and mother before she had received her compensation from the brickworks.

Sefton Merryweather assured Tom that Percy's bark was far worse than his bite and he should know because he'd known him since schooldays.

Vicar Hanley decided to assist by putting on his best community smile and taking a collection box round the village doors so that, in the event of the animal eluding them all, they could purchase a replacement from Amos Farthing across in Flinton; thus keeping everyone happy whilst ensuring Tom got another chance at porcine husbandry.

"What will you do with the money if the pig *is* found tonight?" asked Aggie Sawyer suspiciously, keeping her hand tight around her purse.

"Well," said the Vicar, having prepared himself for such questions, "we will have a community meeting to decide which good village cause it should go to. You yourself complained to me last Sunday that hymns twenty-five to thirty-six were missing from your church hymn book and you had to share with Sefton, who sang so out of tune that he put you off your own most tuneful performance. New hymn books could be one consideration could they not?"

Aggie reluctantly opened her purse and made a small donation whereupon the Vicar gave her a disappointed look and cast his eyes heavenward until she doubled it. Nevertheless, she thought it a little premature of the Churchman to be collecting at the *start* of the search.

The Village Maid public house at Flinton was deserted. Jack Foley had visited earlier in the day to ask his brother Tom, if he could help him out with some supplies as he expected a brisk trade that evening. Word had quickly spread about young Tom Hubbard's predicament, causing the Flinton regulars to reflect that they might as well have a night out in Little Pecking and join in the fun. Amos and Diggory Farthing, the local pig breeders, had quickly organized some farm carts so that even the old timers could go and have a mardle with their country cousins. And so it was that the track to Little Pecking resembled the trek to the Midsummer Ball with everyone in good humour as they trundled along singing and sharing jokes about marauding pigs throughout history.

"What a lot of trouble to put everyone to," said Molly Hubbard as she cuffed Tom's ear and sent him off to join the searchers. "I don't know how we're goin' to thank everyone, we'll be in their debt forever more."

"Gather you all around, me old shipmates," called Abel Sawyer, as the Green began to clear of everyone save the old timers and the womenfolk. It's going to be a long night so we may as well make ourselves comfortable and enjoy ourselves. Hi up, here's Eli Penny look, we don't often see him over here."

Eli was the Flinton baker who delivered bread and cakes three times a week into Sefton Merryweather's general store. He now left a laughing group to join the small assemblage outside The Bell, chuckling as he did so.

"What's tickling you tonight, Eli?" asked Abel, "Or are you just happy she's let you out?" Eli, was well known for being henpecked.

"Young lad came in just afore I shut up shop tonight and guess what he said"...he spluttered into his ale as it slopped down the mug and he tried to stop laughing, "he said...ha ha ha...he said ha ha ha..."

"Spit it out, Eli," said Abel good naturedly, "we can all do with a laugh."

"He said...ha ha ha... he said... ha ha ha... 'Can I have a pennyworth of stale cakes please, Mother say 'but not too many weddin' cakes 'cause we don't like 'em'...ha ha ha," he finished, holding his middle as he tried to get his breath and the group around roared with laughter.

"Thass a good one, Eli," spluttered Sefton, "wait 'til I tell my missus that tonight, ha ha ha...not too many weddin' cakes...ha ha ha..."

"Aggie," called Abel to his sister where she sat talking to Molly Hubbard on the Green, "Come you on over here you two, this'll give you a good laugh."

And so the good-natured conversation went on as Jack and Ada prayed that the pig would not be caught *too* early.

In the event, Arabella decided that there were far too many people abroad in the neighbourhood for her to accompany Harnser in the search, so she went back to Barcada and persuaded her father to join her at the end of the track, where they spread out a rug and watched the activity with interest and promised to look out for the pig, who had, by some village wit, been given the apposite name of 'Trotter'.

Trotter, alas, was not recovered, therefore, in due course, Vicar Hanley relinquished his hold on his collecting box, said a silent farewell to his new hymn books and purchased a new pig for Percy Slater.

CHAPTER FOUR

"I hope you have done this before," said Arabella nervously as Harnser helped her into the boat.

"Of course I have, you are in safe hands," he gave her a cheeky smile, "herons are quite at home on the river."

It was an ideal day for boating with just enough breeze to take the heat from the day without causing discomfort. As Harnser guided the little boat up river he feasted his eyes on his sweetheart sitting opposite. She had on a white, high-bodiced frock, which had a floaty appearance that added to her ethereal beauty and gave her creamy complexion a flush of soft colour. Her rich, chestnut hair was caught and fastened high on the back of her head and fell loosely down in a cluster of ringlets beneath her straw hat. For some reason the ringlets brought to Harnser's mind a raceme of soft wisteria and he had the urge to gently cup them in his hand and bury his face in the fragrance. Admiration shone from his eyes causing a barely discernible smile to play around Arabella's lips as she blushingly caught his gaze time and time again from beneath lowered lashes. She gently turned her head this way and that as she tried to take in the views of the river banks but found her gaze returning always to Harnser and his sparkling dark eyes as they unashamedly made love to her. The rhythmic splash of the oars added to the relaxing atmosphere as they made their way upstream.

Ducks protested loudly as they bobbed around the reeds and hoped for titbits to compensate for the disturbance. Occasionally a Mute Swan or two would sail majestically by with young cygnets in attendance, causing Arabella to ooh and aahh and Harnser would smile happily at the simple things that brought delight to his love. One did not always need money to bring pleasure to a lady.

The sweethearts smiled and nodded to other day-trippers on

the water and along the banks as they searched for a quiet spot to share their picnic.

A suitable riverside oasis was found; a lush grassy spot with surrounding trees to afford them shade from the hot summer sun. "There, you need not have brought your parasol, Arabella, nature has provided us with one."

She allowed Harnser to help her ashore and watched dreamily as he secured the boat and lifted out their belongings; a blanket, some cushions and, of course, the picnic basket, their outer garments could remain in the craft.

"I cannot see anyone nearby," she whispered presently, "apart from on the other side of the river. Look, Harnser I believe they are waving to us...yes they are...shall I wave back?"

"Of course you must," he chuckled at her shyness, "and you need not ask my permission." He took her hand and guided her back from the water's edge where they settled down to enjoy the views and watch the pleasure craft sail by. "It will be completely different tomorrow," he said thoughtfully. "The wherries and cargo boats will be in evidence again. Strange how the ambience of the river can change so dramatically."

"Then let us enjoy *today*, are you going to serenade me?"

"Would you like me to?"

"Of course."

Arabella lay down and closed her eyes while Harnser softly played the ocarina. The water lapped gently against the bank and boat, and the birds sang in the foliage around them and the trees above.

After a while Harnser ceased playing.

"I was enjoying that," she said dreamily without opening her eyes.

"And I am enjoying *you*," he said throatily. "I am in heaven, Arabella, I truly am. What purpose did my life have before I met you? How did I live without you? A few months ago I was unaware of your existence, how can that be when you are the very essence of my life?" He was lying by her side; propped up on one elbow holding one of her hands in his.

She looked up into his eyes; how she loved those eyes, usually merrily sparkling, but now deep and brooding. She lifted his hand to her lips and gently kissed his fingers. "I do not know," she replied softly, "I only know that I feel the same."

He moved his head down and his lips found hers; they touched gently several times with sweet, torturous restraint before crushing together in a passion which took away their breath and very nearly their reasoning. Their world stood still in a moment of ecstasy until Harnser pulled himself away. "I am sorry," he said huskily, "you are so beautiful, I love you, Arabella, I love you...I love you..."

"And I, you. I have never been happier. I will hold this day in my heart forever; a perfect day in our Summer."

A picnic...more declarations of love...a few more tunes... some flowers and grasses gathered...shared secrets.

Promises...kisses...caresses...listening to the birds...watching the river. The afternoon passed in the glorious togetherness of young love.

On the way back they fed the ducks.

Harnser climbed the bank to pick a spray of pink dog roses; perfect specimens, sweetly scented. Some were open flowers, a few still in bud and some were at the pretty half-way stage. He brought them down triumphantly and gave them to his love. "Here, Arabella, pretty and perfect just like you, creamy pink like your complexion. See the petals, heart shaped, symbolic of our love – pretty English roses for my pretty English rose."

"I will press them tonight and add them to my collection. I have pressed every flower you have given me, including the ones we gathered on Sunday from the river bank." She blushed visibly as she said the last few words, knowing that Harnser, like her, would be instantly reminded of their passion.

"How will we manage, Arabella, when we have only our memories and our keepsakes? No," he added quickly, "we will not think about such things tonight, we have months ahead of us to be happy." But all the same, he knew they were both aware that the year was passing quickly – too quickly. He did not know how he would bear to see her in church on Sunday mornings knowing that she would go home with Charles and he would not see her for another agonizing week. It had been hard enough on Charles' visit home, but at least it had been for only a week and he had kept busy making the bench seat. They reached the said seat and sat down. "Do you think of Marcie when we come here," he said suddenly.

"Only when I am sad."

"Yes, it is strange, is it not, that when one is sad one's thoughts tend to wander to other sad occasions, even other people's. You would think that nature would have us think of happy things at those times so that our mood improved"

She smiled at him, "You think of the weirdest things sometimes, how can one think of happy things when one is sad?"

"I do not know," he said thoughtfully, "but it may be expedient to learn how to do so."

He turned to her and asked suddenly, "Do you remember how we met?"

"Of course," she laughed, "you were very deceitful, I am amazed I forgave you."

"There, I have done it."

"Done what?"

"Turned our thoughts to happy ones."

"You," she said, laughing into his dark eyes, "are very clever." She picked up the spray of roses, studying them intently and said softly, "You are also very romantic."

"Arabella, we must go to a photographer as soon as possible, while the wild roses are still blooming, so that I can have a photograph of you holding a spray. And you must wear your white frock – the one you wore last Sunday."

She laughed merrily at his enthusiasm. She loved the two distinct sides of his character. He could be serious, knowledgeable and interesting, as befits a student teacher; or engagingly boyish.

A plan was beginning to formulate in her mind.

Chapter Five

"Well, how are all my old shipmates tonight?" asked Abel as he lowered his head to enter the little room and take up his place in the chimney corner. "Has Trotter been captured?"

"If you ask me," said old Joe sagely, "he's locked up in someone's shed 'til the heat is off."

"No, nobody would've done that with young Tom's job on the line," said Abel.

"I s'pose you're right, thass just my cynical nature talkin', but you would think Christmas had come if a pig walked into your garden wouldn't you. I mean, thass not as if he's a little runt is it?"

"Now look who's come to see us tonight," said Abel setting down his mug of ale and looking toward the little doorway. "Has she let you out tonight, young Harry?"

Harry Greene and Arthur entered the room and found a seat taking great care, as always, not to sit directly opposite Sefton Merryweather and his straining, waistcoat buttons, which they feared could take an eye out should they give up the fight to stay attached.

"You look as though you have lost a shilling and found sixpence, Master Harry. You'll have to cheer him up, young Arthur," he said, turning toward the other young man, "we can't look at that long face all night."

"I was hoping to have help in that direction," said Arthur hopefully, "He's just had a ruckus with Polly."

"Oh, you're having marital problems are you?" said Amos tentatively.

"She say she don't know why I want to go out of a night when I could sit in with her and her mother. I told her a man needs some fresh air of an evening when he's been cooped up in a six-acre field all day."

The group laughed heartily out loud, spluttering into their ale mugs, until Sefton ventured, "I bet young Polly didn't take too kindly to that; she was always sparky."

"She took umbrage and flung a scrubbing brush across the kitchen. It caught me a fair crack at the back of the neck. I told her, with a force like that I was going to enter her for the village games next Michaelmas so she upped and followed it with a bar of carbolic soap. It caught me right alongside my ear. My head's *still* reelin'." Harry rubbed the side of his head as he scowled at the thought of it. The group rocked with laughter as they imagined the domestic scene that he had described.

Having regained his equilibrium Sefton offered some advice. "Well, as a happily married man, who has hopefully learned wit along the path of wedded bliss, I suggest you go home early tonight and apologise, else she'll be cutting off your conjugal rights."

Arthur looked puzzled as he said, "I don't know what that mean but it sound mighty painful."

"It means, young Arthur," said Sefton patiently, "that Polly will be keeping herself to herself, if you get my drift, in the bedroom department."

"Ohh," said Arthur slowly as he absorbed this new information, "I'll have to remember them posh words – I may be able to impress some young mawther with them."

"Now just you be careful about impressing young girls with words like that or you might find yourself in trouble like Harry did. It was thinking about that sort of thing before he should have done that got him up that aisle so quickly in the first place, and now he's got a wife, a baby and a mother-in-law to keep happy. It takes some experience to cope with *one* woman let alone two."

"It must be nice to have your bed warmed at night," said Arthur wistfully.

Harry looked up sulkily, "You can have a warm bed any time you want with a hot brick and a piece of flannel, Arthur."

"Ah, but, that's not quite the same is it, young Harry, that's not like the love of a good woman," said Abel with a faraway look in his eyes.

"I thought you'd never been married, Abel," said Arthur quickly.

"I've had my moments, Arthur and I may have a few more yet. There's many a good tune played on an old fiddle, isn't that right, Joe?"

"Aye, thass right enough," said old Joe nodding his whiskery head sadly, "but I fear this old fiddle isn't goin' to be asked for an encore."

"Now don't you give up so easily, Joe, you know the old adage, 'you're only as old as the woman you feel'. I saw 'Hannah on the organ' giving you the glad eye on Sunday."

"'Hannah on the organ' give all men the glad eye, she remind me of them insects that eat their mates."

"You mean the 'praying mantis'," offered Abel.

"Aye, ever since her husband died she's been lookin' for a replacement, no man's safe when she's around. She'll prey on any man over fifty."

"I think you'll find that's spelt differently, Joe."

"I don't care how thass spelt, Abel, along of me there's only one sort of praying to do in church and I wish she'd remember it, and pay more attention to hitting the right notes."

"Talking about affairs of the heart," said Sefton a little more quietly, "I hear young Alice Hubbard is quite smitten with that musician, they're often seen together, coming home from town on a Tuesday evening and they disappear somewhere every night. Mollie say she'd be quite worried if it was anyone else but young Harnser ought to be trustworthy, him being educated. '*To think*,' she said to me, '*my daughter marrying a schoolteacher. We're movin' up in the world at last, Sefton.*' They're being very secretive though," he added, "they think they're avoiding everyone, but they're often seen at a distance, that chestnut hair can't be mistaken, can it? They'll have to be careful when they're on Estate land, old Sugar Sanderson's been known to take a pot shot at trespassers."

"Thass more in the woods when he think they are after his game, I don't think he'd be too hard on a couple of young spooners; he's not a bad old stick," said Joe in defence of his landlord and erstwhile employer.

"He's quite friendly with the Major," said Arthur presently, to no one in particular.

"Who is?"

"Harnser."

"What make you think that, Arthur?"

"He's bin invited round quite a lot accordin' to Marjie, she should know 'cause she's live-in maid there. She say the Major ask Harnser to escort Miss Arabella when she go horse ridin', I think she might be havin' music lessons too."

"Ohh," said Sefton knowingly, "If he's earning a bit extra doing that sort of thing no wonder Molly is hoping for an early wedding."

The assemblage nodded their heads in unison; it was always satisfying to keep abreast of village news.

Harry was particularly pleased that the conversation had drifted away from his marital problems, his head was still aching from the bar of carbolic soap and he was trying to work out how you could have your conjugal rights cut off. He thought 'rights' were things you were entitled to.

There was more to being married than met the eye

CHAPTER SIX

England in Summer is always beautiful but, England in Summer when love is blossoming as from a bud to a full-blown rose, is truly memorable. And when that Summer must last a lifetime it is doubly beautiful and doubly precious – so it was for Arabella and Harnser.

Old men and women the world over will wistfully verify that the euphoric state of first real love is never forgotten and can be brought to mind and enjoyed at will. Beauty and love are the essence of the romantic spirit.

For the lovers the season wore on in blissful contentment, all things dull and ordinary in a different world. It was as if a rosy haze surrounded them. Their conversations were secretive, sensitive and gently probing, as lover's conversations always are. Gradually they learned all there was to learn of each other; as their Summer of eighteen hundred and sixty-three unfolded. There were horse rides to distant villages, idyllic walks beside streams as the sun played on the ripples and tinkling sounds lulled them into dreamy reverie. There were strolls through woods and across meadows, sweet with summer flowers, warm sun and gentle breezes that stirred the heart and calmed the soul.

There were dreams shared, hands held and lips lightly brushed with tortuous restraint. The spectacular skies of eastern England were enjoyed as the sun rose over the sea and set over the beautiful landscape. The early white mists on the water meadows and marshes as the birds called to their mates and Harnser added to his bird-impersonating repertoire to the delight of his sweetheart. The hazy days of a long, hot Summer passed thus, as the lovers spent every available minute together.

All too soon the crops were harvested, the days grew shorter and the evenings chillier as the cottons and muslins of Summer were reluctantly discarded for the warmer wear necessitated by Autumn. The colours of the countryside changed to reds and russets.

Wrapped in warm woollen outerwear, Harnser and Arabella continued their country walks and occasional exhilarating morning gallops on horseback.

Inclement evenings would see them at Barcada where Harnser would entertain Arabella and her father by playing the flute or the piccolo; or Arabella would softly play the piano as the Major and Harnser pitted their wits against each other at the halma or chess board. If Marjie heard the soft strains of music floating up to her room at the top of the house, she supposed that her mistress was having a lesson. It was common knowledge at Barcada and Oxley House that Arabella was promised in marriage to Charles Sanderson. It was also known that Harnser had become a friend of the Major. What was *not* known was that the Major tended to retire early to indulge his love of reading in bed...and to give his daughter and her young friend some privacy...despite his daughter's betrothal, the older man knew that Arabella and the young musician had become very special friends. He also knew that enforcing separation on young sweethearts tended to make them even more determined to stay together and to encourage rash, and often regrettable, behaviour, he had no desire to see history repeat itself; it had caused enough unhappiness and hardship the first time around. Liking Harnser as much as he did made matters a little more difficult, even so the Major satisfied himself that, when the young couple's summer romance had run its course and the colder weather forced them to follow less romantic pursuits within the confines of Barcada, the ardour would cool and Arabella would settle down to plan her marriage to Charles. The Oxley Estate, after all, was her heritage.

In the distance was Flinton church, its old flint walls sparkling in the winter sun. "It looks very pretty does it not?" said Arabella softly as she snuggled closer to Harnser within the circle of his arm. It was a cold, bright day, a Saturday afternoon in

November. "I do not think it is quite as old as Little Pecking church, shall we go and see if we can find some dates?"

"There is a clock on the tower, we do not have one, do we?"

"No, but we will soon," she said hesitantly.

"Oh?"

"Uncle Henry is planning to donate one to commemorate his son's marriage next year." There was an awkward silence. Harnser was acutely aware that Arabella had supplied the information reluctantly and that she had, by careful choice of words, distanced herself from the subject. He realized that the matter would soon become common knowledge in the village and he would have thought it odd had he learned it from someone else. Why did it perturb him, but he did not really need to ask himself that question. The church is the most important building in a village and on its tower, forever more, would be a constant reminder to him that he had lost his Love to another man.

"I am sorry." Arabella's voice was tinged with sadness as she looked up at him with a pleading in her eyes. A pleading that said, 'do not blame me for this'... 'I have no control over the matter'... 'I do not wish to hurt you'... 'I do not want to spoil this lovely day we are enjoying together.' All these things he read in her eyes as he realized how worried she must have been about telling him.

He smiled resignedly at her worried face. "It is not your fault, darling. It is just one of those cruel twists of fate that make a difficult situation even harder to bear. Let us look on the bright side, Vicar Hanley will have no excuse to run his sermons over time; I am convinced the man never wears a watch. Looking at the matter in its correct context we must admit it's a lovely gesture on the part of Mr Sanderson; one from which the whole village will benefit." He gave her a reassuring squeeze and was pleased to see the worry disappear from her face, but the matter troubled him more than he wanted her to know.

"There is someone sketching in the churchyard." Arabella pointed discreetly to where a young girl was intent on her work. "Shall we ask if we can have a look?" But even as she spoke the girl looked in their direction, gathered up her belongings, then hurried down the path toward the church porch. They were still some way off from where she had been, and took a different, more minor route, to the church entrance. Entering the church at an angle from the side path they were appalled to find the girl in tears.

"Can we help?" asked Arabella gently.

"I am alright thank you," the girl said sadly, "Please do not let me spoil your walk." She returned her handkerchief to her eyes managing to give Arabella and Harnser a brief smile as she did so.

"Perhaps it would help to talk to us," ventured Harnser gently, "we are in no hurry." Whereupon the girl dissolved into floods of tears as she abandoned the pretence of being in control of her emotions.

"It was s-seeing the t-two of you," she sobbed, "It brought my unhappiness to the fore."

With gentle probing by the lovers, the girl began to tell them a heart- rending story of young love; a story about a baby that had been abandoned at birth on the doorstep of the local vicarage. The girl told how she had met the foundling when they both attended the village school. They had become soul mates, spending all their spare time together. The boy had a great desire to travel and the girl, although hating the thought of being parted, had tried to understand this need. She had not thought too much about it, knowing that it was so far into the future that it somehow seemed unreal. She said they had devised a game, a childish game that had turned into a private ritual to make sure they would always feel together, in times of great happiness or sadness, even when apart.

"What sort of game?" asked Arabella interestedly.

The girl's face coloured noticeably as she said, "It is a secret game, just between the two of us, it involves stones."

"Stones?"

"Yes, please do not ask me to explain, I would feel disloyal to my – my…"

"I understand," said Arabella softly, thinking of the situation between herself and Harnser and the secrets they shared, then, "May I ask your name?"

"It is Matilda," the girl said quietly, "Matilda Canham."

"That is a very pretty name, I am Arabella and this," she put her hand on Harnser's arm, "is Harnser."

Matilda's sobs had subsided enough for her to talk to the pair and she continued to tell them her story. She said that one day, out of the blue, Matthew – for that was his name – had been told by his parents that he was being sent away to school to prepare him for entering the Church. He had argued that he did not want to follow that path and that he did not want to go away to school. It was then that his parents imparted the devastating news to him that he had been abandoned on their doorstep when he was one day old and that, unable to find his real parents, they had raised him as their own. In the circumstances he had felt obliged to follow his father's wishes. That was when he was fourteen," said Matilda sadly, "I have not seen him since. I am certain that there is a conspiracy to keep us apart, but I do not know why and neither does he. We do not have the money to visit each other and every Christmas, and at varying times throughout the year, his parents visit him but he never comes home. We write to each other regularly and we are determined to be together again one day but in the meantime I just have to wait and hope. Every year as Christmas approaches I pray that he will come home *this* year but so far it has not materialized. When I saw the two of you together walking up the path, so obviously in love, I felt so alone, I am sorry..." Again Matilda broke down and her voice trailed off.

"My father is a friend of Doctor Miles," said Arabella, "I have heard the story of the baby being abandoned, apparently it was the talk of the villages at one time."

"It is *still* the talk of the village, *this* one at least," said Matilda, "but then that is to be expected, it is all rather mysterious, I wish I could find his real parents; that would make him happy, I would love to solve the mystery for him. He has no hope of doing so himself when he is so far away. He loves his adoptive parents," she said hurriedly, "they are really lovely

115

people, it is just that he would like to know why he was abandoned. He has got it into his head that his parents could be undesirables. I am sure they cannot be, they would never have produced a son like Matthew...he is so good and kind and..."

Her voice trailed off once again as the tears came easily into her eyes. "I am so sorry, I should not be burdening you with my problems."

"Nonsense, we are only too happy to help." Arabella felt an empathy with the young girl sitting so despondently in the church porch and wished that there was something she could say to cheer her but she realised that only one thing would make a difference to her predicament and that was the return of her sweetheart. Nevertheless she did her best by taking a genuine interest in the girl's sketches and remarking on their excellence.

The three young people continued to converse in the church porch. Matilda offered to do their portraits if they cared to meet her again. Her offer was readily accepted and they told the story of their own circumstances and of where they lived.

A bond had been forged but when the church clock struck three Matilda said she must go home – to avoid having to walk in the dark. They said their goodbyes and agreed to meet in the same place the following week. The couple were pleased to see that Matilda's mood was a little lighter as they watched the solitary figure – with pretty, pale gold hair – walk away from them down the church path.

"It is a sad story," said Arabella when the girl had walked a sufficient distance away. "I wonder why they are being kept apart, for surely they *are*."

"I wonder if *they* will ever know the reason," Harnser responded thoughtfully, "and if they will ever be allowed to be together."

"We must keep in touch with her, but most importantly we must tell her if we ever hear anything of any importance about the mystery; *someone* must know who the young man's parents are."

"Do you not find it intriguing, Arabella, that everybody one meets has a life that few know about? I mean, I wonder what revelations we would find if we could see into everyone's mind. We meet people in the street; we nod or say 'good day' never knowing what is going on in their private lives. Us, for instance, how many people know of our problems. People tend to share happiness but keep sadness buried within. Even my family do not know of our problems. I feel guilty about that – my mother and I were always so close."

She squeezed his arm in comfort and tried not to think of the future; as often happened, she lost the fight. Hearing of Matilda's plight had brought their own problems to the fore for both of them. She knew that Harnser's thoughts were running parallel to her own as they retraced their steps down the darkening lanes toward home. A huge November sun was slipping gently below the horizon, the birds were swooping low as they sought their resting places, or singing their last chorus of the day. A pheasant suddenly rose from the field and skimmed the hedges each side of the lane just ahead of them, startling them both and bringing them out of their reveries. They heard the peewit call from afar and turned to one another laughing at last; each remembering Arabella's attempts at imitation and making them snuggle closer to each other in the chill evening air.

"It was a beautiful Summer, Arabella, thank you so much for spending it with me. When I am old and grey I will look back on eighteen hundred and sixty-three as the best Summer of my life. I will see you by the bridge and in the copse; gathering flowers and making daisy chains; running down the banks and along our little stream; galloping through the early morning mists along the sands. I will see you in your summer frocks with that dreamy, happy expression on your face that I love so well and with the wild roses that I will ever associate with my own true love, Oh Arabella, how I love you." He turned her toward him and took her more tightly in his arms bringing his lips to hers in a bitter sweet, crushing moment of passion. She responded hungrily and then buried her face in his clothes, enjoying the maleness of him. The warm smell of the leather and wool he wore mingled with his own intoxicating musky scent, the scent she knew that had impregnated her soul and brought comfort to her when she was alone...she only had to close her eyes...

She was glad he had mentioned the wild roses and her summer frocks. It reassured her that she had arranged the perfect Christmas present for him. She had taken the photographs of herself and Harnser – the ones they had had taken in the Summer – and she had approached the School of Art in Winford. A young student water colourist had agreed – for a modest fee – to transform them into paintings. She was very pleased with the results; two matching eight sided, dark wood frames about fourteen inches high, with a gold leaf trim. The side portions were longer than the others to provide for pretty oval mounts. She had sat for her own painting and had advised on the other as to colour and tones. The artist had persuaded her to put just two roses in her hair and had captured their translucent beauty perfectly against her chestnut colouring. The rest of the spray she had held in her hand, a delicate pink and green decoration for her white bodice. She could barely wait to present them to him. And now as the fallen leaves gently eddied around their touching feet she held him tightly and transported her thoughts to Christmas Day...

It was much, much later when she realized that they never had found the date on the church.

CHAPTER SEVEN

An early-morning hoarfrost had carpeted the world in white, causing the fallen leaves to crackle and jump beneath the lovers' feet. Now a weak winter sun was beginning to permeate the thick, bare branches of the copse as the pair ran through, their breath eddying around their faces in a steamy mist. They came to a halt on the far side of the coppice and gazed in wonderment at the view before them. Rolling white countryside, fresh and pure, covered with a blanket of winter faery, stretched as far as the eye could see. In the distance a soft white mist hugged the marshes and promised a crisp, bright day ahead. A robin flew up to a nearby branch uttering its sharp *Tic* alarm call and to their left they caught a fleeting glimpse of a fallow deer as it leapt back into its wooded hideaway.

"There is talk of snow before the week is out," said Harnser breaking the silence. "It looks as if we might have a white Christmas after all. The children at The Hall are quite excited by the prospect," he smiled down at her before adding, " talking of Christmas, I have an important appointment this afternoon, which I must keep in private, but I will visit you this evening as usual, if that is acceptable to you and your father of course."

"You are being very mysterious, Harnser Elliot, but on this occasion I will not badger you further for I have something important myself to do this afternoon." They smiled at each other, their eyes sparkling in rosy faces flushed by the icy weather as they hugged their Christmas secrets to themselves.

That very same night the talk of snow became a reality. Harnser pulled his collar up high round his neck as he stepped out from Barcada to make his way home through the first light flurry of Winter. "Hurry back inside," he urged Arabella gently, " I will see you in church tomorrow and call again in the evening."

Nevertheless she waited until he was out of sight before closing the door and drawing the bolt. Their lives had taken on a pattern; after church on Sundays they luncheoned with their families before meeting for an hour or two in the evening.

By the time Harnser reached the outskirts of the village the light flurry had turned to a thick snowstorm that was already beginning to lay, the wind had increased in strength since he had arrived at Barcada and now the large flakes were accumulating at one side of the road where they had been blown to the bank. He could feel the odd flake of snow run down the back of his neck as his warm body turned it to water. Pulling his collar tighter and his muffler higher he turned his thoughts to Christmas. It *must* be perfect; it would be their only Christmas together. He was pleased with the present he had arranged for Arabella, he had put a lot of thought into it. For some strange reason then, he thought of Alice and her family; it would be their first Christmas without Arnold. He remembered the first Christmas without *his* father and how lonely he had felt, he thought of young Tom who had grown in stature and maturity since taking on the role left vacant by his father, and he not yet thirteen. His heart went out to them all and he resolved to visit them on Christmas Eve, before church, to deliver his modest Christmas gifts and make sure they knew they were in his thoughts. Although still four weeks away the Holy Day was often at the forefront of his mind. He had promised to give a solo, musical performance in church on Christmas Eve. It was going to be a very special evening for him and his mother for she had met his father when *he* had given a similar recital in this very church on Christmas Eve twenty years earlier.

Of course he would play the flute.

By the next morning Little Pecking church had been transformed into a Christmas card scene, its ledges holding crisp white snow that sparkled like diamonds in the winter sun. The backdrop of trees embellished the wintry picture of breathtaking beauty, causing Arabella to think of her grandmother who had wanted her house to give a similar impression – and she had succeeded – Barcada in snow was equally as beautiful as Barcada at sunset.

Arabella left her father's side to make a detour to the left of the churchyard, her footsteps leaving crisp imprints in the pristine white carpet. She reached the family burial plot and gently ran her fingers over the name of her mother, Eleanor Biddemore. Tears came to her eyes as she thought of how hard she had worked at their little farm and how short a time she had lived in comfort after coming to Barcada – just two years. It was at that time that Arabella had become especially close to her grandmother. Her eyes turned to her right where her grand-parents lay under the cold November ground. Maybe because of the cold, which sharpened the mind, she felt particularly close to them all.

She turned back toward the church and retraced her imprinted footsteps between the gravestones. She paused as she saw Harnser, with his family and neighbours – the Hubbards – walking up the main path. As always she noticed how the girl clung possessively to Harnser's side. She wondered if they would marry one day when this magical past Summer was a distant memory in a corner of his mind. Again the tears came and she brushed them aside hurriedly.

Harnser suddenly became aware of the solitary, cloaked figure standing motionless amidst the memorials to his left. He thought how beautiful she looked standing alone in the snow, a light breeze catching the hem of her lovat green cloak and blowing one side of the fur lined hood slightly across her face. He knew it was a picture he would bring to mind many times in the future. Again, he resolved to persevere with his painting; he had so many images he wanted to preserve in colour. This would be one of the first. He had stopped without realizing, he lifted his hand in greeting to her and was rewarded with a smile and brief salutatory wave. He was not close enough to actually see the smile but he knew it to be there; her face and all its expressions were imprinted on his mind.

Alice had also come to a halt. Following his gaze she felt a sharp pang of jealousy as his eyes lingered on the lonely figure. "When is the big wedding?" she asked, trying to break the spell without Harnser being aware of her feelings.

"Next July, I think," he answered vaguely.

"I suppose, as a friend of the Major, you might get an invitation," she had difficulty keeping the envy from her voice. She wished she were the type of person who could slip so easily into the world of the gentry. How did he manage it, she wondered. He did not even have to try. Not for the first time she wished she were better educated...then without warning she burst into tears, burying her face in her hands.

Harnser tore his eyes off Arabella and swung round to pay attention to Alice. They had fallen behind from the rest of their group and now had the path to themselves. He did not know how to respond to the tears. He knew he should put a comforting arm around the girl but did not know how Arabella would react to that. At his turning, Alice buried her head in his chest forcing him to gently take her by the shoulders and push her slightly away. "What has happened?" he asked, genuinely surprised at the outburst and wondering if he were somehow to blame.

"I–It is n-nothing, I'm sorry," she stammered, brushing her tears away self-consciously. "I don't know why I'm crying. We'd better catch up with the others," and she ran away from him toward the church porch through which her family had so recently passed.

Harnser hung back allowing Arabella to traverse the short distance to the door, whereupon he ushered her ahead of him in a state of utter bewilderment at Alice's outburst.

As they walked up the central aisle the congregation was beginning the first hymn.

The snow continued to fall, off and on, all week. On some days there would be a partial thaw but then another fall would cover the slush or ice renewing the freshness in hours.

Saturday found the lovers having enormous fun in the snow. The copse was a perfect place for snowballing with plenty of trees to hide behind. Harnser had taken the old sledge they used in the Home Wood for stick gathering and had skirted the edge of the village through the woods to reach Barcada from the opposite direction. The pair took the track to Rookery Lane, sometimes running, sometimes walking but always laughing as they made for the privacy of the copse. Once there they chased one another through the snow, hiding and laughing, making snowballs and generally enjoying themselves until they reached the other side. Then, still laughing, they climbed aboard the sledge and slid all the way down the bank to the fields below.

Just across the fields to their right were the Oxley woods and far ahead in front of them were the marshes. Several times they trudged back to the top of the slope and sped down again on their toboggan until Arabella declared she had no more energy to spare if she were to make it home again, to which Harnser replied that he would pull her through the copse on their snow conveyance, and so he did.

Tired but happy they meandered down the lane to Barcada to enjoy tea before a roaring fire. Sarah, their cook/house-keeper always prepared tea before leaving at noon for her afternoon off. She followed the same procedure on a Sunday after lunch. Arabella and her father were not useless when it came to looking after themselves – their days on the farm had made sure of that – anyway, they had always enjoyed their quiet evenings together.

"You two have the appearance of a couple of ragamuffin children," the Major declared as they brushed the snow from their clothes and boots before entering the warm confines of the house. "I need not ask if you have enjoyed yourselves."

It had pleased him greatly these past few months to see Arabella so obviously happy. She had blossomed before his eyes, reassuring him that he had taken the correct course in encouraging the friendship between the young couple. Plenty of time for duty in the future; his daughter was having fun, as all young people should before settling down to the harsh realities of marriage and parenthood. Who knew what the future would hold for his precious darling. It warmed his heart to see her so happy. And he had this young man to thank for it all. He was greatly indebted to him. He suddenly realized how very fond he had become of Harnser, how much he enjoyed playing chess and halma with him; discussing current affairs and getting a young man's viewpoint on matters. He hoped he would continue to call after Arabella's marriage, when she would live at Oxley House. He was not relishing the thought of living alone at Barcada but even so he preferred it to moving to Oxley House. He knew he would be welcome there, but Barcada was his home. He was too old for change and anyway there was no doubt in his mind that Arabella would visit him often. Even so it would be nice to have a bit of company in the evenings...he must make sure he extended the invitation.

Much, much later, after supper by the fire, some roasted chestnuts and mulled wine, Harnser reluctantly left Barcada once again. "See you both in church tomorrow," he called predictably "and again tomorrow evening."

It was snowing heavily as he made his journey home, pulling the sledge behind him. He thought of the fun that he and Arabella had had that afternoon and resolved to take little James out the following day; he would enjoy a ride on the sledge and a game of snowballs. He was feeling pleased with himself for more reasons than one as he trudged home in the snow that night, little realizing how his seeds of thought would totally change his life...

CHAPTER EIGHT

"Do you fancy a game of snowballs with me and James in the woods?" Harnser directed his voice to Walter. "Or shall we go to the Green, there is bound to be a crowd there."

"The woods, please, the woods," shouted James excitedly, "We can play hide and seek."

"You two go ahead," said Walter smiling, "I'll join you a bit later in the first clearing."

After an exciting sleigh ride in and out of the trees around the clearing, and a snowball fight, which Harnser let James win easily, the little boy asked for his favourite game of hide and seek. They took turns to hide with Harnser making sure he indulged the child by pretending not to know where the little boy was hiding. "Give me a clue," he shouted at last, you have hidden yourself too well." There was no answer. "Make the sound of a cuckoo and I will try to locate you."

"Cuckoo."

With sudden panic Harnser realized that the sound was coming from above and spun round and round looking heavenward as he searched the overhead branches. Suddenly he caught sight of James, way above his head crawling along a thick branch. "Keep still," he shouted, panic stricken. "Keep very still, James, I will climb up and fetch you, do not move."

The little boy suddenly lost his confidence and began to whimper. "My hands are cold, Harnser, I can't hold on."

"Yes, you can, be brave. I will soon have you down," he shouted as he began climbing the tree.

It was an easy climb through the thick branches with plenty of handholds. He realized how simple it must have been for the boy to scramble up in the excitement of hiding without being aware of just how high he was climbing. At last, after what seemed an eternity, Harnser reached the branch on which

125

James was standing. He edged nearer to the boy, speaking soft encouraging words as he went, then, with only a yard or so to go, James slipped on the snow and plunged downward as Harnser looked on helplessly.

It all happened in a second or two but to Harnser it appeared to be in slow motion as the fair curls went twirling and twirling and twirling around and a child's scream rang out over the surrounding countryside before suddenly stopping as the little boy hit the ground with a soft thud and the snow rose up around his little frame. Almost at the same time, Walter and Maria appeared at the clearing's edge taking in the scene unfolding before them. Their little boy falling from a great height while Harnser looked down in horror.

Harnser was jolted into action; coming down the tree much faster than he had ascended it. On reaching the ground he began tearing off his coat to cover James.

Walter and Maria were crouching by the boy's side; both were crying. As Harnser approached, Walter sprang at him yelling obscenities. "You've killed him, you've killed my little boy, you'll pay for this you young upstart." He grabbed Harnser by the throat throwing him against a tree trunk in order to gain purchase.

"Stop it, stop it," shouted Maria, "we must help James, he's not moving, he's so cold. His leg is twisted underneath him."

Walter was so incensed he hardly heard her. When her voice did get through to him, he suddenly let go of Harnser, who sank to the ground gasping for breath. "Get help, woman, go to The Hall for a carriage to get him to the hospital while I finish this one off."

"No, leave him, it was not his fault, you know how quick James can be…"

She was not allowed to finish her sentence as Walter turned on her uncharacteristically, grabbing her clothes and pulling her towards him as he roared at her, "Do as I say, go and tell them what has happened, ask for a carriage." He pushed Maria roughly away in the direction of The Hall undoing the buckle on his belt at the same time. He pulled off his belt and went towards Harnser who was still choking and fighting for breath as he tried to cover James with his discarded coat.

Harnser's back was unguarded as the belt went down on him in fury. He jumped back in pain but the blows continued to rain on him lash after lash, cutting through his clothes until his shirt was covered in crimson.

Suddenly Walter staggered backwards. "You'll be a long time before you do any more harm, Harnser Elliot," he gasped, "a long time before you kill another child or father another bastard. You think you're so clever; teaching at The Hall, lapping up your mother's affection, consorting with the gentry; well you're not too good for me. I've lived in your shadow long enough and I'll not live in it any more. If I set eyes on you ever again I'll finish you." His breath was coming in short gasps as he continued, "It's your mother's house, not yours, and I'm her husband so now I'll get the respect I deserve. It's my money that feeds them both, my work that clothes them."

Harnser fought to make sense of what Walter was saying; was James dead? No, he was hurt, badly hurt but not dead, he was breathing a few moments ago of that he was sure. He tried to lift his head but his neck and back were burning from the lacerations…where was the carriage?…what was taking the time?…father what bastard…was he going mad or having a nightmare?

He opened his eyes and whispered, "What are you talking about, what bastard…?"

His voice trailed off; the pain was excruciating.

Walter's harsh voice reached him as if through layers of muslin. "It's no use you acting the innocent with me. It's all out in the open now, Molly has just been round looking for you; that lass is five months gone and you don't need to be a genius to add five months to July when all the village saw you kissing her and giving her fancy presents on the Green. I may be quiet but I'm not stupid, I had a good look at that bench you made for her birthday. I saw the inscription you'd hidden underneath; 'A and H, a year to remember.' Well, you'll remember it now alright; it will be imprinted on your back," and with that he brought the belt down again and again.

Harnser lay in the snow, his back and shoulders on fire, he felt as though he were going mad. This was Walter flaying him, mild mannered Walter who he liked and respected. Why was he accusing him, it was an accident, a horrible accident. He raised his head to look to where James was still lying motionless. Please don't let him die, he prayed, please God don't let him die, please don't let him die…

The trees spun around over him, he felt sick…he was going to throw up…he had to help James…why was Alice blaming him…suddenly he was being hauled to his feet – hauled up and pushed forward. Walter's voice came to him as if from afar… "I said get out of my sight, out of my sight…"

Harnser lurched forward as he felt the hand in his back; he stumbled from tree to tree not knowing where he was going. He was aware of voices, lots of voices…then a great black cloak engulfed him as he sank into oblivion.

Gradually the voices began to permeate the layers; his mother was there and somebody else…was it Silas?…yes, Silas, he liked Silas…more voices…more blackness…again he struggled to wake up.

"James…" he said at last.

"Sssshh, it is alright, James is being well looked after, you must try to rest." It was his mother soothing him with her hand on his forehead, just like she had when his father died, he could hear the flute. He invariably heard the flute when he thought of his father. Tears came to his eyes. What was happening to him, then he saw James crumpled in the snow with his little leg twisted beneath him…

…and the fair curls went twirling,
and twirling, and twirling;
and the fair curls went twirling
and twirling around…

…and the sound of a child's scream rang out over the surrounding countryside.

He awoke with a jolt, sweat running down his face, but he could not see anything. It was some time before he realized he was lying face down.

"He should be in hospital, you know that, Maria." It was Dr Miles' voice coming from afar, muffled and indistinct.

"I can nurse him here with your help, I do not want all this to be public knowledge and, anyway, Walter is at the hospital with James. The mood he is in I would not put anything past him, no, Harnser will be better off here with me. As soon as he is a little improved I will get him away to safety. Nobody knows he is here except Silas and Sally, and you of course" she added, making sure he understood that she did not want the matter going any further. "Walter will stay at his sister's when he is not at the hospital, he told me not to expect him home until... until..." her voice faltered.

"Sit down, Maria, you are exhausted." Silas guided the distraught woman to a chair then turned to Dr Miles. "Maria is not expecting her husband home for a few days. I can stay here in case he *does* return."

The Doctor did not appear satisfied; Silas was not a big man. He was no match for Walter in his present state of mind, but the little boy would be some time before he was out of danger so no doubt Walter would stay by his side.

Twenty-four hours later Harnser fought his way through the influence of medication to find Maria by his bed sewing. "Is that my coat?" he asked weakly. He could not remember damaging his coat; he had only used it to keep James warm.

"I am sewing some money into the lining," she said softly, then her voice breaking, she added, "You must leave here Harnser, at least for the time being. I do not know if James will live...and if he does not...I dread to think what Walter will do..."

Tears were streaming down her face as she continued, "I do not blame you, Harnser, but I love that little boy as my own. I would be with him now if Walter had not attacked you."

"Please do not cry, Mother; go to him, I will be fine by

myself." He struggled to stay awake, "Silas will call on his way from The Hall. We need to know how little James is." He could not get the picture out of his head whether awake or asleep; the little boy lying deadly still, one leg twisted underneath him. He could not seem to keep his mind focused, he kept drifting off to sleep. Then he remembered what Maria had said about his coat. "What do you mean 'sewing money into my coat', what money?"

Was he talking or dreaming?

"I want you to have it, it was your father's money which he left to me." She lowered her head knowing he would protest then added, "He would want you to have it, it will help support you while you continue with your studies, please, Harnser, I *need* to help you; the man I brought into our lives has treated you abominably. I feel responsible…"

"Come with me, Mother," he said weakly.

"I cannot."

"Why not?" He was winning at last, waking up a little.

"My place is with my husband and anyway, little James will need nursing when he comes home." She started crying again and Harnser knew that she was far from sure that James would ever come home again.

He remembered the money, "I cannot take all your money, I can support myself."

"I want you to have it, if you do not need it then deposit it with a bank, but take it, I will feel better."

"Why are you sewing it into my coat?"

"Because there is two hundred pounds."

He gasped, his head pounded, his back stung from the cuts and medication, "No, Mother, not that much, it is yours, twenty pounds will tide me over." He could not believe his mother had so much money in the house. His thoughts were all over the place. "Why is it not in a bank? Does Walter know about it?" He struggled to keep his eyes open and his mind on the conversation.

"Yes, he did not want to touch it; he is a proud man, he told me to keep it for you. It was your father's." she whispered.

"He said that?" Why was he so tired?

"Yes."

Gradually Harnser remembered how embittered Walter had sounded when he had flayed him in the wood 'It's *my* money that feed them both' he had spat at him 'my work that clothe them.' It was all coming back to him; the pieces fitting together and fading again. He has harboured resentment toward father and me for years, he realized now. I must be a constant reminder of Mother's first love, he is jealous of her affection for me. He felt a strange pity for his stepfather. He realized what an ordeal it must have been for Walter when he had been asked to play the flute at the Christmas Eve church service. The performance...he would not be able to...and the house...it was his mother's, even *that* must hurt his pride knowing that she would no doubt leave it to her son. Strange how he had never thought about these things before. He had thought they were all happy living together, but deep inside Walter had obviously felt isolated, and now he was in danger of losing his little son, the dearest person in the world to him.

He was thinking clearer, but it was tiring...so tiring. His back was hurting, he could not move without pain but, he must try to get back on his feet and out of the village so that his mother stood some chance of happiness with her husband. Then his thoughts turned to Alice. She was going to have a baby, or had he dreamt that? No, Walter had said it, she was going to have a baby – how many other people thought he was responsible for her condition? Why was she letting people think such things? He hazily remembered her outburst in the churchyard – at least he now knew the reason for it. It was all too much, he could not think straight...he had to sleep...how was James...he must not die...tears trickled down his face and he tasted them, salty, at the corner of his mouth...as Maria and her busy needle faded away again...

The flickering lamplight leant a friendly ambience to the little room. It was very quiet. He was on his back, how had he turned over? He became aware of the sound of breathing; the regular breathing of a sleeping person. He turned his head to see Silas asleep in the chair; his little spectacles at the end of his nose, strangely it gave him comfort, dear, reliable Silas…his friend… with his little spectacles…

The next time he woke there was a soft grey light coming in from the window. The lamp had been extinguished. He turned toward Silas but it was his mother in the chair with her hand stretched out and lying on the bedclothes. He lifted one of his arms, his back burnt at the movement. He tried to reach her resting hand but fell short. His mother stirred in the grey light, turned her head and went back to sleep.

Harnser stared at the ceiling as it slowly took on the colour of day. First he needed to find out how James was; the extent of his injuries; how could he go away when he would be needed here to help? Then he remembered Walter's furious bitterness toward him. His mother was right, he *must* leave. He also needed to see Alice, to discover the reason for her accusation. He had always treated her with kindness, why would she besmirch his reputation. What about Arabella, suddenly, with horror, he realized he did not know how long he had lain there drifting in and out of sleep under the influence of the strong medication that Dr Miles had prescribed.

Maria stirred, shifted around in her makeshift bed and gradually came to her senses. "Harnser, you are awake."

"Yes, Mother, I am awake. How long have I been here?"

"It is Wednesday morning."

"Have you heard anything from the hospital?"

"James is awake, his leg is badly broken but it is his back…"

"His back? He has damaged his back?"

"The true extent of the damage is not yet known, we are all praying…"

"Are you suggesting he might not walk again?"

"There is some doubt," Maria held her head in her hands in despair. "What are we to do, Harnser?"

"You must go to them, and I must leave as soon as possible."

"Where will you go?"

"It is best you do not know, then you will not have to lie to Walter."

"But I won't know how you are."

"I will write to Silas now and again, just to let you know I am well. I will not tell him where I am. It will be for the best. When he calls tonight I will ask him to take me to the railway station."

"But your back, it needs looking after."

"Doctor Miles is not the only doctor in existence. I can get the dressings changed easily enough, do not worry about me, you have enough on your plate. Walter and James need you. I have medication. Take the mid-day carriage, Mother, you know it makes sense."

"What about Alice?"

"I promise you I am not responsible for her condition. Do you really think I would abandon her if I were?"

"But Walter said…"

"I know what Walter is saying, but the bench was not for Alice. It is very complicated but I will try to explain. I am sorry if I misled you but you will understand why it was the best option when you know the story."

Slowly and gently Harnser confided to Maria the story of his hopeless love for Arabella. She listened amazed until he had finished. He ended by saying, "It was just so much easier to let people think what they wanted to. I did not lie. Alice seemed to want to give the impression we were together and it provided a convenient smokescreen for Arabella and myself. I was going to tell you about it one day. I did feel guilty that you were getting the wrong impression but I did not want you to have to lie on my behalf. You do understand?"

"It is all so sad. I want only your happiness, Harnser. Are you sure there is no hope for the two of you?"

"Arabella cannot go against her family's wishes. There is just too much at stake. The family rift needs to be healed; she feels it her duty to carry out her grandmother's wishes and bring the whole sorry business to a conclusion. Fortunately she *likes* Charles. I have resigned myself to the situation. Life is never easy is it? Anyway, I am a penniless assistant teacher, Charles has

133

money, position and property – it would not be fair to deprive Arabella of her rightful inheritance."

Maria rose sadly to her feet and leant over to kiss her son. "You are a very honourable young man, I am very proud of you," was all she said on the matter.

Maria busied herself packing her son's clothes into a bag and preparing an early lunch. She was not happy that he was leaving so soon, he was not well enough; they both knew that. They also knew that the village tongues would be wagging about the recent events and that the sooner Harnser was safe from Walter, and the false accusations from the Hubbard family, the better.

Silas prepared Nellie and the cart before helping Harnser to dress – he was weaker than he thought. Silas voiced what Harnser was thinking. "You are not well enough to do this," he said worriedly to his friend.

"I must Silas, but I must go to Barcada first to say goodbye to Arabella and her father."

"It is not too bad underfoot but it has begun snowing again. We should not waste any time."

"I must do it, Silas."

Silas could see that his friend was determined, he knew he would not be able to convince him otherwise. He made Harnser as comfortable as possible on pillows in the cart and set Nellie in motion for Barcada, hoping that there would be few people abroad on such an atrocious night.

After a treacherous journey he at last turned into the Barcada gates. Harnser slid himself down the little cart until he was sitting on the back. Silas helped him to his feet and slowly they traversed the short distance to the door. But before Silas had a chance to knock, cold and weakness overtook Harnser as he slid to the ground in a faint.

The Major was amazed at the sight that greeted him when he opened his front door. Recovering his composure he shouted for Arabella and between the three, Harnser was lifted up and taken indoors.

"Explanations can wait, we had better put him in your mother's room." The Major said this to Arabella who was kneeling beside Harnser, where he lay on the sofa looking pale and ill.

"We will need a fire," she said shakily, amazed that her father was thinking of using the room. It had been locked since her mother died. Arabella herself had been in to dust and sometimes just to sit and feel close to her mother. The room was down a long passage and overlooked the back garden. It was a pretty room, quiet, away from the main rooms of the house. Her mother had always loved it and had had a bed there during the last weeks of her life.

"He was hoping to make it to Winford tonight. I do not know if the trains are running but…"

"He cannot travel alone in this condition, he must stay here with us until he is stronger," the Major said with authority.

"Thank you, I really think that would be for the best."

Silas and Arabella prepared the room and lit the fire while the Major sat with Harnser. While they worked Silas told Arabella all that had happened. He finished by suggesting that Harnser's whereabouts were kept secret.

"That will be no problem," said Arabella softly. "I will nurse him myself. I am the only one to use this room. Father will not let the staff near it. They know it is kept locked. There will be no suspicion."

Much later when he had helped Harnser to bed and unloaded his bags Silas returned Nellie to the cottage and made his way home. Under his arm he carried a parcel. It was Harnser's Christmas present to Arabella that he had promised to deliver.

CHAPTER NINE

The logs crackled in the inglenook, sending bursts of red sparks up the chimney, as the snow piled up on the window ledges outside the little snug of The Bell

"Well, my old shipmates, what do you think of that?" said Abel having related his collective news to his chimney corner friends.

"The boy fell, we know that for a fact, and he's in a bad way," said Sefton Merryweather soberly, "but Walter shouldn't have flayed the lad, it's not as if he pushed him."

"Are you sure he flayed him?" It was a worried Arthur that said this.

"My brother's a coachman at The Hall, he drove the carriage that conveyed the little lad to hospital. He said Walter had made sure the young upstart wouldn't cause any more trouble for a good while, he said he'd flayed him with a belt to within an inch of his life."

"No one's seen him since," said Sefton gravely. "He could still be lying in the Home Wood covered in snow, there was a fair bit of blood around at the time according to my brother but with another heavy fall that night it's all covered up. The next day, when they went back there was nothing to be seen."

"I wonder what got into Walter, folk say he's a mild mannered chap."

"Perhaps the lad made it home," said old Joe hopefully.

"He couldn't go home, Walter had warned him about that, he said he staggered off in the opposite direction," said Sefton. "He warned him what would happen if he stayed around."

"We ought to have known sooner, somebody should've told us so we could've looked for him," there was annoyance in Arthur's voice. "Why dint we hear nothin' 'til today?" he added.

"'Cause I didn't see my brother 'til last night so I couldn't tell you any sooner could I? I don't think The Hall wanted to spread it about. He was a teacher to their children. They tried to hush it all up."

"Well, he hasn't committed a crime," said Arthur in defence of his friend.

"Well, don't you go saying that to Mollie Hubbard, young Arthur or she'll have your guts for garters. According to her he's left young Alice in a delicate condition, and her just recently lost her father."

"You mean…?"

"Yes I *do* mean, Walter had only just digested *that* news when he found his boy lying at death's door."

"Harnser wouldn't desert her if he was to blame." Arthur said firmly.

"Course he's to blame, all the village saw him kissing her on the Green and giving her lavender soaps. That's a sweetheart's present that is, if ever I saw one."

"Well I don't agree, he could have just bin bein' kind, he's like that, well brought up and very kind. Anyway we *all* kissed her on her birthday, it was just a bit of fun."

"There's something else," Sefton lowered his voice as he said this, as if it was highly confidential. "Apparently he made a bench seat for Alice's birthday, all carved and inscribed underneath."

"How'd you know that?" said Arthur suspiciously.

"Cause Walter was raving about it on the way to the hospital. Mind you, nobody's ever seen it."

"Well there you are then," said Arthur self-satisfyingly.

"There's a bench down at the stream," old Joe said thoughtfully, "I often sit on it of a mornin'."

All eyes turned to Joe, "Whereabouts at the stream?" asked Arthur.

"By Marcie's Bridge."

"Thass haunted down there, nobody go near it, folks say your grandmother haunt that place looking for her little girl. There's a funny old howling sound round there at night and if you listen carefully you can hear Marcie sobbing under the bridge." Arthur shuddered as he thought of all the ghost stories he had

137

heard connected to Marcie's Bridge.

"I'm not going to be afeared of me own grandmother am I," said old Joe. "I like that place, I feel close to my mother there, it gave her shelter when she was frightened and alone. Anyway that howling is just the wind blowing under the bridge and the sobbing is the gurgling and noises of the waterfall."

It was not like Joe to be sentimental, he rarely spoke of his family so the whole little assemblage was surprised to see a solitary tear trickle from his rheumy old eye as he gave a sniff and put his ale mug to his mouth to cover his embarrassment. "Anyway," he continued a little shakily, "there's a seat down there among the bushes and it wasn't there in the Spring," He pressed his lips together and nodded his head as the little group eagerly waited for any more revelations he might make.

Since none were forthcoming there was a short silence until Sefton ventured, "And is there an inscription on it, Joe?"

"I haven't looked underneath; why would I? I just thought the Estate had put it there. They do that sort of thing don't they? It's on Estate land."

"Well, *you'll* have to look, Joe 'cause no one else dare go up that little lane, nobody need to 'cause there's nothin' there except the bridge and the copse."

"I'll have a look tomorrer," the old man said quietly, "but you've got to admit, it's not lookin' good for the young musician is it?"

Worried looks passed between the regulars as old Joe voiced what they were all thinking, until Sefton Merryweather contributed, "Molly don't know which way to turn so she's sent for her brother. I wouldn't like to be in young Harnser's shoes when he catch him. That family have had enough to bear this year without all this just on Christmas."

"The strange thing is, they were all so fond of him," said Abel. "Molly used to bristle with pride when she talked of the catch young Alice had made and young Tom hero worship him. I don't understand why he's left her in the lurch and Alice isn't saying much; her mother can't make her out, the lass was never a shrinking violet was she?"

"He took the wind out of her sails when he gave her those soaps," said Arthur thoughtfully, "She dint look as though she was expecting a present from him. I think they're just friends."

"Well, you can't afford to be givin' birthday presents to all and sundry can you? She must have meant a lot to him," Sefton said reasonably.

"It must be nice to be bought fancy presents like lavender soap," said old Joe with a dreamy look.

"Now what would you want with lavender soaps, Joe, you never bath."

"I'll hev you know," said Joe indignantly, "That I hev a bath every Summer, whether I need it or not."

They all laughed heartily at this until Joe added with a twinkle in his eye, "Mind you, I sometimes feel suffin' queer afterwards, but I'm usually back to normal by Michaelmas."

The little group were pleased to get back to cheerier subjects so Abel said mischievously, "Whose going to invite 'Hannah on the organ' to Christmas dinner then?"

"Now why would we want to do that?" asked Sefton.

"Because she reckons that something snuck into her garden last night and ate all her sprouts, she'll be lucky, she say, to have one helping left so, unless she get invited out, she'll have to save them for Christmas."

"That'll be Trotter, thass for sure," said Arthur. "He's got a rare likin' for sprouts, thass about four gardens he's cleared in the last fortnight."

"Goin' at that rate," said old Joe quick wittedly, "eatin' all them greens, he'll be Trotter by name and Trotter by nature."

They all laughed heartily into their ale mugs at this until Sefton said, "I wonder who'll catch him; after all, he belong to the village now that we've bought Percy a replacement. I'd like to know where he's hidin' out."

"Maybe he's in the copse," offered Arthur, "He'll know he'll be safe in there since no one dare venture in."

"Thass a point," said old Joe with a smile, "I'll hev to remember to take a rope out with me in future. I knew I'd get rewarded one day for being the bravest person in Little Pecking."

139

CHAPTER TEN

The firelight flickered over the little room.

"I must leave tonight, Arabella."

"You are not well enough."

"Yes, I must. I am not welcome in the village anymore. If little James' back is permanently damaged Walter will *never* forgive me. Mother would not desert them. I just hope he does not take it out on her, there is less chance of that if I remove myself. *I* have sampled his temper; I would not want her to do likewise. I know in my heart I was not to blame, even so I *do* feel guilty – he was in my care."

"You did not expect him to climb trees, it could have happened just as easily if Walter had been with him."

"There is Alice too; she is obviously hoping I will be forced to marry her. I cannot see another reason for making me take the blame for her condition."

Arabella blushed a deep pink. "She must know who is responsible…"

"Then of course there is you, Arabella."

"Me?"

"Yes, it will be better for you if I am not around. How can you get on with your life with me here? You have a wonderful future ahead of you; position, wealth and a man who adores you. I love you far too much to take that away from you – I am penniless. I will always love you, Arabella, you will have a corner of my heart forever, but I cannot deprive you of your rightful inheritance."

He looked up into her face where the warm firelight shadows were dancing.

"I cannot let you go, I will die," she whispered.

"We will always be together in here." He laid his hand across his heart as he continued, his voice breaking with emotion, "We have had a beautiful Summer, some people never know that

140

much happiness in all of their lives, I have so many memories of you. I am going to paint some…"

His eyes were moist, she was bending low over the bed, suddenly she caught her breath and her tears overflowed, dropping on to Harnser's face where he tasted their love. She moved closer and their lips met gently – then more urgently until she was lying beside him on the bed in the firelight. The bittersweet pain in his back brought him briefly to his senses and he pushed her gently away – his eyes never leaving her face, "No, Arabella, we must not…"

With a great sense of loss he watched her leave his side to cross the room to the door but, instead of leaving, she drew the lock and returned to the bed. A few moments later, having watched as she shed her outer clothes, he felt her warm, young body slip into the bed beside him.

"Love me, Harnser, please love me," she whispered against his neck, "I need you to love me, if only the once…"

He turned toward her, holding her with a closeness that would have to last a lifetime, his senses spiralling out of control. He wished he could roll with her on the lush, green grass beside the stream… He could hear the waterfall… and the birds… and feel the warm summer sun on his face.

She could hear the piccolo…and the tinkling stream on a hot sultry day.

The agony of his back and the ecstasy of his love mingled inextricably… until he was unaware of one and completely lost in the other

… "I love you, Arabella…I love you…I love you…"

Slowly they realized that the hot summer sun was, in fact, the warm flickering firelight. The ticking clock gradually permeated their senses…

…the waterfall and the piccolo crept back into the quiet recesses of their minds…nestling once more with wood pigeons, damselflies and sprays of wild roses…

Chapter Eleven

Arabella let her eyes wander around the crowded, Christmas Eve church. Bunches of holly and winter greenery were in abundance. Festoons decorated each windowsill and the gallery. There was much shuffling of frozen feet and rubbing of cold hands. Certain regular worshippers were conspicuous by their absence.

Maria, Walter and James, as to be expected, were not there. And Harnser, who was to have made his Little Pecking musical debut on this very night, was somewhere unknown, spending Christmas alone for the first time in his life. Arabella blinked her eyes very quickly several times in an effort to keep the tears at bay. Her eyes had been permanently swollen for two weeks from her crying. She had roamed the countryside, and the copse. She had stared over the marshes and sat by the stream, she had trudged and cried and worried her father nearly to death. Every evening she had lit a fire in the little sitting room at the back of the house, lain on the bed and stared at the burning logs and dancing flames, turning her head time and time again to bury her head and her tear stained face into the pillows that had cradled the head of her one true love; breathing deeply in a desperate effort to catch some trace of a scent of him. Then she would traipse up the long passage to say goodnight to her father before returning once more to the little room where she would fall into a fitful sleep, wondering how she could face another day.

A hush fell over the congregation as a little group walked up the central aisle to take their usual places. Arabella turned her head to see the Hubbard family, heads held rigidly, eyes straight ahead, walking to their seats; in the midst of them Alice, the plump, wholesome girl who always *had* stood much too close to Harnser. Suddenly Arabella felt a rush of pity for her; her face

142

looked sad and lonely, eyes a little red and swollen, it was obviously taking a great effort for her to face the villagers all together in this way. She felt a great surge of empathy, imagining Alice crying herself to sleep in the little cottage, feeling frightened and alone; worrying about the trouble she had caused and whether she had been responsible for the death of someone she loved – Harnser had still not been found and gossip was rife in the village that, when the snow cleared, his body would be discovered in the Home Wood. Should she waylay her on the way out of church tonight and tell her that he was safe? Tell her that she herself had nursed him, comforted him and loved him? That she had watched as he walked out of their lives to safety in the moonlight on a freezing night two weeks ago, as she had fallen in a crumpled, sobbing heap by the gates of Barcada before dragging herself indoors to begin two weeks of hell? Her heart felt as though it would break as she looked at the poor, pregnant girl who had only a box of lavender soap, a few conversations and a friendly birthday kiss on the Village Green to remind her of her lost dreams, whilst she herself had a whole Summer of memories and love to comfort her through the cold, dark days of Winter.

Flinton's merry little band of fiddlers took up their bows and began playing a haunting rendition of 'In The Bleak Midwinter'. It began a night of carols and musical entertainment that would stay in the hearts and minds of a handful of villagers until they took their inevitable places outside in Little Pecking churchyard.

Chapter Twelve

On Christmas morning the church was, again, filled to capacity. Alice looked a little more confident as she searched the congregation with her eyes, hoping against hope that she would see Harnser. She could not bear the thought of him lying dead in the snow, but that was what everyone were saying – that he was hidden under a drift in the Home Wood. She was dreading the grim discovery. How had she got into this position? Her mother had been so proud of her for attracting such a person as Harnser, she had begun to feel like *someone*, not just a kitchen maid at The Hall. It had all gone to her head, and then, when Harnser had kissed her in public on the Green and given her a lovely present, she had let her imagination run wild convincing herself that he really *cared*, after all he was not walking out with anybody else, was he? There had been wild rumours that he had been seen in all sorts of places with her but she knew it was not true even though she never contradicted the gossip; the sightings were on the outskirts of Little Pecking, it could be any couple, probably from an adjoining village, who were trying to avoid the gossips, much like she herself did. Why had she let it get so out of hand? Because, she admitted to herself, she would have had to admit it was all in her head; that she was a kitchen maid and would never amount to much more.

She watched as the last few stragglers took their seats, her spirits – that were never very high these days – plummeted even more. He was not there; she shuddered visibly as a dreadful thought entered her head. In her mind's eye she saw a coffin being borne up the central aisle amidst the Christmas decorations, would it be this week...? next week...? She shook her head, trying to rid herself of such morbid thoughts but they kept creeping back just the same. Then her thoughts turned to

144

Jack, he had been besotted with her and she had encouraged him, mostly to make Harnser jealous so that he would realize she had other suitors…her wiliness had failed hopelessly but Jack had not given up, pursuing her indomitably, loving her in spite of himself – for he was well aware of where her heart lay. Her heart warmed unexpectedly towards him. She did not have to pretend with him, she did not have to watch her grammar or make sure she spoke softly like a lady. She wondered if he had heard of her condition – they had not seen each other for two months. She felt mild panic, what if he did not want her back? She could not blame him. He could be walking out with somebody else. He had become resigned to the fact that he could not compete with Harnser Elliot so had made himself scarce.

She raised her eyes to the huge stained glass window that looked down on the central aisle and there she saw Jesus looking down at her. In that moment she knew she had to tell her mother the truth. She would do it as soon as they got home from church. She began to feel calmer as Vicar Hanley's voice permeated her thoughts. She found herself listening to his sermon about truth and love. Strange how she came here every Sunday but rarely really *listened* to him. It was almost as though he was talking specifically to her. His voice was clear and kind, there was no condemnation, she found herself feeling particularly humble; she had been very silly, she resolved to go to Flinton as soon as possible to ask Jack if he still wanted her, for all of a sudden, *she* wanted *him* very much.

The church began to clear from the front pews. She watched as the Biddemores walked slowly past toward the door, her eyes met Arabella's; was she imagining it or did the young lady look sad, and maybe a little too pale? She had *everything*, what could *she* be unhappy about? And then she realized that Arabella was smiling at her; not a condescending smile but an empathetic one, she smiled back, it was so easy. She had communicated, maybe not verbally but she *had* communicated. She realized Harnser was not so different after all. He was always just himself, whomever he was with. In just one hour Alice felt she had matured at least five years; there would be no more games.

"There is one more present for you, Arabella, it arrived this morning." The Major was very worried about his daughter's state of mind. He knew he had to give her the parcel but if, as he suspected, it was from Harnser, it could well tip her over the edge.

"It was delivered by Mr Midcote – I think it could be from Harnser," he added softly.

"Do you mind if I open it by myself?" there was a pleading for him to understand.

"No, dear, of course not," he said gently.

He knew she would take it to her mother's sitting room, and he was right.

Arabella closed the door and put the parcel on the bed. She was half frightened to open it. She had only just managed – for her father's sake – to keep her emotions under control for Christmas Day. Slowly she removed the brown paper to find a layer or two of pretty white tissue paper secured by a pink ribbon. Her throat was already feeling constricted as she removed the paper and then she caught her breath and the tears fell freely for, what she revealed, was a dark wooden box, beautifully made and polished. On the top was an inlay of light wood in the shape of a diamond and painted on *that* was a single, pink, wild rose. She ran her fingers lovingly over it, crying unashamedly. She turned the little brass key and opened the lid. On the inside of the lid, again on the inlay, in a beautiful black script, was one word, *Arabella*. The box was lined in a deep red velvet.

Lying just inside was an envelope on which was written her name and underneath that was another tissue wrapped parcel.

She opened the envelope to reveal a Christmas card bearing a pretty winter scene; inside, in Harnser's handwriting, was the following:

> *The heart hath its own memory like the*
> *Mind and in it are enshrined the precious*
> *Keepsakes.*
>
> > *Longfellow.*

146

The card was unsigned. She knew why – so that she could display it openly if she wished. All her hard work was destroyed, her eyes once more red and swollen. She read and read again the lovely words. She put the little parcel on the bed and examined the box. It was so beautiful. She suspected Walter Fennel, the undertaker, in Flinton, had made it; he had quite a reputation for making lovely jewellery or keepsake boxes. Sure enough, on the bottom she found 'W.F.1863'.

She wondered whom he had asked to paint the rose; it was perfect. The small L.C. at the bottom of the stem was barely discernible, then it came to her; Louisa Canham, she was quite well known locally for her paintings of flowers and portraits. *That* made her think of Matilda Canham and *her* problems and she cried all the more.

She hardly dare open the little parcel; whatever it was would exacerbate her tears she knew without a doubt. She untied the pink ribbon and could not believe her eyes, for lying in front of her was Harnser's ocarina, his most precious possession, together with a little book of hand written verse. She lovingly picked up the little instrument and put it to her mouth, she was half laughing and half crying as she played the two notes of the cuckoo – the laughing was near to hysteria. His father had given him this; it was the first instrument he had learned to play, he kept it with him always. This was proof beyond anything else that he loved her more than anything. She collapsed onto the bed, holding the instrument tightly in her hand and sobbed her heart out.

Much later she picked up the little book. It was full of love poems, most of which he had written himself and signed H.E.J.E – his initials. She found the Misty Morning poem and realized for the first time that he had written it. She remembered she had said that one could almost imagine the poet sitting with them. She smiled through her tears. He loved to tease her. Then another caught her eye as she leafed through the little pages:

Snow Maiden.

Solitary
Beautiful
A perfect winter scene;
My Loved One
In the churchyard
In her cloak of lovat green.

She remembered how he had stared at her that day and then turned to comfort the girl. She smiled sadly at the memory as she realized he had written his poems as she had pressed her flowers.

The last poem in the book was:

In My Heart

In my heart I keep my sweetheart
Bedecked in greens and blues,
I can close my eyes and see her
Whensoe'er I choose.

Her hair is richest chestnut
Her skin translucent cream,
Her eyes are sparkling emerald
I see them in my dreams.

Her voice is softest velvet
Her heart is warm and true,
I can close my eyes and see her
For, my darling, it is you.

She wanted to be by the stream, she did not care about the snow and cold. She crossed to the wash stand and splashed her face time and time again before putting on her outdoor clothes.

Once dressed she picked up the ocarina and the book of poems, said goodbye to her startled father and ran all the way to

Marcie's Bridge where she read the book from cover to cover.

She hardly noticed the old man who came and sat beside her; the snow had muffled his footsteps.

"Can I help?" said Old Joe softly.

She turned her head, thinking she must have imagined the voice. "Oh J-Joe," she managed between her sobs.

"Don't you fret none, Miss Arabella, he'll soon be back home."

The late afternoon sun sparkled on the stream and the snow. Millions of diamonds twinkled up at them.

She looked at him blankly, "W-will he?"

"Course he will, he's got to be here for the weddin' hasn't he?" She realized they were thinking of different people as he continued, "When is the weddin', Miss?"

"July, it is in July." She was amazed she could think clearly enough to answer him.

"Time'll fly, you'll see. Christmas always make you miss your loved ones that little bit more."

He was trying to help, she gave him a weak smile, "Are you missing someone?" she asked.

"I always miss my mother, I expect you miss yours too. I come down here every Christmas afternoon. I have my dinner along of Abel and Aggie but I don't like to outstay my welcome so I tell them I've got things to do, then I come here for a little bit of quietude and remembrance…"

He blew on his cold fingers as his voice broke over his sentimental words.

No, please, Joe, she thought, do not tell me about any more loneliness. She looked at the old man and saw him staring at the bridge. She was so lucky compared to him, what did he have?

"I hear we're goin' to hev a church clock," he said presently, regaining his composure.

"Yes," her voice was small.

"That'll be nice, maybe Vicar Hanley won't run over time so much."

She smiled, "That is just what somebody else said."

"Those pews are extra hard when you get old and lose your

flesh. *This* is a nice seat int it? I hear young Harnser made it for his sweetheart."

She dared not respond. "Leastways," he continued "there's a rumour he made a bench with an inscription and this one *do* have an inscription but I can't read so I'm not sure about it. I can write my name," he continued proudly, hoping to cheer her up a little. "Abel taught me to do it. He said it's handy for legal papers; Wills and such like, though I don't think I need make one of them; I int got a sight to m' name."

Feeling a genuine warmth toward the old man, Arabella surprised herself by saying. "I understand it makes good sense to make a Will, it is amazing the value of things we take for granted. Your furniture for example, you must have some lovely pieces; my grandmother said your father was a wonderful craftsman and so, I hear, are you."

"Why thank you, Miss," the old man said shakily with emotion. "I hadn't thought of that."

"We have a beautifully carved newel post at Barcada, Grand-mother said your father did *that* and all the breastsummer beams."

Joe thought his heart would burst with pride, this was turning out to be the best Christmas afternoon he had had in years. He would remember it for the rest of his life, sitting here in his favourite place, feeling close to his mother, hearing wonderful compliments to his father and himself, watching dusk fall on the sparkling little stream. "Thank you, Miss Arabella," he said softly, "I shan't forget your kindness."

He got to his feet with the help of his stick, stamping his feet to warm them. "Now I wonder if you would do me a great favour, Miss?"

"If I am able, Joe," she said rising to her feet.

"If I turn this seat up," he said, as he did just that, "Will you read me the inscription so that I can satisfy the curiosity of the regulars down The Bell?"

One look at the inscription and Arabella burst, once more, into tears.

"Oh now don't you fret so, don't you fret," said Joe not

knowing quite how to handle the situation. Should he put a fatherly arm around her? Or just sit and wait for her tears to subside?

Before he could make up his mind Arabella said through her tears, "It says 'A and H. 1863 A year to remember' Oh Joe, how will I ever cope without him?"

Suddenly everything became crystal clear to the old man. Of course, why else would *she* rather than Alice, be sitting here on Christmas Day? *She* was the chestnut haired young lady seen from a distance with young Harnser. Well, well, *now* what was he to tell the regulars at The Bell?

"I'm so sorry, Miss, I didn't know…"

"No, no one knows," she said wearily, "Except my father of course."

The old man made a quick decision. He could tell them what it said on the bench, it would be what they were expecting anyway, or he could just leave it at what he had already told them, that he could not read it. Either way he *was* sure of one thing and this he voiced to the girl.

"There, there," he said soothingly, "Dry your tears now, your secret's safe with me. If no one know it'll give 'em all the more to wonder about. Now I'd best walk you safely home else they'll be sendin' out a search party."

Fancy that, he thought to himself, life's never what it seems.

The snow was crunching beneath their feet as it froze in the crisp evening air. They reached Rookery Lane, suddenly Arabella took his arm,

"Will you make sure Alice knows he is safe? Perhaps you could tell her that he was seen heading for the railway station. It is true after all. *I* saw him. We had to help him Joe, he was in a very bad way, he collapsed on our doorstep when he came to say goodbye. I-I would prefer that the matter went no further."

A bird flew from a tree overhead sending a flurry of snow down onto them. "Don't you worry, Miss, I'll make sure she get the message; that he was seen leavin'."

"Thank you very much, Joe." She squeezed his arm.

It was quite some time since he had walked a young lady

home. It had been an extraordinary day. "This may seem strange to you, Miss Arabella, but you have made this Christmas very special. I usually spend the afternoon quite alone."

"I have not seen you at the bridge for some time," she said softly.

"I usually go in the mornin' around eleven o'clock; thass when they found my mother, at eleven o'clock," he added again, to emphasize the point.

"I see," she said softly. "I tend to go in the afternoon or early evening."

They reached the top of the track. "You go on, Joe, I will be alright now. You must be freezing."

"I'll see you to your gate, Miss, I'm used to the cold and I enjoy a walk in the moonlight."

They walked on in silence until they reached the gates. The Barcada sign was swinging gently making a creaking sound as it did so. "That sign is a bit like me," Joe said, "it needs a bit of oil on its joints. Now you git indoors, Miss, I can see the Major looking out the window for you."

She invited him in for a Christmas drink, which he declined gracefully. "Thank you, Joe...for everything...I hope you enjoy the rest of Christmas," and then, unexpectedly, she put her hands on his upper arms and kissed his whiskery old face before running to the front door, which the Major was holding open.

Well, mused Joe as he trudged home to his cottage and fire, who'd hev thought it?

On Boxing Day morning Old Joe answered a knock on his door to find the Major, who gave him a bottle of best brandy for seeing his daughter safely home the previous evening.

Closing the door after him he returned to his chair by the fire to continue the task he had started first thing that morning – writing his Will in his head. Tomorrow he would go to a solicitor and have it put down on paper. It was true – he had some very nice pieces of furniture in this house and there was one piece he treasured above all others...

CHAPTER THIRTEEN

Maria packed the last of Harnser's belongings into a trunk and dragged it to a corner of the bedroom. She then moved her own things into the room her son had occupied. Relations were very strained between herself and her husband; she had no wish to sleep with a man who had nearly killed her son. Her task finished, she looked out of the little dormer window. Ahead of her was the Home Wood, a place she had always loved, having spent many happy hours there with her father. The leafless trees stood cold and still in the failing light, their branches heavy with snow. She brought her eyes nearer home – to the orchard and then the garden, which stretched out to the right. Down there, in one of the outbuildings, Walter was putting wheels on an old wicker chair ready for his son when he came home tomorrow. Together, in silence, they had earlier moved James' bed downstairs to the main sitting room, making room by moving some furniture into 'the book room'.

Her grandfather had started the book collection with books he had won playing poker at The Hall. Her father had continued it and she had added Edward's and *his* father's books. She was very proud of her book collection and loved to sit amongst the friendly shelves in one of the two easy chairs that stood facing the window, one either side of a pretty little lyre ended table with a leather inlay. She would often sit and read on summer evenings when James was in bed and Walter and Harnser were out of doors. She would open the two casement windows with their leaded lights, which twinkled in the evening sunlight and sit overlooking the garden to relax after a busy day.

She loved the smell of a summer evening, as the air cooled and the honeysuckles and night scented stocks released their tantalizing perfumes, which served her senses as she read her romantic novels. This was *her* time – a time of reading, memories and glorious garden scents.

Now, as she crossed the almost dark bedroom, she wondered if she would ever be happy again. She had chosen her path – to stay with Walter and care for James – but a large part of her was with her exiled son, with his flayed back and his broken heart...his flute, his piccolo and ocarina...his flaxen hair and sparkling brown eyes...spending Christmas all alone.

She heard Walter outside stamping the snow off his boots then the back door open and close, she steeled herself to spend one last, hostile night alone, with a man who had become a stranger. There was a knock on the front door. Who could be calling on them? She stayed her step knowing that if she moved, creaking stairs would announce her presence. She heard Molly's hesitant, conciliatory voice. What was this? She sat down on the stairs listening as Molly told Walter that Harnser was not responsible for Alice's condition. The girl had confessed all... they were very sorry for accusing him...they knew he was better than that...they felt very bad...please could Walter and Maria find it in their hearts to forgive them... it was Christmas, the season of good will...Alice would never forgive herself...

The voices rose and fell for maybe fifteen minutes. The front door opened and closed. Maria heard Walter go back to the kitchen, she heard him put the lantern on the table, a few minutes later the back door opened and closed. She retraced her footsteps to the back bedroom in time to see the dark shape with swaying lantern making its way into the woods.

Hours later in the darkness, she listened to her husband sobbing in the bedroom next door, but he did not apologize to her for half killing her son for no reason...and she did not go to comfort him.

154

Chapter Fourteen

Harnser's gaze wandered over the room that was now his home. He had been very fortuitous in finding it so quickly and ironically it had been due to his injured back and his need to find a doctor.

Upon being told that Harnser had come to the city to enrol at The Stoneham Training College for Schoolmasters the Doctor had immediately offered him a room in his own house, which he shared with his wife. "I will be able to keep an eye on that back of yours," he had said kindly, then added, "I don't suppose you play chess?"

Despite his low spirits Harnser had smiled, "As a matter of fact I do, I will look forward to it, Sir."

"No need to 'Sir' me, we are Florence and Richard if we are to live under the same roof."

The house was on the outskirts of the city in a rural setting and, fortunately for Harnser, the Doctor was not short of money so the rent was very modest for such spacious accommodation.

Having deposited his money with a bank and enrolled at the college Harnser spent the few days before Christmas familiarizing himself with the surrounding area, it was good to be out of doors again even though his back still pained him. He had found a replacement ocarina, and that had made him think of Arabella. He knew he must try not to think of her all the time but it was difficult. He must concentrate on his studies so as not to waste the money his parents had given him.

In the preceding days to Christmas, Doctor Fisher and his wife attended three different musical drama performances in the city, inviting Harnser along each time. They helped to take his mind off home and, despite all his problems, he quite enjoyed them. The finale of the last show they attended featured a solo

155

singer. The purity of the young lady's voice was indeed a joy to hear. Just before she began singing Harnser caught a movement from the corner of his eye and glanced across to see Doctor Fisher put his hand over that of his wife, turning to her with a soft, endearing look. They had obviously heard this young lady sing before. At the end of the solo performance the singer received a well deserved standing ovation and, to the call of 'more, more', indulged the audience. Harnser had never heard a voice like it. It was the sort of performance that left one stunned; few words were spoken on the journey home.

Christmas itself was a subdued occasion for which Harnser was grateful; Church on Christmas Eve and Christmas morning; a very good lunch and a walk – alone with his thoughts – in the afternoon. There were a few callers at the door for this or that, carollers and suchlike and, was it his imagination, or did each knock at the door induce a slight nervousness in his hosts?

It was almost as if they were waiting for something. Another thing he noticed was that one Christmas gift remained unopened on the sideboard, it had still been there on Boxing Day. His thoughts turned to Little Pecking; had Silas remembered to deliver his gift to Arabella? Had she liked it? He was sure she would have, she would now know that he had written the Misty Morning poem. Would she laugh at his teasing? or would she be too sad to laugh? Yes, he thought, it would be much more likely that she had cried when she opened his gift...cried at the box because it was beautiful...cried at the ocarina, because it had been his father's and she knew it was his most treasured possession...and cried at the poems because he had written most of them for her.

He had not wanted to make her cry, and if they had not had to part so suddenly his presents would have had the desired affect – to make her happy. He knew she had arranged a present for him and wondered what it was. That was something else that would make her sad – she would not know where to send it. But, he reflected, that was for the best; if nobody knew where he was, they could all get on with their respective lives and leave the past where it belonged.

Arabella, he knew, was fond of Charles; given the right conditions they could make a success of their marriage and the long, hot Summer of eighteen hundred and sixty-three would gradually recede to a treasured corner of her mind from where she could resurrect it at will, smile, reminisce, think of him fondly, then let it slip quietly back until another reminder brought it to the fore again.

He knew he must do likewise.

The decision to settle in Stoneham had been an instant one made at Winford railway station. Having arrived there, he had suddenly realized he did not have a planned destination so had bought a ticket for London. On the long journey to the capital he had had plenty of time to think. It was unlikely that anyone would come looking for him, even so, the more distance he put between himself and Little Pecking the better for all concerned. He had prayed that little James would walk again, he hoped that Alice would confess that he was not responsible for her condition and that she would find happiness with the real father of her baby – he liked her – she deserved to be happy. For some obscure reason then, he had thought about Matilda Canham and her enforced separation from *her* sweetheart. It was at that point that he had decided Kent would be as good a place as any to finish his studies. With some strange sort of logic, he reasoned that if Arabella and Matilda were within a few miles of each other, and he and Matthew Johnson were likewise in fairly close proximity, well, there was somehow a sort of comfort in that knowledge...so he was happy with his decision.

He closed his eyes as the troubles of the last three weeks fought for pole position in his head. His mind was a jumble of problems and fears against which he had no weapon. He was exhausted...

> ...and the fair curls went twirling
> and twirling and twirling
> and the fair curls went twirling
> and twirling around...

...and the sound of a child's scream rang out over the surrounding countryside.

He awoke with a jolt, sweat running down his face, the nightmare so real he expected to find himself in the Home Wood with little James' motionless, twisted frame lying in the snow.

He gradually became accustomed to his new surroundings as his eyes took in his lodging room.

His gaze fell on the two photographs on the bedside table. One was of his mother with Walter and James. The other was of Arabella, the one that they had had taken in the Summer. His breathing became more even as she smiled enigmatically from the little frame, he could almost discern a slight lowering of her teasing green eyes...

...and he could smell the subtle perfume of a spray of wild roses...

PART THREE

If Wishes Were Horses…

CHAPTER ONE

The clock on the church tower struck the hour of two o'clock and a cheer went up from the crowded churchyard. The clock had been set in motion to coincide with the arrival of the bride for her wedding to Charles Sanderson. It was the seventeenth day of July eighteen hundred and sixty-four – Arabella's eighteenth birthday.

Arabella had woken that morning full of mixed emotions. This was the day her grandmother had dreamed of – the day the Sanderson family would be joined together once more, she had made it possible by promising to marry Charles; but it was not her future husband that occupied her thoughts as she lay in her bath that morning and recited poetry in her head; poetry that had been written for her by her one true love, poetry that she knew by heart, having read it over and over again as she sat by the stream at Marcie's Bridge. She wondered where he was and what he was doing. Had he seen the wedding notice in the national papers? Was he thinking of her today? Would he be among the throngs that she knew would witness her arrival at the church? Did she want him to be there? Yes, she did; knowing he was nearby would give her strength, but, would it be the strength to walk up the aisle and be joined in holy matrimony to Charles Sanderson? Or would he give her the strength to saddle up her horse and ride off with him as her grandmother had done with the Major? She did not know. Even at this late stage in the proceedings she did not know if she would be able to defy the family with all their hopes, to follow her heart and live in comparative poverty with the man she loved. Surely her grandmother would understand if she chose that path; her mother would understand, even her father, whom she knew was very fond of Harnser, *he* would only ask that she were happy, so why had she not done it? Why had she not left with Harnser on that snowbound night seven months ago when he had stolen her heart and walked off with it in the moonlight? She had been carried along with all the preparations as if in a dream, going through the motions while her heart and thoughts were in some unknown place. All Winter she had felt lonely and cold, she had wandered the copse and ridden the estate and kept company with her father on the cold evenings. She had corresponded with Charles but had had to read and re-read her letters to him for fear that she had written what was in her heart rather than her head. Then, in early March she had received a letter to say he would return in April – to formally announce their betrothal.

The letter was a slight turning point. She knew she must stop dwelling on the past and think of her future with Charles. She had tried to do just that and thought she was winning until this morning – her wedding day.

As her carriage arrived at the lych gate the clock struck twice and she heard the loud cheer. She had been asked to walk from the gate to the church door to allow the villagers and estate workers a good view of the bride. She had agreed readily, hoping to catch a glimpse of Harnser among the crowds, but in her heart she knew he would not be there; there were still people in the village to whom he would not be welcome.

Then she saw Alice.

She was holding her baby and was with a tall, dark young man at the edge of the path. Alice looked happy, she was glad about that, for some reason she had worried about the girl even though she had never spoken to her and, was she a little plumper?

The bride kept her head slightly bowed as she walked up the path on the arm of her father. This open adoration from the crowd did not come easy to her, she knew her colour was high but that she must look at the villagers, who had turned out specially to see her in her finery. The walk seemed to her to be

162

in slow motion, she could hear gasps and whispered comments of how lovely she looked, the crowd lifted her spirits. She lifted her head and looked at the church clock. A photographer, who had set up his camera along the path, asked her to pause for a moment to record the historical moment. As she brought her gaze down again she saw Alice smiling at her in open admiration. She returned the smile wondering what Alice's own wedding day had been like. It had been a hurried affair she knew, she had witnessed the banns being read shortly after Harnser had left. At least the young man had stood by her. She felt a strange affinity with the girl and wondered if she, too, still wondered about their heart's desire.

She continued her walk, there was a fresh breeze blowing and fluffy white clouds were scudding across a blue sky; disappearing on one side of the church tower only to reappear on the other. For some reason that made her remember how she had met Harnser. She remembered him telling her how he had seen her approaching and had scrambled round the corner so that he could meet her as if by accident. She smiled up at the clouds and her throat felt constricted, she felt her eyes fill with tears and blinked rapidly to clear them. She became aware of her father's hand covering her own where it clung to his sleeve; did he know she was thinking of Harnser? Was it obvious? She turned and gave him a brief, forced smiled through her tears. He leaned towards her and whispered, "Are you sure you want to do this, Arabella?"

There was concern on his face, love in his eyes, she could not let him down, could not embarrass him by changing her mind at this late stage. Her mother and grandmother were lying not fifty yards distant; she was approaching a vault, where illustrious Sandersons rested in peace, knowing that Sanderson duty and common sense would prevail this day. "He has gone away, Father," she said softly, "and I am left. What else can I do with the rest of my life?" She paused briefly before adding, "I am privileged, Charles is very nice, I must be the envy of every unmarried girl in the district." He smiled and squeezed her hand as they reached the coolness of the church porch.

She turned her head briefly for one last look at the well wishers, the fluffy white clouds and the sunshine, before stepping determinedly into the familiar vaulted surroundings of the little flint church, where her future husband waited at the altar.

He had not come.

CHAPTER TWO

The room was much bigger than her bedroom at Barcada. The ceiling was high and ornate. Huge curtained windows took up most of one wall. Two doors at each end of the wall – on which the bed head stood – led to the dressing rooms and bathrooms. Arabella had taken her time preparing for bed, brushing her hair for much longer than was necessary. She had extinguished the lamps, picked up the candle and walked nervously to the bedroom door wondering if Charles was growing impatient waiting for her. She was therefore very surprised to find that she had completed her preparations first – opening the door to find that the huge bed was still empty. She set the candle on the bedside table and climbed between the cool sheets where she lay nervously waiting for her new husband. Her mind was working overtime. Would he know that she had lain with another man? What would she say if he voiced his suspicions? She watched the shadows, cast by the lamps, dancing on the walls and ceiling knowing that her heart was racing uncontrollably. She tried to calm herself, taking deep breaths and imagining she could hear the waterfall at Marcie's Bridge and that she was waiting for Harnser to rendezvous with her, but the longer she waited the more anxious she became and even felt slight annoyance that Charles should put her through this torture.

She could hear sounds coming from the corridor outside their bedroom as wedding guests made their way to their allotted bedchambers. She wondered how many guests they were accommodating tonight. Some, she knew, would stay on to holiday on the Oxley Estate – relatives who had travelled some distance to attend the wedding, who thought they might as well take advantage of the occasion to enjoy a little more of the Suffolk countryside. How she envied them at this moment; she would much rather be spending the following two weeks here than in London with its bustle and noise.

It had been a long, tiring day and she had been carried along in a busy programme of events beginning with the wedding, progressing to a banquet and ending with a Wedding Ball in the huge Hall of Oxley. Tomorrow would be another tiring day as they travelled to the capital for two weeks before going on to Carendon Hall in Hampshire to holiday with a good friend of Charles. In all they would be away for a month – but first she must get through tonight...

She heard a slight noise behind her and a little to her right. The door to Charles' dressing room opened slowly, she did not move. Her heart was thumping and she could hear the blood pounding through her temples. Although she stared straight up at the ceiling, she was aware of Charles walking round the room extinguishing lamps. Presently he arrived at her side of the bed, where he bent low to blow out her own candle. As he did so she turned her head to look at him; his gaze fell upon her and he smiled briefly before turning to walk round to his side of the bed. She felt the bed depress on his side as she lay rigidly still. Is it possible to be quietly hysterical? She remembered how eagerly she had lain with Harnser in the friendly little room full of firelight. She remembered how she could not wait for him to take her in his arms and to love her, she could almost hear the fire crackling and smell his musky scent...

...and then, to her amazement, Charles leaned gently towards her, took her hand, kissed her softly on her cheek and said, "You must be very tired Arabella and we have a long day ahead of us tomorrow, so I thank you for a beautiful day, wish you a very good night and welcome you to Oxley House – your new home."

She looked up into his face wondering if her gratitude was evident. She began breathing more evenly, she smiled at him, she was almost crying with relief as she answered, "Thank you, Charles...for everything."

CHAPTER THREE

The honeymoon was over. No sooner had they arrived home than Charles said he must return to London on business.

The marriage was still unconsummated.

Arabella began to wonder what the problem was. Did Charles find her unattractive? She found that difficult to believe considering the compliments he paid her. Did he perhaps think her too young to have a family? She felt restless; she had little to do at Oxley. She kept company with her mother-in-law, who spent an inordinate amount of time singing the praises of her only son, which, Arabella reasoned, was only natural. She rode the Estate, walked the grounds, gathered summer flowers, played the piano, dreamed of Harnser and spent much time at Barcada with her father.

It was in the middle of September that Charles returned from London and, surprisingly, Arabella found herself looking forward to his homecoming. At least he would have plenty to tell her. She could not understand the restlessness she had felt of late. It was alien to her nature.

A carriage was dispatched to meet him at Winford railway station. Arabella thought long and hard over whether or not to accompany it before deciding to remain at Oxley. It reminded her of when he came home after her grandmother had died and he had walked with her in the garden and quoted Samuel Pepys. She tried to recall the quotation about the honeysuckle, '*the trumpet flower whose bugles blow scent instead of sound,*' yes, that was it. Then she remembered how he had surprised her with his own lyrical phraseology and his appreciation of evening garden scents. What had he said? Oh, yes, '*One cannot discern them individually but, collectively, they are amazingly seductive. I suspect the honeysuckles are the chief contributors.*' She smiled as she recalled his words and instinctively walked across to the front garden wall to enjoy the heady fragrance herself.

She hoped that arriving home in the evening would bring back the same memories to him and that it would evoke romanticism. Suddenly she stopped in her tracks. Her thoughts startled her. Did she want Charles to make love to her? Surprisingly she realized she did, but maybe for all the wrong reasons. Her feelings of restlessness, she realized, were because she wanted a child. Someone to love and care for, someone to whom she could feel close. She missed Harnser so much and Charles did not adequately fill the emotional void. She felt a little guilty that she was prepared to be unfaithful to Harnser in order to have a child. Then she thought of Jack – their onetime farmhand at the smallholding – and his words when they had come across the copulating dogs in the yard when she was twelve and when she had voiced her concerns that Poppy had not looked too happy. '*No, she dint*,' he had said, '*but thass the way of life, we all hatta put up with things we dunt like to git on in the world and git what we want.*'

'*What does Poppy want?*' she had said innocently.

'*Why, she want her pups, dunt she? Just like you'll want yours one day – babes I mean.*'

Strange how situations bring people from the past to mind. She had not thought of Jack for months, years maybe, and here he was to the forefront of her thoughts. Yes, you were right, Jack, she acknowledged silently as she peeked into the future and saw herself walking with her baby among the summer flowers...

The air grew chilly and she went indoors to find a shawl. She wondered why Charles was so late; the carriage had had ample time to get home since the arrival time of the train.

Eventually, as dusk fell, she gave up her romantic notions of her husband stepping eagerly into her waiting arms in the garden, to return indoors. A disappointment fell upon her, almost a depression, as she made small talk with her in-laws and watched darkness fall on the outside world.

She went to bed alone and in despair.

The next morning she was surprised to find her husband at the breakfast table.

"I missed the train," he said apologetically after rising to greet her. "I arrived back so late I slept elsewhere to avoid disturbing you." He gave her a weak smile and returned his gaze to his breakfast.

A strange little feeling of worry crept into her stomach. Had he wanted to avoid sleeping with her?

"Never mind," she replied over-brightly, "perhaps we could go riding today, it would be nice to have your company at last." She wondered if he would detect the slight sarcasm in her last words, but he appeared not to notice.

"I am sorry, Arabella, Father and I will be busy all day with estate matters. Perhaps Mother could accompany you." His voice sounded flat and uninterested. Again she felt the worrying sensation, but it turned quickly to annoyance.

"I think I will go shopping instead," she said suddenly, "I will make a day of it."

"As you like, Arabella but make sure you are home in plenty of time for dinner. Mother and Father will be disappointed if we are not all together on my first day home."

She wandered aimlessly around the shops wondering what she was doing there. There was nothing she really needed. She passed the jewellers where Charles had bought her brooch, pausing only briefly to look at the window display. She decided to luncheon at The Royal Hotel, only because it was familiar to her; she had never luncheoned alone in town before. She felt strangely conspicuous at her small corner table, so hurried her meal in order to escape.

Once outside she walked along the promenade in reflective mood. She thought of her early morning rides along the sands with Harnser and of how they had always had plenty to talk about. Even when not verbally communicating they had enjoyed companionable silences; happy to be in each other's company. She craved his presence, she had never felt restless with *him*; only happy, carefree and content, and maybe sometimes a little frightened of the future. With good reason, she thought now.

She found a seat and watched the gulls swooping and soaring, as they called noisily overhead. There were children playing on the sands as they made the most of the late-summer, good weather. She watched the sea sparkling in the sun as it noisily announced its presence to the shore, running up the sands to caress the toes of happy youngsters as they screamed in delight. She looked at her watch; it would soon be time to rejoin her carriage at the agreed meeting place outside the railway station.

She did not want to go home.

She dragged her eyes away from the happy, welcoming scene before her to walk the short distance into town. She located her carriage – easily recognizable with its unmistakable coat of arms – and was about to board when a familiar figure caught her eye. The plump, chestnut haired girl struggling with shopping and a young baby was unmistakable – it was Alice. On impulse Arabella ran towards her, intercepting her route to the carrier cart. "I could not help noticing you are heavily laden," she said self-consciously to the startled girl. "I wondered if you would accept a ride home with me. We will pass your door. I – I am sorry I have not introduced myself, I am Arabella Biddemore, er, Sanderson," she corrected herself shyly. "I – I have seen you in church often – with your family." She had wanted to say 'with Harnser' but refrained thinking it might embarrass her.

"Oh, no, Miss, I couldn't put you to the bother, the carrier cart will be leavin' shortly."

"It is no trouble I assure you, I will appreciate the company, here let me help with your shopping," and to Alice's amazement she took hold of her two bags and began to walk away in the direction of the waiting conveyance – Alice had no choice but to follow.

The journey home began a trifle strained. Arabella had acted on lonely impulse and was now at a loss for a topic of conversation. Alice, meanwhile, hardly knew how she had come to be sitting in an Oxley carriage with its plush interior and leather seats; she hardly dared breathe for fear of damaging something. After several silent minutes of averted eyes and general embarrassment on both sides, Arabella's eyes were drawn to the child. She had little experience of babies apart from longing for one. "What is his name?" she asked presently.

"Arthur Jack," the girl replied proudly. "Arthur for *my* father and Jack for *his*."

There was a brief silence as Arabella wondered whether she should mention Arthur's untimely death, then, "You have had a troubled time of late, losing a parent is difficult to come to terms with, especially when it is so sudden."

Alice warmed to her travelling companion.

"The baby has helped, he don't leave me much time for feelin' sorry for myself."

"I am sure he does not." Her eyes lingered on the chubby little boy.

"Might I hold him?" She had surprised herself by the question but not as much as she had surprised the young mother.

"Yes, Ma'am, if you're sure," she hesitated before adding nervously, "Babies can be a bit...dribbly."

The child was passed over, whereupon he put his thumb in his mouth, stared across at his mother for a few moments then fell asleep, lulled, no doubt, by the rhythmic rocking of the comfortable carriage.

Alice was left to rest her arms and marvel at the situation in which she found herself.

"I shall need to get out soon, Ma'am."

"But we are only just reaching Flinton...and it is Arabella...my name is Arabella," she said softly.

"I live at Flinton now...with Jack's mother," she blushed, "We can't afford our own place yet," she added needlessly.

"Where does your husband work?"

"On Smith's farm, Ma'am. I need to get out now," she added quickly.

As Arabella handed the baby back to his mother she felt an acute sense of loss. He was warm and comforting.

171

"Thank you for the ride, Ma'am it was good of you."

"You are very welcome, Alice and thank *you* for letting me hold your baby, he is a lovely child, you must be very proud of him. I hope one day to have one of my own," she said wistfully.

She is envious of *me*, thought Alice. Who would have believed it – Mrs Charles Sanderson, envious of me. She cuddled little Arthur tightly, took her bags from the driver and set off across The Green feeling unusually pleased with her situation.

As Arabella continued her journey alone she realized that their common link had not been mentioned. Harnser was lost to them both. She *was* however poignantly aware of a faint smell of lavender that lingered in the air...

When her husband leaned over that night to give her his customary goodnight kiss, Arabella was disturbed to catch a strong whiff of brandy on his breath.

Chapter Four

"I am sorry," exclaimed Harnser. The girl had come from nowhere, stepping into his path and colliding quite heavily, sending the contents of her basket flying in all directions. He looked up, from where he was retrieving the spilled goods, to see a small door in the wall; it was the back door of a theatre and was still open from the girl's hasty exit.

He finished his task, picked up the basket and was about to hand it back when he realized how distressed she was. The young lady was leaning against the wall, her eyes were shut tightly, she was biting her lips in an effort to control herself. He imagined her to be in her early twenties. He touched her lightly on her sleeve to remind her he was still there, whereupon she dissolved into floods of tears and ran away leaving him holding her basket; he had no choice but to follow.

He saw her disappear into a park and hastened his step so as not to lose sight of her. "Lovers tiff I expect," he heard a passer-by murmur. He entered the park and saw the girl seated not twenty yards distant.

He approached cautiously, having no desire to make her take flight again. "You forgot your basket," he said gently.

"Thank you," was all she replied, keeping her head bowed.

"It sometimes helps to talk…." he began tentatively.

She raised her head and turned to face him. There was something vaguely familiar about her. "I do not think talking will solve my problems," she said flatly.

"I would like to help if I can, perhaps I could carry your basket for you and see you safely home. My name is Harnser Elliot, I am a student at the Training College for School-masters." He did not know why he had told her that, except that it might give him a certain amount of respectability, after all, he was a complete stranger to her.

"So you want to be a schoolmaster?"

"Yes."

"Is that what you *really* want to be, or what others would have you be?"

"It is my own choice, I suppose I would prefer to spend most of my time playing music but that is not quite so practical is it? It would be an uncertain lifestyle."

"You should follow your dreams."

"I try to have the best of both worlds – I give music lessons, I indulge my passion that way. I must sound very boring."

"You are probably doing the right thing. I followed my dreams and look where it has got me."

He noticed she was wringing her hands together in her lap.

"You have not told me your name."

"Emily – Emily Weston."

Emily Weston, he repeated the name over and over in his head, where had he heard that name before? Then it came to him, she was the singer that had so enthralled him on his first Christmas in Stoneham and whom he had heard a few times since.

"You are a singer," he said triumphantly, "I have heard you sing on stage several times, especially at Christmas. I was in very low spirits myself one time and, for a few minutes, you made me forget my problems. You have an unforgettably beautiful voice."

"Thank you," she said, genuinely pleased at the compliment. Then unexpectedly she burst into tears once more.

Harnser was unsure how to react, he tentatively reached for her hand covering it with his own. "Things cannot be *that* bad surely," he said gently.

"Things are *very* bad, they could not be worse," she responded forlornly. He waited for her to expand. "I have no income, I am shortly to become homeless and I am…I am…"

"You are what?"

"I am unmarried and with child."

There was a long silence until Harnser said, "Where is your young man?"

"My *young* man, as you put it, is an older man who suddenly remembered he had a wife. I am an impressionable fool. I have proved my parents right; they always said I was wilful."

"Love makes us do strange things. Lovers will make mistakes for eternity. We never learn – none of us, sometimes, just sometimes, it *is* best to follow one's heart. You are no worse than anyone else."

"I have only enough money for one month's board and lodgings."

"Perhaps I could help."

"No, you hardly know me, I could not accept it."

"When will the child be born?"

"Next March."

"I have lodgings on the outskirts of the city. It is a large house; perhaps my landlord would give you a room for six months or so, until you can continue your vocation. I will be happy to lend you the money, if you will not accept a gift. Think about it and in the meantime please let me see you home."

He walked with the girl out of the park. It was not long before he realized their steps were leading them to a shabby area of the city. The houses were tiny and cramped together. No more than a rookery, he thought worriedly as they walked the dismal, narrow streets.

"That you, Emily?" a voice called out as they entered a miserable little abode. "You're late, your dinner's dried up."

The hall was very narrow, one wall having been erected to afford the householder some privacy in her tiny front room.

"Go on up, I have to collect my meal," said Emily to her companion, pointing to the stairway. "My room is at the back; take the candle." She handed him the candle that sat on the bottom stair.

The narrow, twisting stairway was treacherous in the dim light that came from the candle and the downstairs room. Reaching the top Harnser opened a door into a cramped room. He set the candle down on a tiny bedside table, one of only a few pieces of furniture, which included a chest of drawers, a chair and a bed. He was aware of a dim light coming through the floorboards. The room below was unceiled, making Emily's room a little less private and a little more drafty.

A voice floated through the floorboards, "Have you got a man up there? I'm not responsible for you, you know. No good will come of it, you'll see."

"He is a very good friend who saw me home in the dark, he will not be here long. We are not romantically involved."

"Be that as it may, I'm not responsible," the woman reiterated, "and put those candles out when you get to the top, you won't need them with the lamp."

Harnser looked around the room for the lamp as Emily arrived at the door with her meal in her hand. "It is on the floor at the bottom of the bed," she said, realizing what he was looking for. "There is not room for everything on the chest of drawers." She sat down on her bed, her plate on her lap. "You must share this with me as I have obviously kept you from your own dinner."

Harnser eyed the unappetizing meal before answering truthfully, "You need to eat it all yourself, you must think of the child. I can eat later." It had not been a difficult decision.

Conversation between the two young people flowed easily and Harnser realized with a jolt that it was the first time he had enjoyed being with a young lady since he had left Little Pecking. Arabella was well and truly lost to him. He had seen the wedding notice in the paper and then a short report of it. He had kept the cutting but did not really understand why. Now and again he re-read it. Arabella had been married for two years and seven months. He still kept her photograph by his bed and thought of her constantly, one day, he promised himself, he would go home to see his mother and maybe catch a glimpse of his erstwhile sweetheart. He thought about James a lot, the nightmares had not ceased. The re-reading of Arabella's wedding report reinforced the knowledge that he had lost her and that he must make a life without her. He looked across from his chair to see that Emily was watching him intently. "I do not usually bring strangers home with me," she said softly.

"I am sure you do not, but perhaps we could meet again," he smiled sadly, I think we could both do with a friend. Anyway I need more time to persuade you to take up my offer assistance. I could talk to my landlord tonight and we could hav you installed in no time. I am sure they would help in such circumstances."

"What makes you think anybody would want to help a wayward girl?"

He looked at her in mock sternness. "You are not wayward, but you *are* in an unfortunate position." Then a thought came to him, "Have you seen a doctor?"

"Yes."

"Good, you see you *are* sensible after all, but that is another good reason why you should live at my lodging house – Mr Fisher is a doctor."

"Doctor Fisher?...you live with Doctor Fisher?" the girl looked aghast.

"Yes, do you know him?"

Emily was once more in tears. "They are my parents, Harnser. They have washed their hands of me because I wanted to go on the stage. You must not tell them where I am, promise me. They will be appalled at my circumstances, I am so ashamed after all my high handed predictions of fame and fortune." She was clutching at his sleeves, imploring him to keep her secret. "I find it difficult to live as they would want me to. I love the excitement and travelling but they think theatre folk are loose-living and decadent. We had so many arguments that in the end I ran away. I can assure you they would not want me back in my condition."

The outburst surprised him. He tried to pacify her. "People change Emily, your parents would want you back whatever you had done."

"No, you are wrong, you must not tell them about me. I have nowhere to go." She was becoming hysterical.

Harnser realized why the girl looked so familiar. Now and again he caught certain expressions on her face that reminded him of Florence Fisher and there was a photograph on the wall at home of when she was younger. Thinking about it now Harnser could see the likeness. They had never mentioned aughter. He wondered if he could persuade Emily to become a go-between to resolve the situation with her s. He knew it would be difficult for him living in the same se with his new-found knowledge. He would feel disloyal to em, especially when they had been so kind to him. He would have to tread carefully. One false move could result in Emily running off again, he could not risk it. He saw the fear in her face as she waited for him to speak. She appeared desperate; a few wisps of her blonde hair having come loose and falling across her face, making her appear vulnerable. He had an overwhelming desire to put his arms around her to comfort her.

"I promise I will not tell them about you, but you must promise that you will not do anything silly like running away. I happen to know that they love you very much and are very proud of you."

He told her of the visits to the theatres at Christmas and how he had seen the love and pride on their faces when she had performed. He also told her of the unopened Christmas gifts and the hope on their faces each time there had been a knock on the door.

"I did not understand any of it at the time," he finished, "but now it has become clear. You would make them very happy by returning. Think about it, Emily, you have nothing to lose."

"So they know my new name," she said resignedly.

"Obviously."

"I have not been as clever as I thought."

"It is obvious they have been to see you many times, which proves that they have accepted your way of life."

"Why have they not tried to see me after the shows?"

"Pride maybe. Some people find it difficult to accept defeat. Perhaps they thought you would get it out of your system and then return home with your tail between your legs."

For two weeks the pair continued to meet and Harnser found himself looking unexpectedly forward to the evenings. They walked and talked, mostly discussing options for Emily's future. He could not get her beautiful voice out of his mind and tentatively suggested a joint public performance. "I would be honoured to play the flute in accompaniment to your voice; the church maybe at Christmas."

He wondered who had filled his place at Little Pecking church and how disappointed his mother would have been. He understood Emily's need to sing. When she talked of the stage her blue eyes sparkled and her face took on a lustre of happiness. Who could deny her that personal fulfilment?

Emily's time at the lodging house was running out, he had still not persuaded her to return to her parents. He pulled his collar up against the biting November wind as he once more made the familiar journey through the shabby streets to the cramped dwelling.

The scruffy woman answered his knock as usual, he had waited such a short time that he imagined she must have been standing the other side of the door waiting.

"It wasn't my fault," she said defensively, "I only reminded her that her money was due like I always do and she went up in the air, very highly strung if you ask me. You've got your hands full with that one. She's left you a letter, come in and I'll get it for you."

"You mean she has gone?"

"Yes."

Harnser followed the woman into her little front parlour where, for the first time since he had begun calling, she motioned him to a chair. "Have a cup of tea along of me while you read it," she said before bustling off into the kitchen.

Harnser realized she was not going to give him the letter until she brought the tea. He did not have to wait long; she was obviously prepared.

"How long have you known her?" she continued inquisitively.

"Not long, a month maybe."

"It's not yours then?"

He looked at her where she stood holding the letter. He felt a rush of impatience as he answered a little tersely, "If you are alluding to the child then, no, it is not mine," then his voice

179

softening slightly, "Thank you for the tea it is very cold out of doors, you must forgive my sharpness. I am quite worried about her."

"She didn't have to up and leave like that, I only reminded her. I don't want her out on the streets in her condition. I've grown quite fond of her in my own way."

"I am sure you have."

He was impatient to leave so that he could read the letter until he realized the woman was looking at him expectantly.

"Well, come on, let's see what she says."

He saw that in her rough way she was as worried as he was. He opened the letter and read the contents.

"Well?"

"She does not say where she has gone, just that it is for the best."

"Oh," a worried frown appeared on the old woman's forehead, "Well I hope you find her, let me know won't you?"

"Yes and perhaps you would let *me* know if she should return here. I will write my address down for you…"

She interrupted him by putting out her hand, "I can't read or write so you are wasting your time."

He realized why she had been waiting for him so eagerly. "Perhaps I could call again then. When is she paid to?"

"The end of the week, then I'll have to let the room."

He got up to leave, suddenly feeling an unexpected warmth for the lonely old lady. He put a hand on her shoulder, feeling the bone through her clothes. He gave it a little squeeze and smiled saying kindly, "Thank you for the tea, I am sure she will be alright, she has friends in the theatre world. I will call at the end of the week."

"It's Connie," she said suddenly, "my name's Connie."

He smiled again, "You take good care of yourself, Connie."

He stepped outside, pulling up his collar again as an icy blast swept down the narrow street. When he got to the corner he turned round to see the little silhouette still standing in the softly illuminated doorway. He raised his hand but doubted she could see him.

He tried not to worry about Emily, after all she was not his responsibility but when he was not thinking of her, he was thinking of Arabella, of her rich chestnut hair, creamy skin... and soft summer nights beside a musical little stream. As usual he forced his thoughts back to the present, back to worrying about a delicate young lady and tendrils of ash blonde hair that tended to escape from their anchorage and fall over a pale oval face, making her appear vulnerable and tugging at his heart strings.

Was he destined to always desire the unobtainable?

Chapter Five

It had snowed for the past three days and showed no sign of stopping. As Harnser entered the comfortable house with Florence and Richard Fisher, he could not help but compare it with the tiny dwelling on which he had called last evening. On impulse he had bought holly, bows, some chocolate and a Christmas card, then taken them to Connie's little house, which he had found bereft of Christmas cheer.

She had cried unashamedly when he gave her the gifts and sniffed and dabbed her way through making the weak tea, while he had decorated the little room.

"There, that looks better, does it not?" he had said brightly when they were both seated.

"You're a good boy, your mother must be proud," she said huskily, frightened she would cry again.

As she put out her hand to get her tea Harnser stayed her, "First you must open this," he said handing her the card.

She opened the envelope and stared at the card, tears running down her face. It was some moments before she said, "I've never had one of these before."

Remembering that she could not read, Harnser pulled up his chair close to hers and read what he had written inside. *For Connie at Christmastime, with my best wishes and love. Harnser.*

She had gone over and over the words with him until she knew them by heart, then set the card on the table beside her while she silently drank her tea.

He was glad he had taken the time to call.

Now, as he watched the flames dancing in the inglenook on Christmas Eve he wondered if the Major and Silas had received his Christmas cards. He always signed the Major's card with just his name. To Silas,as usual, he had written a letter. He had never disclosed his whereabouts, just that he was well and working hard at his studies and that he sent his love to them all, especially his mother. He had then taken the railway into London where he had posted them and bought Christmas gifts for Florence and Richard before walking the streets searching for Emily's name on posters outside theatres.

He had not found it.

As yet more carollers began singing outside, Florence went to fetch another plate of mince pies from the kitchen where she was keeping them warm. Harnser eyed the little collection of gifts on the table beneath the window and wondered which one would remain unopened the following night...

The knock, when it came, was barely audible. The Doctor looked at his wife and Harnser saw the hope he had witnessed on previous Christmases. He wanted to say, "No, it will not be her, she is ashamed to come home." Instead he found himself joining them in their dearest wish.

All three went into the hall. The Doctor opened the door as a flurry of snow swept in to melt on the doormat. The little cloaked form before them said two words, "Hello, Father," before falling in a faint onto the soft snow.

"Help me, Harnser, we will take her to my consulting room, there is a bed there," and as the two men lifted Emily from the ground, Florence ran ahead to open doors.

It was an hour later that Richard joined Harnser in the sitting room, "You have met her then." It was a statement rather than a question.

"Yes, but she swore me to secrecy. I thought I could talk her round but..."

"She has told us everything, Harnser...you are not to blame... no doubt you were instrumental in persuading her to come home...she said as much."

Suddenly the Doctor appeared very old; relief at his daughter's return was tinged with worry by her condition – undernourished and with child. "Her mother is with her, she is having something to eat…" he put his head in his hands as Harnser looked helplessly on, his voice when he spoke was muffled, "She is home, that is the main thing and we have you to thank for it." He straightened his back as the realization hit him. "She is home, this will be a good Christmas."

In February, a month before the child was born, Harnser married Emily. He did not quite know how it had come about. The situation had somehow evolved. He knew that Florence and Richard were concerned about gossip and their daughter's reputation. Since returning home, Emily's behaviour towards her parents had been conciliatory, almost humble at times. When Harnser suggested to her that they marry, she had rewarded him with a grateful, puppy dog look; pleased to have the matter resolved without having to think about it herself. She had become very fond of Harnser, he was everything her parents could have wished for in her choice of husband, she was very aware of the fact, and he *did* love her, she had no doubt about it.

Harnser's love for Emily was not the passionate, heady kind of love he felt for Arabella; that type of experience rarely happens twice in a lifetime, but he did have a deep loving feeling for her. He wanted to protect her without stifling the artistic quality of her nature. She was wilful and a little temperamental he knew, but he was sure that with love, patience and encouragement of her profession, she would mature and settle down. The stage after all was intoxicating; having tasted it, he knew she would not abandon it completely. There were theatrical groups in the city, she need not travel unduly to indulge her passion of acting and singing.

Gradually his thoughts turned a little less often to Little Pecking and a little more often to a future in Stoneham.

The wedding was a quiet, private affair in the local church. The weather was cold, necessitating thick, warm clothing – clothing that all but hid the fact that the bride was soon to be a mother.

There were no guests and if the Vicar had his suspicions he did not voice them.

Two months later, when the same man of the cloth christened Amy Florence Elliot in a similarly private service, he was tactful enough not to mention the recency of her parent's wedding day.

Chapter Six

Amy Florence Elliot could not have been more loved. She had brought out a hitherto unseen maternal quality in her mother, who appeared quite happy to put her theatrical ambitions to one side. The child was doted on by her grandparents and was the apple of her father's eye. Harnser soon discovered that the little girl could twist him around her little finger. She had only to look at him, with the puppy dog expression she had inherited from her mother, than his heart melted. The sorrowful expression was not her only likeness to her mother. Amy was a little replica of Emily with ash blonde curls and pale skin. Her biological father had never been much of an issue. Harnser knew only his name – Robert Sitwell – and that he was a small-time actor of forty something years. Emily *did* possess a photograph of him, which she kept with her personal belongings because she felt – as did Harnser – that the child could one day want to have a likeness of him. This particular conversation had taken place before marriage had been voiced between them, but Harnser fancied that Emily had kept the picture anyway.

Harnser could not have loved Amy more if she had been his natural child, giving him an understanding of why Maria could not have left little James in his hour of need.

To all intents and purposes the family was a traditional one – grandparents, parents and child living happily under one roof. There was only one unusual element which, although rarely mentioned anymore, was none the less of paramount importance... it did not seem likely that Amy would have any brothers or sisters for a while.

At the time of the wedding, when Emily was heavy with child, it was unthinkable that the marriage would be consummated. After the birth, Emily had not been strong, so a loving but

186

platonic relationship had flourished. As time went on Emily voiced her concerns that more children, when she was so fragile and Harnser was still studying, would not be sensible. Harnser had no choice but to respect her wishes. She was, after all, of a delicate constitution; her father – who was qualified to make judgement – often remarked on the fact.

"I would love to get back to the theatre, Harnser."

He looked up from his newspaper to where his wife sat sewing. How long had she been harbouring these thoughts, he wondered. He thought she had settled well to motherhood and domesticity. Their lives were ordered; he taught at the local school, which his daughter would attend in a year or so. He felt uneasy and he realised quite suddenly that he had dreaded those words. Emily would never want more children once she resumed her career – if she were strong enough to resume that kind of life surely she was strong enough to have another child. He tried not to show his disappointment, *that* would cause tension between them and he knew how wilful his wife could be. He chose his words carefully. "How long have you been thinking along those lines?" he asked as casually as possible.

"For quite some time now, but I met an old friend yesterday and she told me they were looking for a singer, she said I would be perfect for the production."

"I had no idea you kept in contact with your theatre friends." He failed to keep the suspicious tone from his voice.

"I do *not* keep in contact," she responded quite hotly, "I met her by chance while out walking with Amy."

Two high spots of colour appeared on Emily's cheeks warning Harnser of her determination.

He laid down the newspaper and joined his wife on the sofa. He took her hands gently in his, assuring her of his feelings before saying gently, "I thought we might have another child before you returned…a playmate for Amy. I have been patient, Emily…"

She blushed crimson; their private life had never before been mentioned. Her father had warned her of having another child too soon and she had supposed he had also spoken to her husband. Why else would he have been so understanding? But Amy was three years old, Emily realised she could no longer use *that* excuse.

"Maybe next year," she suggested lamely, "could I not do one or two more shows in the meantime? It would mean so much to me, I thrive when I'm singing, you know I do. Just another year, Harnser, then I will have lots of babies."

The puppy dog expression won him over. A year would fly by, at least the subject of further children had now been broached; that in itself was progress, he reasoned.

It took a little longer for Emily to convince her parents but they did not put up as much resistance as they would have done a few years back; they did not want another period of estrangement.

Emily blossomed; the productions were local, there was no need to travel.

Amy's fourth birthday came and went, and Harnser looked forward to the following Spring, when he hoped their second child would be born.

"Lord and Lady Brindham were at the show tonight, they came back stage to congratulate us all." Emily's eyes sparkled with life causing Harnser to compare her obvious happiness to the previous three years. She had appeared quite content with her life but the difference in her now was too obvious to miss.

"I am so glad we agreed to wait another year," he said softly, "I would have missed seeing you so happy."

"Thank you, Harnser, I do not deserve you."

"As for Lords and Ladies," he continued light-heartedly, had you forgotten you are married to a titled man? A rather strange, local title, but a title all the same."

She laughed merrily. "No, I had not forgotten," she looked at him warmly, "Perhaps it is time you contacted your stand-in."

He knew she wanted him to write to his mother and Walter; to find out the extent of James' injuries, but he was reluctant to disclose his whereabouts. He was terrified of finding out that

James was a cripple, confined to a wheeled chair for life. It was a subject he tried not to think about, but the nightmares, from which he still suffered, had dictated that he told Emily the cause of them...she had also seen his scarred back. He knew it was cowardly to ignore the matter and he was not proud of himself. His strange marital situation meant that nobody but he, need touch his scarred back. Walter had been right about one thing; his back would always remind him of eighteen hundred and sixty-three. 'A year to remember', he had not realized how much those words would come to mean when he had carved them on Arabella's bench seat. He hoped she was happy with Charles. He tried to imagine how she looked now, and how many children she had. Eight years would not have had any detrimental impact on her beauty, he reasoned. Did she still read his poetry? Did she think of him when she heard the cuckoo?

He suddenly realized that his wife was waiting for a response. "My 'stand-in' as you term him would not want to know that I have such a beautiful wife and daughter and that my life has turned out so well. I think he would prefer to think I have paid dearly for my actions."

"You persuaded me to make amends to *my* parents."

"The circumstances were completely different, Emily. *Your* parents longed for you to make contact. *I* am not held in such high regard in Little Pecking; not by Walter anyway."

"James could be better..."

"It is much more likely he is not." He smiled fondly at his wife. Did her words now mean that she realized the importance of family? He hoped so, next Spring was approaching rapidly, life had turned out better than expected.

Harnser kissed his daughter as she lay sleeping, undisturbed by her mother's late homecoming. He looked lovingly on the little oval face framed by soft blond curls, beside which lay the ocarina he had bought for her on her fourth birthday. Had any man been blessed with a more beautiful child? His heart was full, despite his resurrected thoughts of home. He said a silent prayer, thanking God for his good fortune and promising that, were he *not* blessed with more children, he would still consider himself a fortunate man. He kissed her again, "Good night, little lady, I love you so much." Her eyelids flickered and she opened her eyes briefly, smiling at him contentedly before turning over to resume sleeping.

One month later as Harnser walked from school he began to long for home. He had been thinking of what Emily had said to him about writing to his mother and the idea was becoming much more appealing. Perhaps he should write to Silas first, test the water so to speak. He knew he could trust his friend. Then if James was not confined to a wheeled chair...perhaps a visit could be arranged for the following Summer, providing of course that mother and child were fit to travel.

He put his head back and breathed in the fresh air. He loved this part of his walk when the city was left behind and he could see more fields than houses. He realised that, of late, his thoughts were more in the future than in the past, strange that, he had not really noticed the transition. Sometimes, as now, he had to remind himself that his child was *not* on the way, even so when he thought of the next year he always saw the child that would make their family complete. Would it be a littler boy, or another little blonde beauty with puppy dog expression and soft curls? He did not really mind. What he *was* becoming sure about was that he would want to share his happiness with his mother. Eight years was a long time, James would be twelve. He wondered if the little boy could remember him. It would be awful if the only memory he had of him was of the accident. He shuddered in the warm evening air. If he could see James...see for himself that he had recovered...the nightmares might cease...

No sooner had he closed the gate than the front door opened to reveal both Florence and Richard. Harnser could see at once that something was very wrong.

"What has happened?" he asked worriedly.

"They have gone."

"Gone? Who has?" His mood, that had been so bright and optimistic just a few moments ago, plummeted as the realization hit him. He did not want to hear the answer to his question.

"Emily has gone, she has taken Amy."

"Taken her where?"

He followed them into the house where Richard handed him a letter.

My dear Mother, Father and Harnser,

I am so sorry to hurt you all again but I must leave. I have had a very good offer, which I cannot refuse. I know you all try to understand me, but I seem unable to convey to you that my future is in the theatre. I have tried, really I have, but there is this invisible cord that pulls and pulls at me. I love you all and hope you can find it in your hearts to forgive me. I knew you would try to make me change my mind if I told you of my plans. If you know my whereabouts you will persuade me to return home again. I feel like a caged bird, I must have my freedom.

Take very good care of yourselves and please forgive me.

With all our love, Emily, and Amy.

P.S. I have left photographs.

On the table were three identical photographs of Emily and Amy. Harnser took one look at them and his face crumpled. He slumped into the nearest chair and sobbed uncontrollably.

"Please find them for us, Harnser," his mother-in-law's voice sounded weak and hopeless.

"No doubt it's London," Richard contributed huskily.

Their voices seemed distant to Harnser whose head was full of his lost dream of next Summer; two children and seeing his mother again.

Do unto others as you would have them do unto you.

She was no worse than he himself, how could he have treated his mother so?

He stood up wearily, his jauntiness gone. He picked up one of the photographs from the table and put it into his wallet. Tomorrow he would take it to London, to begin his impossible search.

CHAPTER SEVEN

"Would you like me to speak to him?" The Major was very concerned about his daughter's low spirits.

"No, Father, promise me you will not, I would die of humiliation." Arabella dissolved into tears once more, spluttering as she did so, "He must never know I have divulged such things to you."

"Well then, my dear," the elderly man said, "*you* must talk to him; tell him in no uncertain terms how much you long for a child. He will know to what you are alluding and it will give him the opportunity to give you an explanation. It is a very unusual situation for a young couple who have been married for eight years."

"His mother makes it much worse, hardly a day goes by that she does not mention her desired grandchildren and the future of Oxley. I am sure I shall scream one day and be deemed highly strung or *much* worse. The blame is obviously being placed firmly at *my* door."

Arabella felt hot and uncomfortable, she would not have embroiled her father in her marital problems had he not insisted she tell him her troubles, she would have given him her customary stock answers and left it at that. He had caught her at a low ebb. He knew her very well; he could always sense if things were not well with her. When he had said she would be happier if she were to have a child, she had rounded on him in exasperation, "How will I ever have a child if we do not..." Her voice had trailed off in embarrassment.

"If you do not...?" Her father had probed gently.

"If we do not...have never...not once..."

She could not find the words to explain to her father.

"You mean...?"

"Yes, Father, I *do* mean...our marriage is unconsummated."

There, she had said it.

"But why?"

"That is what I do not know. Charles loves me, I know he does. He is good and kind, gentle and complimentary. He is extremely considerate of my well being but…" She knew she should not be disloyal to her husband, but who else could she confide in?

The Major put his hands on his daughter's shoulders and held her firmly to stop her pacing. "The matter *must* be discussed, Arabella. The situation is harming your health. Have you mentioned it to Doctor Miles?"

"I could not," she coloured afresh, putting her hands up to her burning cheeks, "I could never, never do that."

"Would you like me…"

She cut him short at once, "No, never, never, I should not have told you, Oh Father, what am I to do? I wish I had…"

"Had what?"

"I wish I had run away with Harnser when I had the chance. You could have come with us. It all seems so much easier with hindsight. Would it have been so terrible?"

"Perhaps not, my dear." Choosing his words carefully he continued gently, "Do you still think of him so much?"

"I am sorry, but yes. I know it is wrong when I have a husband who loves me but I know that with Harnser I would have… ," Images of firelight and a warm bed in a cosy room sprang to her mind, she could almost *feel* his presence; just *thinking* of him calmed her soul. "Perhaps I will go for a walk," she finished dejectedly.

"Do you think that would be wise?" the Major asked gently.

"What do you mean?"

"Perhaps it is walking in all your old haunts that reminds you so much of Harnser."

"It is all that I have; of him, and to keep me sane."

"I understand, Arabella. Do what you must, but please talk to Charles, promise you'll try."

"I promise, Father. I will think of how to approach the matter, while walking."

He watched her walk out of the Barcada gates and turn right towards Rookery Lane; her usual direction when in low spirits. She had the whole of the Oxley estate to enjoy; many footpaths, meadows and beautiful gardens, he always knew which way she would leave the house depending on her mood.

He turned his head to the right instinctively, he had heard nothing but, on top of the rise, he saw a lone horseman, stock still, outlined against the vast sky. There was something sad about the sight... he knew it to be Charles.

With a heavy heart Arabella walked down the long corridor towards her husband's study. She had begun her short journey full of confidence and determination but the nearer she got to the door, the more timid she felt. The door loomed large, she took a deep breath and almost lunged at the handle, making her entry somewhat abrupt and undignified.

Her husband spun round from where he had been facing the window. "Arabella," he said, startled. He appeared flummoxed, quickly folding the letter he held in his hand and stuffing it into his pocket. The action did not go unnoticed by his wife. Why, she thought, he looks almost guilty. She noted the brandy glass on his desk. For many years now she had smelled the brandy on his breath at night, when they lay in the huge double bed together. Of late she had caught the odd whiff during the day as well.

He followed the direction of her eyes, where they rested on the glass and quickly made efforts to regain his equilibrium.

"An aperitif," he said guiltily, "will you join me?"

"No, thank you, Charles, I need to talk to you."

"Can it not wait until tonight?"

"It is often quite late when you come to bed nowadays. I would rather talk now, before dinner."

He sensed the determination in her manner, and noted the reference to his late nights. He began to feel uneasy; was this the showdown that he had been expecting for eight years? Eight years – he could not believe that *that* amount of time had passed, what would he tell her? He ran his finger around the inside of his collar, suddenly feeling hot and airless. Had she spoken to her father? He had seen them both at Barcada today. Was he now the subject of gossip and conjecture in the family? It would not be long before it spread to the village. He had thought Arabella too timid and loyal to say anything. Then he remembered how she had shown her mettle when he and his grandfather had first called on her. Yes, she had hidden fire, not often brought to the fore, but definitely there *and*, he remembered, it was a trait he had found attractive. She had been quite submissive lately but that could well be because of the situation to which she had been forced to resign herself.

He waited for her to speak, to bring his world tumbling down in ruins and humiliation.

There was a knock on the door, "Come in," he called, relieved at the interruption.

"Dinner is served, Ma'am, Sir."

He had been saved.

Arabella saw the relief on her husband's face. It was an expression that intensified her determination. However late he retired tonight, she would have her answers.

He knew the game was up.

"It is two o'clock in the morning, Arabella." There was tired pleading in his voice.

"I do not care if it is four o'clock, you knew I wanted to talk to you tonight but still you retire late."

Having had to wait an extra six hours to speak to her husband meant that Arabella had found more courage, fuelled, no doubt, by anger.

"What is the problem?"

"You do not *know?*"

"If it is the servants you must speak to Mother..." he blustered.

"I would like a child."

The silence was deafening.

"I would like a child, Charles," she reiterated quietly "and I know of only one way to have one." She knew her colour was high but, then, so was her husband's.

She watched his face crumple before he covered it with his hands and slumped down in a bedside chair. She felt a sudden rush of sympathy for him. She flung back the covers and crossed the room to him, putting a hand on his shoulder, whereupon he turned and buried his face in her nightdress, holding her tightly as a frightened little boy might, sobbing into her clothes.

"What is it, Charles?" she asked gently, frightened of the response she had evoked.

"I am so sorry, Arabella." He looked up at her with a tortured, tear-stained face. "You are so good and sweet and patient, I love you, my little Arabella, I *really* do. You are my salvation, you have given me respectability and dignity and I have betrayed you by letting my parents think that it is just a matter of time before you conceive, I am so, so sorry."

"But if you love me…"

"I *do*, my darling."

"Do you not want children?"

"Yes, yes, of course I do, for you, for me…for Father…for Grandfather…for Oxley…for England," he sounded slightly hysterical. "The pressure, Arabella I cannot stand it any more, help me…please help me…"

"I do not understand. How can I help?"

He looked up at her, a crumpled, pained expression on his face, which broke her heart and made her wish she had suffered in silence.

"Do not tell, please do not tell that I cannot…cannot…that I am unable …"

The enormity of the situation hit her, what was he saying? She wished her knowledge of men were more; would she never have a child? Would she live in this huge house, barren, for the rest of her life? Her head began to pound, the room spinning around her, she felt the hands clutching her…the voice pleading…she was falling…falling… falling …

When she came round she was lying on the bed, a worried Charles looming over her, peering at her with cold fear on his face. She had never seen her husband look so weak and vulnerable. Conflicting thoughts were spinning through her head. Charles – kind and loving; Charles – strong and handsome; Charles – weak and pleading; Charles dominated by his grandfather, then by his father, doing their bidding, marrying his little cousin because it was his duty, when he should not have married at all...she would never have a child...Harnser, where was Harnser?

Her head was pounding, she flung back the bedclothes, struggled to her feet, willing her trembling legs to carry her. She reached her dressing room door, passed through and closed it behind her as if in a dream. She turned the key and tried to block out the voice of her husband as he pleaded with her to open the door.

She dressed hurriedly giving no thought to her attire then re-appeared in the bedroom to the astonishment of her husband.

"Where are you going? It is half past two in the morning." Then, "No, no please do not go to your father, please, Arabella, please, I would die of shame."

She pushed past him to the door, not hearing him anymore. She ran down the corridors turning and turning about, then down the main staircase and out of the house. She ran and ran, across the gardens, then the fields and the meadows, her hair blowing wildly in the wind. The moon was bright although not full, affording her good light, even so she stumbled, fell, crashed into bushes, tore her clothes but still she ran and ran. She saw owls, eerie in the moonlight; their silent flight at odds with her frenzied running.

All the while she called his name, "Harnser...Harnser... where are you?"

Each time she heard a noise she spun round, was it an animal...? A bird ...? Or Harnser doing his impersonations, teasing her.

He would be at the stream.

She came to Rookery Lane and scrambled down the bank, falling the last few feet onto the road below. She picked herself up and kept running. She ran and ran, into the lane, he would be at the stream she knew it.

She reached the bridge and scrambled down the slope, then stopped dead.

The bench seat stood white in the moonlight. The stream trickled by. The wind blew her hair off her face.

He was not there.

A bird swooped low, or was it a bat? It caught her hair making her gasp and duck. She began calling again… "Harnser… Harnser."

She threw back her head as if it would help her to call louder… "Harnser…Harnser…where are you?"

Having searched frantically all around the bench, beside the stream and under the bridge, she climbed the bank into the copse and continued her running; stumbling and falling many times in her quest to reach the other side…and maybe her lost love.

She did not see the low branch, her hair was blowing across her face…and she was tired…

Harnser would save her she knew.

It was Old Joe who found her early the next morning. At first he did not realize that the bundle of dirty, torn clothes was anything more than that, until he saw her hair, spread out wildly on the copse's ferny floor. He was too frail to carry her. "Don't try to move Miss Arabella," he said gently, "I'll go for help."

Her eyelids flickered, "Joe?"

"Yes, it's Joe, don't try to move, Miss."

Joe's heart was thumping in his chest. He knew he would never make it to Oxley, but he might make it to Barcada – if he paced himself.

He had no need to; Arthur found the old man panting by the roadside.

"What's up, Joe?" he said with concern.

"Get help, Arthur, I'm done for. Go to Barcada, It's Miss Arabella, I've found her in the copse half dead. Don't alarm the Major, he's like me, gettin' old; we can't do with shocks at our age. They'll have to be told at Oxley but that will do later, run now ...and send for the Doctor."

"Go back to her, Joe," Arthur shouted as he ran off.

The Major got up from the chair and put another small log on the fire. Although September, it was not a cold evening, the weather had been warm of late. He returned to the chair beside the bed; the one that Arabella had occupied when Harnser had lain in the same bed in this cosy room. It was becoming an invalid's room, he thought sadly, his wife's little sitting room where she had loved to enjoy quietude whilst watching her garden and the birds.

He laid his head back in the wing of the chair and wondered if he could have done better for his daughter. He had not pushed her into this marriage, although, at the time, he had thought it for the best. His mother would have delighted in seeing the family re-united. But she would not have wanted her granddaughter to be so unhappy and unfulfilled, he acknowledged silently. Divorce was not a pleasant option but, in the circumstances, with Arabella's health at stake, would it not be for the best? Anyway, as he understood matters, it would be an annulment rather than a divorce. His poor little girl, was she mentally strong enough to let the matter become public knowledge? How would the Sandersons react to such a proposal?

The Major had known nothing of his daughter's middle-of-the-night flight until Arthur had arrived on the doorstep that morning, gently telling him that Arabella had had an accident in the copse and a carriage and men were needed to bring her home. He had been appalled at the sight of her; dirty, bruised with her clothes in tatters. He had immediately sent word to Oxley House to inform them of the accident, and that his daughter was in no fit state to have visitors of *any* description that day. He would consult with her on the morrow and give them news of her condition. He had written that he was appalled that she could be missing from home and no one had had the decency to inform him.

He had received a letter from Charles, by return of messenger, that he had wholly believed that Arabella had gone to her father after an incident at home, which he regretted. He looked forward to visiting his wife tomorrow and was truly sorry for the situation that had arisen. He hoped any misunderstandings could be resolved with the minimum of fuss.

I bet you do, thought the Major as he read the letter from his son-in-law.

He knew the whole estate was abuzz with gossip of the morning's happenings. As yet he himself did not fully understand what had caused the flight and the accident, but he had a jolly good idea.

Now, as he looked on the bruised, cut and grazed face of his daughter, his heart was heavy. He did not know how many more years he had left to care for her. He had thought that, upon this marriage, he had handed her into the love and care of an honest, upright man; now he was not so sure.

She stirred, "Father?"

"I am here, Arabella, you are at Barcada. You have slept most of the day. Dr Miles gave you something to help."

"I want to find Harnser, will you help?"

"Try not to fret, dear, we will talk of these things when you are stronger. You are a little battered and bruised."

"I suppose the family is ashamed of me."

He knew she was alluding to the Sandersons and her husband. "I should think they are more ashamed of themselves," he said quite forcefully. "I dread to think how long you would have lain in the copse if Old Joe had not happened upon you."

"I like Joe."

"He is an excellent man, we are indebted to him."

"Do you think Arthur knows of Harnser's whereabouts?"

"I do not think *anybody* knows, my dear. Shall I read to you?" Her obsession with Harnser worried him and he was keen to change the subject.

She thought of her little book of poems, she would love to read it but knew she was too tired. She had never shown it to anybody, not even her father. "Not at the moment, Father, but thank you for offering."

A thought came into her head. "When I am better, Father, would you mind if I put two pictures on the wall of this room?"

"Of course not, but nobody uses this room except you."

"That is the whole idea," she said sleepily.

"Are you going to tell me what the pictures are about?"

"They are about a love affair," she responded sadly, "A beautiful love affair that I will have in my heart and my head forever. Look in the second drawer of the dresser please, Father."

The Major opened the drawer and found the tissue wrapped parcels. He lifted the pictures and took them back to the bed, where he unwrapped them carefully. The first was of Harnser in his countryman's clothes, the ocarina clearly visible. He looked at his daughter where she waited for a response. "He is a very handsome young man," he said gently.

When he saw the contents of the second parcel he shed a tear or two. "I have a beautiful daughter, Arabella," he said huskily, "Of course you may display them."

"Thank you, Father, they were his Christmas present; he never saw them."

CHAPTER EIGHT

"What do you think it's all about, Joe?" Abel watched the face of his old friend with interest, he was not giving much away at the moment.

"How would I know?" Joe answered, acutely aware of his divided loyalties, "I only found her."

"Didn't she say anything?" he probed. "She must have said something, Joe."

"She said one word and that was 'Joe'," the old man replied truthfully. "She was in a bad way, not really up to much talkin'. Her head was cut and bruised, she must've run into a sturdy branch."

"What about her clothes?" said Arthur, joining the conversation outside The Bell, "They were in a state, weren't they, Joe? All torn and muddy, How did they get like that I wonder? And what about the hour; Miss Arabella's not usually abroad at that time is she? She could have bin there all night for all we know. You'd think someone would've missed her."

"Don't your sister Maisie know anything?" ventured Abel, a little put out at not being able to get to the bottom of the mystery. "She work up at the House, she must've heard somthin' about it."

"There's all sorts of rumours flyin' about up there, the young master didn't even go and see her 'til the next day, now that can't be right can it?"

"They seem happy enough..." Abel began.

"Things aren't allust what they seem," reflected Old Joe remembering his Christmas conversation with Arabella of eight years ago.

"I think you know more than what you're lettin' on, Joe," said Abel suspiciously, squinting his eyes and peering closely at Joe.

"I *like* Miss Arabella," the old man said forcefully. "I like the

Biddemores, they're not so toffy-nosed as the other lot, they've known harder times and they don't forget it. They're not above havin' a conversation with you. I often see the late Mrs Biddemore's sister when she come to visit. She likes to walk in the countryside. She allust have a word with me. She allust make at least *one* visit to the churchyard to put flowers on Eleanor's grave. She was very kind to Miss Arabella when she lost her mother. She take her Godmotherly duties very serious. I wonder if anyone's let *her* know about the accident."

This was a very long speech for Joe, and Abel noted with interest how defensive the old man sounded. Yes, he thought, Joe knows a bit more than he's letting on about.

Arthur listened politely to his elders while waiting for an opportunity to contribute again. He now leaned forward into the little group and said mysteriously, "This is just between us now, but, I've heard that he's drinkin'."

"Who is?" said Sefton, who hitherto had remained quiet.

"The young master, there's bin one or two incidents lately when he's had to have a steadyin' hand, if you get my drift. And there were raised voices yesterday comin' from old Sugar's study and Charlie-boy's drinkin' was definitely heard to be mentioned."

"Oh," they said in unison, nodding their heads knowingly, pleased to have had a clue about the goings on.

"That could well be *it* then."

"It dint do no good," continued Arthur, doubling his negatives like most of the villagers, "apparently he went straight from his father's study to his own and stayed there all day drownin' his sorrows."

"Maybe she's left him," said Sefton thoughtfully.

"That'd upset the applecart," said Arthur knowingly. "That was one of the longest engagements known to man, they certainly had time to make sure of their feelin's ."

"You're not saying much, Joe," said Abel.

"When you int got nothin' interestin' to say it's best to keep quiet," he responded, not wanting to betray Arabella or to offend his contemporaries.

"Haven't you got any beds to go home to?" said Jack Foley, coming out of the inn and addressing the group. "You'd rather come and burn my oil than use your own wouldn't you? I don't know if gossip do me any good at all; it bring in more people but you're so busy talkin' you drink less," and he took down the lanterns, hoping to encourage a few of them to find their homes.

"Keep us informed, young Arthur," said Sefton, as he strained his waistcoat buttons further by getting to his feet, "You're our man on the spot you know."

Arthur felt quite important at this but, like Joe, his loyalties were with the Biddimores and he was remembering another incident in the woods eight years ago...and fresh footprints in the snow leading out of Barcada one cold, December morning. He hadn't told his friends all he knew, they probably wouldn't know he was walking out with Marjie; so had a foot in two camps as it were.

CHAPTER NINE

"I'm sorry."

The words were barely audible.

Maria looked across at her husband, where he sat staring into the fire on one of his rare nights in. She had not quite heard Walter but her heart suddenly leapt in her chest at what she *thought* he had said. "What did you say?"

"I said I'm sorry." He looked Maria in the eyes repeating, "I'm sorry for flaying Harnser."

"You are sorry? You wait eight years to say you are sorry and I suppose you expect me to forgive you all of a sudden." Her voice held bitterness.

"It's been hard on me too, knowing what you think of me." He sounded deflated, like he had in all the limited conversations they had had during the past years.

"You knew within two months that your son would walk, albeit with difficulty, *I* have waited eight years for *my* son to return home. I sometimes wonder if I will ever see him again."

"You will, Maria."

"How can you be so sure when you told him you would kill him if you ever saw him again?"

The ticking clock dominated the heavy silence, the fire popped and spluttered as gaseous flames appeared and disappeared on the coals. The subject, now resurrected, would drive a further wedge between them, making life even more difficult than it had been.

It had been a sad little household. Maria had never moved back into the marital bed. Harnser was never mentioned between them although James often brought up the subject to them individually.

On the surface they managed. There was no shouting, no arguments, no voiced recriminations; neither was there warmth between them, as in the old days. No companionable silences, no music on cosy winter evenings, because there was no Harnser. Maria could play, after a fashion, but she did not have the heart. Instead she read, and sewed and worked…and worried.

There had been one bright spot in all the gloom – their son was having a very good, private education.

When James first came home and was confined to his wheeled chair, Maria had had a visit from Lord Haverham from The Hall. He had suggested that James might like to join his children in the schoolroom; it would be less far to push him every day and less chance of his injuries getting knocked about. He had also leant them a custom made chair that was lying idle at The Hall. He had been very fond of Harnser and, in the circumstances, wanted to help Maria. He was actually quite fond of Walter too; appalled that an apparent accident could tear a family asunder.

James gradually learnt to walk again, at first with the help of crutches, then sticks and finally unaided. He did, however, still have a pronounced limp.

When Maria had suggested that James was well enough to attend the local school, Lord Haverham would hear of no such thing. James was very bright, it would be a pity to deprive him of his latin lessons and excellent mathematics master now, especially as his experiences had sparked a desire to study medicine. His education and his daily contact with the children at The Hall were providing him with a grounding to aspire to great things. Maria was pleased for him; it somehow made up for the situation at home.

Now, as they sat either side of the fire, Maria and Walter were lost in their own thoughts.

Walter acknowledged that the accident had been a blessing in disguise for his son. He now had a future. A future that he would never have had in normal circumstances.

Maria's thoughts were with Harnser; wondering if there was anyway she could find him now that her husband had voiced an apology. She would see Silas as soon as possible, to ask if he had any ideas on the subject.

"There are one or two publications published for school-masters," said Silas when faced with Maria's enquiry. "Perhaps we could draft a notice for insertion on the off chance he saw it."

Maria leapt at the chance, slight as it was, of contacting her son. "He is obviously in, or around, London," Silas continued, "his Christmas communications always bear a London postmark."

"Would you arrange it for me please, Silas? I will reimburse you."

"I am happy to help," then lowering his voice instinctively, "Have you heard the gossip from Oxley?"

"Yes, Molly told me; she got it from her Tom."

"Rumour says she has left him and is back at Barcada."

"Fortunately *that* cannot be laid at my son's door; he did the honourable thing, he would have even if the accident had not taken place. Thank you, Silas for your loyalty on *that* subject, at least the matter did not become public knowledge. I dread to think what life in the village would have been like if Walter had known *that* as well."

"There was never any impropriety anyway, but you know what wagging tongues are like, what they have no knowledge of, they fabricate."

"She was not in church on Sunday, did you notice?"

"Yes, the official story is that she is convalescing with her father in the peace of Barcada before returning to the house, her injuries were not minor, I understand. It is still a mystery how she came to be in the copse so early in the morning, there is talk that she might have lain there all night."

"An estate cottager said their howling dog woke them at four o'clock in the morning. They *said* they could hear an eerie, ghostly calling. *That* story has fuelled the Marcie's Bridge ghost stories of course. Tom says most people think Arabella was frightened by a ghost and ran into the branch of a tree. *That* of course still does not explain why she was out in the middle of the night."

"No doubt all will be revealed," said Silas sagely, "these matters have a habit of revealing themselves."

CHAPTER TEN

Arabella returned to Oxley in October having spent a month at Barcada. Although gossip was rife among the servants, and many ears listened at many doors, information and answers to rumoured questions were in short supply.

Arabella spent many hours on solitary walks and galloping over the Estate. Her early morning rides took her to the sands of Cottlefield and Winford, to the marshes and to outlying villages, as they had done with Harnser in eighteen sixty-three. She became obsessed with finding him. Her thoughts went no further than that. She would see a tall, slim, male figure in the distance and convince herself it was her lost love, hurrying her pace or urging on her horse until she caught up with him, only to find herself faced with a complete stranger and forced to make demure apologies.

She found herself loitering at the gates of village schools, walking her horse and engaging in conversations with the locals until she had learned the names of all the schoolmasters. She had convinced herself that, once qualified, Harnser would return to the area so that he could keep a discreet eye on his family. She sat for hours on the bench at Marcie's Bridge knowing she was even less likely to be disturbed there now that ghostly sightings were once more on the lips of servants.

Her old fears of becoming the subject of gossip and conjecture in the village seemed to have been self-prophesying. Even the old images of riding her horse wildly in the moonlight to meet her lover by the stream had not been that far out; except that she had no children slumbering peacefully in their beds at Oxley.

"I will be leaving for London next week," Charles did not look his wife in the eye.

"What is the reason this time?" Arabella had not forgotten the hurriedly folded letter.

"Business, what else would I go to London for?"

"I would like to accompany you."

"You would be lonely, I have agricultural talks to attend, I am sure you have no interest in crop yield, corn prices and animal welfare."

"I could go sight seeing, I rarely go to London nowadays. I will enjoy being by myself in the city."

Charles looked uncomfortable, "Actually I have arranged to share accommodation with Hugo. We will have much to discuss."

"Hugo?"

"Yes, Hugo, I know only *one* Hugo."

Arabella felt a twinge of annoyance, she sometimes thought that Charles preferred the company of his good friend Hugo to that of her own. They had spent their honeymoon with Hugo in Hampshire and had since been many times to visit. The visits usually resulted in Arabella retiring early, by herself, while Charles and Hugo stayed up until the early hours, drinking and talking 'business'. The situation might not be so bad if Hugo was married, at least, Arabella thought, she might have some female company on such occasions. Instead, whether in Hampshire or Suffolk she usually found herself with no company but her own. There had been the odd occasion when Hugo had invited his sister, Cathryn, to join them, but Arabella found her rather haughty and, in her own opinion, poor company.

Cathryn had two children, whom she never brought with her, saying that if she could not retreat to her ancestral home every now and again, to spend time with her 'little brother' Hugo, she would go quite mad. Arabella could not understand the sentiment, if *she* had children, she would want to spend as much time with them as possible, of that she was certain.

"Will you stay at a hotel?" The question seemed reasonable enough.

"Why are you suddenly so interested in my business affairs,

Arabella?" She noticed the slight irritation in his voice and the two spots of high colour on his face, but she stood her ground.

"Why should I not be, I am your wife, I have little else in which to take interest at Oxley. Your mother manages the house with the housekeeper, the gardens are maintained by the staff, you and your father manage the estate, if it were not for my father living close by I think I would go mad with boredom. I know every inch of the countryside within a radius of ten miles having walked it, ridden it, and travelled it, by coach, alone. Am I to believe that you could honestly begrudge me the excitement of a London holiday when you have to go anyway?"

Charles looked defeated, he would have to tread carefully, he did not want her running off again. Their bedroom becoming a battleground of late; he would have to find a way of pacifying his wife.

He crossed the room and took hold of Arabella's shoulders; he turned her gently to face him. He was acutely aware that he rarely touched his wife, apart from brushing her face with his lips when saying 'goodnight' or when he departed on one of his journeys. Since the night of her flight he had felt at a disadvantage when in her company. He knew only too well that she held his reputation in her hands. He had expected his world to tumble down around him but nobody had spoken to him about the incident. His father had demanded at once to know what was going on, of course, but he had managed to convince him that Arabella's longing for a child was having a detrimental effect on her health and that maybe it would be better if no one, especially his mother, mentioned the subject for a while. He was ashamed of himself for perpetuating the belief that Arabella was having difficulty conceiving, but it was as near to the truth as he dare go. He had then retreated to his study to drink the day away, hating himself for what he had become, but convincing himself that he had no choice.

Now, as he looked into the face of his loyal wife, who could so easily have ruined him, he felt genuine sadness for her. "Of course you can accompany me to London," he conceded quietly, "but why not ask your aunt along so that you will not have to be alone so much. I will alter the accommodation arrangements accordingly."

"It is very short notice."

"It is worth a try. Or maybe your father would enjoy a change of scenery?"

"Thank you, Charles, I will ask him."

Peace again, but for how long, he wondered as he watched Arabella go through the door of her dressing room to prepare for bed. He looked around the room. It was no wonder he was becoming less and less inclined to retire at the same time as his wife; this room, though large, was becoming claustrophobic to him. Once in here at night he was at the mercy of Arabella, with her awkward questions and sad countenance. He felt ashamed to be having such thoughts about his beautiful, loyal, innocent Arabella; she deserved better. He had thought two weeks in London with Hugo, away from the Estate and the permanent reminders of his problems, would help him cope a little better, but it was selfish of him, he realized with shame; Arabella needed respite too – they were in this together.

"I think it a wonderful idea," said the Major, pleased to see his daughter actually looking forward to something. "I might not be able to gallivant around London *every* day with you but I am sure we will have a good time, I am quite looking forward to it," he finished with a twinkle in his eye. Then on a more serious note, "I take it things are a little better between you?"

She knew to what he was alluding. "I am *very* fond of him, Father, you know that, and I am doing my utmost to accept the situation. It is not easy."

"The matter has not been resolved then?" he enquired tentatively.

"No, the matter has not been resolved." Her voice was barely audible.

He could see she was becoming downcast again. "Well let us forget our problems for two weeks. Perhaps we could fit in a visit to the Museum of Ornamental Art, I always enjoy that. Mind you," he added smiling, "with every year that passes I feel more like one of the exhibits. It will not do for me to stand still for too long – someone might come along and dust me!"

She appreciated his efforts to lift her spirits and gave him a rare smile.

"That is better," he said beaming, "much more like my Arabella." His joviality, however, belied his inner feelings for he knew not how he could help his unhappy, troubled daughter.

As Arabella and the Major set out on the first leg of their journey to the capital, little did they realise that their summer interlude would set in motion a chain of events that would ultimately change their lives...

CHAPTER ELEVEN

"Will you be staying long, Sir?" The hotelier smiled at Harnser in the way that hoteliers do, welcoming but impersonal.

"Possibly four weeks, maybe a little less, maybe a little more. Does that present a problem?"

"No, Sir, definitely not." He looked Harnser up and down; young, serious, well educated and alone. He assessed his needs quickly. "Perhaps roomy accommodation at the front of the building, Sir, with a table for writing? It is a little quieter at the front, believe it or not, the back ways are always busy...with carriages rattling through..." He hesitated, not knowing if his words were getting through to the serious young man who seemed preoccupied.

"That will suit me very well, thank you."

"I was saying, Sir, the front is a *little* quieter. There are so many theatres around here that all the thoroughfares are busy, especially in the evenings."

They reached the recommended room and the hotelier unlocked the door.

"I am used to a bit of noise and bustle. Do you get much custom from the actors and the like?" He tried to sound casual as he followed his host into the surprisingly comfortable room.

"Oh yes, Sir, a considerable amount of custom. The establishment is very well patronized by theatre goers, producers and performers alike."

Harnser relaxed, pleased with his choice. "I am looking for a relative," he began tentatively, "I have reason to believe she may be in the area." He put his hand into his inside pocket and produced the photograph of Emily and Amy. He decided to be honest with the gentleman as he said. "The lady is a singer, a very, very good one, but there are family circumstances that require her presence at home. I wonder if you recognize her?"

With this he handed over the photograph.

"She *does* look familiar, Sir." Harnser's heart leapt in his chest as he waited for the next words.

"I will keep an eye out for her and tell you if I have any luck."

He supposed it was the most he could expect. He pocketed the photograph, smiled again at the hotelier, thanked him as he left, then stood looking out at the traffic on the street below his window.

This was his best chance yet; he congratulated himself, a small, but good hotel in the middle of theatre land. He had started his search for his wife and child the previous year, spending every available day off and vacation in London going around the small music halls, with no luck whatsoever. A few people claimed Emily's acquaintance but said they had not seen her of late. Gradually Harnser's search progressed to more fashionable, better known establishments, after all, he reasoned, Emily had written that she had had a *very* good offer. Perhaps she was making a name for herself at last.

The search was costing money. Richard was sharing the burden, even so, Harnser did not know how long he should continue searching the streets of London for his family. It was like looking for a needle in a haystack. He tried to second-guess his wife; in the afternoons he would walk the parks, which were frequented by ladies with their children and nannies with their charges. He kept in mind that his wife could have tried to alter her appearance, or that of the child, to avoid being recognized so easily. Amy would have grown. She would be wearing clothes with which he might not be familiar. All these things he bore in mind as his single-minded quest dominated his life. In addition, he was mindful of his duty to Florence and Richard, who stayed at home hoping and praying that he would find the runaways; he therefore wrote often, even though he had no good news.

Now as he looked down on the hustle and bustle beneath his window he wondered how he would ever single out his wife against so much activity.

That evening he took a small, corner table in the dining room from where he had a good view of his fellow diners; he had met a few of Emily's friends, he must stay vigilant. Tomorrow he would start this new phase of his search in earnest.

Two weeks later, weary and dejected, Harnser decided to go home. His search had revealed not one bit of evidence that Emily was in the city. She could be anywhere in England, he conceded silently, or even Scotland. The railways had made travel so much easier.

He turned into St James Park for one last look at the mothers, nannies and children. His steps took him to the edge of the lake. The sun was warm on his back as he looked out over the water. In his mind's eye he saw the sparkling ripples of the little stream which ran under Marcie's Bridge and watched the damselflies at play. Arabella was with him, calling his name softly. Home was tugging at his heartstrings. He had had no time to think about going back since Emily and Amy disappeared.

Arabella sauntered into the park to while away a sultry afternoon while her father rested. She gradually became aware of a tall figure ahead. Her heart began to beat faster, surely she could not be mistaken this time, she would know that walk anywhere. She hastened her step as she had so many times before, she kept her eyes riveted to his back. The flaxen hair...the easy gait...was she imagining it? She half expected the image to fade away before her eyes.

He came to a stop facing the lake and she stopped too. She began to feel faint with excitement. How should she approach...from behind and speak his name, or from the side with a better view of his face? She was half frightened of going nearer. From where she stood she *knew* she was close to her love; a little nearer and he might turn into a stranger, as he had so many time before.

She walked forward slowly, veering slightly to the right as she did so. She stopped by the lake, only ten yards or so from the young man. He was staring morosely out over the lake, seemingly oblivious to his surroundings.

It was *him*, she knew it. Her heart thudded in her chest as she crept nearer. Her throat felt constricted, her eyes smarted, she hardly dared blink for fear of him disappearing.

"Harnser," she whispered. Even *she* did not hear her voice. "Harnser?" she said again.

Should she touch him? Was she seeing things? Why was he not responding?

"Harnser."

Slowly he turned his head, as if he was reluctant to take his eyes from the water, but was becoming aware of someone beside him.

He looked at her, blinking several times as if to focus his eyes before realization dawned on him.

His face softened as he came out of his reverie. He raised his hand slowly to touch her face. "Arabella...? Is it really you?" Tears sprang to his eyes, "Arabella oh, Arabella tell me I'm not dreaming."

"You are not dreaming, but I think I must be."

They stood facing one another, everything else forgotten and then, oblivious to passers by, throwing decorum by the wayside, they fell into each other's arms, crying with happiness.

She could smell the musky scent she knew so well, as she buried her face in his clothes, she gasped it in as a drowning man would gasp air. He buried his face in her hair, saying her name over and over again. Every now and again he would gently push her away, feasting his eyes on her face and then pull her close again, hugging her to him as if his very life depended on it. "I was thinking of you, as I stood watching the lake. I could see the stream, Arabella...and you. I could hear you saying my name softly, and then I turned...and you were there."

She smiled at him, she had no words, it was enough just to be with him.

"Will you come back with me?" he said huskily, "to my hotel room?"

"Yes," was all she replied.

They walked in silence...through the park...through the

217

fashionable streets…each in their own thoughts, frightened that words – any words – would break the spell.

They reached the hotel and turned towards one another, their eyes speaking volumes, before passing through the door. As they walked the corridors and climbed the stairs their pace quickened until the last few yards when Harnser ran ahead to unlock the door. He relocked the door as soon as they were inside and they once more fell into each other's arms.

His back was healed, there was no pain this time, just unadulterated passion, pure and sweet as a sparkling wine. The hunger of nine long years needed appeasing this day, as they clung together at last. They rolled together on the bed as they would have on the lush banks of the stream had things been different and life kinder to them.

"How I have longed and longed for this day," she whispered as their light summer clothes were discarded with abandon. "I cannot tell you how I feel to have found you."

"Arabella, my own Arabella…I love you…I love you…I love you…

Much later having dressed again they each told their stories.

"…so you see," Harnser finished, "I have lost her, lost my little girl who, together with you, has stolen my heart. I was at my lowest ebb when you found me, you have saved me, Arabella. What are we to do? We are both married to other people. I need to find Amy, and when I do I will also find my wife. I cannot believe that we both have unfulfilled marriages. I imagined you happy with Charles, with your children playing at Oxley. How have we come to this, Arabella?"

"I do not know, I am just happy to have found you."

She consulted her watch, mindful of how long she had been away from the Major.

"I must get back to Father, he will be worried about me."

"Will you tell him we have met again?"

"I will have to, he has been so understanding and supportive throughout my troubles with Charles. I cannot let him go on worrying about my unhappiness when it no longer exists."

"I would like to see him again."

"Meet us in the park again tomorrow."

"I was going home this evening."

"And I, tomorrow."

"Stay, Arabella. Stay another two weeks with me here in London. Or we could go to the country; I do not mind where we are so long as you do not leave me. Promise me you will stay."

"I promise, though I do not know what I will tell Charles. To Father I can tell the truth, he will understand and be happy for me."

"I do not want to let you out of my sight again."

"Me neither."

"Tomorrow we will make plans. We must not be parted again."

She smiled sadly, knowing that they *would* have to part again but not, if she could help it, for long.

"Have you heard anything of James?" Harnser asked, half dreading the reply.

"James is very well, Harnser." He has been left with a limp, but even that could improve."

The breath left Harnser's body in relief as he slumped forward and held his head in his hands. "He has been on my mind for so long. The nightmares have never left me and they have been ten times more frequent since Emily and Amy went. This is a happy day for me, Arabella, happier than I thought a day could be without Amy. Have you seen him?"

"I see him very occasionally. When Charles is away and Father and I have the opportunity of having a word or two with Silas after Church. He has kept us informed."

"Of course, I was forgetting you met Silas when he brought me to you."

"You were in no fit state to remember anything that night, I am not surprised you forgot."

"Dear Arabella, you saved me then as you have now."

Somewhere in the back of her mind she heard someone else saying something similar, and a vision of Charles sprang to mind, reminding her of another life, back in Little Pecking.

"Does Arthur know about us?" she asked suddenly, remembering she had good news for him.

"I would not have thought so."

"He seems keen to keep me informed of your family, it is all said quite casually, but, there is something in his expression and his eyes that make me wonder. For instance three weeks ago he caught me in the garden at Barcada, gathering flowers for Father. He approached me and looked all around – as if making sure nobody would overhear – before speaking. Then he told me that Walter had apologized to Maria for flaying you. I got the impression he thought I knew where you were and he was telling me it was safe for you to return."

"Walter has apologized? Are you sure?"

"Quite sure, Maria told Molly, Molly told Tom and Tom told Arthur. Silas is now helping Maria to trace your whereabouts. I know it to be true because I asked Silas myself when on a visit to The Hall."

"It took him some time to say sorry considering James is so well."

"Yes, but apparently he is now seeing that the unfortunate accident had its advantages."

"I do not understand, how can that be?"

"Oliver – Lord Haverham – insisted that James have lessons in the schoolroom with his own children. This of course was when he was dependent on a wheeled chair. He said it would be more convenient for Maria and would avoid any more damage being done to James' back and legs in the rough and tumble of the village school. James has done so well that Oliver thinks it would be a shame to take him away now, especially since he has aspirations of becoming a doctor. So you see the accident has enabled Walter's son to have a free, private education."

"A doctor eh, Doctor James Porter; it has a nice ring to it. I am so pleased he is being given a chance in life. I can also see why Walter's conscience might be troubling him."

"You can go home, Harnser."

He smiled a deeply satisfying smile, looked at her tenderly, nodding as he reiterated, "I can go home."

"And so must I," Arabella said, looking at her elegant gold watch.

"That is a very fine watch you have there."

"It was a present from my father for my eighteenth birthday. See, it matches the bracelet he gave me for my seventeenth."

"Your seventeenth birthday, it seems a lifetime ago, little did we know then what the future held for us."

"We have so much to talk about, we will need the next two weeks to catch up. I absolutely loved my Christmas presents, Harnser. You are so dear to me. I still have *your* presents at Barcada but I am not going to tell you what they are because, very soon, when you visit your mother, you can visit father at Barcada and *then* I will show you."

"I cannot wait."

"Now I really *must* go, I should be packing."

"I will take you back…" he saw the alarm in her face, "no, do not worry, I will leave you before we reach the hotel."

He stepped from the carriage, his fingers lightly caressing hers. "Until tomorrow, Arabella," he said tenderly.

"Until tomorrow…"

Chapter Twelve

Charles returned to Oxley leaving Arabella and the Major in London. He had not seen his wife looking so happy in years. Her holiday was obviously having a good effect.

"Stay as long as you like," he said gently, as he left for the railway station with Hugo. He lightly brushed her face with his lips, noticing with pleasure the warm flush on her cheeks that he had not seen for a long time. He could not now see why he had been so reluctant for her to accompany him. He must take her with him more often, it would give her something to look forward to; take the pressure off a little...brighten up her life...give *him* time to address other matters that were on his mind...

For two glorious weeks Arabella and Harnser enjoyed London, each other and the warm summer weather. For the most part the Major left them to themselves giving the excuse that he was too old to gallivant around the city. Arabella, however, knew different. He was, she knew, giving her a rare opportunity to enjoy herself. All too soon it was time to leave – Harnser to his teaching, Arabella to Oxley. There were tears and promises. "If ever you need me, write to me at the school," Harnser said worriedly, not wanting to send his love back to her unhappy life at home. "I will arrange a visit to Mother as soon as I am able and include a visit to your father but, Arabella, we must be careful. Scandal is ugly; I would not wish it on you. We *are* both married."

"They *will* return, Harnser," she said, alluding to his family. "Maybe not for a while, but they will come home. People always do, heartstrings are very strong. As for me, I can bear anything so long as I can see you once in a while and know that you are well."

"I love you."

"And I love you."

With that he watched her go out of his life again, back to collect her father and their luggage for their return to Little Pecking.

Those strong heartstrings were already tugging at him.

Arabella hugged her secrets to herself and dreamed every night of her August in London. The bedroom had ceased to be a battleground, for which Charles was grateful.

It was in late September that Arabella began to suspect that she was with child. At first she was so excited she wanted to tell the world, especially her father, but within minutes the reality of the situation hit her like a ton of bricks. It would definitely be the end of her marriage. Would Charles publicly shame her as an adulteress? Would she have to leave the district... her father?

Her head began to pound, so she did what she always did on occasions such as this – she went to the stream.

She sat on the bench and listened to the relaxing sounds made by the stream as it tumbled over the little waterfall to her right. She was almost unaware that her finger caressed the carved leaves on the armrest. It was a nervous habit she had developed. Sometimes, when she realised she was doing it, she would smile sadly to herself, thinking that, in years to come, one arm would be worn smooth by her worrying fingers.

It was a breezy day, some of the trees behind her in the copse were beginning to lose their leaves and they fluttered around her like large flakes of snow. Some of them reached the stream where they were carried away, tossing and tumbling like boats on a stormy sea...stormy sea...stormy sea...

Her mind seemed to stop here, and she heard the words over and over again as she thought of what lay ahead. She would be like one of those leaves, tossed and turned not knowing where she would end up. And what of her poor little adulterine child – born into scandal and deception. *What had she done?* To whom would she turn? Her father, she answered herself. Her father, who had worried about her for eight years and would now worry some more. She could not burden him. She would wait until she was absolutely certain about her condition, then she would write to Harnser, tell him her news and wait for his advice.

He had still not visited his mother.

Having made a decision she felt a little calmer. She wanted this child. She was happy about it, she was even happier that it belonged to Harnser. Whatever happened it would be loved. She was far from destitute; she was no Alice Hubbard who could have been deserted without a penny to her name. Her father would leave Barcada with her if he had to – she had no doubt about the matter.

Alice? How was Alice? How did she cope with so many children? The last time she had seen her she had four. She had looked happy – happy, wholesome and plump. Arabella smiled, she herself would not have minded having four of Harnser's children and living in a little house on the Green.

Her head felt a little better now that she had made her initial plans. She decided to go for a walk through the copse, she never met anybody in there. As she walked she remembered the Winter of eighteen sixty-three, and her antics with Harnser and the sled.

The fluttering leaves were again reminiscent of the snow. She followed her usual route along the path that she and Harnser had forged. She reached the other side of the copse and stood, head held back, breathing in the clean, fresh air. Ahead of her lay the marshes, no mist today, just the wide open expanse of sky and marsh. She loved this view, she heard the peewit and smiled. She never *had* quite mastered that sound. She bent down and plucked a blade of grass, stretched it between her thumbs and tried again. That was not too bad she told herself, and then she began to cry – Harnser would make a wonderful father…but would he ever have the chance.

She wondered if his wife and daughter had returned home; maybe *that* was why he had not visited his mother. Then a terrible thought struck her. Had he visited, but thought it best not to contact her or visit her father? Was he regretting their actions in London? Perhaps, if his family had returned they had *all* been to Little Pecking and were making a fresh start as a family. She should be happy for him if that were the case.

She looked at her watch, conscious that she had lost track of time. She would come back tomorrow and the next day…and the next…and the next…

One day she would see him again.

It was on her way back home that she met Arthur in Rookery Lane.

"Evenin', Ma'am," he said politely.

"Good evening, Arthur, I see we are both taking advantage of the lovely weather."

He stopped then looked behind him, much as he had done in the garden. "Harnser has written to his mother, he hopes to visit her for Christmas. Apparently he has a wife and daughter. He's hopin' to bring them too."

"I am so very pleased, she must be very happy." Then remembering that this should be the first time she had heard of his family, she added, "A wife and daughter you say, that *is* good news."

"She heard from him about a month after I told you that Walter had said sorry."

He was watching her closely, she was sure he knew something. Then, "I'll say goodbye then, Ma'am."

"Goodbye, Arthur."

He half turned away and then looked back and smiled, "Thank you, Ma'am," he said quietly.

So he *did* know, but how much? she wondered, alarmed. She consoled herself that he might just think they had kept in touch with Harnser because the Major was fond of him. She would have heard had there been gossip in the village.

"You are looking much better since your holiday, Arabella." Her mother in-law was having difficulty keeping to this new house rule not to mention children. She shot a quick glance towards her son, who was sitting opposite her at the dining table, "Charles must take you with him more often, then perhaps…"

Charles cut his mother short before she had the chance to

mention the future of Oxley – one of her pet subjects. "I have already told Arabella to accompany me anytime she wishes so long as she takes a companion along so that I do not have to worry about her alone in the city."

His mother noted the interruption with annoyance, *someone* had to remind her daughter-in-law of her duties; she could not go roaming the countryside aimlessly forever. She smiled at Arabella, "You have not been horse riding of late I notice."

Arabella blushed a deep crimson. "No, I have been walking instead, the countryside is so beautiful in September it seems a shame to rush through it on horseback."

She suspects, thought Arabella. She is looking for any little sign that I might be with child.

"I thought perhaps you might be feeling a little under the weather?" There was question to her voice.

"No, I am perfectly well, really. Perhaps I will go horse riding next week."

Sarah's face fell noticeably; so much so that Arabella realized she had put her off the scent. Perhaps she should have a gentle ride to Barcada to convince the older woman that she was not about to become a grandmother. If she stayed a while with her father, Sarah would think she had gone for a long, exhilarating ride. Despite her problems she realized she was going to enjoy this little game with her mother-in-law.

By the end of October Arabella was sure about her condition. She did, however, acknowledge that she should see a doctor for confirmation. She could see no other reason for her symptoms, especially as she felt so well, but if she *was* right, she would soon be unable to hide her condition. She hoped to keep the matter private for as long as possible especially with regards to Sarah and Henry. She wanted to have her escape well organised. It was her intention to let Charles explain to his parents – *after* her departure. After all, it was he who had fuelled their hopes for grandchildren; let *him* explain why the marriage foundered at the precise time it should have been cemented – when she was with child.

She wished she knew of Harnser's circumstances, whether or not his wife and child had returned. She supposed they had because Arthur had said he hoped to bring them on a visit to Maria. Arabella was fast coming to realize that she did not really belong to either man. It looked as if her future was with her father and her child.

In the first week in November, she went on a shopping trip to Winford to arrange some suitable clothing. While there she went to see a doctor. He looked at her a little suspiciously as she took a seat in his consulting room.

"You are not one of my patients, Mrs Sanderson, might I enquire why you did not go to your own doctor?"

"I am in town alone and I felt a little faint and since I was passing your door…" It was not altogether untrue; she had felt a little strange.

"Do you have any idea of why that might be?"

"I think I might be with child," she blushed then added, "I *hope* I am with child."

The Doctor relaxed and smiled. After asking her some personal questions and examining her, he confirmed that the baby was due in May.

"Go and see your own doctor as soon as possible, in the meantime I will drop him a line."

"No, no there is really no need for that," she said hurriedly, not wanting Doctor Miles to call on her unexpectedly at home. Then seeing his surprised look she smiled and added. "I want to choose the right time to announce my good news, Dr Miles is a friend of my father's."

The Doctor appeared happy with the explanation and wished her 'good day'.

It was not until Arabella stepped out of his house that the full implications of her pregnancy hit her. Up to a short while ago she knew, although unlikely, that there could have been other reasons for her symptoms.

She decided to go straight home and write to Harnser at his school.

My Dearest Harnser, she wrote,

I hope this letter finds you well. I have some very special news to tell you, which I hope will make you as happy as it has made me. Prepare yourself, my darling for I am overjoyed to tell you that I am with child – your child. Yes, Harnser, I will have our baby next Spring.

Tomorrow I will tell my father then, very soon I will tell Charles.

I have had a long time to think about my plans. I know I will have to leave Little Pecking, at least until the scandal dies down, so I will ask my Aunt Evelyn if I can stay with her. My father may wish to accompany me, whatever happens I will stay in touch.

I know you have your own family to think of and in that respect I ask nothing of you. I know you love your little girl, I would not dream of asking you to leave her.

Arthur intimated to me that your wife and child had returned home, actually, he said you were hoping to bring them to see your mother at Christmas.

I will not cause you any embarrassment, only Father and myself will know my child's paternity. Despite my unusual circumstances I assure you I am overjoyed to be carrying your child.

I will keep you informed.

Take good care of yourself,
My love as always,
Arabella.

The next morning, unable to trust the letter to anyone else, she went into Winford to post it, calling in on her father on her return journey.

"Father I want you to prepare yourself for a shock."

She crossed the room and poured some brandy into a glass. She gave it to the Major, urging him to sit down.

"You are worrying me, Arabella," the elderly man said, not taking his eyes from her face, "What has happened?"

"Father...I – I am going to have a baby."

228

The old man stared at his daughter dumbfounded, then his face relaxed, a broad smile spread over his face.

"But that is *wonderful* news, my dear, I am absolutely delighted. I thought for a minute you were going to tell me bad news, we should be drinking champagne."

With this he set his glass down on a side table, rose from the sofa and took his daughter in his arms, chuckling with pleasure as he did so.

"Father," she hesitated, not knowing how to spoil his happiness, "Father, you do not understand." There was pleading in her voice, pleading that said, 'do not be angry with me', 'I would never have a child with Charles,' 'This is my only chance of happiness and fulfilment.' Instead she said, as she sobbed against his chest, "Please forgive me, Father, please, please do not forsake me, for I could not bear it."

"Arabella, my dear, what is all this. The news could not be better. Why should I forsake you…you are a married woman…why…?"

He stopped in mid sentence as realization dawned, no she would not have done…not Harnser…three months since London…he fell back onto the sofa and, with shaking hand, picked up his brandy glass again.

He was staring ahead trying to absorb the implications of his daughter's news.

She stood rigid, her hand to her mouth, waiting for him to speak.

"Father," she said meekly. "Father, please speak to me."

"Arabella," he whispered, "Arabella, what have you done?" his voice was barely audible.

"Father, you are frightening me, I have no one else to turn to, please try to understand. I love Harnser, I have *always* loved Harnser."

"You are both married."

"Yes." She knelt in front of him, taking his hands in hers, tears streaming down her face. "I would *never* have had a child with Charles, you know that. Please be happy for me and your grandchild. Let me know he is wanted."

"Of course he is wanted."

She raised herself off her knees to sit beside him on the sofa.

"So long as I have your love and support, I will cope, Father."

"We will have to leave the village."

"Yes," she whispered.

"Oh, Arabella, Arabella." He put his arms around her and drew her to him, her head resting on his shoulder. She felt safe, safe and loved.

"Does Charles know?"

"No."

"You will not be able to hide it for much longer."

"No."

"When do you intend to break the news?"

"Soon, but I need to have some plans made. I will have to leave the House as soon as he knows. I will ask him to divorce me."

"There will be gossip and speculation, nobody will understand why you are divorcing in the face of such wonderful news."

"People might understand when they know it is an annulment."

"I will write immediately to your Godmother to ask if we can stay for a while – give us time to think."

"Thank you, Father, I too thought Aunt Evelyn's would be the best place to go."

"It should not take long for her to reply. In the meantime Charles must not suspect."

"I am feeling very well physically, there is no reason why he should."

She thought of her mother-in-law's piercing blue eyes across the dining table, looking for any little sign…

"I am so sorry, my dear."

"For what?"

"For not enquiring after your health, it has all come as such a shock. Are you keeping well?"

"Yes, very well thank you." She smiled suddenly, so relieved to have shared her news. "Actually, I have never felt better."

He took her in his arms again.

"We must look after you, keep you smiling, otherwise it will be bad for the two of you, you are both very precious to me."

"You do not know how happy it makes me to hear you say that."

"Did you ever doubt me?"

He wore a hurt expression.

"No, Father, never."

He smiled at her.

Two weeks later, having heard from her Godmother, Arabella plucked up the courage to make a return visit to her husband's study. She took a deep breath before knocking briefly as she opened the door.

"Why, Arabella, I was about to come and find you." He looked sheepish. Why is it, she wondered, that every time she came to this study her husband looked guilty?

"Oh." She was taken off guard. If she were not careful, her courage would fail.

"Yes," Charles continued, "I need to talk to you about something very important...and very private," he added, lowering his voice considerably.

"Important...? And private...?"

"Yes, come and sit down, you look a little tired."

"I am fine, Charles, I have something important I want to tell you."

"Yes, yes, later, Arabella, now where was I, oh yes, since we went to London I have been thinking of a solution to our problems... and I think I have found the answer."

"You have?" She was nonplussed.

"Er...yes."

Why was she feeling so uncomfortable? She had entered the room so confident, pleased that everything would soon be in the open and she could get away to Essex.

"Would you like a drink, Arabella?" Charles appeared excited...excited but nervous.

"Some water perhaps."

Her mouth was feeling dry, she had no idea what Charles

might be planning.

"Hugo has written to me and..."

She cut him short.

"Hugo? What has Hugo got to do with our problems?"

Charles sounded impatient. "Please, Arabella, will you give me a chance to explain, I am doing this for you as well."

"I am sorry."

"As I was saying," he said gently, "I have had a letter from Hugo, who has a little problem on hand at present, you see...er...one of his maids...er...has found herself in an unfortunate condition..." he shot her a swift glance not knowing how to go on. Arabella waited, not wanting to interrupt again.

"She is very young, Arabella...no money...she is desperate."

"You mean she is with child."

"Yes, yes that is exactly what I mean," Charles sounded relieved.

"What has that got to do with us?"

"Well, Hugo thought – and I must admit, after much consideration I am inclined to agree – that we might like to adopt the child...I-It could all be done very discreetly you see. First of all we could announce your pregnancy, then you could go and stay in Hampshire, and in six month's time we could announce that you have had our baby, then you could both come back here and nobody – not even Mother and Father – would be any the wiser."

Arabella could not believe what she was hearing. Her husband was prepared to adopt a baby born to a housemaid and make it the heir to the Oxley Estate...and all to cover his own embarrassing inadequacies.

He looked at her, waiting for some response.

"Well," he said, "do you not think it a perfect solution? I know how much you want a child."

"Do you mean to say," she said at length, "that you have discussed our problems with Hugo? Has he *also* been led to believe that I am having difficulty conceiving?"

Her voice had risen, uncharacteristically.

232

"Sshh...we do not want the servants getting wind of this."

"No, I am sure you do not; it is a ridiculous idea especially as I have come here today to ask you to agree to an annulment of our marriage."

There, she had said it.

Charles stood aghast.

"Arabella," he whispered, "what are you saying?"

"I am saying, Charles," she reiterated gently, "that we must have our marriage annulled.

"No, please you cannot do this to me, I will be the laughing stock of the county."

"Any alternative is unthinkable."

"But I have just provided you with an alternative."

"No, Charles, your solution is untenable."

"How can you say that?"

"Because, Charles, I am with child."

A deathly silence descended on the room. Charles stood rooted to the spot, incredulity written over his face. He wiped the back of his hand across his mouth; a habit of his when lost for words.

He walked behind his desk, a terrible expression of loss and horror on his face, and slumped into the chair.

Arabella did not speak, then, to her amazement, he began to laugh; awful, hysterical laughing that half frightened her to death.

She began backing from the room. She stood with her back to the door, not knowing whether to flee or comfort him. She felt terribly sorry for him, he was such a *nice* man, maybe a little weak in character, but *nice* just the same.

She watched as he threw back his head and the laughing changed character. She gradually realized he really *was* laughing, he sounded almost relieved.

She did not know how to respond.

Eventually he stopped. "Come here, Arabella," he said gently.

She walked slowly towards him, not knowing what to expect. He took both her hands in his but did not rise from the chair. He looked up at her, his face, more at peace than she had seen

233

it for a long time.

"My little Arabella," he said softly, "I do not know how you have managed it, but you have saved me again."

"Saved you?"

"Oh, Arabella, you cannot know how happy you have made me; this is far better than what I had planned. Now we have a legitimate heir for Oxley."

"B-but the baby is not yours."

"No, but it is *yours*, and you are a Sanderson; your grandmother was my grandfather's sister, the child is a true full-blooded Sanderson. I cannot wait to tell Mother and Father."

He stopped suddenly, "We must be careful, you must not tell the man concerned. This child is the rightful heir to Oxley, nothing and nobody must stand in the way."

"But do you not want to know..."

He cut her short, "There is nothing to know...I have complete faith in you; you will not have had a dalliance with a local farmhand. I suppose it was London...yes of course it was...I am so, so glad I took you with me."

Arabella's mind was in turmoil. Maybe it could work. Harnser was married. He had a child. If she stayed with Charles there would be no gossip. Charles needed her, she suddenly realized she was in a position of power.

"I will stay with you, Charles, on one condition."

"Anything, Arabella, anything at all."

"That you never force me to divulge the name of the baby's natural father."

"I agree to it, the matter is closed already, *I* am the father."

Charles sat in front of his standing wife; he buried his face in her clothes, his arms around her, clasping her tightly to him. She had saved him again, his dear, sweet, little Arabella, loyal and true to the end.

Now he had only one worry on his mind...

Arabella placed her hands on her husband's head, much as she would have done a child's. She stared at the oil painting on the panelled wall in front of her, but she did not see it, instead she saw Harnser, reading the letter she had yet to write...

Chapter Thirteen

"What do you think of that then?" Harry Greene directed his question to Arthur, "An heir for Oxley at last, that should keep our jobs safe for another fifty years."

"It's taken them long enough, I was beginning to think Charlie-boy didn't have what it takes; eight years they've bin married. Strange how that happened just after that business when she was found in the copse. We thought she'd left him didn't we?"

"I expect they had their orders from old Sugar to put a stop to the rumours," said Abel. "The gentry are a strange lot, they'll go to great lengths to avoid a bit of gossip – and I mean that quite literally."

"What do you mean by that, Abel?" said Arthur, always keen to improve his education.

"I mean that they don't often misbehave on their own doorsteps; they like us all to look up to them, speaking of which, I wouldn't let him hear you calling him 'Charlie-boy' if I were you, or you and Marjie will find yourself out on your ears and that wouldn't do would it, with those youngsters of yours needin' a roof over their heads."

"At least we dint take eight years to have our first. I only have to smile at my wife and she fall."

"Well just you watch who you're smiling at, Arthur or you could find yourself in a lot of bother." Then turning to Old Joe, "You're not saying much tonight, Joe."

"I'm still thawing out, I don't know how much longer I'll be able to trek down here on cold winter nights. I don't think I'm long for the top."

"Now don't you go sayin' things like that, Joe, you'll have us all cryin' into our ale in a minute. Christmas is nearly here again and we're all s'posed to be happy; not worrying about being six foot under, pushing up daisies."

"I'll be happy when the Spring come and me bones warm through again," he said as he shuffled a little nearer to the fire.

"Talkin' of Christmas," said Sefton, "I heard a little bit of news today." He took a long draught from his ale mug after he said this, knowing he had got the attention of the whole group and relishing the enjoyment of making them wait to hear what he had to say.

"Well come on, spit it out and we'll sort it," said Arthur, not known for his patience.

"The young musician's comin' home next week for a visit." He beamed as his hand went back to his mug and he pursed his lips in anticipation of his ale and the interest he had generated.

"Harnser's coming home?" Arthur could not hide his pleasure, "Are you sure? Who told you?"

"Molly told me today. He's comin' home to spend Christmas with Maria and Walter."

"It's exactly nine years since he left," said Arthur dreamily as he stared into the fire and thought back. "He should have played the flute at the church 'do', do you remember?"

"That was a rum old do, weren't it? I wonder where he's been all these years."

"I heard he's got a wife and child," said Abel, "Is he bringing them with him?"

"Molly never said, so I don't know but I wouldn't have thought he'd leave them home alone at Christmas. And in answer to your question, Arthur, he's been in Kent."

"Kent! No wonder no one's heard anythin' about him. Thass a long way from home, what's he bin doin' there?"

"He's a schoolmaster, he married a doctor's daughter. They all live together."

"Well I'm very pleased he's done well for himself," Arthur said, smiling. "I always did like Harnser, I'm lookin' forward to seein' him agin. He'll see some changes here."

Privately he was wondering if the Biddemores had heard the news. He would have to make sure he mentioned it to the Major the next time he saw him, then *he* could tell Arabella. Arthur still thought it was the Biddemores that helped him get away, the Major thought a lot of Harnser and so, he knew, did his daughter.

Old Joe was deep in his own thoughts; also of Christmas eighteen sixty-three, when he had found Arabella by the stream. He had made good use of the bench since then and had often met her again there. How was *she* going to react to the news? It was only in the last few months that she had begun to blossom again, she was such a solitary soul, he was very fond of her. He hoped the news would not send her on a downward spiral, thinking she should have run off with Harnser.

Harnser's homecoming on Christmas Eve was a mixture of tension and happiness. He had written that he would get a carriage from the railway station home, because he was unsure of the time of his arrival. He had not told them that he was praying that Emily and Amy would return at Christmas and, if they did, he wanted to be there to welcome them. Emily had, after all, returned home at Christmas once before.

The letter, which had arrived two days before Christmas had informed Maria that he would more than likely be travelling alone, he would explain why when he saw her. Maria had not told her friend Molly this particular piece of information, she had sensed there was a bit of mystery surrounding her son's wife; she had no wish for her family to be the subject of village gossip again.

"You'll wear the floorboards out," her husband remarked not unkindly, as Maria went once more to the window to look out, "James will tell you as soon as the carriage comes into view." James had gone to wait along the road; he could not wait to tell his mother that Harnser had arrived.

"I want this Christmas to be perfect, Walter, I have waited so long to have my family all under one roof..."

James running excitedly into the kitchen stopped her in mid-sentence.

"There is a carriage coming, Mother."

The young boy's face was alight with happiness. For nine years he had been aware that his accident had been the cause of the family rift. Now as he blew on his fingers and stamped his feet to get them warm, his eyes went to Walter, a pleading in them to let bygones be bygones.

Walter read his son's face accurately. "It will be a good Christmas, James, have no fear of that."

The boy smiled, grabbed his mother's hand and pulled her outside where a carriage had lately drawn up. Strangely shy all of a sudden, the three watched from the doorway as the young man alighted with his luggage.

He had grown in stature; this was not the boy that had been hounded from the village nine years earlier. He turned towards the cottage as Maria caught her breath and ran down the path to meet him. They met midway, mother and son, too emotional to speak. Maria almost fell into his arms, oblivious of the moving curtains in nearby cottages.

"Mother, oh, Mother," he murmured hoarsely, I am so happy to see you."

He held her tightly, unashamed of his public tears. James too was crying as Harnser put his arms around the boy and pulled him close.

"You are all grown up, James, I cannot believe you are my little brother." He held him at arm's length, there was no need for more words; their expressions spoke volumes as the tears continued to fall down their faces. Reluctantly he loosened his hold on the boy to turn towards Walter.

"Hello, Walter," he said respectfully, "It is good to see you again."

There was genuine warmth in the young man's voice and Walter responded accordingly, "Hello, son, welcome home."

Walter and James walked back down the path to retrieve the almost forgotten luggage, while Maria and Harnser stepped back into the kitchen with the scrubbed white table. The room, though quite large, looked smaller than he remembered it. He looked at the table where he had sat so many times, turned to Maria and said with a chuckle, "I see you have not changed your ways, it is whiter now than ever."

"It has had an extra scrub for Christmas," she said merrily, pleased he had remembered how proud she was of her kitchen table. "Come, sit down and tell us all your news."

They talked and talked, through the afternoon, through supper and late into the night, first in the kitchen round Maria's table, then in the sitting room around the fire.

Walter did not say much; his heart was full as he watched the expressions on his wife's face as she listened to her son. Why had he been so jealous of him, he wondered now. Harnser was a son to be proud of and Maria should not have been made to feel guilty. He felt very humble as his gaze passed from Maria to James, who sat at his mother's feet avidly listening to his brother's story.

"I hope they come back home to you," the boy said sincerely, "I hope they make you as happy as you have made us."

"I'll second that," said Walter quietly.

"Thank you, all of you," Harnser said, visibly moved, then turning to James, "I hear you want to be a doctor," he said proudly, "that is a fine ambition to have."

"I want Mother and Father to be proud of me," he hesitated, looking from one of his parents to the other, before saying, "like they are of you."

"I will let you into a little secret, James, they are already proud of you – and so am I. Perhaps you could come and stay with me, for a holiday, then you could see what a doctor's life is really like."

"Can I, Mother, Father," he said excitedly, looking form one to the other, "can I go soon?"

"Perhaps," said Harnser tentatively, "you could *all* come – in the Summer maybe, when I will have time to show you around Stoneham."

Maria looked to Walter for approval; she need not have worried. "Why not," he said happily. How much happier it made one feel to give pleasure to others. He wished he had not waited so long to do it.

"Then that is settled," said Harnser happily, "we are not so very far apart now that we have the railway."

Very late that night, when James and Walter had gone to bed, Harnser took his mother's hand, put his finger to his lips, indicating secrecy, and led her back to the kitchen – the room furthest away from Walter's bedroom.

"Is anything wrong?" she asked worriedly as Harnser pulled a chair from under the table and pressed her into it. She noted he had quietly closed all the doors after them.

"I have something to tell you," he whispered as they faced each other over the lamp. "You must not tell anybody else, promise me, Mother, nobody at all."

She saw the seriousness of his face and whispered back, "I promise, Harnser."

"Arabella's baby belongs to me."

He watched as his mother's hand flew to her mouth and she stared at him unbelievingly. "Only you, me, Arabella and her father know the truth, Mother. Even Charles does not know."

He saw the fear in his mother's eyes, fear of gossip and recriminations. He reached out and took her hand in his, rubbing it gently to comfort her.

"Do not worry, it is not as you might imagine, Charles is very, very happy about the situation."

"How can that be?" she whispered incredulously.

Harnser proceeded to tell Maria the story of Arabella's marriage, her unhappiness, her desire for a child and Charles' seemingly inability to consummate the union.

When he had finished he hesitated a while before saying. "This is very embarrassing, but a similar situation exists between me and Emily. Our marriage, too, has been in name only. You and Arabella are the only people aware of this. Arabella and I met by chance in London when we were both at a very low ebb in our personal lives. We are both very happy about her pregnancy. Please be happy too, Mother."

Maria had relaxed a little, the situation was unusual but if Charles was happy... she looked at her son across the table where the lamplight was dancing on his worried face; waiting for her response...for her understanding...for her continued respect and support. She smiled, "I am overjoyed for you both, dear; you both deserve some happiness," she squeezed his hand tightly, "I am so excited about my grandchild, fancy, my grandchild – the heir to the Oxley Estate."

Harnser's face relaxed into a smile, "I have arranged to meet Arabella at Barcada on Boxing Day, we have much to discuss. I cannot wait to see her again. I am not proud of the situation in which I find myself but, in the circumstances, it is the best I can hope for, at least the two of us are not destined to go through life childless. I perhaps, could have coped – after all I do have Amy, who I consider to be my own – but Arabella is a different matter, her health was beginning to suffer. The Major was very worried about her. Strange as it may seem we have managed to bring happiness to quite a number of people, we must focus on that."

"This is the first Christmas Eve I have missed church for nine years; the year you left and the year you returned," Maria smiled, "No doubt your presence will create a bit of a stir tomorrow morning. I think Walter will feel a little self-conscious too."

"While they are talking about us, they will be leaving others alone. I do not think the gossip will be in any way malicious. Folk welcome a bit of juicy news, it is human nature."

"I suppose we should find our beds," said Maria reluctantly, "although I *could* stay up all night talking; it is so good to have you back. Promise me you will never hide your whereabouts from me again."

"I promise. I thought I was acting in your best interests but when Emily left, it brought home to me how you must have felt. Surprisingly, it was she who encouraged me to write home. I had just about made up my mind when she ran away and left me in turmoil. All my energies went into work and searching for them."

"I understand," she looked at the clock over the fireplace, "It is two o'clock."

Sensing his mother's reluctance to go upstairs he said, "We have a week together."

"Yes but…"

241

Maria blushed visibly in the flickering lamplight. "I moved out of Walter's room when he flayed you...tonight will be my first night back...I feel strange...as if I am being disloyal to you."

"I would rather you mended bridges, you have nothing to fear on my part, I have forgiven him, who knows, I might have reacted similarly if someone had hurt my Amy."

"She will return, Harnser, I know it."

"I hope you are right."

They pushed themselves up from the scrubbed, white table to head for the stairway – a new chapter of their lives about to begin.

The Christmas morning worshippers at Little Pecking church had much more to interest them this year. The little vaulted building was bursting at the seams, a scene of great satisfaction to Vicar Hanley as he rubbed his hands together – not only because of the cold – and made a mental calculation of what the collection box might hold later. There was much shuffling, stamping of feet, head turning and whispered speculation.

Harnser and his family had arrived early at Walter's request; even so they were aware of the whispering taking place behind them. Arthur too was an early arrival, keen to welcome his friend back to the village.

"It is good to see you again, Arthur, we must meet up at The Bell before I go home, catch up on all our news. I hear you married Marjie."

"Two youngsters as well, Harnser. We've got more in common now, us both bein' fathers," he whispered, as Hannah struck up on the organ.

The church continued to fill behind them. Old Joe took his place in an aisle-side pew toward the back of the building from where he had a good view of the congregation. He did not know why he should be feeling apprehensive, but he was. He could see the music man and his family standing in solidarity towards the front; two rows behind and across the aisle from where the Sandersons had their reserved seats. Joe's interest was a little different to the rest of the congregation. Whereas the majority was more interested in the situation between Harnser and Walter, Joe was interested in how Arabella would react to the presence of her erstwhile sweetheart. He was very fond of her. He hoped she had been warned that the music man was back, otherwise, in her delicate condition, he could see her publicly fainting.

He heard the clattering as the horse and carriage arrived at the door – it invariably came all the way up in the cold weather. He saw Harnser turn eager eyes on the open door. Old Joe looked behind him, Mr and Mrs Sanderson, as always, entered first, then came the Major with Arabella on his arm, with Charles following at the rear. His eyes turned to Harnser, yes; there was definitely still an interest.

Arabella looked flushed and nervous; her lowered eyes looking up briefly at frequent intervals to look around the congregation… and then she saw him.

Her hand went quickly to her throat and she stumbled slightly, causing her husband to reach forward and put his hand under her elbow. "Are you all right, Arabella?" he was heard to whisper.

"Yes," she answered breathlessly, her eyes never leaving Harnser's face.

The whole episode was over in a matter of seconds and went unnoticed to all but a few. The Sandersons took their places and the Christmas service began.

Now and again throughout the proceedings Arabella turned her head very slightly to the right, where her eyes met Harnser's in mutual suppressed excitement.

Much as he tried, Harnser could not take his eyes from her. She was wearing his favourite colour of green, which suited her so well, her matching hat framing her face perfectly. Had she worn green for him? He liked to think so. She was a little plumper, even so her pregnancy would not have been obvious to the uninformed; no one would have suspected, especially after eight years of marriage.

"She is very beautiful," Maria whispered to her son as they resumed their seats after the first hymn.

Later as holly quivered on the overhead arches in response to the joyful singing of the Little Pecking parishioners, Harnser thought back to the Christmas of eighteen sixty-three and his missed solo performance. He would have been so proud to play for Arabella, as his father had played for his mother. He doubted if he would ever get another chance here at home. Then suddenly and unexpectedly he was filled with optimism. Why not, he thought, what was stopping him from coming home *every* Christmas? He could bring his family with him, if they returned. So far he had been well received, with villagers nodding and smiling warmly as he walked to church. He needed to watch his child grow up; yes, he would return every Christmas and as many times in between as possible. Nobody would suspect anything now that he and Walter had made their peace. He could visit the Major to play chess and halma, two of their joint favourites. Arabella would call in with her child, what would be more natural and seemingly innocent than that? He and his child would not be strangers. He felt happier and more light-hearted than he had since London, as he looked forward to the future. He might even come home permanently, yes, even *that* was a possibility. His heart was positively soaring as he put great vocal effort into the last carol, causing James to look up admiringly at his older brother.

The church began to empty from the front. Charles, who had arrived last, gestured to Arabella and the Major to begin the procession to the door preceded only slightly by Vicar Hanley, who hurried ahead to the porch to bid his parishioners goodbye and wish them all a happy Christmas.

Their eyes met, Arabella's and Harnser's, and spoke silent volumes in the few short seconds of passing, then she was past him – down the aisle, through the porch and into the waiting carriage.

He saw her look sideways briefly, keen to catch a last glimpse of him.

"It is very nice to see you again, Harnser, we must re-arrange your musical debut."

The Vicar's voice was low due to the approach of Walter,

whom everyone knew was responsible for the cancelled performance nine years earlier. Strange how a Christmas so long ago was at the forefront of the minds of all the villagers over fourteen years of age, and all because of the return of one young man.

"Are you sure she will come?" Harnser enquired of his elderly host.

"She will be here." The Major cleared his throat in a nervous manner before adding, "I need not remind you, Harnser, that my daughter's reputation is at stake here, it is imperative that the truth of the situation never becomes public knowledge."

"I am as concerned as you, Sir, for Arabella's happiness. I have told only my mother, and in that respect the secret is as safe as if I had told nobody."

"It is only because of the unusual situation between Arabella and her husband that I can accept such an affair."

"It would never have arisen in normal circumstances, you have my word on that."

"No, no, of course not, I know you better than that. I should be thanking you for making my daughter's life tolerable, I do thank you, son, from the bottom of my heart. You should have run off with her."

"You mean that, Sir?"

"With hindsight, yes, damned insufferable business all this...up at the House...all out of my control...impossible to know how it would have ended if Arabella had not met you again...half dead she was when Joe found her in the copse...I suppose you have heard all about *that?*"

"Yes, Sir, I am sorry I was not around to help."

"Nothing you could have done, he should have been straight with her from the start... no backbone, I cannot understand the chap. There was nothing in the early days to suggest any of this might happen."

"It would not do for us to be able to see the future."

"You are right there. Of course if you *had* run off with my daughter nine years ago I would have been after your hide," there was a twinkle in the old man's eye. "Well perhaps not, not if you had taken me with you; you play a mean game of chess."

Harnser smiled at his elderly friend.

"They both looked up sharply as a carriage made its presence heard on the gravel outside. Two handsome black mares snorted and tossed their heads in the crisp, cold air, sending their warm breath eddying around their nostrils.

Arabella was assisted from the carriage and escorted to the front door before the conveyance circled the frontage and returned from whence it came.

Remembering his manners, Harnser waited for his host to open the front door, he had wanted to rush forward himself to welcome his love, instead he waited in the sitting room doorway, his heart pounding wildly while the elderly man made his way down the hall. And then he was running forward, all else forgotten and much to the Major's surprise took her in his arms, his eyes shut tight, savouring the closeness of her at last.

Her face was cold and fresh against his, he was conscious of a delicate floral perfume, her hair was caught up in a cluster of ringlets beneath her bonnet.

Her face shone with health and happiness. Her joy at being with him again was not lost on the Major.

"There is a fire in your mother's sitting room," he said huskily, overcome with emotion at the sight of his daughter's obvious happiness.

"Thank you, Father," she said turning to give him a warm hug, "thank you so much for your understanding."

Harnser opened the door of their favourite room for her as she removed her bonnet and hurriedly unbuttoned her coat. He helped her off with it, laying it carefully over a chair then once more took her in his arms. "You look radiant, Arabella. You have hardly left my thoughts since I saw you in church yesterday. I would like to tell the world that you are carrying my child, I wanted to take over the pulpit and announce it to the whole village."

"I am very glad you did not," she laughed.

They sat together on the sofa facing the fire, their bodies

turned towards one another, their hands joined. Arabella put up one hand to his face, her eyes looking into his.

"I have missed your lop-sided smile," she said softly. "I cannot put into words how much I have missed you, but," she coloured slightly, the soft flush bringing a warmth to her cool, cream skin, "I have your child, Harnser and that makes our separations so much easier to bear. I have a part of you forever."

"Do you keep well, my love?"

"I have never felt better, I have an inner peace."

"Is everything alright at the House?"

"Mother and Father-in-law are ecstatic. Sarah spends half her time sewing and the other half fussing over me. Henry and Charles are so proud I expect them to burst at any minute. The whole household is vibrant and alive; it is as if the dustsheets have been removed and the cobwebs blown away. We are in the middle of redecoration, not just the nursery and the nanny's accommodation, but the whole house," she laughed here, "and it is a *big* house so you can imagine the upheaval. Of course Henry is adamant that I will have a boy and is urging me to choose a name."

Harnser smiled his lopsided grin, revelling in his sweetheart's light-hearted chatter. "And have you?" he said softly, "chosen a name?"

"I was hoping we might do that today." Her face became serious, "I suppose you realize we will have to give consideration to Sanderson family names."

"That might not be a problem," he smiled secretively.

"Oh, why not?"

"My father's name was Edward Charles. My mother's father was John."

She smiled at the realization.

"You see I have been given the matter some thought, the problem is not insurmountable. Do not forget your father, Arabella, he of all people should be honoured."

"I had always intended to name him for you and father, I would have liked 'Harnser'."

"That is not possible."

"No, I suppose not," she agreed sadly, "but he will always be little Harnser in *my* mind."

"We might have a daughter."

"I think we could be here all night," she said, her green eyes sparkling merrily.

"I could cope with that." He looked into her eyes, love and adoration radiating from his face. "I do not know how I can leave you again."

"Could we write?"

"It would be risky. I feel bad enough at keeping secrets from Florence and Richard."

"From what you have told me of them, they would understand."

"Possibly, but the fact remains I have been unfaithful to their daughter."

"Not before she deserted you."

"It is easy for *us* to find excuses for our behaviour, Arabella. It might not be so easy for them, they are probably not aware that mine and Emily's marriage was in name only."

"It might be best to tell them."

"Perhaps, I will have to see if a suitable opportunity arises."

"There is a possibility that it might ease their consciences."

He smiled, "I suppose there is female logic in there somewhere."

"They are very fond of you. Their daughter has broken your heart by taking Amy away. It may help for them to know you can have your marriage annulled and find happiness elsewhere."

"You could be right. I have no idea how the law stands in such circumstances. I doubt I could get an annulment on my word alone."

"A divorce then, on the grounds of desertion."

"That would be more likely, but," he looked at her tenderly, "if I cannot have you I might as well leave things as they are. Florence and Richard have become very dear to me, and I to them. They need me as part of their family; they are quite alone now."

"Yes, of course they do, we are getting far too serious. There is something I want to give you."

"That is a coincidence."

The Christmas mood had been rekindled.

Arabella crossed the room to the chest of drawers and took out the paintings.

"You should have had these nine years ago," she said softly, handing him the parcels.

He unwrapped the presents and was overcome with emotion. His voice broke as he stared at the two pictures. "They are beautiful, Arabella, *you* are beautiful, how well the artist has caught your ethereal qualities, your inner beauty, as well as your external, is captured forever in a moment of time. It is a perfect likeness of you. Your eyes are full of love, love for me."

"Yes, he did them with the help of the photographs. I looked at the camera and pretended I was looking at you," she hesitated, "I know you did likewise."

He blinked several times to keep the tears at bay. "I kept your photo by my bed until I married Emily. You were the last person I saw before I went to sleep and the first person I saw when I awoke." He took her hands in his, "I would love to take them home with me but it is not possible."

"I understand. After my accident in the copse I asked father if I could put them on the wall in here, I feel close to you in here. He said I could but I think it was only to cheer me up. When I was better I realised it was not such a good idea, they might have been seen by one of the girls, anyway, they are yours."

"I hope one day to be able to display them openly, in the meantime can I leave them here in 'our' room?"

"I think it is the most appropriate place for them."

The pictures were replaced in the drawer, their tissue wrapping once more hiding the secret love affair.

Harnser knelt in front of Arabella. He put his hand in his jacket and took out a small parcel from his pocket. "This is for you, Arabella, I had it made specially when you told me of your pregnancy."

She unwrapped the present carefully, frequently looking into his intense brown eyes, whatever it was she knew she would love it.

The present exceeded her expectations.

When she opened the box she gave a gasp of pleasure for, lying on a bed of dark blue velvet, was an exquisite brooch – a spray of wild roses.

"It is beautiful, Harnser," she said breathlessly, "truly beautiful, I will treasure it always."

He gently brushed the tears from her cheeks with his fingers.

"I never see them in the hedgerows without thinking of you, I love you so much, Arabella."

He stood up and pulled her to her feet, wrapping her in his arms with a tenderness that pulled at his heart. He tilted her head upwards, losing himself in the depth of her green, green eyes, the image of which he kept enshrined within his heart, along with all his other precious keepsakes.

CHAPTER FOURTEEN

"What is it, Arabella?"

The Major hovered over his daughter where she sat pale and drawn. "Shall I send Arthur for the Doctor?"

"I am in the most dreadful pain, Father, it was very sudden." She began to straighten her back slightly before adding, "I think it is easing little...yes, it is easing. I suppose I will have to start using a carriage to visit you, although I do enjoy the walk from the House. There is no need for a doctor...there, it is gone."

The colour returned to Arabella's face as she picked up the huge bunch of daffodils and catkins she had collected on her way over.

"I will put these into vases for you, I could not resist them, they go so well together do you not think?"

The Major smiled at his happy daughter.

"Your mother always put a spray of catkins with daffodils, you remind me so much of her. I do think however that you should stop your flower gathering until the baby is born, it cannot be good for you to bend and stretch so much."

"You are probably right, I promise I will be more sensible, after all it is only six weeks to wait now. I'll put some of these in Mother's sitting room shall I?"

She did not wait for an answer as she set off for the kitchen to fill vases with water that Arthur had drawn that morning.

The Major followed at his own pace.

"Do not get in Sarah's way, you know that she likes the kitchen to herself."

Sarah heard her kindly employer.

"I can always spare a corner for Arabella, it will give us an opportunity to talk about babies," she said cheerfully. Then turning to the expectant mother, "I suppose the nursery is ready and waiting? You must be very excited, Arabella."

"I cannot wait, Sarah, neither it seems can anyone else at the House, I am beginning to feel a trifle claustrophobic with everyone hovering over me. It is so nice to take a walk over here and feel free for a while. Oh, I do not mean to sound ungrateful, Sarah, I know they are only concerned for my well being, but everything is so much more *formal* over there, especially with your namesake."

"I understand, I'm a grandmother myself don't forget, I do my fair share of worrying about my children. They probably think I'm an old fuss pot too."

Arabella put her arm around Sarah's shoulders. "You are *not* an old fuss pot," she said kindly, "you are *motherly*."

The vases were filled and Arabella began to distribute them around the house. It was as she was coming back up the central hall from her mother's sitting room that she suddenly screamed out in pain and fell in a crumpled heap to the floor, clasping her arm around her body as she did so.

Sarah and the Major were with her in a second.

"Can you manage her feet, Major? I'll try to take most of the weight," the housekeeper said worriedly.

"We will take her to the end room, there is a bed in there," the old man said hurriedly, feeling in his pocket for the key.

Having carried Arabella into the sitting room and laid her on the bed the old man began talking quickly.

"We must send Arthur for a doctor, I should have done it earlier, I will never forgive myself if anything happens to her. And the nanny will be needed, she is already installed at Oxley; no doubt she has experience in these matters."

"It is her day off," Arabella said feebly from her position on the bed, "she has gone to Illingham to visit her family. It is alright, Father, I am feeling a little better again."

"Hurry, Sarah, I will sit with her."

The Major ushered Sarah away and once more sat with his daughter in the room that he rarely visited, but which Arabella loved.

"I feel very close to Mother and Harnser in here, Father," she said, as she lay pale and frightened.

"I know you do, dear, I should use it more often, it just seems to hold such painful memories for me."

"It is such a pretty, peaceful room; where my mother last spoke to me."

"That is how I should look on it, instead of thinking it is where she left me."

Please God do not let Arabella leave me here as well, he prayed silently as he held her pale hand in his and closed his eyes tightly.

"Aaahhh, Father, help me please," Arabella screamed as she crushed his hand and doubled over in pain, as another contraction took hold of her body.

"Sarah, Sarah, where are you woman?" the Major called in panic, getting to his feet and crossing to the door.

Sarah came hurrying down the hall.

"I couldn't find him, Major, how is she?"

"She needs a doctor, have you found Arthur now?"

"Yes, yes, he's gone, I told him to hurry and I've put water on to boil, I think the young heir is eager to get here. I should get her undressed and into bed properly, is there any linen down here?"

"The bed is ready, I keep it made up, Sarah." Arabella's frightened voice reached the housekeeper as her eyes peered round the unfamiliar room. "There is linen in the cupboard on the far wall," she continued. "Do you think the Doctor will be here in time, Sarah?"

"A first one usually takes its time, dear. Don't you worry about nothing. Jenny will be back from the village soon; we'll manage between us 'til Dr Miles get here. I've delivered a few babies in my time."

"Really, oh Sarah that makes me feel so much better."

The housekeeper bustled around sorting linen into piles before saying authoritatively, "Do you think you could manage to sit in a chair for a few minutes while I pull this bed out to a more convenient place. As soon as Jenny comes back I'll get her to light the fire."

"I can do that," the Major said, pleased to be of use, "It's laid all ready behind the screen," and he busied himself at the fire place, casting frightened glances at the bed as he did so.

"Good, that's good, then, when you've done that take yourself off next door while I get this young lady to bed."

The Major was relieved to have someone take over.

He was halfway through the door when Sarah added, "Don't forget the Doctor will need letting in, and tell Jenny to watch things in the kitchen. I've got a pie half made for supper in there and the water needs an eye kept on it."

"That should keep him busy and out of our way for a while," Sarah said importantly but not unkindly, sounding far more cheerful than she was feeling. "A delivery room is no place for a man that's for sure. Now, let's get you into bed ready for the Doctor."

No sooner had she settled into bed again than she was gripped by another strong pain.

"Mother, Mother," she screamed in anguish, "Mother help me...help me."

"I'm afraid I'll have to do, Arabella," Sarah said gently taking her hand. "Hold on tightly to me when they come on you, it'll help."

Jenny came bursting into the room, "I've just heard – what do you want me to do?"

"Look after the Major and the kitchen, and make some strong tea, the Doctor will need one, he like his tea strong. Then come back here in case I need you." She turned to Arabella and mopped her sweating brow. "We'll have to send word to Oxley, they don't know what's happening yet."

"No, no, not yet. There is nothing they can do. Arthur can go later when he comes back," she said breathlessly, gritting her teeth against the spasms.

"Are you sure? Wouldn't you like Master Charles here?"

"No, no, he would only worry, like you said, it is no place for a man," Arabella said tiredly, but even as she said it, she wished Harnser was with her.

She began thinking how she would get word to him that his

254

child was making an early appearance when again she was consumed by pain. Her back felt as if it were breaking, as if she were on a rack being pulled in two. How long would she be able to bear it?

Time dragged on, she was vaguely aware of Jenny coming in and out of the room with bowls; she could hear herself screaming, knowing her father would be terrified, but unable to stop herself. She tried to form an image of Harnser in her mind, imagining him there with her, comforting her, soothing her. Then she would be racked with pain again and the image would disappear as Sarah peered at her with cold fear on her face, mopping her brow and murmuring soothing words that were all at odds with her frightened face.

"There, there, Miss, the Doctor's comin', Arthur'll soon be back with him, don't you worry none now, we're all here to help. He'll be here soon and give you somethin' for the pain."

Arabella tried to think clearly, was she shouting for Harnser or her mother? She must not mention his name, whatever happened she must stay in control and not bring shame on them all...no...no...no. "Sarah," she gasped, "Sarah, I cannot do this...give the flowers to my mother...tell him I love him...tell him I love him, tell him I am sorry I cannot bring his child into the world..."

She fell quiet; exhausted and drenched with perspiration, pale and still for a few seconds until once more the pain returned with a vengeance.

"She'll not survive this much longer," she heard someone say, and then, when she thought she could bear no more, she felt the child leave her, smoothly and quickly.

"It's a girl, you have a daughter, Arabella," came Sarah's excited, relieved voice, "She's beautiful, look here..."

"A baby's first sharp cry filled the room, like music to their ears.

Sarah held the baby aloft, a smile played around Arabella's parched lips as she looked on her child for the first time.

A few minutes later having cleaned the baby and wrapped her up, Sarah laid the child in her mother's arms.

Arabella clasped the infant to her with almost a hunger and looked into the face of Harnser's daughter – she had waited a long time for this day.

Half an hour later, when mother and child had been made presentable, the Major was just about to be admitted for the first glimpse of his grandchild when several things happened in quick succession.

The Doctor arrived, but not Dr Miles, who, it transpired, had been out on an emergency call when Arthur reached Flinton, necessitating the young man to ride all the way to Winford to find another.

Having sent Arthur off once more, this time to Oxley to inform them of the child's birth, the Major was halfway down the hall again when he heard his daughter, once more scream out for her mother.

He froze in his steps, what now, she should not be in pain now.

I should never have put her in that room, he thought frantically, it claimed Eleanor and now it looks as if it might claim Arabella too, for two solid hours he had listened to her screaming.

He hastened his step and reached the delivery room door just as Jenny rushed out in tears.

"What is wrong, why is she screaming again?"

"I don't know, Doctor say somethin's wrong, I can't bear to watch."

"What do you mean, 'wrong'?"

"She shouldn't be in pain now, she's all twisted up and whimpering, that room's cursed, that's what it is."

"Get a grip, girl, we cannot all fall to pieces," even so the old man's hands were shaking and he could feel his heart pounding in his chest. He had sat alone in the library, feeling helpless as his daughter's pain reverberated through the house, praying hard for her deliverance and now, just when he thought it was all over, the nightmare was starting again.

He turned to the trembling housemaid, "Has word been left with Dr Miles?"

"Yes, Arthur went there first. He daren't come back without a doctor so he went on to Winford."

The old man held his head and closed his eyes against the screaming, the moaning and the whimpering coming from his late wife's sitting room. "There are two doctors at Flinton, where was Dr Benjamin?"

"I don't know, Sir, Arthur dint say."

"Alright, alright, calm yourself now, none of this is your fault, go off to the kitchen and make yourself busy." He had to show some control in front of his household. "No doubt we will have the Sandersons here any…"

He stopped mid-sentence as a deathly silence fell on the house. His daughter was quiet, his legs turned to jelly and only just managed to carry him to the nearest chair in the library.

Jenny came running back down the hall and stood facing the delivery room door, cold fear written all over her face.

"She's gone, Sir, oh no, she's gone, I knew she would…"

She glanced into the library, through the open door, to where the Major sat rigid, his face set in fear, both hands on top of his walking stick…and then they heard the baby cry.

"Oh, no," Jenny whimpered, "it's crying for its mother, what are we goin' to do, Sir? She's so little, she won't survive without her mother."

The Major stared ahead, numb with shock.

He should never have put her in that room.

Their eyes turned in unison to the door as it opened to reveal Sarah – Sarah smiling at them both. "It's a little boy, a girl and a boy – twins!"

"Twins! Sir it's twins…Sir." Jenny shook the Major's arm.

"Arabella is alive?" the old man whispered incredulously.

"Arabella is alive," Sarah said gently, seeing the shocked state of her employer. "She's bin through the mill, Sir, but she's definitely alive."

Tears flowed down the old man's face. He had not lost her

after all. He felt weak, the room had not taken her. He had twin grandchildren.

He felt Sarah's arms around him, helping him to his feet. "Come on, Sir, I don't want another invalid on my hands," then, happily, "We've got some celebratin' to do tonight, Sir."

"Yes, Sarah, we certainly have...we have some celebrating to do tonight."

Suddenly he began chuckling as relief swept over him, "No supper, Sarah, but plenty to celebrate."

Charles crept quietly into the room and crossed to where the Major was sitting with his daughter and grandchildren. "Is she awake?" he whispered, looking on the spent, pale form of his wife.

"No, they are all sleeping, Arabella is exhausted." Then seeing the worried countenance of his son-in-law, he added proudly, "Well, what do you think of your children?"

She could not have told him, thought Charles, walking round the bed to reach the infants, even the Major thinks I am their natural father. He peered down into the drawer – which acted as a makeshift crib – to where the babies lay side by side; a little girl with a head of chestnut down, and a fair haired little boy. "Twins! I have twins," his voice was barely audible.

The Major watched Charles' face, trying to guess what he was thinking. "No doubt he will go darker in time, it is often the case," he said cautiously.

"Mother is blonde," the young man said quickly, she will be pleased that one resembles her."

"Of course she will, where are they?"

"Waiting in the sitting room, do you think they could come in?"

Arabella stirred and opened her eyes, "Father."

"I am here, dear...so is Charles," he added quickly, frightened that his daughter might make some reference to Harnser. "You have caused quite a stir."

Charles leaned forward and kissed his wife. "Well that should keep Mother quiet for a while," he said gently. Then, more seriously, "Your babies are beautiful, Arabella, we are all very proud of you. Can Mother and Father come in and meet the heirs to Oxley?"

When Charles had gone, Arabella turned to her father with a contented sigh. "I absolutely love this room," she said. "I am glad my children were born here."

"I am warming to it myself," the old man replied with a smile. "Your daffodils look lovely, they are all round the house," he smiled tenderly, "Jenny finished the job."

"Oh yes, I had forgotten, so much has happened since then." She looked across at her babies where they lay in the drawer supported by two upright chairs.

"To think they have a fully equipped nursery waiting at Oxley and here they are in a drawer," she said softly.

"They look happy enough. I do not suppose they mind where they are so long as they are warm and fed. They are very small, Arabella, the Doctor says you must all stay here for a few weeks."

"That will suit us very well," she said sleepily. "I can arrange for their father to visit us…"

"Oh but surely he will move in here for a week or two," said Mrs Sanderson, entering the room and catching the end of Arabella's sentence. "Now where are my beautiful grand-children, come quickly, Henry, oh they are darlings, look, he looks just like me I can see the likeness already. And a little girl, I cannot wait to take them home. You have done us proud, Arabella, how are you, dear?"

Charles watched proudly as his parents admired the babies. Events had worked out well, his mother and father would be more than satisfied with two children. When Arthur had arrived with the news that Arabella had given birth to a daughter he had thought his parents might be disappointed it was not a boy, but they had surprised him. Henry had slapped him on the back and said, "Well done, Charles, you have made a good start, maybe in a few years time you will have a son; if not we must make sure that your daughter marries well."

Whatever happened Charles was relieved that the pressure was off him. Then when they had arrived at Barcada the Major

259

had given them the wonderful news of twins. He would never feel inadequate again. He could hold his head high in the village – he could well imagine what they had been saying about him. Well, he had shown them all, or rather Arabella had. Dear Arabella, he would spend the rest of his life making sure she was happy; he was indebted to her.

As he surveyed the happy family scene, Charles was acutely aware that one person was missing. He had readily agreed to Arabella's condition that he would not insist on knowing the paternity of her babies, now, however, he had an overwhelming desire to know the identity of the natural father. He did not think his wife was conducting a long-term affair; he had kept his eyes and ears open for the past few months and had discovered nothing untoward. It was probably as he had suspected, a lonely, love-starved woman being swept off her feet in London by an aristocratic picaroon, who had long since forgotten the dalliance. He could not broach the subject at this late stage and risk another of Arabella's fiery outbursts or, worse still have her resurrect the subject of an annulment; he owed her a great deal and was in no position to make demands.

"…are you sure, dear? I am certain Charles would not mind." His mother's voice floated across the room to him and he saw that Sarah was looking at him expectantly, as if waiting for confirmation of something.

"I am sorry, Mother, you were saying?"

"That you are quite prepared to move into Barcada for a few weeks …until the children are big enough to be moved."

"Well, er…yes…I suppose so, if that is what Arabella wants…"

Arabella smiled tiredly at him, "There is really no need, Charles. We will be well looked after here; you would have to go to Oxley every day anyway to conduct your business; you might just as well stay there and come here to visit us."

Her eyes closed again, she was exhausted, she just wanted to sleep, to sleep and dream of her babies…and Harnser.

"If you are sure…"

"I am, perfectly sure. Perhaps Nanny could stay here, after all you have engaged her and I cannot expect Sarah or Jenny to take on the fulltime commitment of nursemaid." Again his wife smiled at him. No, he had nothing to worry about; Arabella was completely content now that she had her babies.

Later that night when the babies had been moved to a hastily prepared room with Nanny, so that Arabella could rest, she had the opportunity to speak with her father. "Would you take the paintings up to my room please, Father, I am worried that someone will find them if they remain in the drawer. Put them in my travelling trunk please." She gave her father an apologetic look, "I am sorry to involve you in subterfuge, I hope you do not think too badly of me."

"Arabella, I do not think badly of you at all. I know none of this would have happened in the normal course of events. You do not know what it means to me to see you so happy. How can I compare your happiness now to how you were last year and wish things different? You were being destroyed by the situation; I was extremely worried about you." He patted her hand and said softly, "I will take the paintings and you must get some sleep. Nanny is just next door, ring the bell if you need anything and she will call Sarah. We are all close at hand."

He kissed his daughter goodnight and left the room with the paintings. No, he thought, he could not have subjected her to an unhappy, barren existence, which was beyond her control to change. He was sure she could be forgiven her infidelity in such extenuating circumstances. In the absence of a male Sanderson heir, Arabella's son would have inherited Oxley anyway, even if she had not married Charles.

Now all that was left to do was to inform the children's father of the birth.

Chapter Fifteen

As was to be expected, news of the twins' birth spread like wildfire around Little Pecking. Conversation in The Bell was of little else that night.

"I bet the champagne is flowing up there, Charlie-boy won't be the only one stumbling up the stairs tonight," said Arthur, enjoying his celebrity status. He had not put his hand in his pocket once for a drink, and each time he told the story of his dramatic ride to find a doctor he seemed to remember a few more morsels of embellishment.

"I took Miss Arabella's horse, it's the fastest one in the stables, she went like the wind, Rosie seemed to know her mistress's life was in danger, my, she had some life in her; you should've seen her; mane and tail a-flyin' like the devil himself was after us."

"I reckon the Major will reward you, Arthur," said Old Joe knowingly. "He allust give me somethin' if I do them a good turn, especially where Miss Arabella is concerned, I've had one or two bottles off him, and when I found her in the copse he gave me ten guineas. Yes," he reiterated, "no doubt you'll get somethin'."

"Ten guineas!" Arthur whistled, "Phew, ten guineas, I've never seen that much money in my life. Do you really think he'll give me that much?"

"I wouldn't be surprised, you carried on to Winford didn't you? Accordin' to Sarah it was touch and go when the Doctor arrived." This time it was Abel raising Arthur's expectations.

"I'm in a different position to Joe, I already work for them, they could say I was just doin' my job."

Arthur began to lose his hold on the ten guineas, adding, "I couldn't have refused an order could I? No, I don't suppose they'll give me any extra."

"Now what's all this I hear about you saving Miss Arabella's life, Arthur?"

Sefton Merryweather dipped his head as he made his way through the low doorway into the snug. "I hear you went all the way to Illingham before you found a doctor," he continued, sitting down and straining his waistcoat buttons.

"Winford, I went to Winford," said Arthur, sorry that he had to cut ten miles off his journey. "Well, it was like this... Sarah came running into the stables all of a panicking muckwash and told me Miss Arabella was in dire need of a doctor and likely to die if we didn't get him quick... My this story telling give you a dry throat..."

"I hear they need some more help to look after the babies, Nanny said she was only expecting there to be one and they're so small they'll need extra care. She say she don't want no young lass from the village who's still wet behind the ears, she want a mature woman who knows what she's doin' so that she can have proper time off without worrying about them." Arthur nodded his head importantly, "Thass what Sarah told me, anyway. They're all stayin' at Barcada for at least six weeks 'cause it's the Doctor's orders."

"Well, you can't argue with that," said Abel, sagely, "there's many a littlun don't make it when they *are* a good weight; I hear they're tiny, only about four pounds each."

"I wonder what we'll git for the village this time – we got a clock for the weddin' dint we?"

"No doubt it will be somethin' for the church."

They all fell quiet thinking about what would be most beneficial to the community.

Little did they realize that the same subject was due to be discussed first thing the following morning at Oxley House.

"I think the village end of Rookery Lane would be the best place, Father, there are more outlying hamlets and dwellings this end of the village." Charles was pleased to have something new to focus his energies on, in the absence of having his children under his roof.

"It will have to be subsidised of course; we are only a small community, but with more housing as well…"

The two men surveyed their draft plans with pride. It was the Major that had raised the subject the previous night that what the village needed was its own doctor. "You are quite right, Bertie," Henry had said with force, "Charles and I will initiate the matter first thing tomorrow morning."

Now the rough plans lay before them in Henry's study; a terrace of eight cottages and a large house fit for a doctor, within the region of the church and the vicarage.

The imposing house would be known as 'Edward House'; the pretty row of cottages, 'Eleanor Terrace'. These were the names that had been chosen for the twins, together with other family considerations.

"What is the name of the young man who rode for the Doctor, Charles?"

"Arthur, it was Arthur Osbourne who went."

"And the woman who delivered Eleanor?"

"Sarah Penny."

"They should both be offered a cottage first, agreed?"

"Agreed, Father."

"I heard in the village that you are looking for a mature woman to help Nanny with the babies." Maria's gaze never left the Major's face.

"Do I not know you?" Bertie peered into the face of the woman at his front door.

"You have probably seen me at church, I am Maria Porter," then much quieter but still looking steadily at the Major, "I am Harnser's mother."

"Come in, come in," the elderly man said in a fluster, "this is…er…very embarrassing…I do not…"

"I would very much like the position, for obvious reasons." She looked around making sure no one was within earshot before continuing, "It would enable me to get to know my grandchildren, needless to say I would be discreet, I have no

264

wish to cause trouble."

The Major's mind was working quickly. The woman would be trustworthy; she would have a genuine interest in the infants' welfare. She had also, by all accounts, nursed her own little boy back to health from the brink of death. They would find nobody *more* suitable in the village.

"Do you know my daughter?"

"Only by sight."

"The ultimate decision must be hers, but…"

Maria waited for the old man to continue, but instead he waved her to a chair and appeared to be deep in thought.

"…you have taken me by surprise," he finished lamely.

"I am sorry, perhaps I should have written, but I did not want the post taken before I had applied. I heard that time is of the essence."

"Yes, Maria, as you can imagine twins were a huge surprise," then lowering his voice, "Have you informed your son?"

"I did not know if Arabella would prefer to write first."

"I think she has already written but not yet posted it, it is all very awkward."

"I could do that for her."

"Yes, of course you could, that would be splendid, would you mind waiting while I have a word with her…I will see if I can find you a cup of tea along the way. We are all at sixes and sevens here at the moment."

"Father, that would be perfect, send her through please so that I can meet her properly."

"Do you not think it a bit risky."

"Maria will no more want gossip than we do."

"Nanny will want to be consulted."

" 'Consulted' being the operative word." Arabella raised her eyebrows at her father, "I will have the final decision."

"She can be a bit…" he searched around in his mind for an appropriate adjective.

She laughed finishing his sentence for him, "…overbearing?"

"Ssshh," he held his finger to his lips, "she is only next

door…yes," he agreed, "overbearing."

They laughed together as they each made faces resembling the nanny's stern countenance.

"Apparently it goes with the territory, now, where is Mrs Porter?"

Fifteen minutes later the post had been filled.

"Why did you do that?" Walter was dumbfounded.

"It was a spur of the moment thing. I was in the village shop, heard about the post and thought, why not me?"

"You do not need employment." His disapproval was apparent in his tone.

"I am here alone all day. I will enjoy being busy again. Anyway it will not be for long. They will be moved to the House in six weeks, then I suppose I will be redundant."

"Do I not earn enough to keep us?"

"Of course you do, it is nothing to do with that. James is thirteen, neither of you are dependent on me for all your needs. A woman likes to be needed, it is in her nature, but," she assumed a disappointed look, "if you are so opposed to the idea, I will have to tell them you won't allow it." She shot him a quick glance before continuing, "They were so pleased I applied because they heard how well we cared for James after the accident."

She knew it was naughty to bring up the subject; that Walter's conscience would trouble him enough to make him back down on the issue, and she was right.

"Well, if it means so much to you, it is good to know we have folks' respect I suppose."

She crossed the room and gave him a rare peck on the cheek. "Thank you, Walter, I knew you would not be unreasonable."

She felt a little guilty that she could not tell him the truth of the situation, but she consoled herself with the fact that she had been loyal to him above and beyond the call of duty – she could have left with Harnser. If her son could not be with his children, then at least she would be able to give him news of them.

Life for Maria was not perfect but at least it was improving.

Arthur and Sarah both received an *ex gratia* payment of ten guineas from the Major and a promise of new accommodation from Henry Sanderson.

Edward House and Eleanor terrace were completed in eighteen hundred and seventy-four.

CHAPTER SIXTEEN

One year later...

Emily and Amy had not returned home although Harnser, to a lesser degree, continued to search for them. He was also troubled by the fact that he did not have much contact with his natural children. He often thought of returning to Little Pecking or at least to the area, but Florence and Richard would not move from Kent in case their family returned, and he was reluctant to leave them on their own. He also knew that if he returned home the situation would be unbearable for him; living so close to Arabella and the children but unable to have them with him. He was aware that, if he lived close by, he would have to at least see them regularly and then how long would it be before someone suspected? No, it was better for all concerned if he stayed away.

Strangely, although he knew that James had recovered, the accident nightmare continued to haunt him, especially when he was troubled by other matters, which was not infrequent.

He would go to sleep thinking of his children lying in their beds miles away at Oxley House, and of Arabella lying in the huge double bed with Charles – which, in spite of everything, they continued to share – and he would fall into fitful sleep only to witness the horror over and over again:

...and the sound of a child's scream rang out over the surrounding countryside.

As always he would awaken in a cold sweat, his heart pounding, wondering if he had called out and disturbed his mother and father-in-law. If he did they never mentioned it.

He wondered if the reason for the nightmare continuing was because of his troubled conscience concerning his secret children. He wanted to acknowledge them publicly, at least to Florence and Richard.

So it was, that on his children's second birthday, when he was particularly melancholic – so much so that Florence had remarked on the fact – he sat them down and told them the truth. It was not an easy task, especially admitting that his marriage was in name only.

His story was met with a stunned silence.

"I expect you would like me to move out," he said at length, with sadness.

Florence rose from her chair, crossed the room to him and put her hand on his slumped shoulder. There were tears in her eyes as she said falteringly, "We have been so worried about you leaving us, Harnser. We are well aware of how much heartache our daughter has caused you, you have been patient, kind and loving beyond the call of duty, more so than we ever realized.

"Richard and I have grown to love you as our own. We knew the day would come when you would meet somebody else and want your own family, we were expecting it, but not like this; how have you borne it all alone? No wonder you suffer nightmares," she coloured visibly, "I'm sorry I should not have mentioned that."

Harnser rose and took Florence in his arms, "It is due to you and Richard that I have borne it, I would not have managed without you, I hated keeping secrets from you."

Richard spoke for the first time since hearing the story, "Will you divorce her?" he said brokenly.

"I do not know what to do, I wish I knew if she had left me for another man. She could have fallen genuinely in love and want her freedom," he looked from one to the other of them resignedly, "I do not think that Emily was ever really in love with me."

"Perhaps not, but she was genuinely fond of you," Richard said, "and as far as Amy is concerned you *are* her father; *she* loves you, without doubt."

"And I love her," said Harnser, sitting down heavily again and putting his head in his hands, "I wish I knew she was well…and happy…I wish I could see for myself that all my children are well and happy…"

He began to sob quietly, his shoulders shaking visibly. "It is my children's second birthday today and they are with another man…they hardly know me…I have seen them only four times….I was so happy when they were born…what an awful mess my life is in."

Richard took control, "First of all I speak for both of us when I say we certainly do not want you to move out, we have lost enough already. We long ago voiced our suspicions to one another, and accepted, that our daughter could have run off with another man – she is very wilful and easily influenced and if he had offered her a tempting life in the theatre… Well, we all know how much she wanted *that*. But, Harnser, we still love her, *we* can forgive her most things, no doubt, you will your children. We do however agree with each other that, after all this time, you should be entitled to your freedom, it will make no difference to how we feel about you. You must do as you think fit – either way you have our love and support."

"I am so lucky to have you both," he said softly, "but I am in no hurry to divorce Emily, I live in hope that they will return; it is not as if I can marry my children's mother. We might as well leave things as they are for the present."

He gave them a weak smile, "I am glad everything is out in the open at last, I feel as if a great weight has been lifted from me."

PART FOUR

Where There's A Will…

CHAPTER ONE

London 1878

Fourteen year old Louis Chevalier made his way to his head-master's study with a certain amount of trepidation and knocked gently on the door. Receiving no answering call he was about to use slightly more force when the aforementioned gentleman came striding down the corridor.

"Ah, there you are, Chevalier, I see you received my message."

"Yes, Sir," the boy answered meekly, wondering why he had been called, and trying to think of any misdemeanour for which he could be in trouble.

The headmaster unlocked the door and ushered the boy before him into the wood panelled room, where he stood nervously awaiting his fate. The gentleman shuffled papers on his desk before saying, with slightly more compassion than the boy had ever heard in his six years at the school, "I have some unfortunate news to impart."

He raised his eyes to the boy, hoping he was not going to fall apart – he could not abide weakness of any description and had not the slightest notion of how to deal with tears. "Hum... er...yes, Chevalier, it has been brought to my attention that you are needed at home where your aunt has fallen ill...very ill, I am afraid. In fact it is thought she is approaching the end of her days." He paused then added unnecessarily, "You understand what I am saying?"

"Yes, Sir."

Louis' eyes began to smart and he had difficulty keeping them dry. His aunt was the only person in the world he truly loved; he looked forward to spending the holidays with her, when she would take him to the country to stay in a little cottage with her elder sister. He loved the countryside. He hated leaving her to return to school each term, but she would pack him off amidst oceans of tears reassuring him they would soon be together again. She invariably told him he must work hard at his studies so that he could make something of himself and meet the vagaries of life with fortitude. And all the while she would be dabbing at her eyes and straightening his clothes and he knew she was not taking her own advice...and he loved her for it; she was the only person who had ever cried because he was leaving them. Now he would soon have nobody.

"....straight after supper."

The headmasters voice came to him again as if through layers of muslin, "I said you must pack your trunk and be ready to leave straight after supper."

"Yes, Sir," he answered in a faltering voice.

"We will see you again at the beginning of next term." His voice softened slightly before adding, "We must face these things with fortitude, Chevalier, they come to us all."

Louis blinked rapidly and bowed his head so that he did not disappoint his superior, who had rounded the desk and put an arm around his shoulders to escort him to the door. "My best wishes go with you young man."

Once outside the door the tears fell freely. He brushed them away with his sleeve before hastening to pack his trunk and make his way to the dining hall for a supper he did not want and could not eat.

"The Doctor's just been, Louis, he says it will not be long now. Just sit quietly, we do not want to tire her."

He watched his aunt Ethel's sister leave the room and pull the door closed. He took one of his aunt's pale hands in his, they were almost transparent, the veins clearly visible, they were surprisingly warm.

"Is that you, Louis?" her eyes did not open.

"Yes, Aunt Ethel." He leaned forward in an effort to hear her small voice more clearly.

"I was frightened I would be called before you got here." Still she did not open her eyes.

"I am here now, do not tire yourself." He tried to keep his voice strong so that she would not worry about him.

A good ten minutes elapsed before she spoke again. This time he saw her cheeks were wet, he realized she had not been sleeping but summoning the strength to speak again. "Can you hear me, Louis?"

"Yes, Aunt Ethel."

"I have something very important I want to tell you," she paused to get her breath, "something I should not tell you." She opened her watery eyes to make sure she had his attention. Seeing that she had, she continued, "Your father loved your mother very much." Her breathing was shallow, he could see it was an effort for her to talk but she was determined to do so.

He lifted the pale hand to his lips, the action brought a barely discernible smile to the old lady's lips. "Colette became ill before you were born and died soon afterwards."

Louis listened patiently as the old lady continued her story, how happy and deeply in love his parents were, how devastated his father was when his mother died leaving him with a weak, sickly baby, not expected to live.

"I did not know much about your parents, I was hired as a nanny shortly before you were born."

"But you are my Aunt."

"No, Louis, I was your nanny." She saw his face crumple at the information she was imparting. "I may not be your real aunt but I love you like a son."

The tears were running down both their faces now. The old lady's because she was dying and would leave him; the boy's because the one relative he thought he had was no blood relation at all. Even so he did not want to lose her.

She continued her story.

"About a week after you were born, I heard your mother say to you, 'My little Louis, heir to the great Oxley Estate', then she gathered you close to her and said ' I will never see it, I wonder if you will.'

"Then she asked me to fetch a box from her closet. She took

275

out a document and showed it to me, it was your birth certificate, I saw it with my own eyes."

Ethel closed her eyes again.

"But I do not have any close family, there is only my distant cousin Charles."

The boy thought of the man who occasionally used to visit, who had seemed vaguely interested in him in a dutiful way. He imagined he lived in the city.

The old lady gripped the boy's hand as tightly as her failing strength would allow. "He is not your distant cousin, he is your father."

"But…" The boy was clearly shocked. The blood had drained form his face.

"Yes, Louis, you thought your father was dead."

"But why…"

"I do not know all the details, but once, in a moment of weakness, after your mother died, he told me his life was in turmoil."

Ethel continued her story, punctuated with frequent pauses.

"He said he could not take you home because he had promised to marry his cousin and if his father found out he had married Colette he would be disinherited. He asked me if I would take care of you until he found a solution. I thought it would be for only a short time but I have had you ever since." Ethel smiled at him, "I am not sorry on my part but I wanted you to know the truth before I die."

"If you rest you might get better," the boy knew he was clutching at straws.

"No, Louis I am not going to get better," she said tiredly, "but I have thought long and hard about the situation; you are the legitimate heir to a large country estate. You should fight for your heritage. I still have your mother's box here, the proof is inside…your birth certificate. Take the box, Louis, it is in the closet, guard it with your life, it is yours."

She watched as he fetched the box, wooden, with a brass lock and key. She saw his dejected face, saw how her story had affected him and her heart went out to him.

"Your father is not a bad man," she said gently, "weak in character maybe, but definitely not bad."

"But he has disowned me."

"Not 'disowned'. He pays your school fees and the rent on this house."

"I thought it was all paid from my parent's estate."

"That is what he wanted you to think."

"What should I do, Aunt Ethel?"

Although frail she was the only one to whom he could turn for advice.

"After I am gone you should go to Oxley – the address is on your birth certificate."

"But how should I introduce myself?"

"Tell them that you have been left quite alone in the world and that you are appealing to your cousin Charles for help and advice."

"Will they not wonder how I found them?"

"Say you found the address in your mother's papers, it is the truth."

"But I have no money."

"I am not rich, but I have never been unemployed."

Louis thought of all the prominent people for whom his aunt had worked in London. She had often stopped to converse with them in the parks and streets, reminding them of when she had been their nanny.

Ethel continued, "I have left everything to you, everything I own will be yours." She smiled at the astounded face in front of her. "Thanks to your father, the amount is not inconsiderable, I have not had to pay rent for fourteen years and who better than you to benefit from your father's generosity."

"I do not know how to thank you."

"Thank me by claiming your inheritance, the Oxley Estate."

"I am not a brave person. I may not be able to live up to your expectations. There may be other heirs."

"Not direct ones, not that I know of. I am sure he would have told me."

"If that were the case why does he have to keep me secret?"

"I do not know, Louis, I have never understood it, I am your father's employee. I never wanted to jeopardise my position by being inquisitive, I had grown too fond of you."

"Dear Aunt Ethel," he paused and smiled at the old lady propped up by white pillows. "Yes," he continued, "you will always be my Aunt Ethel. I do not care if we are not related by blood."

"Go to Oxley, see which way the land lies, bide your time, Louis, but do not let anyone take advantage of you, your mother had great strength of character, you are more like her."

The old lady peered at the ceiling and squinted her eyes as if trying to remember something from the dim and distant past.

"What is it, Aunt Ethel? What are you thinking of?"

"I am thinking it would not surprise me if you are the only heir."

"Why is that?"

"Because your father blamed himself for your mother's death. He once told me he would never risk another woman dying due to having his child. It haunted him, Louis, you see, he is not all bad."

She looked lovingly at the boy she loved as her own and added softly, "You are such a sweet-natured, self-effacing person, I am worried you will let people take advantage of you. Promise me you will go to Oxley, Louis."

"I promise, Aunt Ethel."

Louis stared at the entry on the birth certificate. So his name was Louis Charles Sanderson. Chevalier was his mother's name. Fourteen years of age and he had not known his proper name. He wondered what other revelations awaited him at Oxley, more to the point, was he in any hurry to find out?

CHAPTER TWO

As the train rumbled on toward Winford railway station Louis began to lose courage. He went over and over the planned introductory speech he had formulated since his aunt Ethel had died a month earlier. He and Ethel's sister had gone through the house sorting and packing as necessary. He had given Grace lots of bits and pieces but, being elderly herself, and with only a small cottage, there was much remaining in the house. The rent was paid up to the end of the next quarter, so he felt confident in leaving everything in place for the time being. His aunt had told him that all financial matters were dealt with through a London solicitor, he had their name and address, but had not yet informed them that Mr Sanderson's housekeeper had died; he would impart the information personally when he reached Oxley house – the reaction would help him judge the lie of the land.

He stared out of the window at the vast sky and flat landscape, it was all so green and uncluttered; the fresh air coming in at the window had a strange saltiness to it, which he found quite pleasant, so much so that he stood up, putting his face closer to the aperture.

"New to the area are you?" his travelling companion enquired.

"Yes, Sir."

"Thought so, pound to a penny you hail from London."

"Yes, Sir."

"I can always tell, Londoners always get up to smell the salty air."

"It is very..." He searched his mind around for the appropriate adjective, "...fresh," he finished, smiling at the gentleman who had joined the train at the previous station.

"You can say that again, it is even fresher in the Winter with an east wind straight off the sea, fair takes your breath away. The east coast will kill or cure, that's the old saying around these parts."

"I do not suppose I will be here in Winter," Louis said quietly.

Noticing the dejected tone, the traveller smiled warmly, "Spring is a much better time to visit, where will you be staying?"

"I have yet to find suitable accommodation, perhaps you could advise me."

The traveller looked the young man up and down, well dressed, well spoken, expensive looking luggage. "The Royal hotel is very popular with holiday makers, right beside the sea, you would be comfortable there." Then his curiosity getting the better of him, " Will you be staying long?"

"I have not yet made up my mind, a day or two perhaps, I will be looking up relatives in the area."

"The Royal's the place then, just across the river it is, handy for carriages and the railway station. I will show you if you like, it's not far, we are nearly into Winford."

"Thank you, Sir, I am much obliged to you."

Within a few minutes, the train came to a noisy stop sending the carriage occupants back into their seats with a jolt.

"Always get up too early, always sit back down again," the traveller chuckled to his young companion, "good job the seats are soft."

The boy picked up both his substantial bags, but his new acquaintance stayed him with his hand, "You get out, I'll pass them down to you."

The pair passed out of the railway station and turned right, where a harbour full of fishing vessels met their eyes. Hundreds of seagulls whirled and screamed over the smacks, as they dipped and dived for any morsels of fish available.

"Lovely sight isn't it?" The gentleman turned to his young companion.

"Yes, Sir."

"A bit different from London?"

"Very much so."

The gentleman raised his arm and pointed ahead. "Well, there she is, straight ahead look, you'll be comfortable enough there. Enjoy your stay young man, I'll bid you good-day, I've got an appointment to keep for which I am a little late."

"Thank you, Sir, good-day to you."

Louis set his bags down to take stock of his surroundings only to snatch them up again and stagger back as a carriage and pair swept up to the station. Seeing that he was in the middle of a very busy thoroughfare he hastened forward toward the boats, the gulls, the bridge and the imposing building displaying the name 'The Royal Hotel'.

Louis booked into his temporary home under his familiar name of Chevalier. He had decided before leaving London that he would introduce himself to his new-found family by the aforementioned name and let them decide to which part of the family he belonged. He was aware he would have to keep his wits about him. Each time he began to falter, which was frequent, he would bring to mind the vision of his dear aunt Ethel, propped up on her white pillows, her transparent hand gripping his, telling him to fight for his inheritance; an inheritance that he had, as yet, to lay eyes on.

The sky was clear and blue with fluffy white clouds scudding across in a hurry. Although the sun was shining, the air was crisp. Despite the fact that, for sometime now, Louis had been the carriage's only occupant, he sat to one side holding his hands tightly together – an observer might say 'wringing' them together.

Having just passed through Little Pecking village the young heir knew he was nearing Oxley House. Just as he thought he was approaching open countryside he saw a large house coming into view on his right. As he passed he saw the sign on the front gates which read 'Edward House'. A little further on was a terrace of cottages, newly built, bearing a plaque in the middle. He tried to read the writing but the distance and the brisk pace of the horses prevented him from doing so. His prepared speech kept slipping from his memory and he found himself repeating the first words over and over again as he tried to recall the rest of it. His nerves were getting the better of him. He wondered if his father would be at home and, if so, would he recognise him? They had not seen each other for at least six years, though he knew Charles had visited Ethel a few times when he had been at school. She had always related the visits to him – now he knew why.

He had changed a lot in six years. Although only fourteen he was tall, almost six feet. The last time his father had seen him he had been a slight boy of eight years. The thought provoked a slight anger and he felt his face redden, why hadn't his father wanted to see him? Surely he could not blame him too, for his mother's death; he had not asked to be born. Guilt maybe, guilt because he had hidden him away at school under a different name.

"Nearly there now, Sir," a voice called from the drivers seat.

Louis felt the carriage turn and saw, through the window, high ornamental walls each side of a wide gateway – to one side was a lodge.

Then, in the near distance, he saw the house, Oxley House, his inheritance. A huge imposing building, three stories high, clean and bright in the sunshine. He had not known what to expect when he left London, but the building, which stood before him surpassed all his expectations; it was bigger than his school, which housed eighty boys.

They drew to a halt, the driver jumped down and opened the carriage door for him – Louis stood spellbound staring at the house.

The driver coughed politely reminding the young man that he had not paid his fare. The money duly changed hands with Louis' eyes hardly leaving the house.

"Shall I wait, Sir?"

"Er, yes, if you would not mind."

Louis approached the huge front door with trepidation, all of a sudden he felt much smaller then his six feet. He took a deep breath and pulled hard on the bell. He did not hear it ring inside the house, but then if the width of the door

282

was any indication of the thickness, he doubted that anything could be heard through it – even a herd of charging bull elephants.

He felt his lower stomach contract within and was about to turn and flee when the door opened to reveal a maid in white, starched apron.

Remembering his manners he snatched off his cap. "I have come to see Mr Charles Sanderson," he said with more authority than he felt.

"Step inside, Sir, I'll see if he is at home. The maid pulled the door wider and Louis stepped into his ancestral home.

"Who shall I say is visiting, Sir?"

"Louis Chevalier," he answered quickly, before his nerve failed him.

"Would you repeat that please?"

"Louis Chevalier," he said much more slowly.

"Take a seat please, Sir, I won't be long," then asked, "Is Mister Charles expecting you?"

"No, he is not expecting me."

Left alone Louis looked at the huge, marble-floored hall. The walls were oak panelled and held many portraits and landscapes. There was a central staircase which, halfway up, split into two.

On the wall facing the front door where the stairs went in opposite directions was a massive portrait of an elderly man with a long grey beard. Below the painting was a plaque, which was too far away to read. He assumed it to be one of his forebears, the one that built the house perhaps.

His eyes searched the walls for a portrait of his own father; his recollection of him was hazy. He remembered a tall dark haired man, quite well built, who was softly spoken. That could be him, he thought, as his roaming eyes settled on a painting of a young man in riding habit, standing under an oak tree in casual pose. On an adjoining panel, in matching frame, was a portrait of a young woman, a beautiful young lady with a cream complexion and chestnut tresses. Was this the cousin his father had promised to marry?

He saw the maid returning up a corridor to the right of the staircase, she appeared flustered.

"Mr Charles is not at home," she said breathlessly, as if she had searched the house for him in vain, "but Mr Henry Sanderson will see you in his study, follow me please."

She led the way back from whence she had come, turning every now and then to make sure he was still following. His throat felt constricted, he did not feel in control of the situation. He was about to meet his grandfather for the first time in his life – a grandfather he had never heard of until the previous month.

Although he was angry with his father for treating him so shabbily, hiding him away in embarrassment, Louis was acutely aware that there could be innocent people in this house who did not deserve his contempt. He must remember that.

The maid came to a halt and knocked on a door that looked like any other door they had passed – except for the name on a brass plaque, which said simply, 'Henry Sanderson'.

"Come," he heard a muffled voice call.

The maid opened the door and stood to one side for Louis to enter. "Your visitor, Sir," she said self-consciously, before going out and closing the door gently behind her.

Louis thought of his Aunt Ethel and strode purposefully towards the large desk, behind which sat the man who he now knew to be his grandfather.

The white haired gentleman rose from his seat, walked round the desk and extended his arm to the young visitor. "Henry Sanderson," he hesitated then said, "and you are?" But before Louis could reply he added, "You must forgive the maid, she could not remember your name."

"Louis – Louis Chevalier."

"French, eh?"

"My mother was French."

"Chevalier, a noble name indeed, am I right in saying it is the French equivalent of 'Knight'?"

"You are quite right, Sir."

"So, Louis Chevalier, I understand you have come to see

my son Charles. He is out on the estate somewhere, can I help at all?"

Taking a deep breath the young man launched into his prepared speech. "I have reason to believe, Sir, that I am related to the Sanderson family. I have recently had the misfortune of losing a dear aunt, whereupon I inherited some papers belonging to my deceased mother. I found the address of Charles Sanderson amongst them. My Aunt had often mentioned that I had a distant cousin Charles. Being left quite alone in the world I decided to use my school Easter holiday to travel to Suffolk to introduce myself in the hope that I would not be *quite* so alone in the world."

Louis was surprised he had remembered his introductory speech so well, and was pleased to see he had the intrigued interest of his grandfather.

"Needless to say you have taken me completely by surprise. You are an orphan you say?"

"That is what I have been led to believe, I do not know much about my family history."

"So your mother was French, yes?

"Yes, Sir."

"Presumably, your father was also French, er, judging by your name."

"I do not know so much about my father."

"This dear lady you have recently lost, what was *her* name?"

"Ethel Millfield."

"Was that her maiden name?"

"I was never made aware that she had had a husband, but that is not to say she had not."

"Ethel Millfield…" Henry Sanderson stared up at the ceiling while repeating the name over and over again. "I cannot remember hearing of an Ethel Millfield."

"I know she had a sister called Grace," the young man said helpfully, knowing that Grace was a popular name.

"Ah, Grace, now you are talking, I am sure I have heard of a Grace somewhere in the family." Henry cleared his throat in the manner of embarrassment. "There was a family rift you see, many years ago, in my grandfather's day. You know how it is, dear boy, when someone becomes successful and makes a lot of money. There are always those who are jealous and expect to benefit in some way." Henry realised he could be referring to the boy's family and added quickly, "All in the past now of course, I am sure you are not here in *that* capacity."

"My aunt has left me a small legacy and I was told my education is paid for from my mother's estate, as is the rent for the house in which my aunt lived. I – I am not sure what to do about the house, I am at boarding school most of the time."

Louis was almost certain that his grandfather had been kept in the dark as much as he himself had. He was about to continue when there was a knock on the door. His grandfather called 'Come' and the same maid as before entered, "The carriage driver says should he still wait," she said, looking admiringly at the young Frenchman.

"I had completely forgotten…" Louis began, only to be stayed by Henry who said, "Wait here, Louis, I will go and pay him off."

So far, so good, the young man thought. Aunt Ethel would be proud of him. He had told no lies.

The older man returned, clearly having hurried in both directions. Louis took out his purse, eager not to be seen as a sponging individual. Henry waved the offered money away saying, "No, no, keep your money, you will need it. Where are you staying?"

"At the Royal Hotel in Winford."

"You must stay here with us, we have plenty of room, it will allow us all to get to know one another. We cannot have you all alone in the world when we are obviously related. I see no other reason for you finding our address among your mother's papers, anyway I can see a distinct family resemblance."

"You can?"

"Definitely, I would recognize a Sanderson anywhere. Come with me to look at the portraits, you will see what I mean."

And that was where they met Charles.

"Ah, Charles, we have a young visitor, come and meet Louis

Chevalier, a relative of ours from London."

Charles stopped in his tracks. The blood drained from his face as he stood rooted to the spot. Louis no longer felt at a disadvantage, he saw that his presence in the house terrified his father. He strode forward confidently to shake the hand of the man who had disowned him – no not exactly disowned, as his aunt had pointed out – hidden him away like something to be ashamed of, and kept him in ignorance.

Charles looked at his son; he would not have recognized the young man that stood before him. A weird mixture of emotions took hold of him, this handsome young man was the fruit of his loins, the only child he would ever have, were he not so frightened he would feel proud. But he was frightened. How had he found him? How much did he know? He had given Ethel strict instructions, why had she betrayed him?

All these thoughts were spinning around in Charles' head, as the young man strode toward him, hand outstretched with an affable manner about him.

"I am extremely pleased to meet you, cousin Charles." There, that should put him at his ease.

"Louis has just lost his closest relative, Charles, he thought he was quite alone in the world, then he found our address among his mother's papers."

His mother's papers, the words screamed at Charles. What papers, there were no papers at the house, the solicitor had everything. Yes, he was sure he had given everything to the solicitor.

"Are you alright, Charles?" Henry's voice penetrated Charles' overworked mind and he realized he was still staring at the newcomer. He raised his hand and felt it warmly clasped in those of his son…his son…his son…

He needed a drink, he had returned for lunch but he needed a very large drink.

His father's voice came to him again, as if from afar. "I have an appointment in town, can I leave Louis in your capable hands?"

Without waiting for a reply he turned to the boy, "Will you

allow me to collect your bags from the hotel since I will be close by?"

"Thank you, Sir."

"Before I go, Louis look here, at the top of the stairs." Henry pointed to the huge portrait with the plaque that dominated the hall. "That is Obadiah Sanderson, who built this house. He had two sons and four daughters. One of those sons was my grandfather."

"What was the other's name?" Louis asked interested.

"He was Harold. He led a life of debauchery and womanising and died young." Henry shot Louis a warm smile, "I do not think you stem from *that* particular branch of the family. What say you, Charles?"

Charles had said little but his father seemed not to notice as he gave the newcomer a brief account of the family history.

"No," continued Henry, "it is much more likely that you descended from my grandfather's brother. He settled abroad; not sure where, and made a small fortune from wine after a family rift."

Louis had began to see why Henry had accepted him so readily as the older man pointed out various pictures of young men where a resemblance to himself was plain to see. He even mentioned the likeness to his son in the portrait under the oak tree.

"Do you not agree, Charles?" Henry asked, studying the picture with more interest than usual. "Especially the nose and mouth."

"Yes, I can see." Charles thought it best not to disagree; that way the subject might be dropped sooner.

"Not so much across the eyes," Henry continued, unperturbed by his son's flat voice.

No, thought Charles, those eyes are the eyes of my poor Colette, how would he face them across the dining table night after night. He had loved those clear hazel eyes, so open and honest.

"Who is the beautiful young lady?" asked Louis, looking at the portrait of Arabella, which hung on the next panel.

"That is Arabella, Charles' wife, you will meet her at dinner tonight. They have two children, Edward and Eleanor, they are six years old now. You will also meet my wife, Sarah. The ladies and children are all away today in town."

So there *are* other heirs, thought Louis. That will complicate matters. He had no wish to upset the lives of innocent people. If it were not for the vision of his Aunt Ethel, that kept coming to his mind, he would just enjoy a holiday in the Suffolk countryside, then return to his studies. But should his father get away so lightly? Charles knew who he was. His demeanour, when they met, had guilt written all over it. No doubt he was standing behind him right now, plotting how to get rid of him before his true identity became known.

He walked from portrait to portrait, only half absorbing the information being imparted by his proud grandfather. He liked him, he had not bargained for that. He had almost seen the family as his enemy before he arrived today. An enemy that had cast him into obscurity, like a mentally deranged relative they were ashamed to own. As always when he thought along these lines, his face became hot with anger. He was a stranger to confrontation; it was alien to his nature to quarrel. He was not sure if he could see through this quest for his inheritance.

"…so there you are, Louis, we have familiarised you with some of your lost family," Henry finished, "No doubt we will soon sort out exactly where you fit in." He turned to his son, "Look after him until I get back, Charles, show him the estate, it is a fine day for a ride." Then turning to Louis, "You *do* ride?"

Louis thought of the few times he had been astride a horse whilst staying in the country with Grace. Her grandson had taught him the rudiments of riding, but that was around a meadow on an old mare that would not have had the energy to throw him even if she had felt so inclined.

He felt it best to be honest. "To tell you the truth, Sir, my riding skills are negligible."

"Well, that must be remedied at once, we have some docile mares which the ladies ride, my wife's would be ideal. Charles will look after you, you will see quite a lot on a gentle walk. Well,

I must be off, enjoy yourselves. I will see you both at dinner." And with that Henry strode off back the way they had come, leaving Louis at the mercy of the man that did not want him.

Charles looked across at his riding companion who appeared uneasy on his mount. He was almost certain that he had not recognised him, all the same he must use the ride to make sure.

"So you thought you had been left quite alone in the world?"

"Yes, Sir."

"Charles will do since we are related. Who was this relative you have just lost?

"My Aunt Ethel."

"You were close?"

"Yes."

"Please accept my condolences."

So he thought Ethel was his aunt.

Louis shot his father a surprised look; he seemed sincere. "Thank you, Charles."

"It is always hard to lose those you love." There was a faraway sound to his voice.

"Yes."

Was he thinking of his mother? Ethel said he had been devastated.

"You will never forget her, but the pain will ease."

Louis did not answer, his father did not really seem to be with him, but lost in his own thoughts, until suddenly he said. "You must sit straight in the saddle, try to relax a little, you are quite safe on Diamond."

The pair continued with Charles pointing out interesting landmarks, whilst at the same time instructing Louis on horsemanship.

"So when did your aunt pass away?"

"A month ago."

"What have you been doing since?"

"Sorting through the house, packing things away."

"Do you have any money?"

"I understand my school fees are paid from my mother's

estate. The house is rented. I have the address of a solicitor. I suppose I should go and ascertain matters."

He waited for the reaction of the man he knew to be his father.

"You must leave all that to me."

"To you?"

"Well...er...to us, to Father and myself, you are far too young to be burdened by such things. Anyway you are not yet twenty-one – you cannot undertake legal matters."

"But I cannot expect..."

"Nonsense, anyway, we cannot have you living alone in London, we must hire a housekeeper or make alternative arrangements during school holidays. Father and I will look after matters. You concentrate on your studies."

Charles began to panic, he needed to think things through and he could not do that if his brain was addled with alcohol. On the other hand how would he get through this ordeal without a little help...

"I can tell you love this place."

"Yes, I do."

"It must have been wonderful growing up knowing all this would one day be yours."

Charles spun his head round to look at his young companion. Had he said that to make him feel guilty? Was he tormenting him?

But Louis was staring ahead, his eyes half closed against the strong afternoon sun. Again Charles experienced the feeling of pride. Never in his wildest dreams had he thought he would ride this estate with his natural son at his side.

"Your wife, Arabella, is very beautiful. Where did you meet her?

Louis was determined not to feel inferior. If Charles could ask questions then so could he.

"She is my second, or is it third, cousin, her grandmother was my grandfather's sister."

Why had he asked that?

"Does *she* love Oxley?"

"She loves the land, I do not think she likes living in such a big house, she prefers Barcada."

Why was he telling him this? He had this urge to talk to his son, to confide in him. He wanted to tell him about his mother. Tell him how much he had loved her – still loved her in fact. He wanted to tell him that he had not wanted to hide him away in shame but, he had promised his grandfather that he would marry Arabella and unite the family again. All these things he wanted to say but, as always, he held his tongue – held his tongue and drank his brandy...and his whisky...and his wine...

"Barcada?" The boy was looking at him puzzled.

"Yes, it joins the estate, a house and ten acres. My great-grandfather built it for his daughter, Arabella's grandmother. It is a long story. Arabella loves the house, it is substantial but nowhere near as large as Oxley House."

"Who lives there now?"

"Arabella's father."

Why was he so interested? Was he up to something? Did he know he stood in line to inherit?

No, of course he did not, an address would not automatically make him think he had any claim on the family. To his knowledge he did not even bear the name of Sanderson. Charles reasoned that he must keep a clear head and go along with the pretence until he could get to his London solicitor and make sure that no information would be divulged to the boy. He would also have to get his hands on his marriage certificate and Louis' birth certificate. He was sure they were with his solicitor but if they were not... He had been so devastated when Colette had died that he could not remember where the papers had been placed. He would search his study tonight. How had he managed to overlook such vital matters?

In the latter stages of pregnancy, when she became ill, the doctor had told Charles that neither Colette nor the baby would survive. She had begged him to marry her, so that she would not die in shame giving birth to an illegitimate child. In the circumstances he saw no reason to deny her her dying wish. He was very happy to grant it to the woman he had loved so much, and who had loved *him* so much that she was willing to leave her homeland and settle in a strange country, to become his mistress, knowing they would never marry.

At least he had been honest with *her*.

He looked across to his son sitting tall and handsome atop his mount, he was not sorry he had survived, he was part of Colette. There lay the problem. Those eyes – he could not look at the boy without being reminded that he had taken her life by giving her a child. He had found it easier not to see him. Taking the line of least resistance had been the story of his life. He had promised to marry Arabella in the same way. He should have told his grandfather that he had met the woman he wanted to marry, and that it was not his cousin. Why did he find it so difficult to assert himself? Both his grandfather and his father were of strong character, why could he not be like them? Always obedient, always dutiful, he would die doing other people's bidding, of that he was sure. And it inevitably landed him in the mire – always drove him to the bottle…How long would it be before the truth came out? For all he knew this son of his could be planning to make an announcement at dinner tonight.

He must think of a reason why his name should be among Colette's papers…and he must do it quickly…

CHAPTER THREE

The atmosphere at the dining table was one of excitement. Arabella and Sarah were intrigued when told they had a young visitor who purported to be related to the family. The family had assembled a little earlier than usual to meet the newcomer.

"Do you know *nothing* of your family history?" asked Sarah who always liked to get to the bottom of a mystery.

"I have told your husband almost all I know."

"And I have told *you,* Sarah," said Henry patiently.

"Perhaps we are not related," said Charles cautiously.

"Oh no, do not say that," rejoined his mother, "It is much more interesting to suspect we are."

All eyes turned to Charles, waiting for him to expand on his last statement.

"Well, come on," prompted Arabella, her eyes alight with interest. She found the Sanderson family a little too formal and reserved. They rarely did anything spontaneously; Sarah was perhaps the exception, she *did* mostly speak her mind – sometimes without *enough* thought beforehand.

Arabella found her thoughts surprising. Sarah's outspokenness had often irritated her in the past. Now she saw it from a different perspective. Perhaps she was just bored and liked something new to break the monotony of the women's life at Oxley. She had been much better company since the twins had been born.

"Well," began Charles, carefully, "there could be an alternative reason for our address being found among Louis' mother's papers."

"Not just our address, Charles," his father reminded him, "*your* name was found."

Charles felt slightly uncomfortable, was his father getting suspicious? He ran his finger around the inside of his collar, his colour was a little heightened; had anybody noticed his discomfort? He considered his words carefully. "Perhaps I went to school with …er…er…what did you say your mother's name was?" he turned to Louis, ashamed of himself for denying knowledge of his wife.

"Colette…"

"Yes, perhaps I went to school with Colette's brother, or met him on my travels. Perhaps they were *family* papers rather than her personal ones."

"Did your mother *have* a brother?" Sarah asked Louis gently.

"I do not know. I know nothing of her family, although I am going to rectify that as soon as possible. I could have a family in France as well."

He shot Charles a satisfied look, he did not like the fact that he was trying to disassociate him from the Sandersons when he knew his origins better than anyone at the table.

"How do you intend to do that?" Henry asked his young guest.

"I have not thought it out yet, but there must be ways. Aunt Ethel said my mother did not come to England until the year of my birth. Fourteen years is not long…there will be records… certificates…"

"You are forgetting, Charles, Louis' Aunt told him he had a distant cousin by your name," Henry reminded his son.

"Yes, of course, you are right, I *had* forgotten that."

The warmth that Louis had begun to feel for his father whilst out riding was slowly slipping away again. He obviously had no intention of acknowledging him as his son. He felt his colour rise again, as it always did at these times. He felt a rush of pure love for Ethel, whose loyalty had been to him rather than the man who had paid her wages. What was it she had said? Oh, yes, '*your father is not a bad man, weak in character maybe, but definitely not bad.*' He tried to keep those words to the fore, Ethel was a good person, a good judge of character, she had not seemed to want him to hate his father, but then, she had not known the position here at Oxley.

He looked around the dining table, his father definitely looked hot and uncomfortable. Henry, at the top of the table, frequently looked in his direction and smiled. He guessed him to be an intelligent man, he would no doubt make enquiries into the family situation, find out a few facts for himself.

He looked at Sarah, his grandmother, she appeared quite haughty, but she was interested in him, he could tell. She, too frequently looked in his direction, what was going through *her* mind? She seemed friendly enough but he judged her to be inquisitive, *that* could definitely work in his favour.

Then there was Arabella, his stepmother; very young to assume that role, she did not appear to be older than around thirty. She smiled at him a lot, she had a lovely open, honest face; she could not be devious if she tried, he decided.

She caught him watching her. "You must meet the twins tomorrow, they are only six but I know they will want to get to know you. They are very inquisitive, like most children of six. No doubt they will ask you all sorts of questions, they do not meet many strangers. They will want to know all about life in London and what you do at school. Speaking of which, do you have any ambitions for when you have finished your education?"

"I would definitely like to live in the countryside, farm maybe."

Charles looked up sharply, "Surely you would miss city life."

"I do not really see much of it, being at school most of my time, but Aunt Ethel took me to the country almost every holiday and I absolutely loved it." He paused here then added bravely, "It must be in my blood."

There it is again, thought Charles, the boy is playing cruel games with me, he knows who I am and is seeing just how far he can push me. But even as he thought these things, he looked across at his son to find him staring into space. Surely, if he were playing games, he would have shot him a spiteful glance at the time of speaking. The boy was either very clever or entirely innocent. He would have to take charge of him. Take an interest in him so he had little chance of idle conversation with the rest of the family. Arabella had saved his reputation by having the twins. Their future was mapped out, they had village buildings dedicated to them, there was, unfortunately no room for this son of his. Guilt overwhelmed him. Louis was his flesh and blood, how could he do him out of his rightful inheritance. Surely he owed it to Colette to one day make him his heir. He could feel himself getting indigestion. His meal was lying very heavy. He was drinking too much wine and his father was noticing the fact. There would be another argument...and *that* would make him drink more...then the drinking would prevent him from sorting out the enormous dilemma that faced him. He wished he could discuss the matter with Arabella. She was his best friend. She had the ability to see matters much clearer than he. She would, no doubt, find a solution...and it would be a solution so simple that he would wonder why he had not thought of it himself. Dear Arabella, he really *did* love her; she deserved better.

Charles was becoming maudlin and foggy headed, the wine was not his first drink of the day...and the pain was back, that niggling little pain in his side that he had noticed of late.

Henry surveyed his table with interest. The ladies were very animated tonight; happy to have a new interest in the house but his son was beginning to worry him. He had drunk far too much wine and he suspected that he had been at the brandy bottle before dinner. He was the only member of the family that appeared uncomfortable at the sudden, unannounced arrival of their visitor. He tried to recall his son's reaction to the newcomer earlier in the day but he had not taken much notice at the time. Tonight, however, was a different matter, Charles was clearly fretting about something. The ladies would not have noticed because their attention was clearly being held by their, very personable, young visitor. Now what could be disturbing Charles? Did he know more about this young man than he was willing to divulge? Had he had dealings with his family that were an embarrassment? Perhaps he gambled in his young days whilst abroad. Could he have moved on without paying his debts? No, that was unthinkable, Charles was many things but not dishonest. All the same, something was troubling this son of his...

His daughter-in-law's voice broke through his thoughts; she was addressing Louis. "Would you like to come riding with me tomorrow? It promises to be a fine day."

Louis answered sheepishly, "Thank you, Arabella, I am tempted to accept but I am feeling a little...er...uncomfortable." He blushed visibly.

"Oh," she smiled sympathetically, "yes, that is often the case when one has been in the saddle for a long period when not used to it. Charles should not have kept you out so long."

"I enjoyed it, honestly, at the time."

"We must remember to break you in gently. Perhaps a walk then, I love walking, we can get to know one another properly."

"I shall look forward to it." Louis looked appreciatively at Arabella. He was not just being polite, he really did like her. He had the distinct feeling they would become firm friends. Of all the people at the table he felt most at ease with her.

It was another bright and breezy day. Louis glanced sideways at his walking companion. Arabella's hair was blowing wildly in the wind, at times her face was nearly obscured from view. Every now and then she would turn around and let the breeze blow her hair back from her face, she was so beautiful, how could his father have not wanted to marry her?

They walked down the long drive of Oxley House with Arabella pointing out interesting features along the way; the rose garden, planted in remembrance of her grandmother; a cluster of young oaks planted when Charles senior had died. The ash grove in the distance, that Obadiah had planted when the house was built, and far away, in the distance, the row of tall poplars that separated Oxley from Barcada.

"Charles says you prefer the Barcada house." Louis looked expectantly at his stepmother, he felt close to her, he did not feel he was gathering information for his cause, he was genuinely interested in her views.

"I much prefer the house, it is more..." she paused, then finished, "...feminine. It has low ceilings and beams, latched doors and latticed windows. I will show you if you like, we could take a circular walk and return that way."

"I would like that very much."

"It would take some time," she smiled in his direction, "have you recovered from yesterday?"

"Not completely, but a long walk might help." He did not mind how far he walked with her; it was nice to relax away from the house.

"The twins are looking forward to meeting you after their lessons, they each have a swing in the orchard, I think they are hoping to lure you down there."

"A swing sounds fun."

"And I must show you the summer house, and the walled garden with the old wisteria, and the clematis is looking beautiful at the moment, masses of flowers…"

She paused and laughed, "I am sorry, you have probably gathered that I absolutely love gardens and flowers."

"I like them too. Aunt Ethel had a small garden with a brick path leading to an apple tree. She used to sit under it and read in the Summer. I can see her now in her old straw hat."

He had a faraway look in his eyes and Arabella noticed he was blinking rapidly to keep the tears at bay.

"I can see you miss her, you will call upon those memories many times in the future, but it will get easier. I remember when my mother and grandmother died I thought I would never laugh again." She closed the narrow gap between them and linked her arm through his. He looked sideways and slightly down, his sad eyes met her understanding ones, and they both smiled in mutual empathy.

They continued in silence, each in their own thoughts. She was thinking how much like Harnser he was, easy to talk to with a lot of young, male charisma. He even had the floppy hair, though it was slightly darker. He had lovely eyes, almost feminine, with long lashes. Suddenly she really missed Harnser, she had not seen him since Christmas, when he had made his customary visit home. She saw him only twice a year, sometimes three times, always at Barcada. She always wanted to go to the stream with him, but had never dared put her thoughts into actions, for fear they were seen together.

Maria still helped with the children, but only on one day a

299

week when Nanny had a half-day off. She liked Maria; they had become firm friends. The arrangements were working well.

Amy and Emily had never returned to Harnser.

Arabella and Louis reached the end of the drive and turned left, then left again into the long Rookery Lane. She still had her arm linked with his; it felt comfortable.

Louis was full of mixed emotions. He had arrived with hostile feelings for the Sandersons, but now felt a kind of kinship with them, maybe not his father, but definitely with Arabella and Henry...and he had arrived only yesterday. He felt a remarkable closeness to Arabella, he was enjoying walking with her, she was so enthusiastic. She regularly pointed out wild flowers, most of which he would have missed. He loved the sound of her laugh, tinkling with clarity. There was something about her he found dangerously attractive. It was as if she had secrets that she would never divulge, an ethereal quality that he found exciting. She regularly looked up at him and smiled, exerting a gentle pressure on his arm as she did so. He was fourteen, he had never been this close to a young woman before and he was enjoying it. He thought of the dormitory discussions about girls, that had seemed to evolve during the last year or so. Several of the boys had told stories of their exploits with young ladies; one even boasted of having kissed his friend's sister, who was two years older. No one believed this of course; all the same it had been exciting to hear. The boldest revelation had been from a gentleman farmer's son, who had followed a farmhand into a barn where he had met a housemaid...he should not have watched of course, but every boy in the dormitory was glad he had...

Louis smiled down at Arabella; the boy's barn story somehow seemed sordid now. This, on the other hand, was beautiful and he would not tell a soul about it...He realised, with sudden alarm, that he was falling in love with his stepmother. He had never been in love before.

They turned off Rookery Lane to the right, where, about two hundred yards further on, they reached the bridge. They leaned over the warm bricks to watch the stream babble along its way below. The water was clear and sparkling. Arabella remembered the first time she had brought Harnser to the bridge. "Shall we have a race?" she suggested excitedly.

They found twigs and raced their 'boats' under the bridge and down the waterfall several times before running down the slope to the grass beside the stream.

"It is beautiful here, Arabella."

"Yes, it is my favourite place on the estate."

"It is so peaceful."

"Yes."

Louis looked around him. "There is a seat too. Shall we sit down for a while?"

They sat and watched the stream, listened to the birds and closed their eyes in the warmth of the sun. No, the dormitory boys would never believe this.

"It seems incredible that no one else is around," said Louis presently in a hushed voice.

"No one comes here accept me and an old man from the village," she laughed, "Well, and the pig of course."

He looked at her puzzled, "The pig?"

She told him the story of the runaway pig. "Everything to this day gets blamed on the pig."

"Do pigs live that long?"

She laughed, "I have no idea, I do not want to know, it would completely spoil the stories."

"Why does nobody come here?"

"It is supposed to be haunted."

"And is it?"

"Maybe, I do not know. I find it very peaceful here." She suddenly realised she had taken no one but Harnser there before. She voiced her thoughts, "Can this be our secret, Louis?"

"What?"

"That this place is not frightening."

"Of course."

"You see, I know it is selfish, but I would hate to see it crowded."

"Who is supposed to haunt it?"

She told him the story of Marcie and that Old Joe was her son. "Did Joe make the seat?"

"No."

He waited for her to expand but she just stared ahead at the stream.

"Do you know who made the seat, Arabella?" he prompted gently.

"It is rumoured in the village that a young man made it for his sweetheart, but he does not live here anymore."

"And his sweetheart?"

"She married someone else," she said softly.

They sat in silence, her thoughts with Harnser and Louis' with her. It was the nearest to heaven he had ever been.

An hour later after a walk to the far side of the copse and a view of the marshes, they headed in the direction of Barcada. On the way Louis talked about his school, of London and of his aunt Ethel. He wanted to tell her his secret, but did not want to hurt her; he could never hurt Arabella. She was expecting her son to inherit the estate, their future was secure, how could he be the one to rend it asunder? He prayed his Aunt Ethel would understand, but he kept seeing her transparent hands...her watery eyes...and hearing the pleading in her fading voice.

"There is Barcada," Arabella's voice interrupted his thoughts, "Is it not beautiful?"

He could see what she meant, the sun was warm on the mellow bricks, the latticed windows twinkled invitingly. It looked comfortable, nestling among the trees.

They walked the last part of the lane and turned into the front yard. The old sign creaked on its chains in the fresh breeze. Arabella turned towards him and said laughingly, "We have used gallons of oil on that sign, it does no good at all."

He felt a great rush of warmth toward her, he did not want to enter the house, to be with other people, he wanted to keep walking and talking forever with her. He felt even more anger towards his father, who had deceived this lovely woman. He wanted to tell her that Charles was unworthy of her, that she deserved better, that if he himself were her husband he would

302

never treat her so shabbily. Instead he smiled, imagining the huge oil can, and the sign that laughed in its wake.

Leaving Barcada, Arabella and Louis set forth on the last leg of their walk, the mile long track between the two properties.

"Well, what did you think of *my* ancestral home?" Arabella smiled mischievously at her new-found friend, she liked Louis, she felt very much at ease with him. She hoped they would see a lot of him in the future. "Not so grand I admit and not so many portraits but given time…"

He laughed back at her, he was enjoying the day, it was the first day he had really laughed since his aunt had died and it was all down to this lovely lady. "I can see what you mean about it being more feminine, it is a beautiful property. It would be difficult to choose between the two but, on balance, I think…maybe…um…"

She laughed again, "The sign might keep you awake at night?"

"There is that."

"I never really hear it, but when I do it is somehow comforting. Charles thinks I am mad to prefer Barcada but, if I am, my father is too."

"I like your father."

"*Everyone* likes Father, I am very lucky to have him, he adores the children, they were born here, did you know?"

"No."

"Strange really, they were, but I was not."

"No?"

"No, there was another one of those famous family rifts."

She told Louis all about her grandmother running off with the Major and how Charles senior had kept the house from her and then had tracked them down and persuaded the family to return to Barcada.

"That was when I promised to marry Charles, I was twelve."

"Twelve? That is younger than I am."

"Yes, looking back I find it quite amazing but, family duty and all that… I did not think I had a choice." She suddenly realized how it would sound to him. "Oh, I grew very fond of Charles, we had plenty of time to get to know one another." She paused then said passionately, "Make your own choices, Louis, and make them very carefully, the heart sometimes makes sounder judgements then the head."

She was staring ahead at the row of poplars. He felt she had momentarily forgotten she had company. What had she meant? Did she regret marrying his father, and if so, why?

He thought of the stream and the seat. Had she always gone there alone? Who had made the bench? And for whom? He felt the day had given him more questions than answers and all of a sudden he wanted to unravel the mysteries. He remembered the softness of her voice when he had asked what happened to the young man's sweetheart. '*She married someone else,*' she had said sadly. Was that 'someone else' his father?

In two days Louis' life had changed immeasurably. He felt part of this family with all their secrets – he had one of his own. More and more he sensed that Arabella did not know she had married a widower, and he was almost certain that *none* of the family knew that the widower was also a father. He would have to tread carefully.

"Do the children love Oxley?" He did not know why the question had popped into his head.

"That is a strange question considering it is their home."

"I am sorry, I did not mean to pry."

"Not at all, they know little else, they have nothing to compare it with, except Barcada. Edward certainly loves visiting Barcada. I think he is going to be especially musical."

Louis wondered why the two should be linked. Was Barcada synonymous with music? There were times, and this was one of them, that Arabella's thoughts seemed to be elsewhere.

"I understand Charles is going to accompany you on your return to London."

"He is?"

"Apparently so, I think he has taken a liking to you, young Louis," She linked her arm in his again, "As have we all," she finished, giving him one of her lovely smiles.

Two weeks later Charles and Louis returned to London. The boy was loth to leave. His visit to Oxley had not helped him make a decision, in fact it had complicated matters. He had grown so close to Arabella on their many walks and horse rides that he knew he could not hurt her. Whilst he knew that Oxley was not dear to *her*, it was her son's inheritance and, as such, how could he steal it away from him?

But, on the other side of the coin was his father, to whom Louis had found it more difficult to get close. Their conversations for the most part had been polite. Only rarely had they shared any sort of empathy. Louis felt his defences were always up against Charles, he wanted to love him as his mother had done, but there was this anger simmering just beneath the surface, because he did not acknowledge him publicly as his son. Louis wondered what plans Charles would make for him, he was in his hands, although Charles did not realise that he knew it. There was something else about his father that bothered the boy – he frequently appeared to be the worse for drink.

Louis liked his grandparents. Both Henry and Sarah had made him welcome and insisted he spend all his school holidays at Oxley. His father had not appeared keen, and the boy felt that new arrangements might be in store for him; he doubted he would see the inside of Aunt Ethel's house again.

Then of course there were the twins, his half brother and sister. He had had fun playing with them; they were like their mother – easy company, very likable. All of a sudden he felt much older than his fourteen years, and very lonely. It was a long time to Summer when he would see them all again and there was no Aunt Ethel in London. He had promised to write, but that made him sadder, a page of writing was no substitute for the warmth of Arabella's arm linked with his, as they made their way to the stream and the sturdy bench with the secret inscription. Yes, he had examined it thoroughly when alone one day, and was even more sure it had been made for his stepmother.

He could not wait for Summer – and his next visit to Oxley.

CHAPTER FOUR

America 1879

The little girl sat rigid on the chair by the bed, her eyes never leaving the face of the woman that lay there, pale and still.

"Amy...?"

"Yes, Mother, I am here." The girl leaned forward, taking the woman's hand in hers.

The woman's eyes closed again and the child resumed her position on the chair. A door behind her opened and she heard, rather than saw, her Pa. "Come out of there, Amy, it's no place for a child."

"I am not a child, I am twelve."

"In my book that's a child. Your Ma is sleeping, she doesn't know you're here."

"Mother does know, she keeps waking, I want to stay."

"As you like," his voice was unusually quiet and soft. "I've got chores to do, I'll look in later. Make sure you keep the fire up..." His voice sounded husky, causing the child to look up at him. He cares, she thought, he does care, he had spent so little time in the room that she had felt annoyed with him. Now she softened her feelings towards him and felt the impulse to run to him; to put her arms around him and comfort him. She wanted to give him some warm human contact; she also needed *him* to comfort *her*. She needed him to tell her that her mother would get better and that they would all go home to England; to the rolling green countryside, the little grey, flint churches, the music halls and to their kinfolk.

She had never tired of the stories her mother had told her about the theatres and England, but there were some things her mother had seemed very reluctant to talk about. She talked about them going home to their kinfolk, but gave no details of

306

them. When she asked questions her mother would laugh nervously, with vague promises to tell her everything 'one day', and that they must not upset Pa with talk of England. This was something else she did not understand since Pa had folk in the old country as well.

"This is a fresh start," her mother would say determinedly, "We are Americans now." But the resolve never lasted long and, when Pa was out in the fields until sunset, Emily and Amy would look at books from England. The little girl would see the longing in the faraway expression on her mother's face.

"Will you take me to England, Mother?"

"One day."

"Will I see my father again?"

"Pa is your father."

"Yes, but my *other* father, will I see *him* again?"

"Pa is your father."

She always knew when to stop asking questions. Her mother's manner would change and she would feel distanced from her; a cold, lonely feeling that she had no wish to perpetuate. Even so, she hugged the hazy memory of a kind, fair-haired man, who played music to her as she went to sleep.

As the years had passed, Amy had stopped asking questions about her kinfolk. She could talk of England, that was acceptable, but she knew not to ask questions about family…instead she learned to listen when her mother was in melancholic mood. *Those* were the times she was most likely to learn something…if only she could recall her father's name…

She shuddered and suddenly remembered her Pa's instruction to keep the fire up.

She put some more logs in the grate and watched as a flurry of bright sparks leapt up the chimney. She kept staring until she was sure that the logs had taken hold, then returned to her vigil by the bed.

Was it just a week ago that she had been brought into this same room to have a quick peek at her new baby brother? A brother who had struggled for only three days before Parson Alder had been called to minister to him, in case he did not live. And now there was talk that they would be buried together... her little brother Richard and her mother, who seemed to have given up the fight.

Amy felt cold and alone despite the fire and her Pa, who had found so many 'chores' to do outside in the dark during the last week.

She wondered about her baby brother; she had seen him only a few times, but his little face was imprinted on her memory...she knew she would remember him in her prayers forever more. She wondered why he had been named Richard John; John was for Pa, but she did not know a Richard. She made a mental note to ask her Pa...next time he felt able to talk of such matters. Her Pa was not an emotional man, leastways not to her, but he loved her mother, treating her like a fragile doll, and took good care of them both. She wondered how he had persuaded her mother, who liked the bustle of city life, to live on a cattle ranch, miles from the nearest town.

She had never understood that.

Her eyes wandered around the room and came to rest on the trunk. She always thought of it as *the* trunk because it held such interesting things from England. Her mother would sometimes go through the contents one by one, telling her little stories along the way.

The ocarina was in there; a little musical instrument her father had bought for her when she was four years old. Her mother said it should remain in the trunk for safekeeping. If her mother loved England so much, why could they not have stayed there with Father?

"Amy..." The girl was brought back to the present by her mother's weak voice.

"Yes, Mother, I am still here."

"I love you, Amy..." Tears trickled down the pale face, making the child cry too. "Pa and my baby...I love you all."

"I know, Mother, I know, I love you too...and my baby brother."

"Your father..."

She had said 'father' not 'pa'.

"Yes, I remember my father, what was his name, Mother?"

"Your father was Harnser." The faint semblance of a sad smile played around the woman's mouth as her eyes closed once again.

"I remember him, Mother, I remember a tall, kind man with fair hair. When I think of him I hear music...beautiful music."

There was a long silence as the woman gathered the strength to continue. "Yes, he loved music, the flute...the piccolo, and of course...the little ocarina. I am so glad you remember him...he was your *real* father...the one that truly loved you...Robert was..."

"Robert? Mother, who was Robert?"

"Robert was..," her voice faded.

"Mother..."

"A photograph..." Her eyes opened briefly. Robert is a photograph...he did not want us, Harnser saved us..."

Her eyes closed again and it was a full five minutes before she said, "Harnser, The Stick Man of Little Pecking, he loved us, Amy...you must write...write to Harnser...he is quite near...I can hear the music..."

That last sentence was to stay in the mind of the girl forever, for it was the last her mother spoke.

Three days later the woman and child were laid to rest, together in one coffin, in the grounds of a white wooden church, high on a windy hill...

...as soft tendrils of blonde hair blew across a little girl's face.

CHAPTER FIVE

For the next four years Louis spent his holidays at Oxley. He had never divulged his secret, knowing he had time on his side.

The Sandersons became his family.

Charles made sure the London solicitors would not talk to Louis.

Louis never went back to Aunt Ethel's house.

Charles had hunted through two houses to find the elusive birth and marriage certificates but to no avail – he still had his suspicion that his son had them in his possession. He still thought he was playing games with him and this ensured his relationship with the brandy bottle, and almost any other bottle that came his way.

Louis' schoolboy crush on his stepmother gradually matured into a deep friendship – she was the one person who had his total loyalty. He remained fond of his grandparents, whom he knew as Henry and Sarah, and his Uncle Bertie who, like most people, he called Major. Louis also loved his stepbrother and sister.

He frequently wrote to Grace and made visits to her whenever possible – visits that his Suffolk family knew nothing about.

There were three more years until his twenty-first birthday, when he would be free of Charles' jurisdiction.

They were both silently aware of the fact.

Christmas eighteen hundred and eighty-two proved memorable for Louis for two reasons – the first concerned the inevitable showdown with his father.

The holiday began quietly enough, routines had been established over the years.

Just before Christmas, at dinner one evening, Louis sensed

an atmosphere. Charles was tipsy, Henry was angry, Sarah was tense and Arabella was clearly embarrassed. Charles' florid complexion appeared to dominate the table, he frequently dropped his eating utensils and each time the clattering jarred the nerves of everyone present, Charles would stare defiantly at his father – daring him to reprimand his adult son in public.

The ladies made attempts at light conversation and it was one of these brave efforts that finally caused Charles to snap.

"What are your plans for next year, Louis?" Sarah asked in all innocence.

"I think I am expected to travel."

"Expected?"

"Yes."

"I do not understand, dear, expected by whom?"

"By those faceless solicitors who issue me my orders and provide my allowance, I have never met them," he smiled, "I sometimes wonder if they exist."

Charles threw down his knife and fork with even more noise than his previous accidents had caused. "I thought you might actually enjoy it, not everyone gets the chance to travel, but if it is so abhorrent to you, you might like to try working for a living instead."

A silence fell over the dining table.

"I was joking," the young man said, shocked. "I did not know you had arranged it."

"Who do you think arranged it?"

"The solicitors are my guardians, I assumed…"

"You assume too much, young man. No doubt you will all be happy to excuse me."

With a brief glance at his horrified parents, Charles pushed himself from the table and stumbled to the door of the dining room, with Henry in hot pursuit.

"Finish your meal, Louis," Sarah instructed kindly, "None of this is your fault. Charles is tetchy today, Henry will talk to him."

The ladies and Louis continued eating, but the atmosphere was strained until Henry returned.

"Charles would like to talk to you in his study, Louis, when

311

you have finished your meal, of course. He would like to apologize, no doubt. His behaviour was inexcusable."

The knock was barely audible but obviously his father had been waiting for it, for the door was opened almost immediately.

Louis followed his father across the study where he was motioned to one of the leather armchairs beside the curtained windows.

They sat down with only a low table between them. The table held two glasses and a jug of water.

"Would you like some water, Louis?"

"Yes please, Sir."

Charles sighed heavily, "I thought we had dispensed with the Sir."

"I thought in the circumstances…"

"Do you mean because we are in private?" Charles looked levelly at his son.

"No, I mean because I have incurred your wrath."

"I would like to apologize for my behaviour at the table, it was provoked only partly by you."

"Oh?"

"Yes, I know it is no excuse, but I have been in pain all day and have tried to alleviate it by drinking. Waste of time and good spirits of course," he attempted a defeatist smile, which evoked pity in the younger man.

Louis reminded himself that this was the man who was denying him his birthright. He did not want to feel sorry for him.

They faced each other over the table and the water, both at a loss for words until Charles, as the elder, felt it incumbent upon him to break the heavy silence. "You know who I am, don't you, Louis?"

"Yes, Sir."

The Sir had made a comeback.

"How long have you known?"

"Since just before my aunt died."

"*She* told you?"

"Yes."

"So you have been playing games with me for four years?"

"Not games, Sir."

"How would you describe your behaviour?"

Louis wanted to say that his own behaviour had been no more deceitful than his father's, that they were as guilty as each other for 'playing games' as his father put it. He chose his words carefully, mindful that Charles had been drinking, although he now appeared more in control than earlier.

"When I first came to Oxley," he began measuredly, " it soon became apparent to me that your family did not know of my existence. You were aware of it, Sir, so I took my cue from you. I had no wish to cause unhappiness to innocent people, and it was obvious you wanted to leave matters as they were." Louis hesitated here but continued to look his father straight in the eye. "I do not call that 'playing games', Sir."

Charles lowered his eyes and leaned forward for his glass, wishing it contained something stronger than water. This son of his had a presence about him, a strength of character that the older man found attractive although it put him at a distinct disadvantage.

Louis saw Charles' discomfort and steeled himself to continue. "I do not think you would have thanked me if I had announced my relationship to you at dinner, on my first evening at Oxley."

Aunt Ethel's face loomed large in his mind and he heard her fading voice, *Do not let anybody take advantage of you, and remember he is not a bad man.* Her face and her white pillows faded as his father spoke again.

"You are quite right of course," he said quite strongly, and then, before his son's very eyes, his face crumpled, a pained expression gripped his face and he dropped his head into his hands, which were working at his forehead as if trying to erase the tension.

Louis sat rigid, the clock ticked loudly, should he call someone? There was a bell-pull on the wall behind the desk. Suddenly he remembered that Charles had said he had been in pain all day, there was concern in his voice as he said, "Are you alright, Sir? Is the pain back? Shall I ring the bell?"

He was on his feet and crossing to the desk when Charles' weary voice reached him. "Do not ring the bell."

Louis stopped in his tracks, turned on his heel and returned to his former position opposite his father, who now raised his troubled head and looked at him tiredly. "Pain, pain, pain," he said wearily, "Pain in my stomach, pain in my head and pain in my heart – What am I to do, Louis?"

The young man was taken aback; he had never before been asked for advice from an elder, he was out of his depth. He thought it best to keep quiet, he did not want his father to become angry again, he had consumed too much alcohol to be having a rational conversation, let alone to resolve eighteen year old problems in one evening.

"Would you like me to leave now?"

Charles flopped back into his chair, sighing heavily. "I would rather you stayed and talked to me," he said tiredly, "Unless of course you have other things to do."

"There is nothing of importance…"

"Tell me what Ethel told you."

Louis began his story, slowly at first, but as he went on he noticed he had his father's full attention.

Once or twice Charles refilled their glasses and he appeared to be more alert.

"…so you see," Louis concluded, "I felt I owed it to Aunt Ethel to come here and stake my claim to Oxley."

"And will you…stake your claim I mean?"

Louis looked his father in the eyes. "That, Sir, is what I have been trying to decide for four years."

"I have listened to your story with interest, Louis. Now you must listen to mine."

Charles told his son how he had promised to marry Arabella to reunite the family and how he had then met Colette and fallen in love with her.

"I was completely honest with your mother, I told her I was promised to another but…" he trailed off, obviously thinking back. "I loved her so much, Louis, I could not leave her all alone in France – she had no family except a grandmother, who was very old. She pleaded with me to bring her to England and when we discovered she was with child, I felt it was the right thing to do.

"All the time I told myself I would resolve the matter. I was determined to stand up to my father and grandfather, tell them that I could not marry Arabella. You would think it would be easy, would you not? Family pressure can be very burdensome; one gets carried along with what is expected of one until there seems no way out. Oxley is of tremendous importance to my father, to *me* even, you would have to have had my childhood to understand the enormous pressure under which I felt. Then your mother became ill and I decided she was much more important than Oxley…"

Charles' eyes had misted over; the pain was back on his face. "I did not want to reject you, Louis, but I could not look at you without seeing your mother…it was so painful, and always there was the pressure of family duty. In the end it was easier to go along with their wishes. I told myself I would not be of much use to you if I were disinherited, that I would at least be able to give you a secure future. And always in the back of my head was the notion that one day…somehow…I might be able to put matters right." He paused, looking to his son for understanding. "You do not know how much it has meant to me to ride the estate with you. You are my son, Louis. I have never disowned you. I *still* want to resolve matters".

"There was eight years between my birth and Edward's."

Louis was trying to understand why his father could not have resolved the problem long before he married Arabella. "I was not illegitimate, why did you not tell them you had been married and had a son? You could have still married Arabella, kept your promise…"

"No, you do not understand, I did not wait years to marry again, the wedding was already planned for when Arabella was eighteen."

"You mean you married again just after my mother died?"

Charles hung his head in shame. "Yes," he said quietly, "five months later."

He saw the horror on his son's face and continued quickly with embarrassment. "If your mother had lived I would have called off the wedding, I was prepared to do that, I promise you, the pressure, Louis, was unimaginable. I am not a monster. I…"

His son's accusing eyes were unbearable. How much should he tell him? Should he reveal the twins were not his natural children. Did he have his son's loyalty? Or would he expose him to Henry and Sarah? He wanted to tell Louis that he had remained faithful to his mother, remained faithful because he could not risk another woman dying. He had to tell him something, he could not bear the look of contempt.

"I am going to confide in you, man to man."

Louis waited.

"The reason the twins were born eight years after my marriage was because…was because…"

The silence was deafening. Louis could see his father's discomfort. This would have to be good, he decided; if he was ever going to feel respect for this man again.

"… the reason was because our marriage was in name only."

"In name only…"

"Yes…your mother, Louis…I could not forget your mother…"

He was redeeming himself; he was evoking pity again. Louis stared hard at Charles. He knew he had the upper hand. "Are you expecting me to believe that… for eight years…"

"I cannot make you believe it. I only know it is the truth. Why else do you think I drink so much, I am not proud of my past behaviour. I owe Arabella a lot. I cannot hurt her anymore. *She* expects Edward to inherit Oxley and *I* know that it is *your* right. Can *you* see a solution? Because, if so, I wish you would enlighten me."

He believed him, much has he had not wanted to, he believed him. He began to see his father as Ethel had seen him.

Henry was over seventy years old, too old for these sort of revelations and what of Arabella – his best friend, Arabella. No, he could not destroy her ordered world.

I am sorry, Aunt Ethel, he said in his head, I would have done it for you if it had been at all possible, but…it is not…

The two men sat in dejected silence; the fire had burned too low for resurrection, with neither noticing. The water jug was nigh on empty. Snow was beginning to fall silently on the other side of the windows, heralding a white Christmas.

The following evening a subdued family assembled around the dining table for an early meal. All day Charles and Louis had been conspicuous by their absence around the house. They had been out walking; they had been ensconced in the study talking; they had been riding; but the biggest noticeable factor was that they had been together.

They had decided to keep their secret.

The ladies were almost frightened to make conversation for fear that the previous evening might be repeated. They need not have worried.

Gradually the tension eased and talk turned to the Christmas Eve church service. They were looking forward to some entertainment, a tradition in Little Pecking on this night.

As usual there would be the Flinton musicians; the little band of fiddlers that performed at every event of note in the area. There would be solo carollers; the children's choir and, every year, a guest performer, which was always a surprise; a secret that the Reverend Hanley kept close to his chest for at least three months beforehand.

The snow had continued to fall off and on all day, to the delight of Edward and Eleanor, who had spent most of the afternoon out of doors.

This year was to be their first visit to church on Christmas Eve.

They were ten years old.

Lanterns had been placed at intervals along both sides of the church path, sending dancing shadows on to the pristine snow beneath. On every ledge of the church and on the tops of each gravestone was around two inches of snow, sparkling like millions of diamonds in the light of the lanterns, and of the moon, which appeared at intervals between the snow laden clouds. The children could not wait to leave their carriage at the gate; they had chosen to ride with Louis and Nanny and felt very grown up.

"It is beautiful," enthused Eleanor, "why have we not been allowed to come before?"

"Because you were too little, you would probably have fallen asleep half way through, you might tonight," said Louis.

"I will wager I do not," said Edward defiantly. He could already hear the organ music filtering out through the porch door, where a warm orangey glow shone out to greet them.

"I will have no talk of wagers on holy ground," came a voice at their side, "especially on such a sacred night."

"I am sorry, Nanny," the boy said meekly, but almost immediately grabbed his sister's hand, put his head close to hers and whispered, "How does she hear through all that hair and wool?"

"She would not hear if we were being good," Eleanor whispered back.

"Keep up," came the voice again, "remember this is a treat, you should be home in bed."

Louis smiled down on the twins, they were a mischievous pair and heaven help anybody that came between them. Of a sudden, despite the magical atmosphere, despondency fell upon him; he was going to miss this family of his when he left after Christmas. He was inextricably entwined with them now, but, much more important, he loved them all – even his father.

As always on Christmas Eve the church was packed. The Sandersons filed into their reserved pews. Together with the Haverhams from The Hall, they were one of the last families to take their places and one of the first to leave. This ensured that the whole churchgoing community always witnessed their comings and goings.

The service followed its usual pattern until about three quarters of the way through, when the Reverend Hanley announced that their guest performer, a soprano from Illingham was unable to attend due to illness. In her place, he said, he had managed to persuade Harnser Elliot to play the flute and the piccolo for them.

A hush fell over the packed congregation as Harnser made his way to the front of the church. Although asked many times since his first visit back to his home village, he had always declined in deference to Walter, who had ranted so jealously at him in the Home Wood. Last evening however, when Reverend Hanley had called at the cottage to plead with the musician, Walter had insisted that Harnser should play.

As the haunting strains of the flute permeated the little flint church not one person in the building was unaffected. They were held spellbound.

The older villagers were remembering a similar night thirty-nine years earlier, when Harnser's father had captured their imaginations and stolen the heart of Maria Porter.

Tears fell down Maria's cheeks as the haunting melodies and Christmas tunes filled the church. Walter placed an arm around her shoulders, James held her arm protectively, but the tears fell copiously.

A few rows in front and across the aisle, a younger woman was experiencing the same emotions. Arabella too, was crying with a mixture of love and pride, as her children's father held the congregation spellbound. Her throat felt constricted, she could not take her eyes off her erstwhile lover. She was glad she was in the front pew; Maria's tears of joy and pride were to be expected, but how would she explain her own. She hoped Charles, who stood by her side, would not glance sideways. She cautiously took her handkerchief and dabbed at her face, trying to minimise the damage. She shot a furtive look along the line of enthralled faces to her left. Charles, like most others, was staring straight ahead, at the performer but, along the line, Henry was looking in her direction. Not at her, she noted, but slightly above her head, and his face wore an expression she could not fathom, was it amazement – puzzlement? She had never seen it on his face before. He did not know she was observing him. She turned her head to the right, where her children and Louis were sitting looking straight ahead.

Suddenly she realised that the music had stopped and that Vicar Hanley had resumed his position at the front of the church. "And now, for his finale, Harnser is going to play us one of his own compositions, apparently the inspiration for the piece came from a vision in this very churchyard, an earthly vision, I hasten to add. Please enjoy Harnser Elliot's 'Snow Maiden'."

Arabella's heart lurched; he had written music for her. One of his poems to her was called 'Snow Maiden'.

She thought her heart would burst with love as she sat and recited the words in her head while the music swam hauntingly around the little church. She was crying again, she dabbed at her face and dared to look back and across at Maria. Their eyes caught and held in the mutual appreciation of their loved one. As her eyes left the older woman she almost laughed aloud; why had she worried about the tears; almost every woman present had a handkerchief to her face!

"He's every bit as good as his father was," numerous voices were heard to utter as the parishioners filed out into the snowy night. "He won't be forgotten for a long time to come."

"*I* am going to do that one day," Edward announced to his parents as they left the church, "just you wait and see."

He turned to Louis, adding, "*and* I did not fall asleep."

"You certainly did not. Now we know how to keep you quiet and entertained." The two lagged a little behind.

"Mr Elliot is the best musician in all the world," continued Edward to no one in particular.

"Do you know him, Edward?" Louis asked, surprised.

"Oh yes, he is a friend of Grandfather, he helps me and Eleanor with our music."

"Do you see him much?"

"No, not much, only when he visits Barcada."

Something clicked in Louis' mind, he heard Arabella saying to him, '*It is rumoured in the village that a young man made it for his sweetheart, but he does not live here anymore.*'…And Mr Elliot's Christian name was Harnser. Was he the 'H' that went with the 'A' on the bench seat by the stream? If he were a betting man he would lay money on it.

On Boxing Day the snow was even deeper after a heavy overnight fall.

Edward sought out his mother, anxious to get to his grandfather's house. "The carriage is ready, Mother," he took her hand, pulling her in the direction of the door.

Arabella laughed, "It will not leave without us, Edward."

"No, but Grandfather will be waiting for us."

Yes, thought Arabella, and he will be on tenterhooks. Her heart was racing as she stepped up into the carriage to join her children. It had become a Boxing Day tradition for her and the children to spend the day at Barcada. At some point during the day Harnser would visit his elderly friend and the whole group would play parlour games and generally enjoy themselves. It was a day to which Arabella looked forward all year. Today however was going to follow a slightly different pattern, for Arabella had at last given in to her desire to meet Harnser at the stream.

Having delivered its occupants to Barcada, the carriage returned to Oxley; it would collect them again at the end of the day. "Do not be long, Mother," Edward called from the front door, "Mr Elliot may call and you will miss all the fun."

Arabella turned and waved as the children scampered indoors into the warmth. She turned onto the track that led up to Rookery Lane, the snow was deep and fluffy, her feet sending flurries into the air as she walked.

The children were ten and it perturbed her that they did not know that Harnser was their father. When they were born, and there was still a chance that Harnser's wife and child might return, the present situation seemed the best solution. She rarely wrote to Harnser, letters were dangerous; the wrong people could read them. They rarely had the opportunity to talk about their children in private. This Christmas she had been determined to meet him by the stream, so had asked her father to pass on the message. The meeting had to take place in the morning because Arabella knew that Old Joe went down to the bridge in the afternoon. She did not want to spoil Christmas but she *did* want to discuss the future.

She reached the bridge and negotiated the slope down to the seat. She brushed the snow from the seat but did not sit down; she would get cold if she sat still. She walked up and down beside the water; stopping now and again to watch the waterfall, it always fascinated her. Overhead the branches of the trees hung heavy with snow. Every now and again a bird, alighting or leaving, would send a soft flurry floating downwards. The birds were very busy, hunting for any morsel of food not covered by snow. Christmas, for them, was just another day of survival, their offspring were self sufficient – until the next brood. They did not have her weighty problems of heirs, heiresses, natural fathers, secrets, the future of Oxley, the mystery of a young relative and a son who looked more like his father every day – so much so that she was amazed nobody had made the connection. But then, nobody was looking for one.

She wondered if Charles ever thought about his children's origins. He had never mentioned the subject to her, but then, that had been a condition of her staying with him. One thing she found very surprising was her husband's continued drinking; he had been so relieved when she had told him she was with child. She had solved his problems. Why then did he still feel the need to over-indulge? It was the one thing that provoked arguments between them. She thought it set such a bad example to the children and she told him so. She often saw them wrinkle their noses as they kissed their father goodnight.

She was brought out of her maudlin thoughts by a wood pigeon calling from the copse. She smiled as she looked upward. She never could tell the difference between the real thing and Harnser's ocarina.

He came half-running and half-sliding down from the copse, landing at her feet in a dishevelled heap. He stood up, put his hands under her elbows and kissed her on both cheeks. Since the twins' conception, they had never again given into the passion they felt for each other; they were both married.

"Hello, Arabella," he said huskily.

Her misty eyes looked into his, "I was so proud of you."

He knew she was referring to his musical performance of the penultimate evening, "Did I pass muster?"

She smiled at his modesty. "Thank you for The Snow Maiden," she said softly.

"Did you like it?" he had no need to ask the question.

"I loved it, will you send the music to Father so that I can play it on the piano?"

"I will do better than that." He put his hand into his inside pocket and produced a sheaf of papers. "I will leave it at Barcada."

They smiled at each other; there was no need for words.

"Will you walk through the copse with me?" Even as he spoke he ushered her in front, turned away from the bridge, and walked along by the stream, to where the slope to the copse was a little less steep.

"Do you ever think about our antics on the sledge, Arabella?"

"Every time it snows, and often in between."

"I am so glad we kept our year happy."

"It was less than a year, but yes, I agree."

"How are things at home?"

She knew he was not just being polite. He worried about her home life; he was concerned for her happiness.

They walked and talked; they laughed a lot and cried a little. They saw the marshes way out in the distance, spectacular in the snow.

"I want to come home."

She held her breath, how she had longed for those words.

"I do not see enough of the children." He squinted his eyes against the bright sun, reflecting on the white expanse in front of them. "I am going to ask Florence and Richard if they will consider moving to Suffolk."

"Do you think they will? Oh, Harnser it would be wonderful to have you near again."

"I think they have accepted that Emily and Amy are not coming home," he hesitated before adding, "and so have I."

Sadness for him mingled with her own happiness. She did

not speak; she sensed where his thoughts were. She was proven right when he said, "I doubt I would recognize her now. She might not even remember me. She is fifteen years old. We could have passed each other in a London street, unknowingly."

Arabella felt his pain, "I am sure she will not have forgotten you, I can remember back to when I was four."

He smiled sadly, "I hope you are right, but that is all the more reason for me to move back this way so that I do not miss any more of the twins growing up."

Having walked back through the copse, they reached the bench seat again, and sat watching the stream.

Louis was at a loose end. He had never been invited to Barcada on Boxing Day, much to his disappointment.

He asked Charles why the Major did not come to Oxley House instead.

"One day away from home at Christmas is enough for the old chap, he is a bit set in his ways. He loves to have his immediate family all to himself. He plans the children's entertainment well in advance, so they always know they will enjoy themselves."

"Does anybody mind if I go for a walk?" Louis asked the question casually, hoping that no one would offer to accompany him. He wanted to think about his future. Charles was offering all sorts of things by way of compensation. He needed to consider them carefully.

"Would you like some company?" Charles asked, none too enthusiastically.

"I would rather go alone if you do not mind," he gave his father a knowing look, "lots to think about," he added.

Louis wondered whether to set off towards Barcada and hope that he was invited in, but he thought this action might seem a little obvious; they would have invited him had they wanted to. The thought upset him a little. Sometimes he felt very much a part of the family and then at times like this he felt isolated. There were also times when he thought of the family as two distinct halves. He was not sure why this should be because he knew Arabella and Charles were close. He could not quite put his finger on the reason for his misgivings. For four years he had wanted to confide in Arabella, not for any malicious reason, but because he did not like the fact that she was being kept in the dark.

He reached the end of the drive and turned left. At the top of the road he turned left again and realised he was heading for the bridge without having made a conscious decision. Going to the bridge with Arabella was one thing, going alone would probably exacerbate his feelings of isolation, therefore, when he came to Marcie's Lane, he kept on walking, heading for the village.

He wandered up the path to the church wondering whether to go inside, then compromised by sitting in the porch. He thought how different it looked to how it had two nights ago. One or two people were in the churchyard, walking slowly, picking their way between the memorial stones in the snow. He got to his feet and wandered aimlessly around, reading the inscriptions on the gravestones as he went. He found a few familiar names including those of Arabella's mother and grandparents. He raised his head and looked around the almost deserted churchyard. He wondered what the future held for him and whether he would ever take his rightful place here among his ancestors.

He retraced his footsteps down the main church path and turned left toward the village. On his right was the Village Green and the little, snow covered pump house. A group of children were amusing themselves with a game of snowballs, so he sat in the pump house and watched them.

He thought of his Aunt Ethel and the promise he had made her and of everything that had happened since. He wanted to talk to her, discuss his options. He had had long conversations with his father who had suggested several ways forward. He could go travelling, not very enjoyable alone. He could go to university; his father's favoured choice, or he could go to Hampshire to Hugo's estate and learn the business thoroughly; apparently Charles and Hugo had discussed this option in depth.

He was acutely aware that Charles had not suggested he stay

at Oxley to learn the business. This too had caused him hurt, but his father had been quick to point out that if he were to do that it might arouse suspicion within the family. Charles was still promising to try and resolve matters somehow, but Louis knew from past experience that his father was not good at 'resolving matters'. Solutions are not found in bottles of spirits!

Charles had talked vaguely of 'setting him up' somewhere if Oxley – as seemed likely – went to Edward. But Charles was in no position to set anybody up until he was in sole control of Oxley; and that could be many years from now.

Louis doubted he would ever have the cool, calculated drive to take legal proceedings to claim the Oxley estate, he was far too fond of Arabella and her children.

He got to his feet, took one last look at the children playing in the snow and turned toward Rookery Lane.

Since he had no desire to go to Marcie's Bridge alone, he climbed the bank into the copse and made his way to the other side where he stood and admired the view of the marshes. He had grown to love the area. The more he came back here the harder it would be for him to turn his back on his inheritance. He could see himself becoming increasingly bitter as the years went by; for today he had finally acknowledged to himself that, more than anything else, he wanted his beloved Oxley.

He turned away from the marshes and made his way back through the copse, taking a slightly different route that would bring him out further down Rookery Lane.

He had come to a decision; he would turn his back on Oxley, before it broke his heart by turning its back on him.

The resolve lasted all of ten minutes, for it was then he heard the voices…

"…I can see there would be one problem if you returned here to live…"

It was Arabella speaking.

Louis realised he was near to the bridge, the soft snow had muffled his footsteps. He paused, not wishing to eavesdrop, but curious as to whom her companion might be. He had thought her to be at Barcada with the children. The voice continued,

"...Edward is growing to look more and more like you as the years go by – do you not think so? I sometimes wonder if I see it because I know the truth, or if it is actually so. I am worried that Charles might happen upon the two of you together one day and see it too."

"I think we should seriously consider how we might regularise the matter, Arabella. We cannot let the children get too much older before we do something about it. We both have grounds for annulment, don't forget."

Louis' heart was thudding so loudly in his chest that he thought the pair, seated below on the bench, would easily hear it. He hardly dared breathe for fear of giving away his presence. Edward and Eleanor were not Charles' children. He did not know whether he was more shocked or excited. A few moments ago he had been ready to turn his back on Oxley but now...

The full implications of what he had just heard hit him like a ton of bricks. There was only one true heir to Oxley, Charles aside, and that was himself. His melancholy turned to elation, he wanted to shout out aloud. He could almost see his Aunt Ethel smiling. He tried to calm his thudding heart. Surely his father would make him his heir now.

He came down to earth with a bump. How was he going to break the news to his father without causing scandal and mayhem in the family? His thoughts were all over the place. He would never have thought that Arabella could be unfaithful. Then he remembered what Charles had told him about the marriage being in name only for eight years. It was understandable that Arabella could have looked elsewhere for love. But what then? It was highly unlikely that the marriage had suddenly been consummated at the precise time that Arabella was being unfaithful...But if that were not the case his father must know that the twins were not his own.

Louis was getting confused. If both Charles and Arabella knew the truth about the children's parentage, why couldn't Charles bequeath the Oxley estate to him? Nothing made sense.

He leaned against a tree trunk, well hidden if Arabella and her companion should suddenly leave for Barcada. He peeped from his hiding place, trying to ascertain whether the mystery man was indeed Harnser Elliot. He was almost certain it was, although he had heard his voice only a few times in the church on Christmas Eve.

"I must get back to the children, it is nearly lunch time," he heard Arabella say.

"I will see you all this afternoon, I will stay here a little longer, although I do not suppose many people are about."

Louis heard Arabella call goodbye. Her voice came from further away so he imagined her to be up on the lane. He kept still for five minutes or so then peeped out again to see the man leaving the stream.

When he had gone, Louis made his way down the slope and took their places on the bench seat...he realised that they had just presented him with a further option...but was it one he dared to take?

After much deliberation Louis decided to bide his time. If he were lucky, Arabella and Harnser could well solve his problems for him. They had spoken of annulments and of regularising matters concerning the children. If they were to carry out their plans it would necessitate making the whole situation public knowledge – he could afford to wait. When the explosion came, no doubt someone would write to him and tell him all about it – that would be the best time to stake his claim. When Henry realized that the male Sanderson line was about to become extinct, Louis would be his saviour.

In the mean time he would go far away and undertake his father's favoured option.

There were so many secrets at Oxley that he feared he might reveal one by accident.

The way he saw it was that Charles may or may not know that he was not the twin's father, but Henry and Sarah were certainly in the dark.

He and Charles had their own secret which *nobody* else knew.

Arabella had *her* own secret. It would appear from the conversation he had overheard that Charles might know he was not the twin's father but he had no idea who *was!*

How much did the Major know? Louis knew that Arabella was very close to her father, but there were limits to what a daughter might divulge. All things taken into consideration he thought it best to put some time and distance between himself and his complicated family situation.

Despite what he had discovered he knew that the person he would miss the most was Arabella. Her straying was understandable, but his father's continued secretiveness about his first marriage was, in his opinion, unacceptable.

So it was that Louis continued his education in Scotland – and spent his holidays with Grace.

Chapter Six

Six years later...

"I wish I could stay here forever," said Eleanor dreamily.

"What do you mean by 'here'? Edward asked, peering over the marshes.

"Oxley – here at Oxley."

"You could if you wanted to."

"You mean if I remain an old maid." Eleanor grimaced at the thought but the alternative was not attractive to her either – getting married and moving away.

"You might marry someone local, then you could stay."

"There is nobody local that I would want to marry."

The twins were sixteen years old and Eleanor often talked of marriage – to her brother at least.

"You have not met him yet, that is all."

"Can you think of a suitable husband for me within ten miles of here?"

"Not off hand."

"Well, there you are then." She pouted slightly and set her horse in motion. Edward did likewise. She continued, "You know exactly where you will be in ten years time, while I have absolutely no idea where I shall be."

"What about Nicholas? Father would let you marry *him*."

"Nicholas! Uugghh, he is old – and odd."

"He is not *that* old – and not odd really."

"He is besotted by bugs."

"Not just bugs, he is a naturalist, I find him very interesting."

"*You* would," his sister replied scornfully.

"He is becoming quite famous, he has written books and gives lectures all over the place."

"Maybe so, but I have no intention of trekking miles and

330

miles, living in a tent and hunting for rare plants and bugs. He is hardly ever at home, I would never see you, anyway he is too old, he must be nearly forty."

"Do you realise how much time we spend talking about your future husband?" laughed Edward. "I do not know what we will talk about when you are married."

"We will then set about finding *you* a wife." She smiled lovingly at her brother, she could not bear the thought of living miles away from him, in whom would she confide?

"Anyway you know who you want to marry."

Edward's voice was flat. He knew his sister was besotted with Harry Linwood, four years her senior and miles away in Hampshire. Harry's uncle, Hugo, was their father's oldest friend. He knew that whenever Eleanor talked about getting married she was thinking of Harry, even though she constantly denied it, because she did not want to live in Hampshire.

Edward did not want her to live in Hampshire either. He tried not to think about it. Eleanor was older than him by about half an hour. Had she been a boy *she* would inherit Oxley one day and he would be free to do other things…

On the other hand – he glanced across at his beautiful twin – he loved having her as a *sister*. His train of thought led him to Henry. "Did you know Grandfather had another bad turn this morning?"

"Yes, Mother told me."

"He should not work so hard, Father is quite capable of running the estate, I could leave school and help him."

"Grandfather will never willingly relinquish his hold on this place, he loves it too much."

"I do not think I will ever get the satisfaction from Oxley that he does," he paused, "I would never dare tell him of course."

"You might feel as he does one day, when you are older."

"Maybe."

They stopped on the rise of the hill, looking down on their ancestral home. "You must admit it is beautiful, Edward."

"Yes, it is, we are very fortunate, don't worry, Eleanor, I shall look after it when the time comes, and there will always be a home for you here, I promise you."

She smiled lovingly at her twin, "I'll race you home," she said, by way of answer. But as they galloped toward Oxley House, she was thinking of Harry – and how she could possibly have *both* her loves.

Chapter Seven

One year later…

Charles put his binoculars back to his eyes to survey the estate for other storm damage. He had ridden miles after the ferocious storms of the previous night. A weird, still atmosphere hung over the damage. Branches lay everywhere, fences were down.

Suddenly, into his field of vision, came a lone horse and rider. He could not make out who it was, but they were coming from the direction of the house – and they were in a hurry.

He spurred on his horse and rode toward the rider. He stopped. Looking again through his binoculars he recognised his daughter – she was galloping much too fast for the storm-ridden terrain. Fearing for her safety, he increased his own horse's pace.

They met at a gallop, slightly passing each other as they reined in their mounts.

"Are you trying to kill yourself?" he shouted accusingly, with the concern of a father.

"Father, I have been searching everywhere for you," Eleanor said breathlessly, "Edward is out looking for you too. You must come home at once, Grandfather is very ill. He is asking for you. The Doctor is with him."

"Is it his heart?"

"Yes, we think so, I did not wait to hear what the Doctor said."

Nothing more was said between the pair as they raced for home.

Charles knocked on the door of his father's room, but did not wait for an answer. He crossed to the bed, where Henry was propped up on pillows, with Sarah sitting by his side. She rose and rushed to greet him. "Thank God you are here, Charles, your father wants to see you in private." With that Sarah leaned over the bed, kissed her husband on the forehead whispering, "Charles is here, Henry, do not tire yourself."

She left the room.

Charles did not like what he saw; his father looked ten years older than he had at breakfast. His white hair hung low on his forehead, even *that* appeared lifeless. His brain, however, was as alert as ever, his first concern was for the estate. "Much damage?" he said, looking straight at his son.

"Nothing that cannot be fixed, I will attend to it, you must rest, Father, Eleanor told me what happened."

Henry's piercing blue eyes looked hard at Charles and he said with as much strength as he could muster, "He is your son isn't he?"

Charles was taken aback, of everything that had been going through his mind, as to what his father might say to him, this had not entered his head. He wondered if Henry was in full control of his mental faculties. He must not assume that Henry was talking of Louis. He was very ill. Charles knew he must not cause his father any more anxiety.

"Are you talking of Edward?"

Annoyance crossed Henry's features, "Louis, I mean *Louis.*" He put stress on the last word.

Charles felt hot, the room was stifling and he had just galloped for miles, he felt a little light-headed and very uncomfortable. This was not the ideal time to talk of such matters. He was terrified his father would have another attack. Should he lie and put the old man's mind at rest, or tell the truth and risk making him more ill than he was already?

"Well?"

Charles knew he had to tell the truth, he would not be able to live with himself if he lied to his father on his deathbed. For once he must not take the easy way out. He swallowed hard, looking fearfully at Henry. "Yes, Father, he is my son."

"Does he know?"

"Yes."

"Does anybody else?"

"No."

"Not even Arabella?"

"No."

"I knew it." The old man closed his eyes, Charles was frightened that he had killed him. He sat erect by the bed, looking for any sign of life. After what seemed an eternity, Henry opened his eyes again.

Charles sighed with relief.

"Tell me all about it," the old man said wearily, "and leave nothing out." It was not a request; it was an order, one that Charles felt duty bound to obey.

Hesitantly he began his story, choosing his words carefully. Henry lay still and quiet with eyes closed, but Charles knew he was missing nothing of what he was saying. When he came to the part of his first marriage, he stopped, fearing the reaction of the older man.

Henry opened his eyes; Charles saw the impatience there. "Father I am going to tell you something that will upset you."

"You already have," the old man said wearily, "I want no exclusions."

"I married Colette."

"You what!" Henry tried to raise himself off the pillows, he clutched at his chest, then fell back again.

"Are you alright, Father? Shall I call Mother?"

"No, I want to know everything."

"She was dying, I could not let her die in shame. I was told they would both die. It is the most honourable thing I have ever done. I cannot be ashamed of it."

"Louis is legitimate." It was not a question.

"Yes."

"You know what that means."

Charles knew all too well what it meant.

"You must sort out the whole affair, Charles and you must do it quickly. I cannot die like this."

"I am so sorry, Father."

"Carry on please."

Charles spared his father nothing. He was relieved for it to be in the open between them. Throughout the story he was frequently in tears. When he finished he looked to his father for forgiveness. "Please forgive me, Father. It was not my intention to cause hurt, especially to you, Mother and Arabella.

"Oh, Charles what have you done? I suppose all this is the reason you drink so much."

"Yes."

"I know we have had our differences, but do you not think you could have told me all this long ago?"

"I knew how much it meant to you and Grandfather that I should marry Arabella. *She* was expecting it too, and when Colette died I thought I should still go ahead with the marriage. I thought I was doing what you all wanted."

"But your child, Louis. Did you think you could keep him a secret forever?"

"I did not know what I thought. I wanted to please everyone and I have made a mess of it all." He held his head in his hands, miserable and exhausted.

The silence hung heavy in the room. He felt his father's hand on his arm, "Despite everything, I love you, Charles. You are my only son. We have had our differences I know, but that is probably because we are so alike."

"Alike!" Charles raised his head to look at the man he had revered all his life. The strong, dependable, respected man, with great strength of character, whom he could never live up to.

"Yes, we are alike. You have got yourself into more trouble that is all. You are not weak, you are kind, always wanting to please; that is not a bad trait to have."

"I have handled it all so very badly."

"Maybe."

More silence.

"Your mother will have to be told."

"Yes."

"And Arabella."

"Yes"

"It is Edward I feel most sorry for, he has grown up expecting

336

to inherit the estate some day. I do not envy the task you have before you."

Charles did not reply. His father had taken his news well, but then he remembered that it had not been news to him.

"How did you find out, Father?" he asked suddenly.

The old man tried to smile. "In church," he said, softly.

"In church?"

"Yes. It was when Louis was here last time."

"But that was seven years ago!"

Henry looked abashed, "You are not the only one who tries to avoid confrontation. I hoped you would tell me before I had to ask."

Charles could not believe his father had known so long. "But you did not tell Mother?"

"No, you see, I could have been wrong."

"I do not understand how you found out in church."

"It was Christmas Eve. We were listening to that flautist. I suddenly realised what an awe-inspiring effect he was having on everyone. I glanced sideways and saw the two of you in profile, you and Louis; it was quite uncanny, like he was your shadow. As I stood there surrounded by the haunting music, I suddenly thought, He is Charles' son, my grandson. There was no doubt in my mind at all at the time."

"But you doubted later?"

"Not really, but I did not know how to tackle the subject. Arabella and the children are very dear to me and Louis did not appear to be aware of the fact, so I let it rest, hoping that you would confide in me."

"I let you down again." There was despondency in his voice.

"We cannot alter the past, Charles, but we can put things right for the future. This is your chance to put right, past wrongs. I am counting on you. I am too tired to explain all this to Sarah and Arabella; I must leave that to you. What I do want to do is see my grandson again."

"Louis?"

"Yes, Louis. I do not think I have long. If I get over this attack I will probably have another one in the not too distant future. I want to talk to Louis – about Oxley. Write to him Charles, get him here as quickly as possible for me, please. In the meantime we must think about Edward."

Edward – suddenly Charles remembered that his father had another shock coming to him. Edward was not his grandson. If he told him this too, it could well bring on another attack – if he did not tell him, he could die not knowing the truth. Surely it would ease the old man's conscience if he knew that Edward should not inherit anyway. On the other hand, could he take away his father's grandson? A grandson he loved so much. Would it really be so terrible to let him die thinking Edward was his own? Why not leave things as they were and let his father die happy, with three grandchildren to ensure the future of Oxley.

Once again Charles was in turmoil. If he told his father he would have to tell the twins. How would they react? He would lose their respect for ever. He suddenly realised that he had almost forgotten they were not his natural children. He could not love them more if they were. No, it was better to leave matters as they were. He would wait for the right time to tell his mother and Arabella about Louis. In the meantime he must write to him.

Within the week Louis arrived at Oxley. He was twenty-five years old.

The first person he saw as he stepped onto Oxley soil was Eleanor – and he immediately lost his heart.

"Louis?"

Eleanor had purposely hung around the front of the house knowing that their young relative was due to arrive. She remembered him with affection, but nothing prepared her for the effect he was now having on her. Her colour was high; she had forgotten how handsome he was. She had been ten years old at their last meeting – he had been a distant relative. She had hardly thought about him at all during the intervening years.

He stood among his luggage. He had been so absorbed with looking on the house again after such a long time that he had not seen her until she had spoken.

She held out her hand, he took it and kissed it in greeting, his eyes never leaving her face. She was just like a young Arabella. Should he kiss her on the cheek? He suddenly realised he was staring.

"Eleanor?" he said incredulously.

He took her other hand; he now stood holding both her hands in his. She smiled, totally smitten by the man who stood before her. She was, for once, at a loss for words.

"I–I know it is stupid of me," he said in a daze, "but I have always thought of you as a child."

She continued to smile.

"You *are* Eleanor?"

"Yes."

"I cannot believe how beautiful you have grown."

She smiled again; she had done little else.

He realised he was still holding her hands. He kissed her on both cheeks and reluctantly let go of her as somebody picked up his luggage.

He remembered why he was there. "How is Henry?" he asked.

"He continues to improve."

"I expect you know he has asked to see me."

"Yes"

"Do you know why?"

"No."

They did not know what to say to each other, so were slightly relieved when Arabella appeared on the scene.

"Louis," she exclaimed, "how lovely to see you again." He kissed her warmly. "Henry is looking forward to seeing you, he was always very fond of you. Why have you stayed away so long?"

Before he could answer Charles appeared to greet him, and the whole group moved towards the house, full of mixed emotions.

Louis had come to see Henry but now could not get Eleanor out of his mind.

Charles knew that time was running out. He had got to talk to his wife – before someone else did. He was not looking forward to it. For years he had known he had to compensate Louis for losing Oxley but, now it was Edward to whom he had to make amends. How would the boy react?

Charles drew his son to one side, "Father is eager to talk to you. He knows everything."

So this is it, thought Louis, the day I have been waiting for since I was fourteen. The day I am accepted into the family as heir apparent.

The elation he felt was spoiled only by the fact that Edward was in for a massive shock – and that his grandfather was so ill.

There was nothing he could do to help Henry, but he must encourage Charles to compensate Edward. He did not want to be the cause of another family rift.

His thoughts returned to the present. "Does anybody else know my true identity?"

"I – er – I have not yet told Arabella or the children – or Mother," he added, his embarrassment clearly showing.

Now why did that not surprise him? The old anger was boiling up again.

"I am trying to decide whether to tell them separately or all together," Charles continued, as they hurried along the corridor towards the ailing, old man.

"For what it is worth, *I* think you should tell Arabella first." He did not add that he thought his father should have told his wife before he married her. Why did his father always have to prolong the agony? He made a silent promise to himself that he would never shirk his responsibilities. Then another thought popped into his head, a very pleasant one, of how *very* happy he was to know that Eleanor was not his father's natural daughter. He had gone only a few more steps when he suddenly stopped; *he* knew Charles was not her father, but *she* did not!

He must talk to Arabella, he must find out if Charles *knew* her children did not belong to him. He would have to confess to her that he had eavesdropped on her conversation by the stream.

His head was reeling – so many secrets – so many revelations about to be made – what would be the outcome?

340

There were servants, villagers – the gossip would be horrendous. How would they all survive it?

"He is just along here." Charles' voice penetrated his thoughts, urging him to resume walking.

They reached their destination, Louis took a deep breath; this was going to be one of the most difficult and also the most enjoyable conversations of his life; talking to his grandfather, man to man, about Oxley – with no secrets between them.

If only he were not so ill.

"Have you seen him?" Eleanor asked, excitedly.

"No, he is still talking to Grandfather, what can they be discussing?"

The twins were in the garden, having escaped from the house at Eleanor's request.

"He is so handsome, Edward, so tall and so…" she hesitated, searching around for the appropriate adjective, "…French," she finished triumphantly.

"He is English, Eleanor.

"His mother was French, he told us long ago. His father must have been French too, otherwise he would have an English name."

Edward laughed at his sister's enthusiasm. "What happened to Harry?"

"Harry?"

"Yes, Harry Linwood."

"Oh, Harry and I were never really sweethearts."

"You could have fooled me, you have talked of little else for the past year."

"This is different, Edward. You will understand when you fall in love yourself."

"You have hardly exchanged a sentence with him."

"I did not need to," the girl said dreamily, "I cannot explain it, but I am going to marry Louis."

"He might already be married."

She looked aghast, "He cannot be, we would have heard, surely."

"He might not tell Mother *everything* in his letters."

"His Christmas cards are always signed with just *his* name."

"That is true."

Eleanor breathed a sigh of relief, she had met her future husband – nothing must come between them.

"I thought you did not want to leave Oxley." Edward enjoyed teasing his sister.

"I do not."

"Louis might one day return to France."

"He would not go if it made me unhappy."

"You are very sure of yourself."

"I can *feel* it, Edward. I know he feels exactly the same about me as I feel about him. Anyway I would grow to love another home."

Edward gasped, "That is the first time I have ever heard you say that."

"I have never been in love before," she answered simply.

When Louis entered the breakfast room the next morning both Arabella and Charles were missing. He looked around the table, sensing an atmosphere; Eleanor gave him the briefest of smiles then turned her eyes back to her plate. "Is Henry worse?" he asked worriedly.

"Henry is a little better today, he enjoyed seeing you yesterday," said Sarah, kindly. "He hopes you will spare him some time later today."

"Of course."

Nobody spoke.

"Is anything wrong?" he ventured, looking from one to another of his eating companions.

"You might as well know," said Sarah, when no staff were present, "Charles and Arabella have had an appalling argument; most distressing when Henry is so ill. I hope I can rely on you all to keep it from him. I expect they will sort things out between them."

So he has told her, thought Louis frantically. He would have to find her and explain that his father had wanted him to keep it all a secret, that he had not been a willing party to the deceit.

"Do you know where Arabella is?" Louis asked his grandmother.

"She saddled her horse and left about thirty minutes ago. Charles is distraught. No doubt she will feel better after a good gallop. It is best we keep out of it. She likes to be by herself at times like this."

Another brief smile from Eleanor, which he returned with as much conviction as he could muster.

He knew he should stay at the table- so many of the family were missing from it already – but all he could think about was finding Arabella.

"Would you like to come riding with me today?" asked Eleanor, "I mean *us*," she added, seeing the look her brother gave her.

"I would love to, Eleanor, but there are things I must do today," he gave her a smile, "Can we go another day instead?"

He saw the disappointment on her face but dare not surrender to her charms.

"Yes, another day then," Eleanor agreed reluctantly, wondering what was more important to him.

Louis saddled his horse in a hurry. He had a very good idea where Arabella would be, so made his way straight to the bridge. He rode past the entrance to Marcie's Lane and entered the copse further along Rookery Lane, where he could approach the bridge from the opposite direction. He thought it very unlikely she would have company so early in the morning, all the same, he wanted to make sure she was alone before he approached her.

He dismounted in the road and led his horse up the bank to the copse, then made his way toward the stream.

She was alone. Her horse was tethered about twenty feet distant.

He tied up his mount and made his way down the bank a little further upstream. She did not hear him. The stream was gurgling on its way having tumbled down the waterfall to their right.

She was staring ahead.

He caught his breath, her face was tearstained, he began to doubt his actions. Then she turned her face towards him.

Her face crumpled in pain. "Oh, Louis," was all she said before lowering her head into her hands.

He swiftly went to her side. Putting his arm around her shoulders he pulled her to him in comfort. "I am so, so sorry, Arabella. I wanted to tell you years ago, when I first came here, but Charles...er...Father...would not hear of it. It must be such a shock for you, and I dread what Edward will make of it all. You cannot imagine how dreadful I feel; I never wanted to oust Edward from Oxley, but it is all out of my hands now..."

She raised her head, causing him to stop abruptly; the look on her face was unimaginably painful. She pushed him away from her, studying his face as if she were seeing him for the first time. "What are you saying, Louis... What do you mean 'oust Edward from Oxley'?"

In a flash it came to him that she did not know.

She shook his arm, horror written all over her face. "What do you mean, Louis?" she asked again in a strangled whisper.

"I thought he had told you, I thought that must be what the argument was about..."

She continued to stare at him.

"...Charles... er... Charles is my father, I thought he must have told you."

Her hand came out and grabbed his sleeve, she had turned deathly white, she swayed slightly before regaining her balance. She did not speak.

He moved closer and took her hand in his, his eyes never leaving her tortured face. "I am so sorry, Arabella," was all he could say.

"I cannot believe this," she said at length, "after everything I have been through...what has he done to me?"

"I wanted to tell you, it pained me that I could not."

Her brain was working quickly, trying to work out how it could have come about. But you were born before I married Charles."

"Yes."

"I–I do not understand."

"He was married before – in France, to my mother."

Her hand flew to her mouth in horror. "You knew you were his son when you first came here?"

"Yes, but I quickly realised that none of the family knew of my existence. Even Charles did not own me. I found out from my Aunt Ethel – incidentally she was *not* my aunt; she was employed by Charles to take care of me when I was a baby. Aunt Ethel told me the truth as she lay dying. She made me promise to come to Oxley and stake my claim on my rightful inheritance. But I grew to love you all, I could not do it. Then when I was eighteen there was that terrible performance at the dinner table – do you remember? When Charles was drunk?"

"Yes, yes I remember," she said, as if in a dream.

"He asked to see me in his study. He asked me if I knew I was his son. I told him I did and we had a long talk about it..."

"Your mother...?"

"She died shortly after I was born."

"Does everyone know but me?"

"No, no, Arabella, no one knows except you and me," he hesitated, "and Henry," he finished quietly.

"*Henry*, Henry knows?"

Apparently he realised the truth one night in church. It was Christmas Eve, the last time I was here. We were listening to the flautist..." he hesitated, remembering he was referring to Arabella's lost love. "You remember the night?"

"Yes...yes, I remember."

"Well, he looked sideways and saw me and Charles in profile. He said it was at that moment that the truth hit him. He said it was like looking at Charles and his shadow."

Somewhere from the depths of her mind, Arabella recalled the look she had seen on Henry's face – the look she had not been able to understand, and had since forgotten about – until now.

"I saw it," she whispered.

"You what...?"

"I saw it," she repeated, as if in a daze. "I saw Henry look along the line of the family. I saw the look on his face… I had forgotten all about it."

A silence fell between them.

"Is that why you never came back? Did Henry banish you from Oxley?"

"No, not at all, he never mentioned it to anybody until recently. He thought he was dying and asked Charles if he was right about me. Charles confessed and Henry asked to see me. It was Charles and I that decided I should stay away. He promised me he would resolve matters."

"Charles? Charles never resolves matters, he seems quite incapable of facing up to his problems."

"I am sorry I have told you all this… I assumed the argument…Charles should have told you…"

"I am *glad* you have told me. Charles never would have."

"He would, Henry told him he must, that is why I thought…he was waiting for the right time…"

She turned and looked him straight in the face. "And when, pray, did you think that would be? We have been married for twenty-five years." There was bitterness in her voice, which he did not like to hear.

She was biting her trembling lips, staring straight ahead, unseeing. Then she closed her eyes as tears squeezed their way from under her eyelids, flowing down her cheeks and dropping onto her coat. She did nothing to stem them. His heart went out to her; he did not know what to say to help her.

She opened her eyes and turned to face him, "Did Charles also confess…"

"Also confess what?"

"Nothing…it is nothing…you would not know…" she bowed her head.

Louis swallowed hard, he might as well confess all to her; there would not be a better opportunity.

"I know your secret, Arabella," he said simply.

Her head shot up.

"I know your secret," he reiterated.

She stared at him unbelievingly.

"I know that Charles is not the natural father of the twins."

He waited for her reaction; she did not speak, but kept staring at him, her face awash with tears and pain.

"I overheard you talking to their father...here on the seat...last time I was home. It was Boxing Day... I did not mean to hear...it was only a word or two, about Edward growing to look more and more like him. I promise you I did not linger. I was so confused about everything...all the secrets...I thought it best to stay away..."

She saw the pain on his face. Up to this point she had thought only of her own distress, suddenly she realised what this young man had gone through, all alone in the world except for this troubled family, who had not known his true identity.

She put her arms around him and pulled him to her as she would a child. "Oh, Louis, I am so sorry, you must have felt so alone through all of this. What are we to do?"

"Were you going to ask me if Charles had confessed to Henry about the children?"

"Yes."

"So Charles knows."

"Of course."

"Yes, of course he would, you are honourable, Arabella."

She blushed, "It had nothing to do with honour, he knew the children could not belong to him; our marriage was never consummated."

She dropped her chin onto her chest. "I should never have let things get this far."

"It was because my mother died, Arabella. He told me he could never risk another woman dying through having his child."

"I see," she whispered, "I have never known, but then, it seems there is much I do not know."

"We must put that right at once."

She looked at him, her face sad and tearstained.

"I will tell you all I know, Arabella, here and now."

When he had finished she felt as sorry for him as she did for herself. She was also very angry with Charles.

"I need to think, Louis I cannot go back to the house until I have thought things through…decided what to do…I am so grateful to you for telling me all this, I can see you were put in an impossible position."

"Do not do anything rash, Arabella. I care about you so much."

"And I, you, Louis. Do not worry about me. I just want to be alone for a while."

"You have not eaten."

"I will not starve. I will make my way to town…walk by the sea…I can buy something to eat…I *must* think things through before I face Charles, it is no good leaving matters to him to resolve."

Louis smiled wryly in agreement. "You *will* take care?"

"I promise, but, Louis, please do not tell Charles that I know. Please do not tell anybody."

"As you say, Arabella."

He left her there by the stream looking sad and lonely. He did not want to go but he had great faith in her, that she would come up with a solution – she always did.

He wondered how he could go back to the house and face his father, perhaps he should follow Arabella's example, and go for a long, solitary ride.

Arabella's head was reeling. How had it all come to this? She should have eloped with Harnser when she had the chance. She thought of him, miles away in Kent, as lonely as she was – Richard and Florence had never agreed to move to Suffolk.

She untethered Rosie and led her back to the lane. Everything was coming back to life in the countryside. The May blossom was already in abundance, heralding warmer weather. It would not be too long before the wild roses were flowering again. Tears came back to her eyes, blurring her vision and running off her face.

She remounted and turned Rosie in the direction of Cottlefield, where she would ride along the sands to Winford, as she had on many a summer morning with Harnser.

The beach was almost deserted when she reached it. It was still far too cold for bathing. The gulls screamed and wheeled overhead, circling and diving as if nothing had changed at all. She thought of Charles. Only this morning she had felt she could not be angrier with him. He had retired to bed the previous night the worse for drink. He was seldom completely sober by nightfall. She had pleaded with him to curtail his drinking, especially when Henry was relying on him so much. The request had been repeated this morning, but by then he was not so mellow, rounding on her with a ferocity she had rarely seen. Telling her that he would, no doubt, soon be out of her hair for good, that she had no idea of the problems he had, and that she lived a life of cocooned luxury, whilst he did all the worrying.

She had not understood him at all then. He had stormed out of the house shouting at her that he had let everyone down and nobody was more aware of it than he.

She wondered how much the staff had heard; she had not been able to face people at breakfast. Now she knew what was on Charles' mind. Why could he not have told her he was in love with someone else? But then she thought of her Grandmother and the promise she had made her. No doubt Charles had felt just as obligated to his grandfather. She did not hate her husband, she decided, as she watched the waves running up the shore and shrinking back again in the spring sunshine. She was infuriated with him but, as always, she realized he had not wanted to hurt anyone. He was probably out looking for her at this very moment to apologize for his bad temper this morning.

By the time she reached Winford her tears had subsided and her head felt clearer. Now all she had to do was find a solution to their problems. A solution that would suit everyone – an idea was beginning to germinate in her fertile mind.

It was late afternoon when Arabella returned to Oxley House. She had stopped off at Barcada on the way home to inform her father of the latest developments in the family...she had also told him of her plans...

The dinner table was quieter than ever. They were all in their own thoughts, oblivious to the monotonous clinking of silver on china. For once Charles appeared sober – much to Arabella's relief. What she was preparing to tell him later would need his full concentration.

Louis and Eleanor regularly exchanged guarded looks and brief smiles. Sarah occasionally commented on the excellence of the meal and made sure they were all adequately fed. She was aware that nobody seemed very hungry. Charles kept his head bowed for most of the time, acutely aware that everyone blamed him for the strained atmosphere. He shot one or two quick glances in the direction of his wife, whose sad, set face was worrying him. He really did not want to cause her more unhappiness, but his father was getting impatient with his prevarications. Next his glance fell on Edward and he almost choked on his food. His throat felt so constricted that he quietly laid down his knife and fork, bowed his head and gripped his hands together beneath the table. It was Edward he was worried about most of all; he was such a fine, honest boy – intelligent, hard working, sensitive and, surprisingly, musical. He wondered where he got his talent from, but then Arabella had arranged lessons for the children from an early age.

Arabella...he was not looking forward to their talk that evening, but he had promised his father that he would put it off no longer and then...when he had told her...he must make an announcement to the rest of the family...

His whole insides contracted at the thought of what lay ahead. Henry was improving, he was eager to call in the solicitors and get things moving...

It was Edward they were worrying about.

They faced each other over the table.

The same low table that had separated Charles and Louis seven years earlier, the customary jug of water and glasses waiting.

Charles was stone cold sober.

He poured some water into each of the glasses, keeping his eyes lowered. Arabella knew she would have to initiate the conversation.

"I know what you want to tell me, Charles."

He swallowed hard picking up his glass as he did so; his throat was dry, as always on these occasions. He had heard what she said, but knew she was mistaken – she had been out all day, she had not seen his father apart from briefly with other people present – no one else could have told her...apart from Louis...and Louis would not have done...would he?

"I think not, Arabella, not this time." His voice was flat, his heart heavy. He did not want Arabella to go off again, as she had that morning ...and as she had years ago, when she had been found in the copse.

He must choose his words carefully.

"This is going to upset you dreadfully, Arabella; but please do not run off. It would solve nothing – we really have to have a deep discussion this time. Father is very weak, we must do nothing to make him worse."

"It is never *my* intention to upset Henry. I have always wanted complete honesty in the family. If you remember I asked you for an annulment before the twins were born."

There was slight accusation to her voice, which he did not miss. He already felt at a disadvantage.

He took another long draught from his glass and refilled it. She knew he was playing for time.

"I know that Louis is your son."

His eyes shot up to look her in the face, his heart was beating rapidly, so she *did* know, he was lost for words, his prepared speech momentarily forgotten.

"Well, are you going to deny it?"

"No."

"Did I deserve to be treated so shabbily?"

"No, no, Arabella you did not," his voice was barely audibly, there was a pained expression on her face. "I never wanted to hurt you," was all he could manage.

"Eighteen years ago, when I found I was with child, you had

351

the perfect opportunity to tell me you already had an heir for Oxley. You made me feel as if the whole future of the estate depended on me remaining married to you." There was bitterness in her words, something he had never heard before. Her face was contorted, he could see she was having great difficulty controlling her emotions.

"I had promised Grandfather and Father; they were expecting *our* child to one day inherit the estate, that was their dearest wish, you know it was."

"But Edward is *not* our child Charles, so what is the difference?" She sounded exasperated and very tired.

"Father *thinks* he is, *that* is the difference."

"And now?"

"What do you mean?"

"Does he still think Edward is your child?"

Charles lowered his gaze in shame. She saw it for what it was. She knew her husband very well.

"Yes," he whispered.

She stood up and paced the room; running her fingers through her hair, her eyes closed against her disappointment in her husband.

"I thought he was dying...I could not take his grandson from him on his death bed. Please, Arabella, see it from where I stand."

"I have tried to see things from your side for twenty-five years, Charles. It is time you started thinking of other people."

"I know, I know." He too ran his fingers through his hair, as he watched her pace.

"We must tell him now."

"No."

"Why not?"

"I cannot do it to him; it could give him another attack."

"If he dies in ignorance you will feel guilty forever."

"Do you think I do not know that?"

"Oh, Charles," she sat down again, heavily. A silence descended on the room.

"Who told you?" he asked at last.

"Louis."

"He had no right."

"He had *every* right."

"When?"

"This morning. He came looking for me. He thought the argument this morning was because you had told me everything. He found me in tears. He tried to comfort me. He told me he had not wanted to keep me in ignorance."

"That is true, he did not."

"Do not fall out with him over it, Charles. I might never have found out the truth had he not told me."

"You would have, Father made me promise to tell you tonight."

"Why can't you ever make these decisions yourself?"

"I do not know, I do not like to hurt."

"A few small hurts along the way might avoid the big hurts later – you must see that."

"Yes," was all he said, dejectedly.

Silence again.

"Help me please, Arabella, tell me what to do; I will do anything you want but please do not tear the family apart."

"You ask a lot."

He looked at her pleadingly, like a lost puppy dog. Had he been drunk she would have lost her temper with him, but he had made an effort – today anyway.

"Can you think of a solution?" he asked pitifully.

"I have thought of nothing else all day," she began hesitantly, "but my solution would cost you dearly."

"There is a lot at stake, Arabella. Our reputation in the community not the least of it. We built a house and a row of terraces in honour of our heirs."

"Louis was not illegitimate, there is nothing for you to be ashamed of in making him your heir. We can ride out the gossip if we are united."

"But are we, Arabella...united I mean."

"We could be...with care."

He refilled his glass, eager to hear her plan.

"You have thousands of acres here at Oxley, how would you and Henry feel about losing a few hundred?"

His brows knitted together. What was she getting at?

"Tell me more," he said, interested.

"I would like you to give me two hundred acres – and enough money to build a school. I mean a large school, a superb school."

"A school!"

"Yes, two hundred acres and a school."

He was dumbfounded, his wife never failed to amaze him.

"I would like to found a school, Charles. A very good school, which excels at everything, especially music. I want it to be renowned throughout the country, and I would like it built adjoining the Barcada ten acres. It will have good grounds and be superbly conducive to study. The rest of the land can be farmed; I liked living on a farm, Charles. We might have looked poor to you when you found us in Essex, but we were happy living simply.

"Edward is gifted in music, I think his leanings are more in the direction of music and education than in running a large estate. Eleanor will make a good marriage, hopefully."

He stared at her. Had she worked all this out in one day? It was a good solution, especially if Edward approved, but did it mean she was leaving him to return to Barcada?

"It sounds good, Arabella, but why a school?"

"We have seen little of Louis because he was away at school for years. I thought then that we should have a really good school in the area. But more importantly I think that is where Edward's future lies, and *I* am very excited at the prospect. I visualize the entrance a half mile down the lane. It will be beautifully landscaped with sporting facilities."

"And music?" he reminded her, unnecessarily.

"Yes, especially music."

"Tell me, Arabella, does Edward get his musical talent from anyone in particular?"

She coloured, he had promised not to ask about the twins' father.

"I-I am sorry, I should not have asked that."

Would it hurt to tell him? she wondered now. He had had a child without her. She knew who Louis' mother was.

"Yes, Charles," she said forcefully, Edward gets his talent from his father and, as we are at last sharing secrets, perhaps you would like to know who that is."

Did he want to know? For years he had wondered about it, but now when the information was being offered to him, he was somehow reluctant to hear it. What if it were someone he knew? There was a certain amount of bliss in ignorance, he acknowledged silently. He had always told himself that a London scoundrel had taken advantage of his wife.

"I do not think I want to know, Arabella."

She was pleased.

"Do you plan to leave me, to return to Barcada?"

"I have not thought that far ahead."

It was his turn to be pleased.

"Do you think Henry will agree to my solution?"

"I have the feeling he might, after all, it will still be in the family."

Henry agreed.

Solicitors were brought to Oxley.

All that remained was for an announcement to be made to the rest of the family…

CHAPTER EIGHT

"The Frenchman is back then," said Abel to no one in particular, "We haven't seen him for a few years, have we?"

"He's set all the ladies hearts a-flutter, from what I hear, especially Miss Eleanor's," said Arthur knowingly.

"How old is Miss Eleanor? I always think of her as a child," said Sefton disappointed that he had not kept abreast of matters at the House.

"She's seventeen, she's blossomed in the last year or so, very slender still, like Arabella was at her age. The same thick chestnut hair as well," said Arthur.

"I only see her when she's out riding and it's not often she comes our way."

"You see her at church," said Arthur.

"She's allust got a hat on then, and all her finery. Anyway I allust take more notice of the older members of the family than the children,"

"She wouldn't like to hear you calling her a child, as far as she's concerned she's all grown up."

"So she's set her cap at the Frenchman, has she?"

"Aye, she has, and by all accounts he's very taken with her as well."

There was a lull in the conversation as this news was absorbed.

"How is old Sugar? I hear it was touch and go for a while," said Sefton, keen to get some more news to encourage custom in his shop.

"He's improvin' every day, but there's somethin' fishy goin' on," said Arthur mysteriously.

"What do you mean by fishy?" asked old Joe from his position on the corner settle.

"Well, for a start why did the Frenchman come back after so

long, it's not as if he's close family – some distant cousin, I heard once. You'd think old Sugar would want to be quiet, not entertain houseguests. And then there's all the arguments – Arabella disappeared for a whole day not so long ago, remember."

"Does he still drink too much, Arthur?" Sefton asked.

"Like a fish, can't understand that either, he's got no reason to be miserable. If I had his money I wouldn't waste it on drink, I can tell you."

"What's that you've got in your glass then, Arthur, thass a funny old colour for water, you'd better ask landlord to have his well checked," said Joe amidst laughter from the group.

"You all know what I mean," said Arthur, a trifle put out at being made fun of. "If you don't treat me kinder I might keep my information to myself, then where would you all be?" he sniffed importantly.

The group knew that their drinking companion was well liked at Barcada, and often found out snippets of gossip that staff at the House missed.

"I'll tell you what," chuckled old Joe, "Just to show you there's no hard feelings I'll buy you another half of Adam's Ale."

Arthur relented, "Make it the real stuff and I'll forgive you all," he said good-naturedly. "Seriously, though, there's somethin' afoot up there. All the staff are of the same mind, but they can't find out what it is. They say the family go quiet when one of them enter the room, now that's not normal, and Arabella has been at Barcada much more than usual." He looked around the ale house to see who was within earshot before leaning forward in his seat and whispering, "Don't let this go any further." He turned again to look behind him, knowing he had the undivided attention of the whole assemblage before saying very quietly, "They've had the solicitors in."

A silence descended on the chimney corner drinkers before Abel suggested, "Perhaps he's changed his Will. People often do when they are ill."

"Maybe he's decided to leave the Frenchman a little

something, especially if he's taken a shine to Miss Eleanor," said Joe sagely.

"There's somethin' else," whispered Arthur, repeating the performance of looking behind him. He looked at them all in turn to make sure he had their attention, "They've bin measuring."

"Measuring!" said Sefton over loudly.

"Ssshh," said Arthur putting his finger to his lips."Do you want me to lose my job for gossiping?"

"Measuring what?" asked Abel.

"Land," said Arthur, nodding his head and pressing his lips together.

"Where?" asked Abel.

"Adjoining Barcada."

"And you say Arabella's been there more often than usual," said Abel, trying to get things straight in his mind.

"Much more," confirmed Arthur. "There's somethin' afoot, you mark my words."

"It'll have somethin' to do with the Frenchman then, else why is he back?"

"I'll agree with you there," said Sefton draining his glass, eager to get home to share the mystery with his wife.

"Now don't you go spreadin' what I've told you," instructed Arthur, as Sefton strained his famous waistcoat buttons getting out of his chair.

"The wife won't say anything."

"Make sure she don't, we should keep this quiet 'til we know a bit more." Arthur had begun to wish he had not shared his news. He liked to think he was loyal to the Biddemores.

"It'll all come out in the end," said Old Joe, sensing Arthur's misgivings.

"Aye I s'pose you're right."

Arthur told himself that he had not divulged anything that others could not have observed for themselves. He had kept the most important piece of information to himself and that was how much personal interest Arabella was taking in the 'measuring' – out in the fields with her husband.

CHAPTER NINE

It was, unusually, a morning meeting.

Henry had insisted on being present – 'to give Charles support' as he put it.

The whole family congregated in Charles' study.

"Do *you* know what this is all about?" asked Eleanor of her brother, as they waited for their grandfather.

"I have absolutely no idea," he answered.

"Do you know, Louis." The girl turned to the man who had stolen her heart. She had not spent as much time with him as she would have liked. On the occasions he *had* agreed to ride with her, he had always invited Edward along as well, and he had appeared preoccupied. She knew he liked her, he could not hide the fact, but she could not help thinking that something was troubling him.

He appeared embarrassed, he could not lie to her, "Yes, I do know what it is about, but I am not at liberty to tell you," he said sombrely.

"It sounds serious," said Edward to his sister.

The door behind them opened and they all turned to see Henry being wheeled into the room by Charles.

They took the seats that had been arranged for them and waited to see who would address them.

Charles stood nervously beside his father's chair.

"I have asked you all to be present this morning because I have an important family announcement to make. It is something I should have told you long ago; something that will affect some of you more than others." Charles' gaze flickered over his entire family, then came to rest on Edward. He swallowed hard and gripped his father's shoulders, looking squarely at his mother before saying quietly, "Louis is my natural son."

Sarah's hand flew to her mouth as she stared unbelievingly at her son. But it was Eleanor who attracted all their attentions when she stood up, screamed something unintelligible, then collapsed on the floor in a faint, as both Edward and Louis flew to her aid.

Edward's head was full of unanswered questions as he helped lift his shocked sister from the floor.

The room was full of babble. Sarah in tears, demanding to know why no one had warned her of the matter. "How could you do this to me?" she was heard to wail, clutching at her son's sleeve, while Arabella was escorting the two young men who carried her daughter out of the room.

"Take her to the drawing room, Edward," she instructed, running ahead to open doors. "Then go back to hear what your father has to say."

"I have heard enough, Mother," Edward answered angrily glaring at Louis as he spoke. "I am obviously not so important to Father as others are."

His sister struggled and moaned in his arms. "Just relax Eleanor, we will take care of you," he said gently, pulling his sister from Louis' grasp. Then turning to the Frenchman, "leave us please."

"I need to talk to you, Edward…to explain…" Louis began.

"You are the last person I wish to speak with," Edward answered, bitterly, "you have betrayed me and my sister."

"No, you do not understand."

Arabella's exasperated voice cut into their conversation. "Take your argument elsewhere, please, Eleanor does not need to hear it."

Edward hesitated, looking worriedly at his sister's pale inert form but his mother turned him around forcibly saying, "Go and hear what your father has to say."

With one last look at Eleanor, Edward turned reluctantly and left the room with Louis hard on his heels.

"I have told you to leave me alone," he shouted uncharacteristically at his young relative, "I want to be by myself."

360

Louis stopped, "Come back to the study, Edward."

"No."

They were making a scene. Shocked staff were scurrying in all directions, trying to look busy, but hoping to find out what all the fuss was about.

Louis returned to the study where Charles and Henry were still trying to pacify Sarah. As if pleased to have someone else to blame other than her son she rounded on her grandson. "How could you do this after we befriended you?" she said, coming at him with all the anguish she felt unable to direct toward her perfect son or her ailing husband.

Louis put up his hand to shield his face, certain in that moment that Sarah would scratch his eyes from his head. Her face was so contorted with hurt and anger that he felt pity for her. Charles rushed to his aid, holding his mother tightly against him as he stroked her hair and murmured soothing words of comfort. It was a tender side of his father that Louis had hitherto not seen.

Sarah was sobbing against her son's chest, "What are we to do, Charles, and your father so ill – it will kill him."

"Sshh, Mother, Father knows all about it, he is not going to die." Then, in a show of rare strength, Charles added, "The only person to blame in all this is me. I am solely responsible and I do not want anybody to be unkind to Louis, I have hurt him more than anyone else."

The sobbing paused as Sarah lifted her head to look into the face of her son. He gave her a weak smile; pleased to feel he was taking control of the situation. "If you come and sit down, Mother, I will tell you the whole story and you will see that you should not be angry with anyone but me."

Sarah allowed herself to be led to one of the leather arm-chairs, where, at her son's insistence, she sat quietly to hear what he had to tell her.

Charles told his story with truth and humility, so much so that, by the time he had finished, Sarah felt that *she* must comfort *him.*

"I'm sorry, Louis," she whispered to her grandson.

He smiled at the old lady, whose usual poise and dignity had been swept away from her, revealing a frailty that tore at his heart.

It was in the quiet lull that followed that Arabella came rushing into the room. "Both Edward and Eleanor are missing," she announced worriedly, "I cannot find them anywhere, and the household is whispering behind doors everywhere."

Louis took control of the situation. "Come in here and look after Sarah and Henry, Arabella. I will have some tea sent in and then Charles and I will go and find them." He looked to his father for support and was not surprised to get it.

"Do you have any idea where they might be?" Louis asked his father, after arranging the tea.

"I suppose they could have gone to their grandfather at Barcada, they are very close to him."

"Do you think we should organize some help?"

"Edward will look after Eleanor, they will come to no harm. I think it best to keep the matter private for as long as possible. It is understandable that they are upset but it is best that we find them so that we can explain more fully. We should go to Barcada first, if they are not there we should split up and search separately."

On reaching the stables they found the situation more worrying than they had first thought; the twins had not left together, but more importantly Eleanor had not waited to saddle her horse.

Charles became angry, as parents do when children put themselves in danger. "What the devil is she playing at, her horse is spirited at the best of times."

Leaving Oxley in the direction of Barcada Charles pointed heavenward, where ominous black clouds were gathering in the west, threatening a break in the hitherto warm weather in the run up to Easter.

As the pair galloped towards Barcada they frequently looked round to see if the storm would pass them by.

A few minutes later their horses thundered into the Barcada

yard, kicking up dust and gravel. They had to rein in sharply to avoid a carriage that had recently arrived at the front door, where the Major was greeting his visitor.

Louis immediately recognised him as Harnser Elliot.

Louis dismounted and ran toward the two men at the door. He nodded briefly to Harnser as the Major said, "What the deuce is going on, you are frightening the horses."

The carriage driver got his horses back under control as Louis gasped out, "Have you seen Eleanor or Edward?"

"Not since yesterday, is anything wrong?" But even as he said it, he was remembering the revelations made to him recently by his daughter, he had thought of little else since.

Briefly Louis explained that the pair were missing after an upset at the house. "They are both distressed and Eleanor was not feeling well so we are anxious to find them as quickly as possible."

Louis could not miss the look of grave concern on Harnser's face. Mindful that he was in the presence of Eleanor's father he said considerately. "I expect we will find them, we will keep you informed. If they do come here perhaps you would let The House know at once."

"I'll come with you," Harnser offered at once. Louis looked at the old man, leaning on his stick in the doorway. "I think you should stay with the Major, we will let you know later if we need more help."

As he spoke a low rumble of thunder rolled across the heavens, and the first few spots of rain hit the dusty ground.

The storm raged all afternoon and, after three hours of searching, both Louis and Charles had returned to Oxley for dry clothes and fresh horses.

There had been no word from Barcada.

A hurried meal was prepared as Louis and Charles donned more appropriate clothing to continue the search.

A group of hardy estate workers were assembled and sent out on foot and horseback after being told only that the twins were missing after the morning ruckus.

The searchers left in pairs with blankets and lanterns, whispering among themselves that the situation was reminiscent of when Arabella had run away and been found in the copse. After the morning's events there were many willing hands willing to work late… and hopefully discover what had torn the family asunder.

As dusk fell early, due to the raging storm, a lone horseman approached Oxley.

He dismounted and climbed the steps to the front door as lightening streaked across the sky and thunder crashed overhead.

The household was on alert for any eventuality, so the door was answered almost immediately.

"I need to speak with young Mrs Sanderson."

No sooner had the visitor spoken than the maid flew down the hall in search of her mistress.

Arabella only just stopped herself from falling into Harnser's arms. "Come this way," she said hurriedly, ushering him into a small reception room off the hall.

"Have they been found?" he asked before she could speak.

"No, neither of them, oh, Harnser what have we done to them? And Eleanor is riding bareback."

"Bareback!"

"Yes, she was distressed, she could be lying anywhere out there."

"Edward will look after her, try not to worry, Arabella."

"No, you do not understand, they are not together," she sobbed wretchedly.

Arabella hurriedly told Harnser of the morning's events.

"I'll get back out there." He took her firmly by the shoulders, looking deeply into her eyes. "I will find them." He spoke with more conviction than he felt.

"Take a fresh horse, Harnser…take my horse…Rosie."

She led him through the house towards one of the back doors where she grabbed an outer garment to show him to the stables.

As they reached the door it was opened…by Edward.

364

"Edward! Where have you been? Is Eleanor with you?"

"Eleanor?"

"Everyone is looking for you, we have been so worried." She put her arms around her drenched son and pulled him close. "You must have a hot bath, Edward. Explanations can wait, we must find Eleanor."

Edward peered over his mother's shoulder. "Mr Elliot! What are you doing here?"

"I am helping with the search."

"I will get changed and come with you"

"No, Edward, you have not eaten all day." Arabella instructed her son.

"Will you wait while I dry off and have a bite to eat?" the young man implored.

Harnser turned to Arabella, "A few minutes will make little difference," he said reasonably, "he wants to help."

Twenty minutes later Arabella, after informing her in-laws of Edward's safe return, watched father and son leave to search for their loved one.

An hour later Eleanor's rider-less horse was brought home.

"We saw her from Rookery Lane, she was nearly as far down as the bridge," Arthur informed Arabella.

"Marcie's Bridge?"

"Yes."

"That's not too far away."

"The men don't like going round there, Ma'am,"

"But this is an emergency, Arthur, surely they will make an exception."

"I'll see what I can do, Ma'am."

"Thank you, Arthur. Edward has returned, he has gone back out to help the searchers. If you see him give him the news." Then she had an encouraging thought. "Did you look *under* the bridge, Arthur?"

"Yes, Ma'am, I did, she wasn't there." His mind went back to how he had felt duty bound to go down to the haunted bridge alone to have a quick look underneath, trying to keep in his mind that if the bridge was haunted it was Old Joe's grandmother he was likely to see. All the same he had not stayed long.

Harnser turned to his son. The black clouds had rolled away to the East leaving a clear moonlit sky. "I think we should go home, Edward, they may have found her."

"There is an old byre along here, I think we should look as we are so close. It is well known to Eleanor, we used to come here as children."

"I think she is in there," Edward exclaimed as they drew nearer to the dilapidated building, "I *feel* it."

"I hope you are right, by all accounts she has no warm clothing with her," Harnser said worriedly.

"Eleanor…Eleanor…" they both called softly as they approached the byre, not wanting to frighten her if she were within.

They dismounted and walked the last few yards.

They both heard the whimpering and hastened their step.

Huddled in a corner, covered with straw and bits of old blanket they found her.

They knelt by her side uttering soothing words…reassuring her…comforting her…

"Come, let us put this around you," said Harnser gently, unfolding a blanket, "We will soon have you home, dear."

"N-no, please I – I do not want to go home," she stuttered through clattering teeth.

Harnser held her to him, rubbing her back and arms through the blanket to warm her. His daughter… how he loved her…he could so easily have lost her had she not been found. She was wet, cold and hungry. He closed his eyes against his anguish and held her tightly.

Edward watched silently, he had always been slightly in awe of this man. He was a man's man in every sense of the word and yet there was this sensitive side to him. The side which played beautiful music, loved nature and who held his sister so strongly yet gently, soothing away her fears.

He watched as Harnser gathered her up in his arms and strode out into the moonlight. He followed, leading the horses.

Eleanor whimpered and protested feebly, but could do nothing against the strength of her father. "It is alright, dear, we will take you to Barcada, we are nearer to there anyway, would you like that?"

The exhausted girl relaxed against the rhythmic movement of his body.

"Ride ahead, Edward and ask the Major to have the downstairs sitting room prepared, there is a bed in there."

"But Grandfather does not usually…"

"He will for Eleanor. Make sure there is a fire…" he shouted after the disappearing form.

The wind had dropped, but Harnser could see more black clouds on the western horizon. He was strong, but it was a good half mile to Barcada. He wished he could tell Arabella that their daughter was safe, but he knew Edward would either ride over or send someone else; most of the Oxley workforce was out looking for her.

He was glad he had decided to spend Easter in Suffolk. He had wanted to tell Arabella his good news in person.

He came to the end of the footpath and turned right into the Flinton Lane. He passed the stables and strode into the Barcada yard. The old sign creaked in greeting and he could not help but smile wryly.

The door was open, for which he was grateful, his arms were leaden with the weight of his daughter.

"Bring her straight through, Sir," Sarah instructed, bustling ahead of him purposefully, while the Major stood in the hall, leaning on his stick with a worried countenance.

The fire was in its infancy, but the room was not cold, he knew this room was rarely cold, facing the way it did with the afternoon sun on its walls.

"We've lots of hot water and we've warmed the bed," said Sarah importantly, "good job you were here, Sir," she continued as Harnser lay his daughter on the same bed that both he and Arabella had used for recuperation purposes. The bed in which

367

they had consummated their love…and where this precious daughter of his had been born.

"We'll take care of her, Sir, you go and get out of those clothes, there's plenty of hot water, we've been boiling up all day. I'll have some sent up."

"I must go to Oxley, Sarah…"

"No…Edward's already gone, they'll be here soon, you'll only pass on the way."

He saw the wisdom of her words and mounted the stairs to make himself more presentable.

Bertie's voice came to him from the hall. "Stay here tonight, Harnser, there is no need for you to turn out again, Maria's not expecting you, is she?"

"No, it was going to be a surprise."

"That is settled then, Arabella will want to see you."

He saw the maid from the corner of his eye and added quickly, "She will want to thank you for finding Eleanor."

Where's it all going to end, the old man thought anxiously, they have still got more shocks coming to them.

Bertie loved his grandchildren dearly, and it tore him apart to witness such upheaval in their lives. He had been worried ever since he had been told that the twins were missing. He thought of his old friend Henry recuperating after his heart attack, upsets like this would not help his recovery.

Forty-five minutes later Harnser was back downstairs with Eleanor.

"You look much better now," he said gently, taking her hand in his.

"Thank you, Mr Elliot," she replied, flatly. "For bringing me here, I mean."

"You were born in this room," he said, as if to himself.

"How strange that you should know that," she whispered.

He realised he had thought aloud. "You would be surprised what I know about you," he said smiling, "I have known your grandfather for years."

At this point a knock came upon the door and Arabella entered with her husband.

Harnser dropped his daughter's hand, but not before the scene was witnessed by Charles.

Oblivious to the surprised countenance of her husband, Arabella rushed to her daughter's side, bending to kiss her forehead. "Thank you so much for finding her, Harnser," she said gratefully, looking him straight in the eyes.

Charles was still by the door. He was acutely aware that his announcement that morning had driven his daughter away. He was not sure how she would receive him. Added to that was the scene he had witnessed a few moments earlier. He had seen Harnser Elliot a few times through the years, mostly at church, and he was aware that he was a young friend of Bertie. Now something else was stirring in his mind.

Mr Elliot often visited the Major at Christmas; the children had mentioned the fact...and Mr Elliot was a musician...a very accomplished one...and tonight Mr Elliot had spent hours looking for Eleanor, in a raging storm.

And wasn't Mr Elliot holding Eleanor's hand a little possessively, when he had entered the room?

Mr Elliot could well be the natural father of his children.

Eleanor's voice permeated his thoughts.

"I do not want to go back to Oxley, Mother, my life is ruined." The girl was in tears, whimpering weakly to her mother.

Charles stepped forward as if in a daze. "You can stay here for now, Eleanor, but we must talk soon."

"We have nothing to talk about, Father," she responded coldly, "You have ruined my life."

She turned away , her actions speaking a thousand words.

"I cannot see how giving you a brother has ruined your life." Charles appeared embarrassed; wishing this conversation was a little more private. He voiced his thoughts, "We will talk tomorrow, in private," he said, looking directly at Harnser. Then Charles leant down and kissed Eleanor on her forehead. "Goodnight, Eleanor," he said quietly, "Until tomorrow then."

She did not answer and kept her face turned away from him. He nodded to Harnser, "Goodnight, Mr Elliot, we are indeed indebted to you."

369

He turned and left the room, resigned in the knowledge that his wife would not be returning to Oxley that night, just as Edward appeared on the scene.

Edward too gave him a cold accusing look but said nothing.

"Edward, please…" Charles began, looking beseechingly at his younger son, but a second cold glare made him turn and hurry through the door, knowing in his heart that he was leaving a natural family together in Bertie's sitting room.

Louis arrived as Charles left by the front door. "Unless you have a stout heart I would go no further, Louis. The atmosphere is very hostile in there."

"I must see Eleanor and Edward – try to explain."

"They are in no mood to listen. Eleanor is exhausted and sounds dreadfully melancholic. Edward is angry. Best come home with me and try again tomorrow."

"I must see her, Charles…er…Father, you do not understand how I feel about her."

"Feel about her?"

Louis did not want to get into another heavy discussion so tried to minimize the damage of his words. "I feel responsible for her predicament," he said, lamely.

"As you like," Charles conceded, letting himself out.

Sarah knocked on the sitting room door and waited to be asked in. "Mr Chevalier is here to see Eleanor and Edward," she announced.

Eleanor's tears were once more in evidence as she grabbed Edward's hand, "Please send him away, Edward. I will die of shame if I see him."

Edward left the room, only too happy to send the Frenchman on his way.

"There is nothing for *you* to be ashamed of in all of this, Eleanor," her Mother said gently.

"I do not want to see him, I do not want to live," she said flatly through her tears.

Sarah arrived with hot soup for the invalid.

"I do not want it," the girl said sadly.

"You *must* eat, Miss Eleanor," Sarah admonished looking to

Arabella for support.

"Just a little please," her mother coaxed, "to help warm you through."

"I *am* warm now." She closed her eyes against the soup, against the pleading and against her future.

"Have something to eat, Eleanor," Harnser said firmly. "Sarah should have been in bed long ago, and I did not carry you home for you to starve yourself to death."

Eleanor opened her eyes to begin crying afresh, but she hauled herself up the bed and took the proffered dish, to begin force-feeding herself.

"Thank you," said Harnser more gently. "Things may not look so bad in the morning after a good night's rest." But even as he said it, he looked knowingly at Arabella, doubting that tomorrow would be any better, in fact, he acknowledged silently, it would probably be twice as bad. Gossip would be rife in both houses and around the village. Servants always got to the bottom of gossip somehow, and when they got to the bottom of *this* particular situation there would be no holding them.

Arabella watched her daughter forcing down the soup, spluttering and crying as she did so, her tears falling into her bowl.

Arabella took a handkerchief and brushed away the tears then turned to Harnser who was sitting forlornly, wearing a pained expression. Arabella knew it was because he had had to talk firmly to his distraught daughter, but he had achieved a result. She knew the children liked Harnser very much, all the same she felt a little guilty for what she was about to ask.

"Would you have a word with Edward please, Harnser. He is so unhappy about this morning's news. He did not wait to hear the rest of what Charles had to tell him."

"Would it have helped?" Harnser asked doubtfully.

"Yes, I am sure it would have, tell him I will explain tomorrow, to both of them. We are all too tired tonight."

Harnser looked at her enquiringly.

"I have something important to tell you too," she said intriguingly.

371

He thought of his own news that he had been eager to share with her when he had arrived that morning. Somehow it seemed to have paled into insignificance during the traumatic day.

He raised himself from his chair and smiled at his daughter, the sad, pale daughter that he wanted to wrap in his arms and protect from all of life's vagaries. "Goodnight, Eleanor," he said softly, "It will be alright, I promise you."

She looked at him pitifully, he was such a nice man but he did not know why she could not return to her beloved Oxley, and the man to whom she had lost her heart.

"Goodnight, Mr Elliot," she whispered, "I am truly sorry to have caused you so much trouble."

He smiled again, and went off to find Edward.

Early the next morning Arabella entered her daughter's room to find her two miserable children comforting one another. Eleanor's face was red and swollen; Edward's pale and drawn. Neither looked as if they had slept.

"Eleanor!" she exclaimed, horrified at her daughter's appearance, "have you been weeping all night?"

The girl looked up at her mother as Edward came to her defence. "I do not think anybody realises just how hurt and unhappy Eleanor and I are," he said firmly. "We have been deceived and will be the laughing stock of the county let alone the village. I have had it hammered into me since birth that I will one day inherit Oxley and all the responsibility it entails and Eleanor…Eleanor…Eleanor has found…" he stopped as his sister once more burst into tears, imploring him not to continue.

"Eleanor has found what?" Arabella asked, putting her arms around her distraught daughter.

"Eleanor has found that she has fallen hopelessly in love with her own brother," he finished miserably.

"Oh, no, no, no," Arabella cried, holding the girl tightly and rocking her to and fro, "No, it is not what you think."

None of them heard the knock on the door or heard

Harnser until he was with them by the bed. "What has happened now?" he asked worriedly, "Has she relapsed?"

Arabella looked at him in anguish, still holding her daughter. She released her hold, took her daughter's hand and reached for Edward's too. "It is not as you think," she said, looking from one to the other. "Louis is not your brother."

"I do not think Father would tell us Louis is his son were it not the truth," Edward said resignedly.

Arabella closed her eyes, grasping both her children's hands tightly in her own, then she looked back towards Harnser who was standing behind her, before saying softly, "Louis is not your brother because...because..." she faulted, knowing she was about to give them another terrible shock.

They were staring at her, puzzlement written all over their faces, waiting for her to continue, when Harnser suddenly stepped forward and said, "What your mother is trying to tell you is that Louis is not your brother because," he moistened his lips, then continued, "because Charles is not your natural father."

They stared at him dumbfounded. Eleanor's tears stopped flowing. Edward looked aghast at his mother. Arabella lowered her eyes and said softly, "It is the truth."

"Mother, what are you saying?" Edward looked appalled, his sister began breathing heavily, as if to get air into her lungs to stop herself fainting again at the new revelation.

"If Father is not our father, then who is?" whispered Edward, shocked beyond belief.

"I am," said Harnser forcefully. "I am your father."

They stared at him, both feeling as if they were dreaming and would soon wake up in their beds at Oxley to find that none of it had happened.

They were still staring when Sarah knocked on the door, then opened it to announce that breakfast was ready.

"I know it was all a terrible shock for you both, but now that you know the details can we call a truce and live together happily in the house again?"

The twins had just heard the whole story from a shamefaced Charles.

"I was going to tell you about the school and the farm at the same time I told you about Louis, but you did not give me the chance."

"And we will major in music?" Edward asked, hardly able to contain his excitement.

"Apparently so," said a relieved Charles, "You must discuss it more fully with your mother; it was her idea."

Edward could see the school in his mind's eye, a beautiful, classical building, rivalling Oxley House, nestling among trees like Barcada. It would be renowned throughout England, and he would one day be at its helm.

Eleanor's thoughts were with Louis, who only yesterday had declared his love for her. She had been devastated to learn that Louis was Charles' son, but elated beyond words to find that she could have her sweetheart after all.

Charles waited patiently for their answer. "Well?" he asked, "Can we all be friends again?"

"Yes, Father," they said in unison. They had known him as 'Father' for far too long to change their manner of address.

Charles put an arm around each of them. "I will try to make up for all my faults," he said conciliatorily.

"It is weird having two fathers, do you think everyone is gossiping about us?" reflected Eleanor to her brother as they sat in the garden. "We never guessed did we? All those Boxing Days with Mr Elliot…"

"There is absolutely no doubt about the gossip," answered Edward wryly, "The servants seem almost as embarrassed as we are."

"Is it not strange how things work out," the girl continued, "almost like there is some great divine plan for us all. We are both happier now, after all this upheaval, than we were before. Imagine…Mother and Mr Elliot…lovers. Do you think it is all in the past?"

"He has lived away for years…he was married…"

"There is still so much we do not know, Edward."

"I expect they will tell us, in good time."

"But I am intrigued."

"You *always* are," her brother chuckled, giving her an affectionate push.

Although he had progressed enough to be dressed and sit in a chair, Henry was still considered to be an invalid.

He sat now, looking grey and ill after his son's latest revelation. His face was void of expression, his eyes sad and empty. Sarah was crying into her handkerchief, as she held her husband's hand.

"Speak to me, Father, please," implored Charles, "even if it is only to berate me."

"There was a time," the old man began, "when I wondered myself about the situation. It happened in London didn't it?"

"Yes, Father."

"After that accident in the copse?"

"Yes."

"I thought it strange at the time...after eight years...but as time went on...I thought I saw a likeness between you and Edward...so I stopped wondering..." his voice trailed off feebly.

"Arabella *is* a Sanderson, there was bound to be a likeness, Father. The twins are still your family." Charles shot a quick look at his mother, who for once was at a loss for words.

Henry smiled weakly, "Yes, you are right, Charles, thank you for pointing that out to me. What relation does that make me to them?"

"You are their Great Great Uncle."

"So I am...that's not so bad is it?"

He looked at his wife. "That's not so bad is it Sarah?" he reiterated, then to Charles, "I love them so much."

" I know you do, they love you too." Charles blinked rapidly, trying to keep his tears at bay; he did not like to see his father looking and sounding so frail.

"Will you ask them to come and see me please? I would like to reassure them of my love."

"I will, Father, I will do it now."

Charles looked at his mother, where she sat pale and still. After the initial shocked gasps and exclamations she had said little, more worried about her husband's reaction to the news than anything else.

She watched Charles leave the room before saying soothingly, "You must not worry about all this, Henry, promise me you will not."

" I am too tired to worry, my dear. At least it's now all out in the open. Who knows, Charles might ease off the drink – I'm glad he told me before I die."

"He should have told us years ago," his wife said, unable to keep the anger from her voice.

"Let it go now, Sarah, the boy has suffered enough for his mistakes. We all need a little peace."

CHAPTER TEN

"The Frenchman!" they all exclaimed in unison.

"The Frenchman," Arthur confirmed importantly. "We've never seen nothing like it. No one can believe it, the Frenchman is Charlie Boy's son."

"So that's why Miss Eleanor ran away," said Abel solemnly.

"That's why they both ran away, only Edward came back of his own accord."

The chimney corner regulars were amazed at the latest revelations from the House... all except one.

"So we'll have a Frenchman in charge of us all one day," said Harry with a worried look on his face.

"He's still a Sanderson," Arthur reminded him, "I don't s'pose he's much different; only half of him's French."

They clasped their mugs of ale as if the feel of them would give them understanding, and all took long draughts, as their foreheads furrowed deeply.

"How's young Edward taken the news?" asked Joe from his corner seat. His voice sounded frail to them all and he gave substance to this by his next words, "I'm far too old for shocks like this," he said, wiping the foam of his ale from his whiskers with the back of his hand. "They'll kill me off with all this, I'll be six feet under, pushing up daisies before long."

"You've bin sayin' that for years, Joe," laughed Arthur, "I reckon we'll have to shoot you before you give up."

"I'm aimin' to reach me century, fat chance of that though with all this goin' on. Anyway, you dint answer me, how's Edward taken it?"

"Well, believe it or not, surprisingly well, but that could be because of somethin' else I've just heard, mind you this is strictly between ourselves." Arthur paused and looked over his shoulder, as he was wont to do in these circumstances. "This is just a rumour mind but it's good and juicy. Hold on to your ticker, Joe," Arthur leaned forward, anticipating with relish the look on their faces when he imparted the best news of the night.

"Well...spit it out," said Harry, "we're waitin' "

"There's a rumour that the twins *don't* belong to Charlie Boy...there, what do y' think of that!?"

Arthur sat back with a satisfied look on his face.

He had their attention, three pairs of eyes stared at him, three mugs were suspended in mid air, three mouths were agape, only Old Joe appeared unfazed.

"Are you havin' us on?" asked Sefton, a look of disbelief on his face.

"No."

"Where did you get it from?"

"Can't say," whispered Arthur.

"More like 'won't say', said Harry disappointedly.

"That's as maybe. Suffice to say it's from a reliable source."

"Oh, listen to him," mocked Abel chuckling, "...suffice to say...I think that new house and ten guineas went to Arthur's head." He paused then said kindly, "I'm glad your educated friends are having a good effect on you."

"I can talk proper when I want to," Arthur said indignantly.

A frail voice came from the corner. "Who is the father then?" Joe wanted to know just how much was public knowledge.

All eyes turned to Arthur. "I was hoping you wouldn't ask me that," he said, suddenly serious.

"Well, who is it then?" asked Harry, reluctant to let the subject drop.

Arthur paused, not sure whether to divulge his knowledge or not. The whole group waited expectantly. They were his friends and he had not been told that the information was confidential. "It is Harnser Elliot," he said measuredly.

"The musician?"

"Yes, the musician."

"Well, I never, who'd have thought it?" said Sefton, eager to get home to share the news, but not wanting to miss anything

378

else that Arthur might reveal.

Old Joe was the least surprised of the chimney corner regulars. His old heart had leapt in his chest when Arthur had made his revelation wondering how they would all react. It was still going a bit faster than usual. He was pleased that Arabella's children belonged to her erstwhile sweetheart, especially now that it turned out that Charles had deceived her. What he did not say was that Arabella had confessed to him herself only yesterday, down at Marcie's Bridge, telling him it would soon be public knowledge anyway.

"You're not saying much, Joe," said Abel to his old friend.

"I'm thinking all the more," said Joe quietly.

"There'll be some changes now, I'll be bound," said Harry thoughtfully.

"How sure are you that the musician is the father?" asked Abel, wondering how safe it was to tell his customers.

"Very sure."

"I thought you said it was just a rumour," said Harry indignantly.

"I didn't want you to go shoutin' about it, I'm not sure who else knows."

"Tell us who told you," challenged Harry, "You can't expect us to believe you if you won't tell us who you got it from."

Arthur sighed heavily, "Harnser told me himself," he confessed reluctantly.

There was stunned silence as the group absorbed this.

"Did he tell you to keep it to yourself?" asked Abel.

"No, I found that surprising. Perhaps he wanted me to spread the news."

"You've always got on with him, haven't you, Arthur?" said Abel unnecessarily.

"I have, he's a nice chap, I like to think of him as a friend."

"Well, he obviously thinks of you as a friend too, else he wouldn't have told you."

Yes, thought Arthur, and I hope I haven't just betrayed him.

"You have told Arthur!" Arabella was a trifle surprised.

"Yes, it was bound to get out anyway. It is best they hear the truth than think you have behaved shamefully."

"I suppose so." She was thinking of her own conversation with Old Joe, it was important to her that Old Joe would not think badly of her.

"The sooner it is all out in the open, the sooner it will become yesterday's news."

"You are right of course, we will just have to ride out the storm."

"Henry took it well, considering the state of his health."

"Yes, I think it helped enormously that the twins are still related to him."

"The school was a marvellous idea, Arabella."

"Will you run it?"

"Me?"

"Yes, you; who else do I know capable of doing the job?"

"Would Charles approve?"

"Supposing he does, would you run it then?"

"I would be honoured, but I doubt he will."

"It will be our school, Harnser. Ours to leave to Edward. Leave Charles to me, there is a good chance I can talk him round. He is feeling quite pleased with how things have turned out."

"My news seems light by comparison."

"What news is this?"

"I have at last persuaded Florence and Richard to visit Suffolk, with a view to moving here permanently."

"But that is wonderful."

"I have also obtained a divorce."

"How do you feel about it?" she asked, suddenly serious.

"I think I have done the right thing, it was never a real marriage, Florence and Richard are in total agreement."

"Then I am happy for you."

They looked longingly at one another.

"If only…" he whispered.

"Yes," she said softly, "if only…"

It was, after all, a peaceful Easter as the houses returned to some semblance of normality.

Harnser returned to Kent.

Two weeks later, Henry suffered his final heart attack... and Charles was inconsolable.

"I have killed him, Arabella. He was improving until I told him about the twins."

"He continued to improve a little afterwards," she insisted, terrified at the way her husband was seeking solace from the bottle again. "Henry has been ill for some time, it was not your fault he developed a bad heart."

"Mother blames me."

"Has she said that?"

"No, but I feel it."

"You are imagining it."

"I am *not*." He lurched across his study to refill his glass.

"Please, Charles, no more," she implored sternly.

He slumped into his chair, a pained, defeated look on his face. "I am glad it was not a casual affair in London," he said unexpectedly.

Her face coloured visibly.

"I love you, Arabella. I have always loved you."

"I love you too, Charles, we are second cousins."

"Do you remember the day we met?" tears rolled down his cheeks, he did nothing to stop them.

"Yes, I remember it well." She knelt by his side, taking his hand in hers.

"Do you still have the sovereign we found on the beach?"

"I have it, Charles."

She started crying too and lifted his hand to her face, "I am so sorry for your loss."

He squeezed her hand. "Do you forgive me, Arabella?"

"We must forgive each other, put it all behind us."

"You have always been wise, yes, that is what we shall do... forgive each other...because we love each other..."

She closed her eyes, the sadness of the situation breaking

her heart.

"I am going riding."

She looked up sharply, "I do not think you should, Charles, you have had rather a lot to drink."

"It is something I must do, for Father."

"I will come with you."

"No, really there is no need. I must do this alone, Saxon will look after me." He smiled sadly, but wryly, "he is used to me, he knows the way home."

"Wait until tomorrow," she said gently.

"I must ride the estate today, Arabella. *This* is the day my father has entrusted it to my care."

Louis found Charles' broken body at dusk; he had obviously misjudged a jump. Loyal Saxon was close by.

He should have taken his wife's advice...and waited until the following day...

...instead he shared a double funeral with the father he loved so much, before they were laid side by side in Little Pecking churchyard.

CHAPTER ELEVEN

The chimney corner regulars were solemn.

"He said this lot would see him off," said Abel, trying to keep his voice steady.

"Poor Old Joe, he didn't reach his century, did he?"

"Ninety two's a good age," Sefton said trying to raise their spirits a little.

Their glances regularly went to the empty settle where their old friend had always sat.

"I'm goin' to miss 'im somthin' dreadful," said Arthur, brushing a tear or two from his cheek.

"Who'd have thought he'd see young Charles out?" asked Abel to no one in particular. "We won't forget this lot in a hurry will we?"

Their hands went round their ale mugs as they stared straight ahead, all with their own thoughts of Joe.

"He never did catch that pig, did he?" said Arthur.

"I don't think he wanted to," said Abel, "He liked to think of it roaming that copse of his."

"Poor Old Joe," they sighed, one after the other, "Poor Old Joe."

"He's goin' to be put alongside Marcie," Abel informed them, "He put it all in his Will."

"Have you told Mrs Sanderson, Arthur?"

"She'd already heard, but we had a cup of tea together this mornin', she's upset about it, she was very fond of him. She's comin' to the funeral."

"I thought she would," said Abel, nodding his head and looking back to the settle.

"She told me this mornin' that everytime she's heard that Barcada sign creak since he died, she's started cryin' again. He once told her that sign was like him, needed oil on its joints.

She's very fragile at the moment, I felt sorry for her."

"They've had their fair share lately, I'm surprised the Major hasn't suffered," said Abel.

"He's a strong old chap, Arabella's allust backwards and forwards to keep an eye on him. Not many a day go by that I don't see her there."

"Do you think she'll move back there, Arthur?"

"I wouldn't be surprised, not yet of course, it wouldn't be proper. She's very cut up about her husband, and the old man, terrible that... both on the same day. Old Mrs Sanderson hasn't left her room apart from to go to the funeral...yes, a very sad old do...and now Old Joe too."

After a solemn service in a packed church Old Joe was laid to rest beside his mother and father.

Abel took off his hat and approached Arabella and the Major. "We wondered if you would like to come back to the cottage, Ma'am, Sir, Aggie's put on a bit of a spread." He hesitated, looking down at his feet before adding, "We'll understand of course if you're not feeling up to it..."

"I would like to come, thank you, Abel," she turned to her father, "Father?"

"Yes," the old man said respectfully, "but I cannot walk with you."

"I'll see Father into a carriage if you can wait for me."

"She's goin' to walk with us," said Abel rejoining the group.

The solemn procession set off down Rookery Lane with the carriage bringing up the rear.

"We're sorry we can't accommodate everyone," said Abel apologetically as one or two more carriages joined the back of the procession, the solicitor's among them.

Arabella reassured him, "The children did not really know Joe very well, they will carry on, just Father and I will join you inside."

"...and to Miss Arabella Biddemore of Barcada I leave my lady's chair, that my father made for my mother..."

"Oh, Joe…" Arabella burst into tears as the bequest was read out, causing Mr Flowerdew to pause in his reading of the Will.

"That's the one you're sitting on," whispered Arthur, knowingly, "No one's sat in that chair since his mother died."

She wiped her tears from her eyes. "I will treasure it, I will put it into the sitting room overlooking the garden at the back, it is my favourite room at Barcada," she looked to her father, who nodded in agreement.

No one else was surprised at the bequest.

The reading of the short Will continued, followed by Aggie's spread, and many reminiscences of Old Joe.

A new era was about to begin.

Chapter Twelve

Five years later...

Arabella ran her hands down the front of her gown and checked her appearance in the looking glass. She wanted everything to be perfect this evening for her husband.

She had a house full of guests; Florence and Richard who had just arrived from their home in Winford; Maria and Walter; Dr James Porter and his family; Silas and Sally. Then there was Matilda and the Reverend Richard Johnson – yes, after much heartache, Matilda had found happiness with her childhood sweetheart's brother.

At any moment now, Arabella was expecting her son, Edward, from The Barcada School and College of Music. She smiled and walked down the central, upstairs hall from where she could see the school a half mile or so away, clean and bright in the early evening sunshine. She checked her watch, "Do not be late, Edward," she whispered.

Her father was in the library, trying to keep an excited Richard calm with a game of chess – two old gentlemen, who had become the best of friends. Florence was bustling about with Sarah, the housekeeper, putting unnecessary touches to an already perfect fare.

Only Sarah Sanderson would be missing; she rarely left the House nowadays...her mind tended to wander. Losing her husband and son in one day had severely affected her mental health.

Arabella knew that Harnser and Arthur would not be back from Winford for some time, even so she rushed down the central staircase and made straight for the front door, which she opened, then stepped outside to take another look...just in case. "What time is the train due?" Arthur asked unnecessarily.

386

"Half past five."

"We're goin' to be early."

"I did not want to be late."

"You look nervous."

"I have never been so nervous in my life."

"Give us a tune."

"What!"

"A tune…on the ocarina, that'll calm you down a bit. I remember when I first met you, it was when old Mrs Biddemore died – you played 'Abide With Me' to us all on the Village Green."

"That was a long time ago, Arthur."

Arthur laughed, "Can you remember what the Vicar said?"

It was Harnser's turn to chuckle. "I can indeed, he said, '*I will know where to come if my organist is ever sick.*'" The mimicry was quite superb.

"And some bright spark muttered, 'Yis, and 'e might not make quite as many mistakes.' Poor old 'Hannah on the organ,' she got it right most of the time didn't she?"

Harnser began playing as they travelled happily on their way to Winford railway station.

After a while he stopped, "Can you smell the sea, Arthur?"

"Lovely int it?"

Ten minutes later they reached their destination; it was five o'clock.

"Told you we'd be early," said Arthur.

Harnser smiled at his friend then put his hand in his pocket where he felt the letter…the letter he had read and re-read so many times that he knew it by heart. He took out the envelope, it was addressed simply:

To Harnser
The Stick Man of Little Pecking
England.

He was amazed it had reached him. Never in his life before had he been so pleased to be known by the quaint title; to think he had, in his foolish, young day, thought it demeaning.

The title had brought his daughter home to him, it had been 'odd' enough to stay in her mind since her mother died. Today especially he was ecstatically happy to be known as The Stick Man.

He took the letter out of the envelope again.

Dear Father, he read,

You will, no doubt, be surprised to get a letter from me, especially one from America. I have wanted to write to you for many years; ever since my mother died when I was twelve years old. In fact I did write, but I did not know how to send it, so I gave it to Pa – I found it among his possessions when he died last year. It was with a note explaining that he could not send it because you might have taken me away from him...I was all he had of my mother.

Pa was good to Mother and me. He loved her very much and blamed himself for her death – giving birth to my little brother Richard, who is buried with her in a pretty cemetery beside a white wooden church on a windy hill.

Pa has now joined them.

I can understand now why he did not want to lose me as well; I resemble my mother closely. I was, however, pleased to learn that you may not have ignored my letter, as I had begun to think – although I knew there was a chance it may not have reached you. I have so little information about you.

Pa came out here with his father in eighteen sixty-three, they took advantage of the 1862 Homestead Act. Are you familiar with it, Father? For ten dollars each they could both claim one hundred and sixty acres of free land. They added to the land over the years.

It was a new beginning for them after they had lost their kinfolk – mother, two girls and a boy – to an outbreak of Cholera. After that Pa liked open spaces, convinced that cities harboured all the ills of mankind. England held so many unhappy memories for him that he rarely talked of it, but Mother told me all about it – England, with its rolling green countryside and little grey flint churches – how I have longed to see it.

Pa left the ranch to me and I was happy here with my husband and son – little Harnser... Yes, Father, I named him after you.

Six months ago my husband was killed in an accident when cattle stampeded in a storm – I miss him dreadfully.

I know my mother always dreamed of seeing the old country again. Her infectious enthusiasm for it must have rubbed off on me, so, when my husband died, I decided to write to you again.

If by chance my letter reaches you – and in the event of you replying to tell me I still have kinfolk in England – I will sell the ranch and return home. We have lost all our dear ones here.

You may like to know that Mother was very happy with Pa, whom she met on one of his very rare visits to the city, when her travelling theatre company came.

I know so little of my family history; it was a subject about which Mother seemed reluctant to talk. I do know she was very fond of you because, with her dying breath, she told me that you loved me and that you had 'saved' us. She implored me to write to you – it was only then that I learned your name. 'Write to Harnser,' she said, 'The Stick Man of Little Pecking.'

I never forgot you, Father. In my head I have a hazy image of a tall, fair-haired man, who loved music

I have found two photographs in a trunk belonging to Mother, I think one is of you. The other has 'Robert Sitwell' written on the back. Perhaps you could enlighten me. Is this the 'Robert' who did not want us; that Mother spoke of, as she lay dying?

I have so many things I want to ask you.

I am praying hard that my letter will reach you, and that the father I have in my head and keep in my heart will want me to return home.

I am praying, Father.
I sign this letter with hope in my heart.
With love,
Amy and Little Harnser.

P.S. I still have my ocarina.

Harnser folded the letter and replaced it in his pocket. Neither he nor his companion spoke.

Arthur could see the tears in his friend's eyes. "Won't be long now," he said at length, although there was still fifteen minutes before the train was due. "Best get on to that platform so they don't miss you." His voice was gently husky, due to the emotion he was feeling at the situation.

Harnser watched as the London train came into view. His heart was thudding in his chest with happy anticipation.

The train made a slow rumbling entrance into the station and came to a noisy, hissing halt.

He strained his neck as the passengers alighted.

He started walking as a lady stepped down from a carriage.

He began running when he saw her reach up to lift a small boy down onto the platform.

She saw him and smiled.

The small boy hid behind his mother's skirts.

Harnser came to a halt in front of her.

"Amy?"

"Father?"

He took her in his arms as the tears rolled unashamedly down both their faces.

The woman took the boy's hand and pulled him round in front of her. "Harnser, this is your Grandpa," she said through her tears, with a distinct American accent, pushing the child forward.

Harnser knelt on one knee and took the boy's hand, then pulled him to him and hugged him warmly. No matter how hard he tried, he couldn't stop the tears.

"Your luggage, Ma'am," they heard a porter say as he reached them, pushing a luggage conveyance carrying two large trunks.

"Oh, yes of course, thank you," she answered in the American accent that Harnser found strange to hear on her. She smiled at her father, "I am afraid there is much more to follow."

"We have a carriage waiting," Harnser told the porter.

"I'll bring it out, Sir, and help you load it." They both smiled warmly at him. They loved the whole world that day.

"I am so happy to have you home again, Amy. I cannot put in to words what it means to me."

"I think I can guess," the young woman said softly, "I know how I feel myself."

"Your grandparents cannot wait to see you both."

"I knew nothing of them until I received your letter, but I now know why my little brother was named Richard."

"Let us get you both home, there is a welcome party waiting for you, there are so many people waiting to meet you."

Harnser's step was light as he ushered his family to the waiting conveyance. It was a beautiful evening; the carriage top was down, which would allow him to point out everything of interest on the way home.

He pointed out the fishing boats in the harbour surrounded by swirling gulls, then The Royal Hotel.

They paused to watch the sea as it whispered and ran ashore. Little Harnser did not want to leave it.

They took the seaside road as far as Cottlefield, before turning inland through the green fields of early Summer.

He pointed out pheasants and partridges as they hastily fluttered back into the fields, away from approaching danger.

They saw rabbits and birds and hawthorn blossom. Buttercups, corncockle and wild roses, all pointed out excitedly by Harnser to his delighted family.

He chatted happily, he felt young again, his heart was singing.

His daughter laughed merrily at his enthusiasm, while his grandson watched him shyly.

Somewhere at the back of his mind were thoughts that he would have to tell her that he was not her *real* father, but that could wait, he knew it would not matter.

Later he waved to people as they went through the village.

He felt like royalty.

He asked Arthur to stop outside the church so that Amy could have a good look at it.

They slowed down as he pointed out Edward House and Eleanor Terrace, named after his children. She looked puzzled, he laughed, "I have so much to tell you," he said happily.

They turned into the track leading to Barcada and he was instantly reminded of the *first* time he had done so. Once again there was a vast, spectacular, pink and orange sky to the left; a magnificent backdrop to the wildflower meadow, that Arabella loved so much, and ahead of them, slightly to the left, were the trees; horse chestnuts, oaks and beeches, that hid the house in Summer.

They were coming home.

"You will see it soon, Amy," he said excitedly, lifting little Harnser onto his lap and pointing ahead.

And then it came into view, the beautiful old red brick house nestling between the trees, with the soft evening sun caressing its mellow walls, its latticed windows glinting in the sunlight.

He remembered how he had felt the first time he had seen it – like he was coming home – home from somewhere unknown, where he had triumphed over adversity – home after a long absence, bringing peace to his inner being.

It all made sense now. He must have travelled this lane a hundred times, but never had he seen the house so much like that first time – until now.

"It is beautiful," breathed Amy, "truly beautiful."

"I knew you would like it, I fell in love with the place in eighteen sixty-three, when I was seventeen."

Harnser asked Arthur to stop the carriage.

"Are we going to live here?" a small voice asked.

"I think your other grandparents are hoping you will live with them, at Winford, by the sea, where the railway station is, do you remember?"

"With the boats?" he asked excitedly.

Harnser laughed, "Yes, with the boats, lots of boats."

"He has developed a love of boats and the sea," explained Amy, "since we crossed the Atlantic."

"You can visit as often as you like, it is only three miles away," Harnser assured him.

Suddenly Harnser opened the door and jumped from the carriage. He climbed the bank and plucked two sprays of wild roses from the hedgerow. He gave his daughter one and held the other aloft. "For Arabella," he said, by way of explanation, "They are her favourites."

Arabella stood by the door. She saw the carriage come into view, and then she saw it stop. She smiled; she knew exactly why it had done so.

She watched as Arthur set the horses in motion to finish their journey, the sun glinting on the brasses as they jogged along.

Her whole life seemed to flash before her as she watched the scene.

Living at the farm with her mother, father and grandmother.

Her first meeting with Charles when they had laughed in the orchard, sitting on the log.

The move back to Barcada, where her grandmother would tell her stories of her elopement, as they sat by the fire on winter evenings.

Her mother's death, in the sitting room, overlooking the back garden.

Losing her grandmother.

Her first meeting with Harnser, when they searched for the elusive cuckoo.

Their beautiful, long, hot Summer – the morning rides by the sea and to the marshes; their day on the river; the photographs and watercolours. Walks in the copse, and, of course, their meetings at Marcie's Bridge on her bench seat, that he had made for her, where they had watched the stream, the waterfall and the damselflies.

The wild roses.

Cavorting in the snow together with the sledge.

Harnser's dramatic arrival at Barcada after being flayed by Walter.

Their lovemaking...and their parting, on the cold snowbound

night when she had watched him disappear in the moonlight.

The Christmas gifts that had broken her heart afresh: the keepsake box, the poems…and his ocarina.

Her marriage to Charles, when she had searched the crowds for Harnser and saw Alice, the plump, wholesome girl, who always *did* stand much too close to him.

She remembered watching the fluffy white clouds as they scudded behind the church tower and out the other side as if playing a game of peek-a-boo; a last look for Harnser…he had not come.

Her early, barren years of marriage, when her nerves were at breaking point and she had run away in the middle of the night, hoping in vain to find Harnser by the stream…then being found by Old Joe…dear Old Joe.

London – seeing Harnser in the park, hardly daring to breathe in case he disappeared.

Their lovemaking.

Her children's births, when she was sure she was going to die, in the same room as her mother had.

She saw Charles – poor troubled Charles, with his secret wife and secret child – who led a guilt-racked life which destroyed him – inheriting his beloved Oxley for only a few hours…before dying on the same day as his father.

Louis – dear Louis, who had arrived out of the blue – setting hearts a-flutter – to claim his birthright.

Dear Old Joe who bequeathed her his mother's chair…and shared her favourite place by the stream.

She saw her father, proudly walking her up the aisle, to at last be joined together with Harnser, her girlhood sweetheart.

She saw Edward, walking over the threshold of the newly built school, with his father by his side.

Eleanor and Louis on their wedding day.

Yes, it all flitted through her mind, culminating in the letter from America, addressed to The Stick Man of Little Pecking.

She watched as they drove into the yard, past the creaking sign that drank oil by the gallon.

She ran across the yard to greet them.

He took her in his arms then reached up to get the spray of wild roses he had picked along the way.

She accepted it with her heart full of love.

He helped his daughter from the carriage, a man full of pride and happiness.

Arabella touched his arm to alert him to two approaching horse riders – their daughter and Charles' son.

She looked to the heavens…it may be a generation late, Grandmother, but the family is happily united again.

Harnser reached up to lift his little grandson from the carriage. He whirled him round and round in his arms…

…and the fair curls went twirling
and twirling
and twirling
and the fair curls went twirling
and twirling around…

…and the sound of a child's *laughter* rang out over the surrounding countryside.